DESTROYER

HIDDEN PLANET: BOOK ONE

ANNA CARVEN

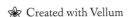

PROLOGUE

KNEE-DEEP SNOW BLANKETED the floor of the ravine, stretching between the sheer stone cliffs like a fine *vooli* pelt. Ares pushed back his hood and stared up at the violet sky as it deepened into black.

"Going to be a cold night," he muttered. The Dagger was visible again, its familiar black outline pointing toward the wide waterplains of the Ardu-Sai. Behind it lay a tapestry of stars, their brilliant glow muted by the dark veil of the Shadowring.

Go back, it seemed to say. *Leave this place.*

That wasn't an option. He glanced over his shoulder. Twenty-five Vradhu followed him, their dark faces grim. The ivory points of their war-spears carved through the deepening shadows, bobbing up-and-down as if floating on an uneasy pond.

Like Ares, they moved quickly and silently, propelling themselves over the snow with the help of their *kratok* bone skis.

As was customary, their leader, Maki-ku-Rathra, brought up the rear, guarding his pack with sharp-eyed vigilance. They were deep in kratok territory now, and although the beasts were supposed to be in the midst of their winter hibernation, one never knew when a lone male might catch their scent and emerge from its burrow.

This was the Highfold, a place of sheer cliffs, deep ravines, and bitterly cold winters. Before the Shadowring had appeared in the sky, the warm season would see a complete melting of the snows, and the blanket of ice under their feet would turn into a river of startling blue, its crystalline waters revealing a submerged forest of ancient logs.

At least that's what Ares had heard. He'd never seen a true Melting in his lifetime. The warm season still came, but its power was muted by the shadows in the sky.

Ares crested a ridge and nimbly swerved around a grey boulder, using the small downward slope to build momentum. Cold air rushed past him, caressing his face and the bare sides of his scalp, tugging at his long warrior's braid. A faint roar reached his ears, growing louder as he neared the Source.

They had almost arrived at the base of the *Matya*, the highest peak in the imposing Esskar range.

This was Ares's territory. He was *khefe*—a lone Hunter —and he had earned the right to venture here alone, but even he was hesitant to trek deep into the Highfold during winter. The Vradhu were a warmth-loving species, and like all of his kin, Ares hated the cold.

He had bitter memories of the cold.

Angling his skis, he carved a vicious half-circle in the snow, throwing up a spray of white powder as he came to a halt. He held up a hand and the Hunters behind him stopped in a similar fashion, quickly removing their skis and strapping them to their backs. Ares removed an *ankre* pod from his pack and snapped it open.

Darkness had fallen, and all he could make out were the whites of his clan-brothers' eyes.

Soft pink light formed a halo around the pack as the bioluminescent pod flared to life. Ares nodded in the direction of the cliff face, where ancient steps were carved into the stone wall, marking out a precipitous path to the top. He exchanged a knowing look with Maki and began to climb.

"I still don't see the point in going all the way to top," someone down the line grumbled. "It'd make better sense to check downstream first—"

Maki silenced the dissenter with a hiss. "There are dead things all the way from the river mouth to the Clanlands. We don't know how far up the chain the poison goes, so we will start at the Source and trace our way down through the Seeli Caves. We can't afford to miss anything."

Ares turned and glared at the insolent warrior, a lowlander named Baku. *Don't you understand anything?* He had half a mind to beat some respect into the idiot, but Maki had his own subtle way of dealing with these things. Several Hunters returned his stare with hostile looks of their own.

Pureblooded fools. Around half the pack was new, replacing those who had died during the last kratok hunt. Out of all of them, only Ares and Maki had a decent number of hunts under their belts.

Maki had five. He was once-blooded.

Ares had seven, the magic number. He was thrice-blooded, having killed three queens—a record for this generation of Hunters. The last queen he'd killed had been ancient, her eyeteeth as long as his arms. He'd taken the teeth as his prize and had them fashioned into *krivera* by a revered old weaponsmith.

Nothing was quite as sharp and strong and beautiful as a pair of kratok-fang blades.

The very same krivera were now strapped to his back as he climbed the walls of the Highfold, moving by feel more than sight.

Ares didn't even need the *ankre's* light, for he knew this ascent like the back of his hand, but he let it shine for the benefit of his brothers. They didn't have time to rescue any Hunter who slipped off the icy path.

The faint roar grew louder. "It's beyond the boulders," Ares shouted, mindful of those who had never been here before. "Follow me. Careful. The rocks are slippery here." A luminous blue mist rose from behind the massive rocks, which were nothing more than dark silhouettes.

He hauled himself up the rocks, muscles straining, his bare hands protesting as they came into contact with the freezing stone. Ares climbed quickly, by feel more than sight. Moving through the ancient stone formations and crevasses of the Highfold was as natural to him as breathing.

After all, this was his hunting ground.

As he reached the top, a gust of warm air hit him in the face. Moving quickly, he turned and traversed a narrow path that led down to a flat embankment of smooth rock.

Ares looked up at the waterfall as he waited for the others to catch up. As always, the Source was a breathtaking sight, a torrent of heated spring water rising from some unknown place within the mountain and cascading down an impossibly sheer cliff. Steam rolled off it, lit up by the brilliant glow of luminescent blue algae. The waterfall disappeared into a giant hole in the rock, where it became the underground riverway they called the Seeli Caves.

When the snows melted, he wouldn't even be able to stand here. This place would turn into a raging torrent of water.

As Maki and the others reached his side, Ares raised his arm and pointed at the waterfall. Strange green lights flickered behind the curtain of water, followed by a ripple of shadow. "See there?" he shouted, making sure they could read his lips in the glow of the *ankre*-light. "There's someone or *something* behind the waterfall."

A deep cave extended behind the cascade. Ares had spent many a night there, taking advantage of the natural warmth that seeped through the rocks.

"Who dares?" Maki hissed, his dark eyes narrowing in anger. The deep black *ankhata* on his face accentuated his fearsome expression.

"If they are the ones responsible for poisoning our waters, I will tear their eyeballs from their faces and rip out their tongues, so they have no choice but to walk blindly and mutely into the Underdark." A vicious smile curved Ares's lips as he contemplated his revenge.

"Hold, brother." Maki put a hand on Ares's shoulder. "Put a leash on that famous temper of yours. We don't know what we're dealing with."

"Doesn't matter. I'll destroy them."

"*Now* I remember why you don't work well with others, Ares-*rai*."

"I'm just thinking like a Hunter."

"The absence of caution can get you killed."

"So can overthinking. I haven't survived seven hunts by being scholarly."

"Truth. But you are also unfairly gifted."

"Merely shaped by Aethra's will, my Lord."

Several of the new warriors hissed as they witnessed Ares's familiarity with the pack-leader, but Ares was beyond caring about formality and protocol. Maki might be a Lord of the Two Clans, but he was also his friend.

Ares dipped his head in a show of respect. "I will go first and find out what is—"

A sleek vessel flew out from behind the waterfall, slicing through the torrent of water.

In unison, the warriors whipped their war-spears from behind their backs. "*Magrel!*" one of the purebloods hissed.

Ares drew his *krivera*—his twin bone swords.

The vessel looked like something straight out of the glyphs depicted in the Ancient Stones; a double-winged ship the size of a youngling kratok.

It drifted toward the embankment and descended in front

of them, seemingly soundless against the backdrop of the roaring falls. Ares held his blades low as the cursed machine landed on a flat area of stone. A blast of warm air hit him in the face, fluttering the edges of his cloak.

Curled around his left leg, his tail twitched in anticipation.

"*Naaga*," Maki growled, loud enough for only Ares to hear. "Now it makes sense. They poisoned the Source to draw us out of hiding."

"What could they possibly want with us? There is nothing of value to them here." A low hiss left Ares's lips. "How did they learn of our existence? We withdrew from the outside world eons ago. Perhaps it is best to just kill them and be done with it."

"Caution, brother. They obviously lured us here with some plan in mind. The Made Ones will be anticipating our violence."

"Feh." Ares took a step forward, raising his blades. "Just *let* them try and take advantage of us." Anger unfurled in his chest, making him want to decapitate the first Naaga he saw.

Young race of fools. They deserve to die slowly and painfully for what they have done to us.

They had tracked the poisoned waterways all the way from the Clanlands to the Highfold. He'd seen the destruction first-hand; the dead trees and plants, the lifeless *sarukark* floating belly-up in the rivers, the desolation across the wide waterplains. Their people had been forced out of the Clanlands and into the dense *sekkhoi* forests, where they carved out a meager living off sekkhoi fruit and rainwater.

This was not how they were supposed to live.

The Vradhu Hunters had been sent to find the source of the corruption and deal with it.

They hadn't been expecting *this*.

A door opened in the side of the ship. A ramp slid to the ground. Out walked a group of Naaga, six in total. They wore long robes that concealed their bodies from head to feet. Only the lower halves of their blue faces were visible.

"White-eyed devils," someone hissed. They had never seen the Naaga in real life, but they all knew what they looked like. They'd all been made to study the Ancient Stones, which depicted the long and bloody history of their peoples.

Ares was already moving, ignoring Maki's warning and sprinting across the flat rocks until he was face-to-face with the Naaga. He raised his swords. "Leave and take your cursed poison with you. This is *our* territory, Naaga."

He would defend it to the death.

The Naaga responded with silence. They didn't even flinch.

The group slowly parted. Another Naaga emerged, clad in shimmering armor made from thousands of tiny metal scales. A faceless helm concealed her features, but Ares could tell it was a *she* from the way she moved and the shape of her body.

The others respectfully moved aside.

A rush of feet and the collective flare of two dozen killing auras told Ares that Maki had assembled the pack behind him. His tail became a black blur as it uncoiled from around his leg and wrapped around the female's neck. He pressed the venomous barb against the underside of her chin.

He spotted a weak point there; a gap where the edge of the helm was supposed to connect with her scale-armor. Ares could punch his barb through it in an instant. She would be dead as soon as the tip punctured her skin.

Vradhu venom was incredibly toxic to all species on Khira. It was why they kept their tails so tightly leashed.

To further emphasize his point, Ares leveled the tips of his swords at her chest. According to the Ancient Stones, the Naaga possessed two hearts.

One on the right, and one on the left.

"*Tek a tek,*" she said.

What the fuck did that mean?

"Why did you poison the Source?" Maki roared.

No response. The Naaga pulled something from the belt at her waist; a round metal orb attached to a chain.

Realization struck him. "They can't understand us. Old Verthe once told me they are unable to speak any tongue but their own. The Drakhin designed them that way."

"Then what's the point of—"

A pungent, sickly-sweet smell filled the air, mingling with the earthy-wet scent of the Source. Faint white smoke poured from the orb. The female swung it back-and-forth, inclining her head.

Weakness flooded through Ares. His legs started to quiver. His grip became loose. "Poison!" he gasped.

He slammed his tail-barb home. It pierced the soft skin underneath the Naaga's chin. The effect was instantaneous. She fell to the ground, dead. The orb dropped from her hands and rolled around on the glistening rock.

At the same time, Ares and his clan-brothers dropped to their knees. It was as if all his muscles had been turned into stone. He couldn't move, not even to turn his head to look at Maki and the others.

Were they going to die here?

Why the fuck would they lure us up here, only to kill us?

That final thought trickled through his mind as the remaining Naaga swarmed around them, metal restraints appearing in their hands.

His anger turned to horror and outrage, and then...

Nothing.

Consciousness returned. Ares gasped. His eyes flew open. Excruciating pain drilled through his head, from the base of his skull right up into his temples.

An oppressive grey ceiling arched overhead. He couldn't

move. Something held him down. *Where is the sky?* A bolt of panic shot through him. They'd taken him somewhere. He was *trapped.* Where was Maki? Where were the rest of the Vradhu pack? He tried to sit up, but restraints cut into his flesh. Ares screamed in frustration.

Cold hands touched his bare skin. Suddenly, a Naaga hovered over him. Pearlescent white eyes without pupil or iris dissected him.

"I'll fucking *kill you*," Ares spat. He tried to move his tail, but it was bound tightly around his leg. Although he desperately wanted to strike the Naaga, the venom in his barb was depleted and would take several days to replenish.

The Naaga shrugged. "You are truly as dangerous as they warned, aren't you? Oh, do not look at me like that, barbarian. Understand that your people survive at our mercy. The moment you stop being useful to us is the moment we obliterate the Ardu-Sai. If you do as we say, you and your clansmen will be treated fairly, and we will reverse the contamination."

"*Fairly?* Y-you poisonous... bastard..." Ares's speech came out jumbled. He shook his head, trying to make sense of it all through the thick fog in his mind. Of course, the Naaga spoke only Naaga, and for some reason, Ares understood him perfectly well.

How?

"Since we are unable to speak any other tongue, all of our subjects get the language implant." The Naaga sighed. "Yours is not grafting well. Too much aggression, you have. Try to calm down. Here. This will help."

Ares raged against his restraints, but it was futile. Something cold and hard came into contact with the bare skin of his lower arm. A needle prick.

Then darkness.

Ares rubbed the area at the base of his skull. A small, faintly tender ridge protruded from his skin; the only remaining evidence that *magrel* had been forced into his brain.

Now he could communicate in perfect Naaga. *All* of the Vradhu warriors could, thanks to their blue captors.

Despicable creatures. If only the cursed Drakhin were still around to take responsibility for their unruly race of slaves.

Ares caught Maki's eye. The Lord of the Two Clans returned his stare with a forlorn look. "They have us caught between the kratok's jaws." He rolled his war-spear back-and-forth along bare, callused palms.

At least they'd been given their weapons back, along with their kratok-hide armor. "*So you can hunt effectively,*" they said.

"There is nothing on my mind but blood-rage." Ares tried to still his twitching tail. "We should kill them now. What can they really do to us apart from poison our lands? Our people are safe in the sekkhoi, and I don't trust these white-eyed devils and their false bargains." Fury turned his heartbeat into a rapid staccato. The dull remnant of pain in his head only added to his anger.

"Ares," Maki said slowly, rising from his seat. "If the Ardu-Sai is destroyed, where will we go? The Naaga have spread uncontrollably across Khira. They vastly outnumber us. We can't afford to do anything rash."

Ares walked across to the only window in their cell, a narrow slit revealing the dark, glittering vacuum of space. He stared outside. "Especially now that they have thrust us amongst the stars?" Unease unfurled in the pit of his stomach. He'd never thought he would enter space, and now they were on a Naaga ship, bound for the Dagger in the sky.

Of course, the Dagger was actually a vessel, an ancient destroyer left behind by the Drakhin when they abandoned the lush paradise that was Khira. The Drakhin word for it was *Hythra.* No one really knew why it was still stuck in Khira's orbit, and even the scholars who constantly pored over the Ancient Stones—Ares's father included—had been unable to learn its true origins.

The Dagger was an enigma, and it was currently occupied by the Naaga, the blue-skinned creatures that had once been slaves to the Drakhin.

Everything their masters had left behind, the Naaga had taken over.

"Control that famous temper of yours, brother," Maki whispered as they momentarily became weightless. The gravity in the cell had been fluctuating ever since they left the surface of Khira. Ares cursed as his feet left the ground. "We have our weapons and our armor and our venom. Let us enter this destroyer and act at completing this *task* they have set for us. All the while, we will wait and observe and learn. We are Vradhu, and their combat skills pale in comparison to ours. Surely the opportunity to escape will present itself."

Gravity returned, and Ares, Maki, and two-dozen Vradhu warriors dropped to the floor again, their bare feet making barely a sound. The others, especially the younger purebloods, appeared spooked.

None of them had been in space before.

"The transporter will be docking soon. As soon as your holding cell opens, you are to exit the vessel through the rear entrance."

"What?" Vanu, the youngest of the pack, thrust his spear in the direction of the cold, detached voice. It came from the ceiling. "Show yourself, bastard!"

"They are speaking through a machine," Maki said quietly. "Save your energy, Vanu."

The warrior's face darkened like a towering storm, but he dipped his head in acknowledgement and backed down, even though outrage twisted the black *ankhata* on his cheeks.

"You will be released into the most heavily infested sector of the Hythra. Do not bother looking for us, because you will not

find us. Your task is to hunt the Corrupted. Full decapitation is necessary in all cases. Fail in this task, and the consequences will be dire."

"They plan to use us like animals," Vanu hissed. "To hunt their own vermin?"

It made sense. The Vradhu were the most supreme natural hunters on Khira. Of *course* the Naaga would want to use them to eliminate pests. Ares shook his head as he stared out of the small window. The bleak edges of the *Hythra* were coming into view. A strange kind of anticipation coursed through him as he caught sight of the ancient ship.

Some said the Dagger had been the floating residence of the Dark One himself.

As they drifted inside the *Hythra*, entering through an open portal in her metal hull, the feeling grew stronger.

Dark energy. That's what it was. A ripple of static along his skin. Whispers in his mind. His heart clenching and twisting.

Welcome, Hunter.

Had the language implant turned him mad, or had a voice just spoken in his mind?

What?

He tried to elicit a response, but all he got in return was an emptiness as vast and desolate as the *Hythra* herself.

So be it. It was pointless to dwell on what he couldn't change. Things only made sense to Ares when he moved forward. *Do not dwell. Act.* He felt for his swords, making sure they were secure at his back. He checked his bone-daggers, making sure the large serrated one at his waist easily slid free of its scabbard. He flicked his tail, willing his poison-barb to regenerate.

Then he closed his eyes and waited, vowing never to let anyone, Naaga or otherwise, get the better of him ever again.

He would *not* be owned.

His will was his own.

Oh, you will do just fine, Hunter.

There it was again. The voice in his mind—was it male or female?—spoke something else, some language in-between Vradhu and Naaga, and somehow, he understood.

Truly, this translator-thing in his brain had damaged his sanity. Perhaps killing some of those wretched Naaga would make him feel right again.

As they disembarked from the transporter, Ares's heart pounded like a skin drum. As *khefe*, he went first, his krivera drawn and ready.

Ever since they'd woken inside that cramped cell on the transport, they hadn't seen a single Naaga. The white-eyed devils worked remotely, using threats and physical restraints. He suspected it was because they lacked the ability to fight.

By their actions, they showed that they feared the Vradhu, as they should.

Ares walked down the ramp, taking in his surroundings. They were in a massive square chamber bordered on all sides by grey walls. The walls possessed a strange reflective quality, capturing the light and throwing it back at them in the form of glittering skeins of silver. As he stared at the metallic surface, it seemed to writhe and shift, as if responding to his scrutiny.

The sensation in his chest intensified into a solid thrum. Energy rippled across his skin. Out of the corner of his eye, he caught movement.

There. In the corner. He whirled. The Vradhu pack moved in unison, following Ares down the ramp. They spread out in a defensive formation, with Ares at the front.

He *was* the spearhead, after all. His father had named him well.

"These are the so-called Corrupted?" Maki growled. "*This* is our prey?"

Three Naaga stared blankly at them.

"They want us to kill their own kind?" A deep and thorough sense of disgust filled Ares's heart. He couldn't understand these Naaga at all. They fought without weapons and traded in secrets and lies. They bargained without honor and their promises were laced with hidden barbs.

And now they would use Ares and his clan-brothers like trained *shuklak*-beasts, to exterminate their brethren?

"We have to find a way out of here," he whispered. "This is madness."

"Look, Ares. There's something wrong with them."

As Ares stepped onto the floor of the cavernous chamber, heat radiated through his bare feet.

What is this? Was the floor actually warm, or was the air around them frigid?

Pulsating vibrations rippled across the soles of his feet. The surface of the floor felt soft and pliable, and it seemed to actually *caress* his bare skin as if it were a living thing.

His heart thudded in his chest like a war-drum.

The three Naaga lurched forward, walking with an uneven gait. Maki was right. There was a *wrongness* about them.

Their pale blue skin had lost its lustre. The plumage covering their heads was gone, replaced by a crown of shimmering grey metal that twisted and swayed as they walked. The very same metal substance marred their skin, forming small jagged patches—as if they had caught a flesh-eating disease.

"Unngh." One of the Naaga moaned, a flat, desolate sound that made Ares's tail stiffen.

Corrupted. Now Ares understood. These creatures were no longer alive. They were little more than soulless husks, consumed from the inside out by some malevolent metal demon.

How? What is this sorcery?

A dull hum echoed through the chamber, and the ramp

extending from the Naaga vessel started to withdraw. Ares snapped his head toward the sound, staring at the *magrel* vessel.

The Naaga ship was simply a much larger version of the craft they'd encountered at the Source. Curved wings extended from a sleek metal hull shaped like an arrowhead. Thin slits representing port-holes appeared along its midsection, disappearing where the hull widened at the rear to accommodate four long tubelike projections. They were as big as ancient tree trunks and emitted an unnatural green glow. Apart from the rear exit, there were no other visible doors. They had never seen the Naaga who piloted the cursed thing.

For such a large vessel, it was unnervingly quiet, hovering about a man's height above the floor.

Thin metal arms extended from the belly of the ship, depositing a black box onto the floor. *"Supplies. Enough to sustain you for the duration of your Hunt."*

There was that creepy fucking disembodied voice again, amplified from some hidden source within the ship.

The ship emitted several blasts of hot air and reversed.

"Yo, they're leaving us here?" Vanu broke from the pack and ran toward the ship as it retreated. The rear wall opened, revealing another cavernous chamber.

"It would be foolish to try and follow us, Vradhu hunter. Those who set foot on the Hythra are never allowed to leave. If you take another step forward, we will activate the airlock and all of you will die."

The way the insolent Naaga threatened death, one would think the Vradhu were little more than animals.

"Vanu!" Maki reached the young warrior's side and dragged him back.

Vanu froze.

The rear wall slammed shut with deafening finality, cutting them off from the retreating vessel—their only escape.

These Naaga think they can toy with us? The thrumming

in Ares's veins became a steady pulse, deep and resonant and powerful. Its heady, intoxicating nature reminded him of the Vradhu war-dance.

The Corrupted moaned.

Ares hissed and drew his swords. He ran forward, the pack moving behind him in strict formation. They might resent him, but they knew how strong he was. They knew *what* he was.

Spearhead.

Several more Corrupted joined the horde. Two broke away from the group, sprinting forward with unnatural speed.

Ares ran faster. His blade found the neck of one, slicing through flesh and metal. *Doof.* The blank-eyed head dropped to the floor and rolled onto its side.

The other Corrupted evaded him, going straight for one of the young purebloods.

"Aargh!" The Vradhu's scream split the silence as the Corrupted raked metal-taloned fingers across his chest. Panicking, he uncoiled his tail and sank his barb into the creature's back.

Still, it kept moving. The potent paralysis toxin in the Vradhu sting failed to take it down.

That was unheard of. A Hunter's poison always felled its prey.

Maki arrived in a flash, swinging his war-spear in a brutal arc that severed the Corrupted's neck and sent its head toppling to the ground.

Ares ignored the twitching headless body on the floor and swept through the horde of Corrupted like a tempest as more and more of the wretched things piled into the room. Maki and the pack followed his lead, countering the speed of the Corrupted with the deadly grace of the Vradhu war-dance.

Shik. One of Ares's blades snagged a limb.

Crunch. The other went through a neck.

Whoosh. He evaded another frenzied attack, his long braid swinging wildly.

All the while, his bare feet flirted with the metal floor. Each step was met with a surge of warmth, as if he were drawing energy out of the *Hythra* itself.

Finding a lull in the battle, he paused to take stock of his situation. His breathing was rapid, his pulse frantic, his senses stretched taut. The world moved in hyper-real slow-motion; he felt as if he could streak through it at the speed of light. Even the tiniest vibration could be felt through his blades, which had become an extension of his body.

This was bloodlust. This was when his heart sang. This was when he felt most alive.

This was his duty.

He was made for the hunt. Hunters didn't get to enjoy the simple pleasures of clan life. Once the *ankhata* emerged, marking the onset of manhood, the warriors were sent to the outer reaches of the Ardu-Sai to guard against kratok and protect the hidden Clanlands from discovery. Never again would they enjoy the warmth of a female's nest, and as for the prospect of finding a mate...

What sane female would want to bond with a Hunter?

Hunters didn't get mates. Death was their betrothed, and battle was one of the few pleasures they could enjoy.

Boom. A tremor shook the floor. The surface went from pleasantly warm to burning hot. Ares started to move, but the floor had become soft under his feet, like mud.

His feet sank in.

What? Impossible!

The burning sensation in his feet turned into pain, as if thousands of tiny needles were being pushed into his soles.

The floor rippled outwards.

The floor rose up.

The floor around him turned into shimmering liquid metal.

Welcome, Hunter.

Ares tried to leap away, but the shifting stuff had a good

hold on him now, sending vines of liquid metal up his legs. Writhing tendrils pierced his skin, drawing out rivulets of blood.

The other Vradhu ran to his side, shouting in alarm.

Magrel. Unnatural. Disgust and horror coursed through him.

The very substance of the *Hythra* herself *invaded* him, eating him alive. Was he doomed to meet the same fate as the Corrupted?

As Ares sank into the floor, he begged the fates for a miracle.

The living metal rippled under his skin, shooting through his chest, his arms, his face, even his fucking *eyes*.

He screamed.

CHAPTER ONE

CALEXA CROSSED her arms and stared up at the Primean, refusing to be intimidated. The woman who had identified herself only as "S" regarded her with an even gaze, her elegant features revealing only detached curiosity.

Calexa resisted the urge to roll her eyes. S was as Primean as they came; genetically perfect, as cool as the inky blackness of space itself, and blessed with that infuriating and oh-so typically *Primean* combination of haughtiness and benevolence. Somehow, she'd escaped Calexa's notice, following her into the lower decks.

A muffled *boom* reverberated throughout the cabin, accompanied by a great metallic groan. Calexa balanced lightly on her feet as the floor tipped sideways. Lights flickered. The walls shook. Shrill alarms of varying pitch and intensity warned her of things she could do nothing about. Pressure was dropping. Gravity was decreasing. Somewhere above their heads, oxygen escaped through a broken seal.

S didn't even blink. She lost her balance, broke her fall with her hands, righted herself, and straightened her flowing sea green tunic—the same color as her striking eyes—all in one continuous, seamless motion. If the alarms bothered her, she didn't show it. "What's our status, Captain Acura?"

Captain? Ha. Only a Primean would use such an old-fashioned term. Calexa was more accustomed to the things they called her in the Fiveways Bazaar, names like: *metalbones, Khral-slayer,* and *blood-digger.* Those were hard-earned names, and they could be terms of endearment or vicious insults, depending on how they were spoken. When people had attempted the latter, she'd been known to separate digits and limbs from bodies.

"The Paxnath are firing on us. They've given us two options: surrender, or get blasted into oblivion." Calexa shrugged, making a conscious effort to appear calm when she was seething inside. The Paxnath stealth-cruisers had taken them by surprise, appearing on their tail without warning. Somehow, the cunning Paxnath had seen through the *Medusa's* cloaking. "That's what happens when you travel outside the designated spaceflight lanes." She ducked as a ration canister broke free of its housing and hurtled toward her. It smashed into the rear wall, spilling its contents—sealed packets of fragrant *aphernium* tea—across the metal floor. "Raphael!"

"Cal." Her navigator's deep voice filtered through her comm, forming a pillar of calm amidst the swirling chaos. "We need to get out of this killspace right now. We're leaking power and our shields won't take another mega-hit like that. The bad news is that more Paxnath have joined the fray. We're outnumbered five-to-one."

"Throw some fire at them, abort the flightpath and eat some distance. What's the nearest J-point?"

"Unknown."

"Unknown? Are you fucking kidding me?" Calexa groaned, pressing her hand against the wall to steady herself as the ship lurched. S looked her up-and-down in that calm, analytical way of hers and copied her movements, swaying elegantly to one side as the *Medusa* rocked back-and-forth.

"*I've located one, but it isn't mapped. I don't have any reliable data on its endpoint. It could take us back to the Solar System, or it could spit us out on the other side of the fucking Universe. I don't even know if it's stable.*" Raphael paused, and the silence—mere seconds—grew long and tense and almost unbearable. Finally, he spoke. "*Do we have any other options?*"

"Go. Take the J-point, Raf." It was a no-brainer. Get blasted to smithereens, get captured by Paxnath slavers, or enter a random jump-point and ride the freaky Netherverse to the middle of nowhere. Slavery was a fate worse than death, and it was *much* worse than surfing an unmapped jump-hole to parts unknown.

Boom! Another blast sent a vicious shudder through the ship. This time, the force came from behind.

"*That was one of ours,*" Raphael informed her. "*I fired back.*"

Calexa fervently hoped the *Medusa's* powerful triticore missiles had bought them a sliver of time. She'd spent a small fortune on the damn things.

"I need to get to Torandor," S said, her voice cracking ever-so-slightly. Maybe there *were* real emotions beneath her flawless porcelain exterior. "Is there any way around this mess?"

"The only way out now is to jump," Calexa snapped. "I warned you about the dangers of taking the unguarded route."

"I signed the agreement-waiver. I was willing to take the risk. So were you."

"Yeah." For the amount of credits the Primean had offered, Calexa and her crew would have flown to the depths of hell and back. With three Grand Maximums, one could buy a livable planet in the Nykrion System, install a decent planetary defense unit, and comfortably retire. "Too bad the *risk* comes in the form of Paxnath slave-hunters. Do you even *know* how they treat their body-slaves?"

S kept quiet. Secrets swirled in her eyes, but it wasn't Calexa's place to tease them out. It would be highly unprofessional of her to ask why a pure-blooded Primean and her entire retinue of human servants had hired Calexa and her crew of mercs to ferry them to the refuge-planet of Torandor.

No questions asked. That was one of the cardinal rules of the Fiveways, and it was the reason small mercenary outfits like theirs could charge big bucks. The bigger the risk, the bigger the price. Danger money was always tempting, but it was also a gamble.

This time they'd been unlucky.

"Should've stuck to killing Paxnath," Calexa muttered under her breath. S raised an eyebrow. If there had only been one Paxnath stealth-cruiser, they could have returned fire, crippled the damn thing, and boarded it. But five fully armed Paxnath ships was too many to handle.

"Sorry about the turbulence. I'm nearly at the J-point, Cal." Raphael was still on the comm. *"You sure about this? I don't even have rough co-ords. We're going into completely unknown territory."*

The walls shook with the force of another blast.

"Do you even have to ask, Raf? Do it." As she gave the order, Calexa watched S closely. The tall woman's stance was deceptively relaxed. Her slender arms hung loosely by her sides, and her unnaturally green eyes were clear and serene. She radiated... nothing. No panic, no fear, no tension. That hint of desperation Calexa had detected earlier—that tiny, almost imperceptible *crack*—had vanished. Perhaps she'd imagined it.

"Where will the jump take us?" The Primean's voice didn't waver as the *Medusa* rode the shockwaves, shaking violently. They dropped to the floor.

"Wherever the Netherverse decides."

A thrill of uncertainty coursed down Calexa's metal-impregnated spine. They hadn't been forced to make a Panic Jump in a long, long time. What they were about to do was incredibly dangerous, but if they didn't go now, they were dead.

"*Incoming!*" Raphael yelled. "*Our shields are fucked. I'm going to go.*"

Calexa grabbed S by the shoulders and rolled as a wave of energy smashed into the *Medusa's* starboard side. She found a handhold and hauled the Primean into her landing seat. "In you go," she grunted, her bionic joints absorbing the impact. The automated restraints came down, locking S into place.

Boom! "Come on, Raf!" Calexa hung onto the handhold with all her strength as the *Medusa* shook like a piece of space-junk in an asteroid storm. "What are you waiting for?"

Silence. Raphael was probably concentrating, or maybe they were already touching the edge of the Netherverse. The comms always went dead when they entered the Silverstream.

Calexa's suspicions were confirmed when a faint electric tingle rippled across her skin. Beside her, the Primean had gone still. S lifted a shaky hand to her mouth, as if she were about to retch.

A loud roar engulfed the cabin, drowning out everything else. Then, as quickly as it had started, the sound died away. Calexa hauled herself into the seat beside S. "First time riding the Netherverse?"

Unable to speak, S merely nodded. Despite the fact that S was a self-righteous, stuck-up, untouchable Primean, Calexa felt a sudden stab of pity for the woman. "For some reason, your kind don't tolerate inter-dimensional travel well." Her voice softened. "Take a deep breath and close your eyes. Trust me, it gets better. In a moment, you won't feel like emptying your guts all over my floor."

"H-how did you know?"

"I just know." The debilitating nausea Primeans experienced when entering the Netherverse was something she'd learned about from the two halfbreeds on her crew, but Calexa wasn't about to spill the beans on the twins. Primeans got all funny when it came to things like genetic purity, and breeding with humans was strictly forbidden.

For 'ethical' reasons, the offspring of such unions rarely survived.

A low hum reverberated throughout the cabin, and suddenly the whole damn ship—the seats, the floor, and the metal walls—bristled with a faint static charge. If they were near a viewport right now, they would see a stream of silver-blue light outside. Calexa's scalp tingled as her short brown hair rose into the air. She couldn't see her reflection, but unlike S, whose braids curved over her head in neat, orderly rows, she probably looked ridiculous.

The hair-raising static was just one of the strange effects of riding through the Netherverse—nicknamed the *Silverstream* —a parallel dimension where thousands of light-years could pass in the blink of an eye.

"Don't worry," she said dryly, "we'll be back in the Universe soon. We're probably already there." Was it possible to be in two places at once? Inter-dimensional travel did funny things to the space-time continuum. Fudge the co-ordinates and one could overshoot the mark by a thousand light-years. There were even reports of spacecraft existing in two places at once. Like most space phenomena, the Netherverse was poorly understood, but some were crazy enough to ride it anyway, throwing their fates to the mercy of the Silverstream.

"There's no way of predicting where we'll end up, is there?" S had regained her composure a little, but her voice was taut with apprehension. She'd probably never encountered anything like this in her sterile, predictable, *perfect* Primean world.

"Nope. Just pray that we end up close enough to some semblance of civilization."

And beg the stars that the aliens we encounter won't be of the enslaving, flesh-eating, or kill-on-sight varieties.

Calexa's thoughts ran to dire places, but out of consideration for her paying customer, she kept her mouth shut.

CHAPTER TWO

─────────────

"*WE'RE DOWN to backup power and reserve oxygen,*" Raphael was back online, but his voice was faint, the transmission patchy and crackling with static. "*Our main powerbank was damaged by a blast-surge. It's nothing Monroe can't fix, but it'll take some time. You'd better rug up, because I'm going to kill the heat, and as you've probably already noticed, I've dimmed the lights and reduced the internal gravity.*" He sighed. "*Jumping through the Netherverse uses a lot of energy, but at least we shot out of there at phenomenal speed, so we'll keep moving without too much effort. I'm running a location scan. I'll give you an update as soon as I get our bearings. In the meantime, try not to breathe too much. Monroe's located the air-leak and plugged it, but we lost a big chunk of our air reserves. Space sucks.*"

"It's one hell of a vacuum," Calexa said dryly as she jumped down into the armory, bypassing the ladder and landing lightly on her feet. She'd left S in the main passenger bay with her terrified human servants. The Primean had been unexpectedly gentle with the women as she tried to calm them down.

Zahra greeted Calexa with a lazy half-wave. She was

standing in front of a neatly arranged row of weapons racks, her grey-green eyes narrowed. "The blast-cartridges are all fully charged, but once they're depleted, we won't have any juice left until Monroe gets the powerbanks back online. We'll be down to naked blades and our fists... that's if we actually encounter anyone to fight in the first place. Why do I always assume everyone else in the Universe is hostile?"

"Comes with the territory." Calexa scanned the impressive collection of weapons, her lips quirking into a wry smile as she attempted to lighten the mood. "Remember when we couldn't even afford a decent armory? You were so desperate for a blast-weapon you stole a Zarakian warlord's photon multiplier."

"That thing ended up being a total piece of shit." Zahra rolled her eyes. "Those Zarakians aren't really as badass as they look. I don't get what all the fuss—"

"*Hey, Cal?*" Raphael's voice cut through their conversation like a lightblade. "*Are you near a monitor?*"

"Yeah. What's up?"

"*Turn it on,* now."

"What's the problem?"

"*I don't know how that thing evaded our surveillance. It just appeared out of nowhere.*" Raphael's subdued tone sent a warning prickle down the back of Calexa's neck. Her navigator was normally as cool-as-ice, but now he sounded... afraid.

Calexa waved her hand across the surveillance monitor to activate it. No response. She slammed her fist into the wall and the ancient thing flickered to life.

"Oh, bloody *hell*," she whispered, going still.

Zahra swore.

"What the hell is *that*?" Calexa croaked. She stared at the screen in disbelief. Maybe she was seeing things; a side-effect of the dropping oxygen concentration.

A ship floated before them. It was unlike anything she'd seen before.

The monitor seemed to strain under the weight of the

immense craft. It glided past silently, ominously, an endless mass of smooth metal and slow-blinking lights.

A chill ran through Calexa, raising goosebumps along her forearms. The cabin's rapidly plummeting temperature didn't help. "Zoom out. I want to get an idea of how big this thing is."

"Hold on..." Zahra played with the controls, entering a swift string of commands. "Let me just..." She frowned, a look of intense concentration crossing her features. She zoomed out once, then twice, then three times.

The alien ship completely filled the screen. It had no beginning and no end. It had swallowed the stars.

"How big *is* this thing?" Calexa rubbed her arms, trying to ward off the cold. She shifted on her feet, ignoring the dull ache that started at the base of her spine and wormed its way into her shoulder blades. It was a familiar sensation. Cold and fatigue didn't sit well with her bionic vertebral implants.

Zahra shook her head in disbelief. "It's bigger than any spacecraft I've seen before, and I've been around." Nothing much could faze Zahra Maleki, but now she looked totally spooked. "It's strange that they haven't tried to make contact yet. If they're anything but hostile, I'll eat my fucking combat suit." Her voice dropped to a whisper. "I don't recognize the design, Cal. I've seen everything from giant Bardak freighters to those spooky Vor Dhanu battleships, and this ain't none of those. What the hell are we supposed to do now, Captain?"

"We're running on backup power. We've taken critical damage. I've got a passenger bay full of terrified humans who are indentured to one weird-ass Primean, and we don't have fixed co-ordinates..." Calexa turned away from the monitor and began to pace. Her bionic joints loosened with the movement, her strides becoming fluid and powerful as kinetic motion kicked in. She massaged her temples, trying to clear her thoughts. "For once, I've got nothing. There's no way we can fight *that*. We can't outrun it either. We don't have enough energy left to power the jump-drive."

"In other words, we're screwed." Zahra wasn't the type to sugar-coat things.

"I'm sorry, Zahra." Frustration coursed through Calexa as she locked eyes with her friend. "I'm out of ideas."

Before them, the massive alien ship continued to drift across the monitor. Calexa didn't give voice to the obvious.

Space was a dark and empty place indeed, and out on the far reaches of the Universe, ships went missing from time to time. They could die here, or worse. Beyond the stars, there existed fates worse than death.

Especially for humans.

Zahra placed a consoling hand on Calexa's shoulder. "It's not your fault, Cal. There was no way we could have predicted those Paxnath would appear out of nowhere, or that they'd be traveling in a bloody fleet. They *never* travel in fleets. We barely made it out of there in one piece, but at least we're alive."

"For now. Fucking Paxnath. We should have waited for a safer job. Anything involving those goddamned Primeans always ends up getting complicated."

"Don't beat yourself up over it, Cal. The higher the risk, the higher the reward. If not for that Paxnath ambush, we would have pulled it off and found our way out of the Five-ways for good. It was a big-money job for a reason, a once-in-a-century kind of thing."

"Shit." Calexa grappled with fear and self-doubt. "I was hoping to get them to Torandor within the fortnight, not deliver our passengers into the jaws of some mysterious alien super-race."

"Super-race?"

"Look at that thing. What kind of beings do you think are capable of creating something so *huge*?" She could see the edge of the ship now. It was all straight lines and sharp angles, a giant blade slicing through the obsidian fabric of the

Universe. No living creature should be able to create something so monstrous.

A metallic groan echoed through the cabin and the *Medusa* listed to one side. As the floor went diagonal under Calexa's feet, she glanced at the navigation screens in alarm. "What the hell's happening?"

"*Something's overriding our momentum.*" Raphael sounded eerily detached. Suddenly, the dim backup lighting died and the charge-lights on the weapons rack went out, shrouding them in shadow. "*Don't mind the blackout. I'm temporarily redirecting all power to the thrusters, but the drag-force is too—*" Abruptly, the comm died.

The alien craft on the monitor grew bigger and bigger, swallowing up the screen.

"It's pulling us in, isn't it?"

Zahra nodded. In the faint silvery glow of the monitor, her expression was calm, but her hands trembled slightly. "Some sort of electromagnetic drag-field would be my guess."

The monitor blinked out.

"Shit."

Squinting in the near-darkness, Calexa pulled her PX-45 from its holster and checked the energy clip. She did it without thinking, the reflexive action giving her a fleeting sense of control. A thin row of blue lights flickered along the clip; it was fully charged. She snapped it back into its receiver and selected another weapon—a frag-grenade—from the weapons rack before turning toward the bridge-side exit. She needed to get to the observation dome so she could see what the hell was going on.

"Maybe they'll be friendly?" Zahra's teeth flashed in the darkness as Calexa looked over her shoulder. "A benevolent species with higher intelligence. I've always wanted to encounter a race of enlightened beings."

"When has that *ever* turned out to be the case? The

Universe is populated with assholes and you know it. All we can do is prepare for the worst."

"And hope for the best?"

"And try to get out of this alive... and *free*."

"And if that's not an option?"

They shared a silent look of understanding. "You know *all* my hangups, Zar. I don't deal well with subjugation."

Neither of them dared say what was really on their minds; that deep down, they were absolutely terrified of what would happen next.

CHAPTER THREE

THE MONSTROUS SHIP that had swallowed the stars now swallowed the *Medusa*. A gaping black maw of an entrance opened up in its side, and some mysterious, irresistible force dragged them toward an uncertain fate. They were utterly helpless against it. Raphael had given up on resistance. Feeding what little juice they had left into the thrusters was a futile waste of energy, and as for the idea of using their remaining missiles...

Against a vessel of this size, that would be insanity.

From her vantage point inside the bridge's observation dome, all Calexa could do was stare as they flew into the abyss. Raphael had chased them away from the navigation pod, demanding absolute silence so he could concentrate on keeping the *Medusa's* failing systems online.

Their usually laid-back navigator was tense. They were *all* fucking tense.

"We're totally screwed. I mean, we've been screwed before, but this time we are *screwed*." Beside her, Mai let her Irradium cannon drop to the floor with a heavy thud. The bloody thing probably weighed close to a hundred pounds, but Mai carried it around as if it were as light as a feather. Like

Calexa and Zahra, Mai had undergone enhancement therapy on that shit-hole of a planet called Dashki-5. Her bones had been coated in a metal composite, enabling her to carry some *very* heavy things around.

Calexa didn't know what to say, because Mai was absolutely right. She shook her head as she pressed her palm against the cold surface of the observation window, trying to see beyond the small halo of light that surrounded the *Medusa*. The ship's navigation lights could only penetrate so far into the inky blackness.

Darkness engulfed them, obliterating the glittering tapestry of space. Without the familiar backdrop of stars, Calexa felt anchorless and rudderless. They were in freefall, and it was utterly terrifying.

Calexa's breath misted in the frigid air as she exchanged a look with Mai and Zahra. The dim light was unkind to her companions, accentuating their tired faces, deepening the dark circles under their eyes, and highlighting the pallor that came from too many days spent away from the warm caress of a decent sun.

They were wide-eyed, ashen-faced ghosts.

She had no doubt she looked just as bad. A good night's sleep was a luxury she hadn't enjoyed in years. In real life, there was no such thing as a deep, dreamless sleep. There were only snatches of fitful rest, stolen in-between visits to grim, charmless destinations.

"Do the girls in the passenger bay have enough thermal gear?" Instead of worrying about her chronic insomnia, Calexa turned to more practical matters.

"Monroe magicked some thermal skinsuits and blankets out of God-knows-where." Zahra said absently, her attention held hostage by the inescapable void.

"*Monroe* did that? Since when has he been even remotely approachable?" The Primean half-breed could fix anything and everything, but he was the surliest individual Calexa had

ever met. It wasn't unusual for him to go for days—even *weeks*
—without speaking a single word to anyone. She couldn't
imagine him doing anything nice for *anyone*, let alone a group
of humans who had pledged their loyalty to one of the
Primeans he so despised.

Calexa tensed as a dull groan echoed throughout the
cabin, followed by an eerie metallic tapping sound. The ship
listed to one side, throwing Calexa off-balance as Mai's Irradium cannon rolled around on the floor. Mai swore as it hit the
wall with a heavy, metallic *clunk*. An odd sensation—like
gravity being pulled out from underneath her like a rug—
churned Calexa's stomach as the *Medusa* dropped.

"Grab a safety hold," Calexa barked. They all scrambled to
the corner of the cabin, fighting the topsy-turvy motion of the
ship. They should have been strapped into their landing
chairs, but because flight monitor-screen was down, Calexa
had been unable to drag herself away from the observation
dome. She *had* to know what was going on. It was like
watching a multi-freighter wreck in slow motion; she knew
disaster was imminent, but she couldn't look away.

She curled her hands around the nearest safety hold and
waited. The ship rocked some more, then a deafening crash
shook the cabin. It was accompanied by a series of powerful
shudders.

The three of them didn't say a word until the movement
stopped and everything went quiet.

Calexa took a deep breath. "I get the feeling we've landed." With a sigh of relief, she released the safety hold. The
impact hadn't been as bad as she'd feared. Raphael must have
worked his magic and had the presence of mind to drop the
landing gear.

She looked outside and saw nothing but endless darkness.

There was no sound, no light, and not a single sign of life.
She was acutely aware of the heavy rasp of her breathing and
her thundering pulse.

"This really fucking sucks," Mai whispered.

Zahra let out a cynical snort. "I've changed my mind. I've decided I *am* afraid of the dark."

Calexa nodded in agreement. There was no way in hell she was going to lead them out into the darkness, not when they had no idea what they were up against.

All they could do was wait. Eventually, whoever—or *whatever*—was out there would show themselves.

CHAPTER FOUR

THE THRONE of thorns writhed in response to Ares's presence, its sharp *ilverium* tendrils curling around his arms and legs in a painful caress. Occasionally, they would penetrate his skin, burrowing beneath the surface like newly forming arteries, pulsating in response to the ship's innate rhythm. The biometal could harden like stone or become as fluid as water with merely a thought. Ares was no longer a simple creature of flesh and bone and blood. The ever-shifting living metal had infiltrated his flesh and transformed him into a monster.

It was filthy *magrel*—unnatural metal—and his body was full of it. At this rate, he wouldn't be surprised if he was turning into one of those cursed Drakhin.

He was never supposed to have bonded with the *Hythra's* semi-sentient networks. The ones chosen to pilot the ancient Drakhin ships—the only ones who were supposed to be compatible—were the Naaga.

Then Ares had stepped onboard, and everything had gone to shit. For some inexplicable reason, the ship had *chosen* him.

He didn't know exactly how long they'd been trapped on this infernal ship. Without the seasons to guide them, time blended into an endless stream. He estimated they might have been here for an entire hunting season, but he couldn't be sure.

The pain of discovery had been sharp, the lessons brutal, and the experience terrifying, but the bonding had given him power, and the *Hythra's* thousand-odd Naaga residents—those who *hadn't* been corrupted—had quickly learned not to mess with the Vradhu warrior who controlled the ilverium.

After he'd wiped out several hundred of them, they'd succumbed, answering *all* of his questions.

Ares had no problem killing the creatures that had so callously degraded his homeland. Now they carried out *his* bidding, having quickly understood that when Ares was displeased, he struck hard and fast.

The Vradhu were ruthless toward their enemies, and Ares was no exception.

He closed his eyes and extended his senses, becoming one with the ship. As soon as he'd discovered that the chair allowed him to control all compartments of the ship with merely a thought, he'd set about isolating the Naaga, cutting off entire sections of the ship by activating the giant ilverium-powered barrier doors.

He'd cut off their communication channels, too.

But for all his power, he couldn't find a way to get off the ship. It was as the Naaga had said. There were no escape vessels. Those who set foot on the *Hythra* stayed on the *Hythra*.

They were trapped.

"What in Aethra's cursed abyss have we caught now, my Lord Commander?" Maki's booming voice dragged Ares out of his semi-trance, forcing him to open his eyes and peel his consciousness away from the destroyer's vast networks.

Maki said the last part with a sardonic curl of his dark lips. He looked down at Ares, a strange combination of affection, pity, and partly concealed horror swirling in his black eyes.

Ares understood that look all too well. To the Vradhu, technology was an impurity; an affront to their way of life.

"Idiot. That's not my title," Ares growled, hating the sound of his own voice. Whenever he sat in the command seat, which he'd mockingly named the *throne of thorns* after the prickly sekkhoi thickets that bordered his homeland, his voice changed, becoming deep and metallic. "I'm not one of those Naaga *pyshtana*."

"I know, Ares." Maki inclined his head, spreading his hands in an apologetic gesture. "I was only speaking in jest. You know me. My jests are rarely received well."

"So it seems. There's a reason you have not yet managed to find a suitable bed-partner. *You* of all people." It was Ares's turn to laugh, and his transformed voice filled the entire command pod. It was an eerie, unnatural sound, part Vradhu and part machine, imbued with the blood-curdling sorcery of the Drakhin.

"I'm a Hunter." Maki shrugged. "Females don't exactly gravitate toward our kind."

"But you are of the Blood. That negates the usual excuses. I am surprised the females haven't been throwing themselves at you like rabid *pikki*. You are only a *little* ugly." He was no Breeder, but Maki was considered handsome by Vradhu standards.

"Good to see you still remember how to drag a man through the proverbial sekkhoi forest." Maki feigned a hurt look. "Vradhu females are proud, complicated creatures. Even royal titles do not sway them." He smiled, idly fingering the torc at his neck as complicated thoughts danced behind enigmatic black eyes. "But enough with the character assassination. I came here to ask the *Hythra* what she has dragged into the lower docks, and since you see what she sees and speak on her behalf, maybe you can sate my curiosity."

"Ah." Ares closed his eyes again and accessed the *Hythra's* surveillance feed, seeing and sensing everything, like some sort of fucking oracle.

In the dim background of his thoughts, the ancient destroyer whispered incessantly, taunting him with seductive memories of fallen civilizations and long-dead kings. She told of how the Drakhin and the Vradhu had once counted each other as kin.

That was ancient history now. Ares ignored the voices inside his head and focused.

The alien ship he'd captured appeared in his mind's eye. It was a tiny thing, barely bigger than a Naaga transport pod. Although it was symmetrical, its grey body was blunt-nosed and bulky—almost brutal in its construction—and various box-like appendages protruded from its metal skin. At the rear were two raised rectangular structures that were separated from the main body of the vessel. These must be the energy sources.

"It is a curious thing. Just appeared out of nowhere, and it doesn't match anything in the *Hythra's* memory. I found it drifting in space under its own inertia. They didn't resist the attraction field at all. I think it has taken serious damage."

"An unknown floating object." Maki raised an eyebrow. "A Naaga commander would have obliterated it without asking questions. A Vradhu elder would have avoided it at all costs. A Drakhin..."

"I am not Naaga, brother, nor am I an elder, and I am *certainly* not Drakhin." He returned Maki's wry look. "In this case, I think the elders would forgive us for violating clan law. We need an escape vessel. These aliens have one, even if it is a half-broken wreck."

"But..." A shadow of frustration crossed Maki's face. "What about you? You've tried to break the bond countless times and failed. It would be a great shame to return without our generation's only *khefe*. You are needed on Khira."

"The Naaga are growing my new body as we speak. If the

Hythra refuses to release me, I will just step into another body."

"Is it that simple? How can you trust that they will re-make you correctly? They're treacherous bastards."

"They have already seeded the *temundra* with my bone-blood, and Seke and Radu are keeping close watch. I have seen them grow their own kind. It works. Whatever body comes out of there, I will take it. If I can transfer my consciousness to it, then so be it. If the process fails, I will stay and destroy every last one of those white-eyed devils while you escape. Aethra knows I have the means."

Maki shook his head. "You are a braver soul than I, Ares-*rai*. Too curious for your own good. That's what father always said. Perhaps that's why the *Hythra* chose you."

"Speculation is pointless," Ares said softly, not wanting to be reminded of the horror he'd felt when he'd first realized what was happening—when the *Hythra* had started *bonding* with him. "One cannot change what has already been done. Just pray these newcomers have what we need." Steeling himself, he prepared to disentangle from the sekkhoi throne.

Release me. The thought exploded from his mind with malevolent force. As if to taunt him, the chair's ilverium limbs shifted and tightened. He could feel the *Hythra's* presence at the back of his mind; silent, insidious, and all-powerful.

What do you want from me?

As always, she didn't answer.

The ancient destroyer was an enigma. When Ares was a child, his father's father, Verthe the Wise, had told him stories about the black dagger in the sky.

If we saw it at dawn, we knew the Hunters would return with a good kill. If it was still there at dusk, it would be a bitterly cold night.

It was the dagger Naktar, the Dark One, had thrown at Aethra when they'd fought in the skies above Khira. She'd suspended it amongst the stars with her magic and banished her former lover to the Underdark for eternity.

Feh. In truth, that was just a fanciful mythtale. The Ancient Stones had revealed the real origins of the black dagger. She was a ship from another world. A *magrel* thing. A Drakhin thing. Large enough to be visible from the surface of Khira and capable of great destruction.

And now Ares was bonded to her.

Each time he took the throne, it became harder and harder to detach. When he was out of the chair, he could only control the ilverium in his immediate surroundings, but when he sat in the chair...

That feeling of absolute power—of the *Hythra* becoming an extension of his mind and body—was terrifyingly intoxicating. Sometimes, he swore the Drakhin warship was intentionally teasing him, tempting him with dark promises of eternity.

Feh. Ares had no interest in such pointless things. What sort of delusional idiot would want to live forever?

Release me! He clenched his fists and pulled his arms upward. Slowly, the ilverium tendrils uncoiled and retreated. As Ares stood, the living metal uncurled from his torso and thighs, and the ilverium trapped beneath his skin became soft and pliant.

Once again, Ares was temporarily freed of the *Hythra's* clutches. The writhing ilverium tentacles withdrew, shifting back into straight lines and sharp edges.

Once again, the command seat was just a chair.

"Gives me the chills every time." Maki was looking at him strangely. "How is it that you are still in possession of your sanity, Hunter?"

"The Naaga succumb to corruption and madness because they are weak." Ares retrieved his twin swords from their resting place at the foot of the throne. He shook himself, loosening his tense muscles. Whenever he sat for too long, the ilverium made his body feel heavy and sluggish. "I am Vradhu."

He was Vradhu, and he would *never* succumb to the will of another.

"To the core." In acknowledgment, Maki pounded his chest with his fist—a gesture of solidarity from one warrior to another. "I am sorry, Ares. I didn't mean to belittle your circumstances. It's just that my simple hunter's brain sometimes struggles with the... strangeness of it all. Perhaps I am *too* Vradhu for these weird and modern times. Who would have thought our people would end up in such a predicament?"

Ares responded with a soft, derisive snort as he picked up his combat helmet. He didn't need or want any pity from Maki. "Notify your pack, Maki-*ku*. I am going down to inspect this new acquisition myself, and I would appreciate the support of your men. As always, it is merely a request." He would never presume to issue orders to Maki, who was of the Blood—the only Hunter who outranked him.

Neither could Maki tell Ares what to do, because Ares was *khefe*—a Hunter who worked alone.

But Maki was also his friend, and he never abused the privilege of his birthright. The Lord of the Two Clans dipped his head in assent. "You don't even need to ask. I will send an advance guard down to secure the hold."

"I would prefer that they do not approach the alien ship until I arrive."

"Have some faith, Hunter. You think we cannot handle whatever is inside that tiny vessel?" Maki bared his teeth.

"It's not that." Ares slid the helmet over his head, obscuring his features. The display on the inside of his visor came to life, lurid green Naaga characters and numbers illuminating the screen. He strode across to the charging dock and selected a suit of light Drakhin battle-armor. Perhaps it was overkill, but it was better that he concealed himself this way. Maki's warriors were spooked enough by his appearance already. There was no need to constantly remind them of his unnatural state.

The Vradhu were a superstitious people. After he'd transformed, many of them had flatly refused to look Ares in the eye.

"I caught it, Maki. You know what that means." *Hunter's Rules.* Ares entered the outfitting dock and stood with his arms extended by his sides and his tail raised. The Drakhin apparatus did its thing, its long metal arms bringing segments of flexible armor-plate close to his body. As the plates met, the strange scaly material joined together at the seams. It flexed and tightened, leaving just enough space for his trousers underneath. As was customary, he curled his long tail—which had been left exposed—around his left leg like a vine. "It was my prey. My catch. It is mine."

The Vradhu were possessive by nature, especially when it came to the things they caught.

"For now." Maki raised his war-spear and followed Ares as he made for the exit. "But we still don't know what's inside. If the occupants are hostile, then we will—"

"Do what is expected. I know. I would do the same."

The Vradhu could be ruthless, too. After all, they'd been born and bred in the Ardu-Sai.

CHAPTER FIVE

SHE WATCHED. She waited. Time passed. Nothing happened. Their nerves became more frayed with every passing minute.

"Someone's approaching." Raphael's bass voice crackled through her comm. *"I've got multiple heat signatures."*

"How many of them are out there, Raf?" Calexa gestured to Mai and Zahra. They nodded in acknowledgement, their oxygenated helmets partly obscuring their faces. They were down in the exit-dock, clad in full combat-gear.

They started to move toward the airlock.

"Hard to say... power's failing. The external monitor keeps going offline. Around twenty or thirty souls is my estimate."

So they were significantly outnumbered. That was no surprise. They'd just been swallowed by a spaceship bigger than anything she'd seen in her life.

"What's the atmosphere like out there?"

"Livable, according to the sensors. At least twenty percent oxygen. Seems... tropical."

"Tropical?"

"A little humid, a little warm. You'd probably find it pleasant, Cal."

"Huh." They reached the airlock. Calexa punched the manual override and they stepped inside.

And waited.

A small port-hole was their only window to the outside. Unable to contain her curiosity, Calexa moved to the side and stared through it.

Darkness stared back at her.

"What's that saying, Cal?" Zahra was right behind her. "If you gaze too long into the abyss..."

"I've heard that one, I think. She who fights monsters, or something like that." Calexa placed her hand against the glass and tried to clear her mind of frantic thoughts.

What the hell is out there?

Whatever it was, she wasn't letting them—or *it*—onto her ship without a fight.

In the blink of an eye, darkness turned into light, revealing a cavernous space. A horde of faces stared back at them.

"Whoa."

The faces were... violet. Deep, dark violet, like a fading Mars sunset.

Violet and black.

"Holy hell," Mai said. "Who turned on the lights? I have *not* seen the likes of those guys before, and I thought I was pretty well traveled for a human. What the hell... *are* they?"

"I don't know." Calexa's voice was barely a whisper. "I don't recognize the species." She scanned the crowd outside, trying to get a sense of their intentions.

Raphael's estimation of numbers was accurate. There were around two dozen of them, and they stood in a defensive formation, watching the *Medusa* with solemn expressions. Without exception, they were all armed to the teeth. Various knives adorned their bodies, and the long spearlike weapons they held had vicious looking white blades affixed to one end.

"They look like a fucking handful," Zahra remarked, her tone uncharacteristically subdued. "I am *not* excited about taking them on. Can we please try and avoid that scenario at all costs?"

Calexa had to agree. "We'll wait until they initiate communication. I'm not opening the doors without a bloody good reason."

There was something strangely primal about the appearance of these aliens. Their features were stark and elegant. High, noble foreheads and sharp cheekbones framed slanted obsidian eyes, and they shared a unique hairstyle. Long, gleaming black hair was drawn into a braid that ran down the center of the head. On both sides, their scalps were shorn, giving them a wild, rakish look.

Their powerful bodies were encased in dark grey armor unlike anything Calexa had seen before. It was constructed from a series of plates, some large, some small, which were all connected in an organic, asymmetrical fashion. The effect was striking, the armor forming a sculptural sheath around their lean, powerful physiques. Artfully placed spikes and horns protruded from their shoulders, and around the left leg of each warrior, there was a strange looking black coil; a thick, rope-like thing that curled around the limb from thigh to ankle.

What was most fascinating, however, was their skin. *Royal violet* was the term that came to mind. The rich hue was accentuated by black markings that varied from face-to-face, forming distinctive striped patterns that coalesced around the eyes, mouth, and cheeks. No two warriors possessed the same facial markings. The intricate patterns appeared to be as unique as fingerprints.

"What a pretty shade of purple," Mai remarked. "Not that there's anything lovely about *them*..."

Momentarily transfixed, Calexa could only nod in agreement. For some reason, she got the sense these strange warriors didn't *belong* on this enormous spaceship. They didn't match their surroundings, which were cold and grey and empty.

A commotion started at the back of the group and rippled through to the front. Slowly, the wall of warriors parted.

They were making way for someone.

The leader of this unit, perhaps?

Two figures emerged through the crowd. The first was a warrior like the others. He carried the same long blade-tipped weapon. The only thing distinguishing him from the rest was the fact that he wore no armor.

He wore very little at all, save for a pair of loose black trousers. His broad chest was bare, revealing a powerful, muscular body. The pigmented markings on his face continued down his arms and torso, creating a fascinating interplay of color and darkness.

Around his neck was a thin silver torc. A symbol of rank, perhaps? He wore his state of undress with a regal sort of indifference, as if he expected the Universe to fall into line around him.

"That's the boss right there," Zahra said. "See how they make way for him?"

"And the other guy?" Mai's voice held a note of trepidation.

Calexa studied the second alien, who walked alongside the bare-chested guy.

Zahra groaned. "Bad news, that's what he is."

She was probably right. Alien number two looked... sinister. Although he was of a similar height and build to the others, he seemed completely different.

His armor was different. It was dark grey, and it shimmered under the bright lights. It was fluid and seamless, and it appeared to be constructed of thousands of tiny scales.

A pair of curved blades hung at his side. Strangely, he didn't carry any sort of gun.

She could make out nothing of his features. His face was hidden by a very tech-looking helmet which was at odds with the garb of the warriors surrounding him.

He came to a standstill alongside his companion and looked up at the *Medusa*.

A strange sensation rippled down Calexa's spine. It was as if the alien could see through the reflective surface of the port-hole window. He seemed to be staring straight through her.

But that was impossible, because the super-reinforced window was one-way glass.

"There's something odd about that one. See how the others give him a wide berth?" Zahra's grey eyes widened.

"It's almost as if they're... scared of him."

"Hm." Between the sinister one and the bare-chested warrior-chief, it was hard to tell who called the shots.

Warrior-chief said something to the mysterious one. Mysterious One shook his head, crossed his arms, and waited.

"About fifteen minutes."

"What?" Calexa blinked, not quite comprehending Raphael's warning. The big navigator could be unintentionally obtuse at times. That was one of the drawbacks of supposedly possessing 'higher intelligence'.

"That's how long we've got until our backup power supply starts to get seriously low. Pulling out the landing gear sucked up more energy than I thought. The systems are already unstable. I'm going to have to down-cycle the cabin lighting soon, but I'll try and keep the ventilators on for as long as possible. We're cycling external air now. Our endogenous oxygen's completely gone."

"I'm guessing the pulse cannon won't fire, and unleashing a triticore missile in here would be a bad idea, wouldn't it?"

"Correct. There would be significant blowback."

"So we're virtually defenseless?"

"I wouldn't exactly call you three banshees defenseless, but you are between a rock and a hard place."

"Huh?"

"Old Earth saying. Sooner or later, we're going to have to set foot out there. Preferably sooner, before the ventilator system

fails, and before our power gets so low that we can't open the airlock."

"How far has Monroe gone with the repairs?"

"He isn't going to get the main powerbank up and running within the next fifteen minutes, if that's what you're asking."

"How *long?*"

"An hour if we're lucky, and that's just because it's Monroe, and he's a freak. That sort of job would take an advanced repair-bot half a day to complete, you know."

Calexa swore. Full automation had its advantages and its drawbacks. In this case, the *Medusa's* seamlessly integrated networks were about to disable the entire fucking ship.

She turned to Mai and Zahra. "You two get down to the passenger bay and stand guard. I'm going to ask Raf to open the airlock."

"What? We can't open it. Not with those guys just waiting—"

"Go and guard our passengers. We don't have too many options right now. The ship's systems are about to go dead." Calexa set her PX-45 to live-mode. With her other hand, she unhooked a frag-grenade from her weapons belt. "I'll handle it from this end."

"Cal..." Zahra regarded the frag-grenade in Calexa's hand with a dubious expression.

"Relax," Calexa said in what she hoped was a calm, reassuring manner.

"Why is it that whenever you say *'relax'* in that tone of voice, I always get the feeling you're about to do something downright insane?"

"I'm going to make first contact, that's all. Don't worry. I'll *convince* them that the last thing we want is a fight. This," she opened her fingers to reveal the dull metal grenade, "is just for... insurance."

Just in case something got lost in translation.

Considering there was no way their databases would have

a translator algorithm for whatever language these aliens spoke
—hell, Calexa didn't even know what *species* they were—that
was a very real possibility indeed.

"We're not leaving you to face them on your own." Mai
swiveled slowly on her heel, aiming her Irradium cannon
through the tiny port-hole window. "If Raf's going to open the
airlock, then maybe I could fire a warning sho—"

Calexa shook her head. "Get down there and guard our
passengers," she insisted, her voice softening. "I'm the gate-
keeper, the test case, the sacrificial lamb. We don't know what
they want with us, and they don't know what we're capable of,
so let me dip my toe in the waters first. I'll try and buy us as
much time as possible so Monroe has a chance to fix the
powerbank. That way, we'll know for sure whether their intentions are hostile or—"

"You're not going to give yourself up, are you?" Zahra was
aghast.

"I have no idea *what* I'm going to do, but I won't be taken
as a helpless captive, and I'm damn hard to kill."

"Princess isn't going to be happy about this."

"S has no say in the matter," Calexa snapped. "My ship,
my rules. You two go down there and keep them safe. What
you decide to do next depends on what happens to me. Just try
to keep everyone on the *Medusa* at all costs. It's our only line
of defense."

"You're nuts, Cal." The resignation in Zahra's voice was
mixed with affection.

Calexa shook her head. "Sanity is a relative thing in our
universe. Whatever happens, I trust you both to keep it real."

Zahra and Mai nodded grimly, exchanging a knowing look.

"We have a reputation to maintain, don't we?" Mai
smirked, and her expression alone—a great *fuck you* to the
circumstances they found themselves in—warmed Calexa's
scarred heart.

CHAPTER SIX

THE AIRLOCK SLID open with a hiss. Calexa stood behind the wall, not wanting to expose herself just yet.

"What are they doing, Raf?"

"One of them is approaching."

"Only one?"

"Yes."

"Let me guess. He just-so happens to be wearing a dark helmet?"

The Primean's voice became fragmented. *"I'm losing you, Cal... breaking up..."*

"Hey, Raphael?"

There was the harsh crackle of static, then silence. The connection had died.

"Shit." Calexa tensed as footsteps reached her ears. The *tap, tap* of the alien's gait was slow and measured; a cold, hollow sound that grew louder with every step. Her neural framework went into overdrive and her enhanced muscles tensed.

Her body switched into fight-mode.

Stay calm, she told herself, suppressing the urge to spring from her hiding spot and rush the intruder. Her instincts screamed at her to fight first and ask questions later.

That method was effective in their usual line of work, but this wasn't some under-the-table Fiveways mercenary job, and these aliens weren't just low-rent criminals. This was uncharted territory, and she was way out of her comfort zone.

The footsteps stopped. Calexa's breath caught. Her trigger finger twitched. With the silence stretched taut, every passing second became a bizarre kind of torture.

What was the alien doing? Even if he was standing just below the airlock, he'd have to haul himself up to her level if he wanted to enter the ship, because Raphael hadn't extended the landing ramp.

A faint hiss emanated from below, followed by a strange scraping sound. The fine hairs on the back of Calexa's neck rose.

The footsteps started again, growing louder and louder until they were almost on top of her.

What the hell? There was no ramp. The intruder wasn't supposed to be able to *walk* up to her.

She pressed her back against the wall and raised her gun. From what she could hear, the alien was going to come through the airlock any second now, and even though she was supposed to try and negotiate a peaceful arrival, there was no way she was going to let him get the jump on her.

Maybe she could take him hostage. That would give them some leverage until they got a handle on the situation.

A booted foot appeared in the doorway, followed by a leg encased in seamless scale-armor, followed by the rest of him in all his sinister glory. He was like a shimmering mirage, moving fluidly like water and teasing her eyes with his strangeness. He was of the same height and build as the warriors she'd seen earlier, and he had the same black snake-like *thing* coiled around his left leg, but that was where the similarities ended.

His armor was different. His swords were different. The air around him bristled with dark energy. It was as if the very essence of him was too much for his physical body to contain.

The Mysterious One. Of *course* it had to be him. Trouble incarnate. She'd known it the moment she'd laid eyes on him.

What sort of being is this?

Calexa froze. Time slowed. In her hyper-alert state, she became obsessed with every little detail.

The way the light reflected off his armor, splitting into a thousand shimmering points. The way he moved, sinuous and graceful. That damn impenetrable helmet of his.

She could see herself reflected in its glossy surface.

In turn, he was staring at her. He inclined his head ever-so-slightly, but she couldn't read his body language.

Hostile, or just curious?

Calexa kept her gun trained on him, her arm perfectly still.

"*Vysh ku agete,*" he said. Although it was a little distorted by the helmet, his voice was unexpectedly rich, and it sent a wicked thrill through her.

"Well, hello there," she replied, knowing perfectly well that he couldn't understand a word she said. "I assume you're not going to try and kill me, because if that was your plan, you probably would have done so already. I don't know what you want with us, but if you try and harm my passengers or crew, I'll pump five-thousand *negas* of supercharged atomic particles up your ass."

It was wishful venting. Calexa didn't really know what she would do if things turned ugly. She was poised on the knife's edge of danger, and the only useful thing she'd learned in all her miserable years on Dashki-5 was how to fight.

The alien didn't react. He just looked at her as if she were mad. She wasn't quite sure how he managed to give off that impression when she couldn't see his face. Perhaps it was something in his stance. He seemed completely unperturbed, almost to the point of arrogance. His arms hung loosely by his sides, his hands were open, and he made no attempt to reach for his weapons, even though she was pointing a gun at his head.

Without raising a weapon in anger, he'd put her on the defensive.

Movement below captured her attention. Calexa's eyes nearly popped out of their sockets.

A metallic grey substance shifted and writhed on the floor, making a soft scraping sound as it slid over the alien's feet. It wasn't quite liquid or solid. It was somewhere in-between, and it was identical in hue to his odd scaly armor. The strange *matter* flowed around his boots as if it were magnetically attracted to him.

What sort of crazy technology *was* this?

The substance extended along the floor and out of the airlock, where it solidified into a ramp-like structure that became continuous with the dark grey floor. Was that how he had managed to get up here without too much commotion? With the aid of that *stuff*?

The Mysterious One raised his hand and crooked two fingers, beckoning her in a simple gesture.

The meaning was universal: *come.*

No fucking way. Calexa shook her head slowly, hoping he understood. *You're asking me to trust you?*

She was not going to walk out there at the request of some obsidian-faced mystery alien when she had no idea what she was getting herself into.

Not when there was an unknown metallic *thing* snaking around his feet.

Not when she had no idea what this strange, dangerous-seeming creature wanted.

He shrugged, as if to say: *suit yourself,* and muttered something low and unintelligible.

The solid-liquid-metal stuff started to move. It slid across the floor, becoming fluid and tendril-like. It came straight for her, and it was damn *fast*. As it coalesced and gained speed, Calexa momentarily forgot about the gun in her hand.

Fear hit her like a punch in the gut. It was fear of the crippling, paralyzing kind, the sort of dread one felt when faced with the terrifying unknown.

The kind of fear she thought she'd left behind on Dashki-5.

If she were young and inexperienced, she might have frozen, but Calexa was intimately acquainted with fear, and she'd vowed never to let it control her again.

The liquid-metal stuff raced toward her, reaching her feet. Calexa suppressed a scream of horror as it touched her booted foot. In less than a second, it coiled around her ankle, forming a twisting rope that stretched along the floor from her leg to the Mysterious One's feet.

It slid up her leg. It engulfed her other foot. It tightened.

What the hell am I supposed to do now?

Her options were limited. One, she could wait and let the metal stuff continue to creep up her body. *Hell, no.* That didn't seem like a good idea at all. Two, she could surrender and follow the alien, but that would mean leaving her ship and its passengers, and that didn't sit well with her when she had no idea what his intentions were.

Three, she could try and overpower him without killing him. That would give her some leverage. It was the only option. *Take him hostage. Show them that we're not toothless.*

When one was completely powerless, one had to carve out an advantage.

Find something they want and use it against them. If you can't think of anything they want, create *something and* convince *them they need it.*

She'd learned that in the damp, frigid underground Arena

prison on Dashki-5, where no quarter was given and the slightest hesitation meant death.

It was a huge risk, but Calexa was all about risk-taking. When death was a constant shadow, risks didn't feel like risks anymore, but more like rational decisions along a thorny, ever-shifting path toward survival. In her universe, inaction was the biggest risk of all.

But first, she had to deal with this sliding, shifting, *living* metal-stuff, which seemed to be completely under the alien's control.

What the hell was he? Some sort of fucking telepath?

Calexa regained her senses, pointed her PX-45 at the moving target, and fired.

Boom! The powerful blast rocked the floor and split the moving metal-stuff into a thousand tiny shards. Whatever the substance was, the particle beam had seriously disrupted it.

To her horror, the shards softened and came together like a million droplets of water, merging into a torrent.

Calexa leapt aside, dancing out of the moving metal's path. The power generated by her enhanced legs propelled her to the opposite side of the airlock. She spun and raised her gun, still clutching the frag-grenade in her other hand. Fat lot of good it did her now. Blowing herself up in confined quarters wasn't exactly part of the game-plan. She'd envisioned using it as a threat against a hostage, or lobbing it out of the airlock as a warning.

She pulled the trigger again. The metal stuff exploded again, splintering into tiny pieces.

"Argh!" She cried out in alarm as some of the fragments hit her legs. They fell to the floor, liquefying as they merged with the shifting mass at her feet. Again, the substance surged toward her.

Relentless. It just wouldn't stop.

Calexa danced backwards and found walls on either side of her. The bastard had backed her into a corner.

"Hey, Cal, what's happening?" Mai's alarmed voice crackled through the comm, sounding patchy and indistinct. "I thought I heard a shot go off. You okay? Want me to come up and sic Beauty on them?" Beauty was Mai's nickname for her Irradium cannon.

"Stay down there," Calexa ordered. "Guard the passengers at all costs. If they get past me, you're it."

"Understoo..." Mai's voice faded away as the unreliable comm went dead.

Calexa was determined to make this alien understand that even though she meant him no harm, she wasn't about to just lie down and let him have his way with her, and she there was no way in *hell* she was going to let herself be engulfed by that shifting metal substance—whatever it was.

She wasn't a damn fool.

"*Kuch ka,*" the alien muttered. He sounded irritated. Calexa was pretty sure those were curse words.

"Fuck you too," she growled. She aimed her gun at a spot on the floor. Undeterred, the Mysterious One started to advance, the grey metal swirling at his feet.

She squeezed the trigger for a third time.

The particle-blast was deafening. Droplets of dark grey liquid-metal exploded in the air.

A shower of metallic glitter filled her vision. Impossibly, the damn stuff had surged up off the floor as she'd fired, forming a narrow column that had very effectively blocked her shot.

It had *protected* him.

The glitter turned into a dark blur as it fell, and suddenly Calexa was staring at her reflection in the alien's gleaming black faceplate.

"What the...?" She prepared to fire again, but his hand was around her wrist, squeezing hard. In the blink of an eye, he was all up in her face, powerful and inscrutable and overwhelming.

Too damn fast... when did he...?

There was a soft crunch as his strong fingers made light work of her combat suit's exterian reinforced sleeve. Calexa hissed in pain as his fingers dug into the semi-flexible material. Although she'd undergone countless rounds of enhancement therapy, she was still human, and she still had some of her pain receptors.

The Mysterious One's grip fucking *hurt*.

His free hand came up. She raised her other arm to block him but diverted at the last nanosecond, remembering that she was holding onto a goddamn *frag-grenade*. The thing still had its safety on, but if it were to suddenly get hit with great force...

It wasn't as if she could just drop it, either.

Calexa didn't want to die just yet, so she pulled her grenade-arm out of harm's way and allowed him to slap the PX-45 out of her gun-hand. The particle weapon clattered to the floor.

Still, the alien didn't let go of her wrist, although he eased his crushing grip just a little.

Strong. And *fast.*

"What do you want?" She ground her teeth in frustration as she tried to wrench free of his grasp.

"*Tvach*," he growled.

Calexa yanked her arm backwards, trying to distract him as she clipped the frag-grenade back onto to her weapons belt in a single swift movement.

Now that her left hand was free, she swung hard, her fist connecting with the side of his helmet.

"*Tch*." He made a soft sound of surprise but didn't go down. He barely flinched, and the next thing Calexa knew, his other hand had encircled her left wrist. He was trying to bring her arms down by her sides.

He seemed to want to restrain her, not kill her.

Calexa was having none of it. She raised her leg and delivered a swift, powerful kick to his torso. There was a jarring sensation as her boot connected with his hard body. The impact sent him reeling backwards, forcing him to release his grip.

She pressed her advantage, following through with a flurry of punches. As she moved closer, she brought her elbow up, smashing him in the face.

"*Kuch*," he snarled, bringing up his arm to block her. Her hand crashed into his forearm but he held fast, resisting her attack.

Before she could comprehend what was happening, he modified his attack, dancing inside her range. He hooked his lower leg behind hers and sent her off-balance.

She toppled to the floor.

Calexa fell onto her back, and the alien came tumbling with her. He broke his fall by slamming both palms into the floor on either side of her head.

"Fuck," she growled. If he could swear in alien, then so could she. It infuriated her that he'd used some cheap, sneaky wrestling tactic to get the better of her.

He was on top of her, his armor-clad body pressing into hers. He was damn heavy, even when he was using his arms to bear most of his weight. Only now did she begin to appreciate how seriously *big* he was.

Calexa wasn't exactly a small woman in human terms, but the alien on top of her made her feel delicate, which was ridiculous.

Curiosity burned away her restraint. "Why do you hide behind a mask? What the hell are you?"

But he couldn't understand a word she said, and even if he did, Calexa wouldn't have given him time to form an answer.

She didn't like being pinned down like this.

Correction: she absolutely *hated* it.

A torrent of unpleasant memories flooded through her.

"Aargh!" With a cry of anger, Calexa pressed her hands into the floor, gaining purchase as she harnessed all her strength.

She slammed her forehead into his, headbutting him.

Her combat helmet smashed into his dark visor with a bone-jarring *crack*. The force of the impact reverberated through Calexa's biometal-reinforced skull, momentarily disorienting her.

"*Kuch ku vydak,*" the alien snarled. A thin fissure had appeared in his helmet, running diagonally from the top of his visor to the left edge.

Calexa didn't waste time. She headbutted him again. It fucking hurt, but she was a tough cookie, and she was used to experiencing—and inflicting—pain. The crack in his helmet's visor became wider, but the opaque surface didn't break.

Suddenly, she couldn't move her head. His hand was on her helmet, just over her forehead, holding her down.

"*Temek ka,*" he growled. He sounded more frustrated than anything else. To her surprise, his words were followed by a short, exasperated laugh.

"Is something funny?" Calexa wrapped her legs around him and squeezed hard, removing any trace of amusement from his voice. He grunted in pain as she twisted her body, using the momentum to topple him onto his side.

They were both lying on their sides now, facing each other. Calexa squeezed harder. Her bionic joints and enhanced muscles gave her immense power, and she used her strength to lock the alien in position.

The leg-lock was a crude old wrestling move. She'd picked it up in the Arena stables on Dashki-5.

A regular opponent would have been screaming in pain by now, but this guy just went still. There was no give in his strange scaly armor, and despite the fact that Calexa was trying to crush him like a python, he didn't appear in the least bit distressed.

At least her head was free now, as was her left arm, which was extended above her head. As her hand slid across the cold metal floor, her fingers brushed against something.

Her PX-45.

"Got you now," she said softly as she brought the gun into her line of sight. She pressed it to the side of his head. "Freeze, or I'll blow your fucking brains out." Her voice was cold and harsh. Surely he'd be able to understand her intentions, even with the language barrier.

In reality, she had no idea whether his helmet could sustain a blast from a close-range particle weapon, but either way, she was bound to do some damage.

Just shoot him. A sinister little voice in the back of her mind told her to get it over and done with, but she held back.

She couldn't kill him. Not when there were two dozen formidable black-and-purple warriors waiting in the wings. She didn't want them to go nuts.

And not when she got the feeling that he was... holding back. So far, he'd been on the defensive, blocking her attacks and using his hands to fight instead of his weapons.

Her legs were still wrapped around his torso. The fact that he hadn't yielded was testament to his strength and skill, because Calexa was a freak, and she was used to taking on many opponents at once.

But he was alone, and he'd been able to match her blow-for-blow.

Not anymore. *She* had the upper hand now.

To drive her point home, she tapped the end of her gun against the hard surface of his helmet, eliciting a loud, hollow crack. His only reaction was a minuscule shake of his head, followed by what she *swore* was a sigh.

He muttered something unintelligible, and suddenly there

was pressure around Calexa's neck. *Something* cut into the flexible material between her helmet and her shoulders.

It was a weak point in her combat-suit. After all, her neck had to move. Although impervious to blades and blasts, the material there was malleable, made of thousands of tiny exterian links.

Therefore, it was also compressible.

What the hell?

He hadn't moved his arms. He hadn't moved at *all*. Grunting with exertion, Calexa tried to squeeze her legs tighter, but the *thing* around her neck wouldn't budge, and she was starting to get a little light headed. She coughed, struggling to breathe.

A strange metallic scraping sound echoed in her ears. It was the noise made by that *stuff*; that creepy liquid-solid moving metal. She'd momentarily forgotten about it, and now it was around her neck, choking her.

Restraining her.

It spread, moving down her neck and across her shoulders. It extended down her arms.

No, not that! A familiar old feeling rose up inside her. Fragments of memories flashed through her mind.

Her neck stuck in that god-awful, too-tight collar. Agonizing pain shooting through her arms and shoulders, the result of being bound in the same position for hours-upon-hours. The sharp sting of fresh cuts on her arms and face. The coppery scent of her own human blood.

The anger burning inside her, all pent-up with nowhere to go.

As the sliding metal tightened, Calexa's mind went blank and panic set in. All she knew was that she had to get free.

She released her leg-lock and tried to wriggle away, but the *stuff* tightened.

Mysterious One reached out toward her gun.

No!

Something wild and frantic exploded inside her. She would *not* be restrained. Never again! Calexa closed her eyes and blindly pulled the trigger.

Blam! At close quarters, the noise was deafening. A faint ringing echoed in her ears.

Then everything stopped.

Is he...?

Her eyes fluttered open, and she saw the alien lying several meters away from her, his hands crossed protectively over his face. He must have rolled away as she'd fired, although how he'd moved so far so *fast*, she had no idea. The metal substance was scattered across the floor in the form of various blobs and shards that twitched and quivered.

Calexa went still. Her eyes widened. Her heartbeat thudded in her ears. Was she seeing correctly?

Part of the opaque black surface had caved in, revealing a tantalizing glimpse of his face. Through the crack in his visor, she saw a single silver eye, surrounded by obsidian skin. His pupil was a narrow black slit.

His gaze was cold, yet curious. It wasn't the look of someone who'd just been shot in the face.

She gasped for air. The pressure around her neck didn't relent. She couldn't move up off the floor. An unknown force held her down.

The alien stood up and walked toward her. Calexa tried to raise her gun, but the liquid metal substance along her arm had solidified, forming an unbreakable restraint. She growled, her frustration turning into crippling fear as the Mysterious One came to a halt beside her.

She was helpless, defeated by an alien that possessed power and technology far beyond her understanding. He squatted on his haunches beside her, studying her with his odd gaze.

His lone visible eye drew Calexa in, and for a split-second, she forgot her fear as fascination took over.

"Mvarak ku bea," he said softly, and perhaps Calexa was imagining things, but she thought there was a note of admiration in his voice.

But that made no sense, because the *thing* around her neck tightened, and her vision blurred, and she couldn't breathe, and...

Everything went black.

CHAPTER SEVEN

"A FEMALE WHO FIGHTS." Ares shook his head as he stared down at the unconscious alien. She'd fought damn well too, and he'd told her so, even though she hadn't understood a thing he'd said.

Then he'd tightened the ilverium noose around her neck, and she'd passed out.

He should have done that at the start, but stepping off the metal floor of the *Hythra* onto the alien ship had weakened his powers, and she'd caught him off-guard with that damn blast-weapon of hers.

She had caught *him* off-guard. Ha. Even in his temporarily weakened state, that was a formidable feat.

He couldn't restrain his curiosity any longer. With gentle hands, he reached down to remove her helmet. Although her eyeshield was transparent, the lower half of her face was concealed behind a protective casing of black metal.

From the very beginning, her eyes had entranced him. They were clear, glittering *blue*, like the mountain streams of the Highfold.

So this is... an offworlder. The Ancient Stones told of

distant places beyond the Shadowring, where strange races built vast civilizations and traveled between the stars.

The Ancient Stones were full of warnings. Vradhu weren't supposed to have contact with outsiders. It was forbidden.

Feh. Since when had he taken those foolish elders seriously?

He was dying to see what the rest of her looked like.

Ares fumbled with the clasp mechanism at the base of her helmet until it gave way, detaching from the mesh-like protective collar around her neck. He pulled the ungainly thing over her head, revealing her face for the very first time.

Sweet Aethra.

He inhaled sharply, fascinated by her alien appearance. He'd never expected to see such an exotic creature up close. He was struck by the odd hue of her skin. It was light brown, and it glistened with a faint sheen of moisture. It appeared soft; he wondered what it would feel like under his bare fingertips.

Her hair was a deep, rich shade of brown. It was tied up high on her head and braided into a long tail—a warrior's braid.

There was no mistaking it, she was a warrior. There was a fierceness about her that spilled over even when she was unconscious. It was in the proud lines of her features. A sharp but once-broken nose, stubborn chin, and full, luscious lips made her a study in contrasts. It was in the scars on her cheeks—two sharp, defiant slashes that stood out against her otherwise unblemished skin.

Ares exhaled as he allowed the ilverium to release its grip on her. The silver-grey tendrils withdrew, retreating into his body.

As always, ilverium sought to return to the whole, yearning to become one with the body of the ship. It took considerable willpower to resist its magnetic pull. Ares couldn't hold out much longer. He needed to plant his feet on the *Hythra's* floor.

"I told you to come with me." Ares shook his head in amazement as he bent down, preparing to lift her into his arms. "I wasn't going to hurt you."

He'd expected this, though. She'd been on the defensive. She'd been terrified. When he'd pushed the ilverium toward her, she'd fired her weapon. Of *course* she had. He just hadn't expected her to move so fucking *quickly*. The ilverium was supposed to have immobilized her *before* she had a chance do any serious damage, so he could take her away and avoid all this drama.

Ares slid his arms underneath her and drew her close, rising to his feet. He grunted with the effort. She was much, much heavier than she looked.

What in Aethra's cursed abyss was her body made of? Fucking metal?

He strained as he hefted her over his shoulder. Her armor-suit added even more weight and bulk to her frame, but Ares had spent many a moon hauling kratok carcasses through the Highfold, and he was used to such things.

He took a moment to turn and take stock of his surroundings. He was in a small entrance bay. On either side of him was a sliding door. Both doors were open, which struck him as odd. As he turned toward the exit, heavy footsteps reached his ears. Someone was running toward him.

Another alien appeared in the doorway. This one was dressed similarly to his catch, in an ungainly grey armor-suit and oval-shaped helmet, but she had a different weapon; a giant cannon-like thing that she carried over one shoulder.

"*Tch*," Ares shook his head in disapproval. These strange brown-skinned creatures were strong, almost as strong and fast as a Vradhu warrior in his prime, but they depended on *magrel* weapons.

The alien yelled at him in an angry, high-pitched voice. She raised her weapon but didn't fire. She wasn't going to shoot him, of that Ares was certain. After all, he had her comrade draped over his shoulder.

He held up a hand and summoned the ilverium. It poured in from the outside as Ares retreated. He formed an image of a wall in his mind and the ilverium obeyed, creating an impenetrable barrier between him and the shouting female.

The summoning took more effort than usual. Ares didn't waste any more time. He reached the doorway and jumped, bypassing the metal ramp he'd constructed earlier. The structure had allowed him to reach the entrance of the alien ship, but now he had no use for it, so he dissolved it in his mind. It collapsed, falling to the floor, where it merged with the very substance of the *Hythra* itself.

He bent his knees as he landed, maintaining a tight grip on the unconscious alien. Dozens of curious eyes turned toward them.

Ilverium surged at his feet in a welcoming caress, and he felt his power return. At his bidding, the writhing metallic substance flowed into the alien ship, sealing off the doorway, piling on thicker and thicker until an impenetrable barrier was created.

He could no longer hear the small alien's shouting voice.

Boom. A dull explosion reached his ears. The ilverium barrier bent outwards before snapping back into place. The alien inside must have tried to blast it open.

Crazy female. Had she actually *fired* that thing?

It didn't matter. She wouldn't escape, and he'd gotten what he came for.

He only needed one of them, after all.

Ares ignored the commotion and walked toward the pack. Maki had been as good as his word and kept his warriors at bay. Vradhu could be cruel at times, especially if they sensed weakness.

It came with the territory.

"What have you caught this time, Hunter?" Maki inclined his head, scrutinizing Ares's prize. He raised an eyebrow in surprise. "What is *that*? It is... female, yes?"

Ares nodded. Her features were distinctly feminine, and her armor failed to conceal the alluring swell of her breasts and the roundness of her hips.

A murmur rippled through the pack. To the Vradhu, the notion of a female warrior was almost unthinkable. The others stared at his exotic catch in fascination.

They weren't used to aliens. Aside from the cursed Naaga, who had ruined everything, they hadn't encountered any other intelligent species.

Appearing mildly impressed, Maki met Ares's gaze. "She fights well?" He was undoubtedly taking in the damage inflicted on Ares's Drakhin-tech helmet.

"Well enough," Ares shrugged. "Even though she uses *magrel*." He used the Vradhu word that meant *false weapon, unnatural,* and *forbidden,* amongst other things. Of course, he was referring to that infernal blast-weapon of hers.

The warriors spoke amongst themselves in low, disbelieving tones. Although they feared what Ares had become, they knew what he'd been like before the *Hythra* had taken him, and they knew very well what he was capable of as a warrior.

Like all of his kind, he didn't give praise lightly.

"And there are... others like her?" Vanu stared up at the strange alien ship, his black eyes gleaming with curiosity. The young warrior's kratok-hide armor was still dark and shiny. He'd killed his first giant beast less than a tenmoon ago, and he was still breaking in the tough, impenetrable hide. Over time, the surface of his armor would grow dull and fade as it hardened in some places and grew soft in others, molded and shaped by the natural movements of his body.

Unlike the others, Vanu didn't try to avoid Ares's gaze. His lighter coloring and the markings on his face—three distinct stripes on each cheek that ran diagonally from cheekbone to jaw—indicated that he was a descendant of the Outer Tribes, and like most of the outer Vradhu, he wasn't as traditional or rigid as some of the purebloods under Maki's command.

Ares rather liked the young warrior.

"There are others," he confirmed. Behind his smashed helmet, Ares's lips curved upward in amusement. "If possible, I would rather you leave them be until this one has been programmed. It will be easier that way."

"And if they attack?" Vanu waved his war-spear suggestively.

Ares acknowledged Maki with a small nod, stopping just short of deference. "I would request that you try not to kill any of them, but that is your choice to make. If the others are anything like this she-demon, then you may encounter some... difficulties."

"Where are you taking her?"

"To our *'masters'*." There was a note of irony in Ares's voice. Of course, he was referring to the Naaga.

Cursed creatures.

If they didn't carry out their orders and rid the *Hythra* of the Corrupted ones, the Two Clans would lose their precious homeland. It was a fool's bargain, but they had no choice. The Naaga were not known for their compassion. To the white-eyed devils, everything was calculated.

Ares growled deep in his throat as he remembered the disgraceful manner in which they'd been lured and captured. The floor around his feet rippled, reacting to his anger.

The warriors hastily stepped aside as he passed. Although his shoulder was beginning to ache—this Aethra-cursed female weighed as much as a damned kratok carcass—he didn't waver. He may have become a monster, but he still had his pride. "I will make them implant the translator-thing into her, just like they did with us. Then our existence on this cursed prison might just become interesting again."

"You're nuts, Ares." Maki's low voice followed him across the hold. "The Naaga sci-people won't agree to fit her with an implant. We don't even know if her kind are compatible with their technology."

Ares grunted. Maki was correct. He *was* nuts, and the longer he remained trapped in his own shifting metal prison, the more he desperately yearned for the wide-open water-plains of the Ardu-Sai. "Who said anything about *agreeing?*" His smile turned bitter. When Ares requested things, people obeyed, because they all knew very well that the power of life and death was contained in the metal running through his veins.

He wasn't worried about the alien's compatibility in the slightest. If the smooth metal bumps along the back of her neck were anything to go by, then she'd had *magrel* things inserted into her body before. Surely she could take a little Naaga inter-ference. After all, Ares and the others had survived the process, and this strange being had just gone toe-to-toe with a Vradhu warrior and come out alive.

That spoke volumes about her toughness.

Ares was rather pleased with his catch.

The creature in his arms began to stir, making murmuring noises that were rather soft and vulnerable and... appealing.

It made sense that she would be starting to rouse. He'd tightened the ilverium noose enough to render her temporarily unconscious, nothing more.

"Better hurry," he muttered to himself. He didn't want her regaining her senses just yet. This one... If he didn't make her *understand* the situation soon, she would be difficult to contain, and it would be a damn shame if he had to kill her.

"What about the rest of your catch, Hunter? You have earned dividing rights." As usual, Maki was the voice of reason, reminding Ares of his duties to the clan.

Claim your prize, take what you need, divide the rest between your brothers. That was the Vradhu way.

The situation was... awkward. In his current form, Ares was stronger than Maki—in truth, he'd *always* been the stronger one—but Maki outranked him, and there was no way he would dare presume to tell the Lord of the Two Clans what to do. That would be a terrible mistake. He would instantly lose face.

Ares glanced over his shoulder as he exited the hold. The Vradhu stared at the alien ship with looks of burning curiosity. Who knew what they might do? *Feh.* Who cared? Ares couldn't be in two places at once, and he already had what he needed. He would leave the business of handling the aliens to Maki. "Take what you wish, Maki. Try not to cause any more damage their vessel—or to those who could possibly repair it," he called out. "I am sure you know what I mean."

Maki smiled at him, revealing brilliant silver teeth. His expression was nothing short of predatory. "Naturally. It came in from space, so hopefully it can go out the same way. I am on your leaf, Ares-*rai*." He slipped in the term of endearment as he regarded Ares' catch with an appraising look. "Try not to ruin the alien."

Ares let out a soft snort as he spirited the female away, heading for the sci-labs. What did Maki think he was—some sort of wanton youth? As alluring and fascinating as the female was, he wasn't interested in *that*. Not when they couldn't even understand one another.

Insidious, heated thoughts entered his mind. He quickly crushed them.

She would need the language implant; the very same one that was inside his head, enabling him to speak and understand Naaga. It would be painful at first, but she was strong enough to handle it. There was no way around it, and the only ones who could do it were the Naaga themselves.

They would agree to his demands, because he was the host

— the *commander*— of this infernal ship, and he held the fate of everyone in his hands. Of course, the Naaga were just biding their time, waiting for the *Hythra* to swallow him, but Ares wasn't going anywhere soon, and he was going to use every damn advantage he had to try and break out of this unnatural mess.

CHAPTER EIGHT

PAIN.

It was all Calexa knew as she regained consciousness. The pain speared her temples and stabbed her eyes. It pounded the back of her head, as if someone were brutally trying to crack open her skull.

She hadn't hurt this badly since she'd undergone enhancement therapy. Too bad the pain receptors in her head were mostly unaltered.

Her eyes snapped open. Bright light flooded in. She gasped in agony, blinking furiously as her world came into focus.

Her memories were hazy. "Wha—?" She flailed about like a madwoman as she tried to regain her bearings. With a groan, she pulled herself up into a sitting position.

Grey walls surrounded her. She closed her eyes again. The pain was too intense. It was a sharp, stabbing, throbbing kind of pain, and it was all in her head. *Literally.*

She grabbed the sides of her head with both hands and found a thick band wrapped around her skull. It felt... rubbery underneath her bare fingers.

And her hair. What the hell had happened to her *hair?*

Her armor-gloves were gone. So were her combat helmet and her weapons and her exterian armor. She wore nothing but her skintight thermosuit.

Memories returned to her like a tidal wave crashing onto a rocky shore. A ridiculously dangerous mission to Torandor at the behest of a crazy Primean. Paxnath slavers turning the entire thing into one huge clusterfuck. A frantic Panic Jump into the Netherverse. Engine failure. System failure. A giant ship, bigger than anything she'd thought possible, drawing them in against their will. *Aliens.* They were purple and black, with *tails.* A species she'd never seen or *heard of* before. She'd fought furiously, *viciously,* with that dark scaly-armored warrior.

Strong. Fast. Inescapable. That's what he was.

Oh, shit. She'd toyed with death again.

On the upside, she was still alive.

For now.

A tingling sensation ran along the backs of her arms, alerting her to a presence. Summoning all of her willpower, she pushed the pain to the back of her mind, opened her eyes, and looked over her shoulder.

And came face-to-face with...

Him.

It was him. The Mysterious One. She knew it with every fiber of her being. His scaly armor was intact, but his helmet was gone, revealing his face.

Whoa.

How magnificently striking he was. Calexa could have become mesmerized by his molten eyes, but anger got the better of her.

"You fucking—" She flew at him, one fist raised. "What have you done to me?" Pain became her weapon, sharpening her rage.

She was on her feet, jumping off the cold metal bed and

launching her powerful body into the air. Her bionic joints tensed, ready to unleash a barrage of pent-up kinetic energy.

Her anger was white-hot and undeniable as realization coursed through her. She'd been violated somehow. These strange creatures had done something to her while she was unconscious.

She didn't know what they'd done, but something felt different. Her head was heavy. The pain was excruciating, to the point where she felt she might pass out. Her thoughts were fragmented, disjointed, scattered. The thin veneer of her self-control had been stripped away, leaving only the primal things: instinct, impulse, and rage.

Oh, she'd been here before. She knew this place, and she *hated* what it did to her.

As for the one who was responsible for all this, she would beat him fucking senseless.

Calexa's fist flew toward his face. Her attack was wild and unfettered, driven by anger. She put all of her strength into the blow...

And met resistance.

His hand closed around her fist, and for a moment they were trapped in a battle of wills.

Silver eyes narrowed. "Stop."

Calexa gritted her teeth and pushed forward, wanting to break his resistance.

"Stop," he said again, his deep voice cutting through the haze of her anger. "Do you understand me?"

A thread of sanity took root in her mind. She blinked, wondering whether she was still dreaming. "What?" The word sounded strange as it dropped from her lips.

What did I just say?

She was no longer speaking in her native tongue.

The meaning was the same, but the word was different.

What. The. Fuck?

"This possible... how?" Her question felt clumsy.

"*How is this possible?*" The alien corrected, his tone dry. "It takes time to get the syntax right, but now you speak the language of slaves."

"No slave," Calexa spat. "Not for you, not for anyone."

"You misunderstand," the alien said, maintaining his grip on her hand. He was a strong bastard, there was no doubt about it. "This is the *language* of slaves. Clearly, you are not ideal slave material."

Calexa's arm grew heavy as the pain in her head intensified. "Observant, you are." She shook her head in frustration as her thoughts seemed to correct themselves. "I meant to say: *you are observant.*" Sarcasm dripped from every word.

His hand was rather large and warm, even when it was encased in that strange scale-armor. Funny that she should notice such things when he held her fist in a bone-crushing grip.

"What have you done to me?" This time, the sentence came out correctly. Somehow, she just *knew* it was right. She understood every word of this strange language, even if she was still struggling to master the grammar and syntax and the different intonations. "What *is* this?" With her free hand, she attempted a swing at his face, but the debilitating pain behind her eyes disrupted her speed and accuracy. Her knuckles grazed his jaw and kissed air as he moved his head to the side, evading her blow.

He was *fast.*

"Stop fighting," he growled. "I won't hurt you... *if* you cooperate."

"Not... hurt? Then why my head feels like this... this..." She struggled with the alien tongue, searching for the right word.

"*Pain,*" he offered. "Fucking hurts, doesn't it?"

"Yes." Calexa ground her fist into his palm, trying to force him to release his grip.

Like a damn rock, he didn't budge. She couldn't do

anything to him. Considering her own immense strength, that was rather scary.

He was more than a little scary.

"Your brain is rewiring. The language is integrating. You're still disinhibited. If you try to stay still and stop fighting me, I can get you something for the pain." His tone was stern but not unkind.

His voice had a strange effect on her. It cut through the haze of her anger and diluted her pain.

She blinked, taken aback by the oddness of it all. With a sharp intake of breath, she absorbed him in all of his silverdark glory. His face was so close that she could see tiny tendrils of liquid metal swirling in his irises.

Swirling. What?

He possessed the same deep violet skin as the others, but the unique black markings on his face were imbued with silver. The metallic stuff shifted and writhed beneath his skin, making his face appear a hundred different ways all at once.

"Wh-what you are?"

What are you? That's what she meant to say, but it came out sounding awkward and broken in this odd new tongue.

Naaga. That was what the language was called. Somehow, the word came to her unbidden, solidifying out of the torrent of information they'd forcefully rammed into her brain.

The alien frowned, his brows drawing together in a wicked scowl. The dark patterns on his face made his expression seem all the more fearsome.

Calexa's breath caught. Had she offended him somehow? But then he smiled, revealing two pairs of sharp canines. Like the rest of his teeth, they were silver, and they gleamed wickedly in the harsh light, curving from top and bottom like the teeth of a wolf. The effect was unnerving. "I am Vradhu, still." If irony were universal, perhaps there was a trace of it in his voice.

"Still?"

He tipped his head in response to her question but didn't elaborate.

Vradhu? She'd never heard of that species. "Wh-where are we?"

"On a Drakhin destroyer, in the orbit of Khira. You are just beyond the Shadowring."

His words didn't make any sense, and it wasn't just because they were speaking a new language. They were probably well beyond the charted territories of the Universe, and that was more than a little worrying.

Correction: it was downright *terrifying*.

Calexa decided not to dwell on it.

The Vradhu squeezed her hand, his touch surprisingly gentle. "If I let go, will you promise me you won't try and hit me this time?" He shook his head slightly, still baring his teeth. "You have hard hands, woman."

"Calexa," she corrected. "Me, Calexa. I..." She closed her eyes, struggling to find the right words in Naaga as she clenched her teeth and fought the throbbing pain in her head. It was like doing complicated sums without an AI. The solution was there, but it took all of her concentration to arrive at the answer. "My *name* is Calexa, and I won't hit you, but only if you promise not to strangle me with that, that..."

"*Ilverium,*" he supplied as the silver stuff trapped beneath his skin rippled and momentarily disappeared, turning his stripes black. Calexa stared at his face in wonder, entranced by his alienness. His eyes were rimmed with black, and the obsidian pigment extended over his sculpted cheekbones as two distinct slashes; symmetrical twin daggers tapering into fine points.

Black on violet. It was the most decadent thing.

Like his features, his markings were severe and unmistakable, and if she were crazy enough, she might even describe them as *beautiful*.

"That moving metal..." Calexa shuddered. There was no question that he controlled it somehow. "What is it?"

"A curse." He shrugged and let go of her hand. For a split-second his eyes flashed black, his pupils momentarily disappearing. "Do not ask again." A dark undercurrent entered his voice. "In my culture, such familiarity between strangers is unacceptable."

Abruptly, he stepped back, creating distance. His action had the same effect as a gust of icy wind, cutting through the shred of familiarity that had sprung up between them.

She froze. She'd almost forgotten that this alien was fucking *dangerous*.

He must have sensed her unease, because he raised a hand and spread his fingers wide in an appeasing gesture. His ominous expression evaporated. "I don't want to hurt you."

"You knocked me out and *abducted* me." This time, her words flowed more naturally, spurred on by her indignation. The unknown device they'd implanted in her brain seemed to be integrating at a rapid pace.

"If you'd just come with me in the first place..." He shook his head, appearing mildly exasperated. "You shouldn't fight me."

"What did you expect me to do? You were hostile. You tried to restrain me." Accusation crept into her tone.

"It was the only way." The alien's eyes gleamed with the promise of violence as the silver hue returned to his facial markings, swirling amongst the black lines. "If you want to survive in this place, do not fight me again. You should *never* fight me."

Calexa stared at the Vradhu, taken aback by the force that radiated from him. The floor around his feet seemed to quiver, threatening to turn into liquid metal.

Back off. That's what he was telling her. His entire demeanor was a threat.

Friend or foe? She couldn't tell.

"What about my people?" Calexa touched her ear in alarm. Her comm was gone. She had no way of communicating with the others. "Promise me you won't harm them."

"I have no intention of harming them, and as long as they don't do anything foolish, my clan-brothers won't, either."

"As long as they don't do anything foolish..." Calexa shook her head in frustration. "Not good enough." There was too much room for misunderstanding, especially when Mai and Zahra were involved. *Especially* when none of them spoke a word of Naaga. "I have to go back." It was urgent. The girls were notorious hotheads. She shuddered as gruesome and disastrous possibilities flickered through her mind.

She looked the Vradhu up-and-down, taking his measure. Could she get past him? There was an open doorway behind him. Beyond the threshold, the shadows deepened into darkness. The eerie blackness was punctuated by the slow pulse of a flashing green light.

She became keenly aware of the fact that they were alone.

She became aware of his sheer physical presence. The scale-armor encasing his body left little to the imagination, accentuating the powerful contours of his arms and shoulders. His body was broad and lean, and his honed torso tapered to muscular thighs. His tail—at least she *thought* it was a tail—was tightly coiled around his left leg. She followed the odd, sinuous thing down to its tip, which rested against his lower calf. It flickered slightly, suggesting impatience.

He was surely built for power and speed. Nature had given him these gifts, and he wore them effortlessly, unlike Calexa, who had twisted the arm of fate to get her enhancements, fighting every single step of the way.

She was a scrapper. In comparison, that made him a thoroughbred.

She was staring.

He was staring.

This was too surreal.

"What the hell *are* you?" His voice had become a little bit hoarse. He was watching her with undisguised curiosity, and his *ilverium* tainted eyes seemed to see right through to her metal-coated bones.

She disguised a shudder as she wondered whether he was some kind of sorcerer.

Sorcery? Impossible. She pushed the ridiculousness out of her mind. Even the infinite Universe had rules, although they kept getting broken.

"I'm..." She wasn't entirely sure what she was anymore. Those who stayed on Dashki-5 long enough inevitably became mixed up and messed up. "I'm human."

Am I?

"Human?"

"Standard-issue *sapiens*. Nothing fancy." She'd acquired a few extra bits along the way, but that was beside the point. With her temper and her vulnerabilities and her penchant for violence, she was as human as they came, and she wouldn't have it any other way.

The alien looked at her as if she were speaking another language. He'd obviously never heard of her species before.

Holy hell. That meant they were *very* far from home, because humans were well known throughout the Universe. They were prized for their soft skin, average intelligence, and manual dexterity. Not too smart, not too stupid, and compared to most alien species, they were physically weak.

That made them malleable, and perfect for certain... purposes.

"*Human.*" The Vradhu's eyes slid down her body, absorbing every last detail. "And *female*, yes?"

"In the same way that you are *obviously* male. Does it matter?" Her Naaga was growing more fluent by the minute. It was actually easier to find the words when she was angry.

He raised an eyebrow at her prickly tone but said nothing. Like a terrible itch she couldn't scratch, Calexa's impatience grew. She glanced toward the doorway, her worry over the *Medusa's* crew and passengers growing with each passing second.

The alien's tail-*thing* flickered. "You will come with me." It was an order, iron-clad and absolute. People skills obviously weren't his strong point. The sheer arrogance in his voice made her bristle, but what stung even more was the fact that he *was* in a position to issue orders. She had absolutely no bargaining power here.

"My crew," she said softly. "Promise me your people won't harm them."

He gave her a long, measured look, but said nothing.

That infuriated her a little. "You can't guarantee it, or you *won't*?"

The pain in her head was still there, but it had faded to a dull throb. Fragments of Naaga-speak swirled through her mind as her understanding of the language solidified.

Sorcery or not, that implant-thing *was* fucking magic. It beat any of the translator nodes she'd ever owned.

Ignoring her question, the alien shook his head and turned toward the shadowed doorway, at once both arrogant and dismissive. "Follow me."

Ooh, the audacity! Calexa clenched her fists tightly, grinding her fingernails into her palms. The pain helped her resist the urge to grab that long, gleaming, proud warrior's braid of his and yank him backwards until he gave her a decent fucking answer. The pain helped her focus her thoughts amidst the swirling mind-fog of Naaga-speak.

The language of slaves. There was a reason he'd called it that. *Why?* The answer was at the periphery of her consciousness, just beyond her reach.

She shook her head, hesitating. He passed through the doorway and into the shadows, leaving her behind. The Vradhu didn't glance backwards or speak to her. He simply expected her to follow.

Every fiber of her being screamed at her to resist. *Fight him and escape.* It was almost second nature; she'd been running on adrenaline and fear for most of her life, and she'd been fighting back ever since she was born.

The fear was still there, simmering just beneath the surface; an old, familiar companion. Normally, she would draw on it, channeling it into violence, but not this time. She'd tried fighting, and look where she'd ended up.

Calexa closed her eyes, exercising restraint. Slowly, she unclenched her fists, took a deep breath, and stepped forward.

Follow me.

She didn't know what he wanted. She didn't know where they were going. It went against her very nature to blindly follow his orders, but she was in no position to argue. She'd gotten a glimpse of what he was capable of. He'd defeated her with terrifying ease, and Calexa was no pushover. The thought made her shudder. Had he *really* been fighting her, or just toying with her?

Something wrapped around her waist.

It was heavy and warm and strong and strangely familiar, almost like an arm. The air in front of her moved, and she gasped as the *thing* tightened.

Her eyes flew open. He was *there*, right in front of her, barely inches from her, and yet no part of him touched her except for his...

How the hell had he moved so fast?

She froze.

His tail!

His black tail curled around her waist. It was as thick as her wrist and it felt like coiled steel. She forgot to breathe as its tip snaked up toward her neck, coming to rest at the hollow above her collarbone. There was something sharp and spiky at the end of his tail. It dug ever-so-slightly into the thin material of her thermosuit.

Calexa's trigger finger itched, and she mentally cursed the

alien for taking away her weapons. Without them, she felt naked and vulnerable. Against an opponent of this caliber, she needed every advantage she could get.

"Understand this," he said, his voice low and soft. "I do not wish to restrain you, fight you, or hurt you in any way."

The ground around his feet became liquid, swirling like a miniature vortex. It made a soft, metallic scraping sound as it rippled and undulated, lapping at his feet. It was as if the very heart of the ship itself were under his command.

Calexa couldn't figure out whether his words were supposed to be reassuring or threatening. "What do you want from me?"

"I want you to accept your situation. You have no power here."

Calexa stared at him, not quite understanding his words.

He moved forward a fraction, his tail—she couldn't *believe* it was actually around her—tightening in an unbreakable loop. Reflexively, her hands dropped to her waist, her bare fingers curling around the strong, snakelike limb.

His skin felt like rough velvet. It was surprisingly warm and soft, and she had an absurd desire to stroke it.

But then he was right in her face, shattering any notion of softness or warmth. His eyes burned with a delicious intensity that was so startling against the inky blackness of his marked skin. "You will not catch me by surprise again. You are strong, but I am far stronger, and this is *my* domain. You are not in a position to demand *anything*. When I tell you to follow me, you *follow*. Do you understand?"

Shit. A dozen questions rose to her lips, but she bit them back. He was a creature from another world, unpredictable and unfathomable. She couldn't read him at all. She didn't understand his culture; why he reacted the way he did to certain things. The only thing she knew for certain was that he wanted—no, he *expected*—her to obey him without question.

Obey? Ha.

The last person who had demanded her complete obedience had ended up dead in his own bed.

"There is a storm in your eyes." The barbed tip of his tail traced up-and-down the hollow of her neck. Slowly, his tail slithered upward until it was completely wrapped around the base of her neck. "You are an intelligent lifeform, are you not? Understand this. Your life is in my hands, and this place is unforgiving. If you want to survive, you must quell the storm. I see it in every fiber of your being, and I want it gone. I am not interested in fighting you."

He didn't tighten the noose around her neck. He didn't have to. As tendrils of shifting liquid metal began to coil around her ankles like rapidly growing vines, Calexa understood.

She saw it in his eyes. They glowed with deep, hidden power. She got the feeling he could end her life in a heartbeat if he wished.

Whoa. Her instincts screamed at her to be careful.

Why did he suddenly seem so much more dangerous than he had when they'd fought inside the *Medusa's* airlock?

His tail flexed. With a soft gasp, Calexa realized she was still holding onto it. Her first instinct was to wrench it away, but she forced herself to be still. "I understand," she said softly. The moving metal continued to slide up her legs. It took all of her self-control to remain still when her body was primed and ready to fight. Her muscles tensed. Her bionic joints were wound tight. Her breathing was rapid and slightly hoarse, her palms clammy. Her hands shook.

She was actually trembling.

"Good." Slowly, the Vradhu withdrew his tail. "I will make sure you have deep, painful regrets it if you try anything stupid." Calexa exhaled in relief as the noose uncoiled from around her neck. The black loops of his tail slid across her waist in a deliberate, almost insolent manner. The moving metal—the so-called *ilverium*—melted away, releasing her from its unnerving grasp.

All the while, he stared at her, the harsh light turning the liquid metal in his eyes pale and iridescent, like platinum. The message was obvious. *Don't fuck with me.*

He'd just succeeded in intimidating the hell out of her, and he hadn't even raised a weapon in anger. The twin swords at his waist remained hidden in their sheaths.

Calexa didn't know whether to feel insulted or terrified. Normally, *she* was the one who did the intimidating, but for now she would have to bide her time until she learned more about this strange new world and its terrifying inhabitants.

The Vradhu's tail returned to its resting place—coiled around his left leg. "Come."

This time, she fell into step behind him as he turned, his long warrior's braid swinging above impossibly broad shoulders. They passed through a dim room where various objects—machines of some sort—glowed an unholy shade of green. Unable to bear it any longer, she broke the silence. "You have a name, don't you?"

He stopped so abruptly that she almost crashed into him. Her breath caught in her throat. Had she angered him somehow?

Slowly, he turned, and when he met her gaze, his expression was distant. "You may call me Ares."

Ares. For such an exotic being, that was a damn *Earthian* sounding name. It resonated deep in her metal bones, feeling ancient and familiar and powerful, like an Old Earth name, one that came from a time when their planet was a lush green paradise where men and women could only gaze up at the stars and dream of gods and monsters.

So why did he look almost... forlorn?

Before she could respond, he turned away, becoming a blur of black and violet and molten silver. The scales of his shimmering armor rippled over his broad shoulders as he stalked gracefully across the dark room, wrapping himself in silence and power. "Follow me, human," he said. "You will be my translator."

"Translator?"

"Your people have something I want, paleface." The metallic echo in his deep, resonant voice made her shudder.

He sounded so damn *alien*.

"Speak for yourself, inkface," she muttered quietly under her breath as she followed the mysterious Vradhu with the Earthian sounding name, hoping he wasn't leading her to a fate worse than death.

Most aliens in the Universe only wanted humans for one purpose, and she would rather die than go down that route again.

CHAPTER NINE

ARES'S TAIL still tingled from where he'd held the human. Impatient with her hesitation and stirred up by the fire in her eyes, he'd turned, and before he knew what he was doing, he'd taken her in a hold that was somewhere between a mating caress and a death-grip.

What had he been thinking?

Take her!

The ilverium in his veins had roared in approval, and he'd almost succumbed to the dark desires of the Drakhin.

He could have devoured her soul there and then.

Wait... What the fuck was that?

Such a thing had never happened before. Having the human in his grasp hadn't helped. To his surprise, she was softer than she looked. Her narrow waist was the perfect size for his tail to coil around, and she radiated warmth.

How could he have had any doubt as to her gender? She was distinctly *female,* in a way that stirred his deeply buried instincts.

He shook his head as his cock stirred. *What a fucking idiot you are. Such a horny Hunter.* That's what the idiot Breeders snidely called them behind their backs.

Ah, she was a strange thing. She bristled at his commands and fought at the slightest provocation. She was tough and fierce and loyal—her concern for her fellow humans told him that much—and yet beneath the hard exterior, she possessed a softness that defied his understanding.

Quick to anger and full of defiance. Were all humans like her? Vradhu males of the warrior caste possessed similar traits, and although there were rare exceptions, most Vradhu females considered them unsuitable as life-mates.

It wasn't uncommon for Vradhu warriors to die young and alone. It was simply their fate. They lived to fight, and the enemies on Khira were dangerous and many.

The tip of his tail flicked back-and-forth, snapping impatiently against his left leg as he struggled to maintain it in the neutral position. A Vradhu's tail rarely left its resting place, but this soft-skinned alien was making him all kinds of restless.

Her curious stare burned into him from behind as they walked through the sci-labs, passing closed doors. The Naaga sci-people were hidden behind those innocuous grey entrances, resentfully carrying out his bidding.

In a prelude to speech, the human took a deep breath, but then she hesitated. Ares could sense her fear. *Good.* It was important for her to be afraid. Fear was a leash. Fear equalled caution. Without it, she'd be impossible to control, and he didn't want to fight her again. She was dangerous. Impulsive. Unpredictable. She'd almost gotten the better of him once— granted, he'd been weakened—but if they fought again he would probably kill her, and that would be a shame.

"You may ask," he growled after a brief pause. He hadn't meant to let her speak until they reached the command pod, but his curiosity burned like a solstice flare.

"Huh." A soft huff escaped her. Ares could hear her perfectly well as she muttered something under her breath in her native tongue. He couldn't understand the words, but the indignation in her voice was obvious.

"How did you know I was going to ask a question?" Finally, she spoke in Naaga. Her command of the language was improving rapidly; she seemed to be tolerating the neural graft quite well.

Ares was impressed. He hadn't been so lucky. They'd had to sedate him three times after the graft, and when he'd calmed down enough that he was no longer a threat to the sci-people, he'd spewed verbal nonsense for days.

"You are an outsider, thrust into a world you know nothing about. Of course there are going to be questions."

"Huh," she said again, sounding a little bemused. "And some things, like: *'what are you, really?'* are off-limits, huh?"

Ares kept quiet. He was being a little unfair with her, but he didn't want her getting too comfortable in his presence just yet, especially when he knew next to nothing about her or her kind. The Vradhu were secretive by nature. A Vradhu's trust was not given lightly, but once earned, it was even more difficult to break.

"What do you want with me?"

"You will be my link. You will convey our wishes to your people. The situation we find ourselves in is precarious, and there is no room *whatsoever* for error. That is why I took great pains to make sure you can understand us."

"Y-you want me to act as a translator?"

"Yes."

"That's... it?" She regarded him with a suspicious look. The crystalline brilliance of her eyes made his heart clench a little.

"For now. There will be other things."

"Such as?"

"I haven't yet decided." He didn't want to reveal his plans just yet. Although he'd done his best to seal the Naaga away, they were too numerous to contain. They could be listening.

Besides, he hadn't decided whether he could trust this alien. What principles did her kind live by? Was she as honor-less and confounding as the Naaga, or were these humans a noble race?

Only behind the dense, resonating walls of the command chamber did he truly feel secure. There he could sit on the sekkhoi throne and extend his senses, becoming one with the ship.

He would take the human there and interrogate her. Then he would decide if she could be of any use to him outside her role as a translator.

As they reached the end of the corridor, Ares lengthened his stride, filled with a sudden sense of urgency. He'd been away from the throne of thorns for too long. He had to go back and join with the *Hythra's* consciousness.

Dangerous.

That feeling—*omnipotence*—was becoming addictive, like a drug. This cursed bond was changing him in ways he couldn't fathom, and part of him was terrified of what he might become. The *Hythra* welcomed him with open arms, whispering sweet, dark truths about the Vradhu and the Drakhin and their shared history over the course of a million sun-kissed orbits.

You are kin-people, Hunter. You can't escape blood.

Dra. *Treacherous*. Khin. *Blood*.

Oh, he *knew* what the word truly meant, but there was no way he was going to succumb to the *Hythra's* pull. She had no idea who she was trying to seduce. If all went to plan, he would soon be free of her.

Just a little longer.

He had one chance to escape this floating hell forever. One chance that he might see the revered plains of the Ardu-Sai again in this cursed life. One chance to rescue his brethren from living out the rest of their existence onboard this lifeless prison. Kratok-hunting season was about to begin, and without Maki's warriors, the Two Clans would be in deep trouble.

Ah, the Hunt. How he yearned for it. A vivid memory entered his mind. It was the warm caress of the *Mengash*—the great southerly winds—across his face as he stared up at the glorious snow-capped Esskar range. As he'd scented the air, which was thick with the musky spoor of the great beasts, a savage thrill of anticipation had coursed through him.

His homeland called to him. Even from beyond the Shadowring, he felt the pull of the brutal, beautiful, and utterly wild Ardu-Sai. No Vradhu could comfortably stay away from Aethra's cradle for too long. Their existence here on the *Hythra* was a slow kind of torture. If they didn't leave soon, they would die.

The Naaga were counting on it.

What they hadn't counted on was the arrival of these strange brown-skinned aliens.

"Perhaps you will be our salvation," he whispered under his breath in Vradhu as they passed into the main vault. The Human matched his pace perfectly, keeping exactly two steps behind him. She moved with the natural stealth of a trained fighter, her footsteps silent on the metal floor. He was close enough that he could feel her through his connection to the *Hythra*.

Tap. Tap. She walked as gracefully as a black-footed *tikkrit,* her feet almost caressing the smooth grey floor. Tiny vibrations rippled through the sentient surface, and in his hyper-aware state, Ares became acutely aware of the way she balanced her weight on the balls of her feet. She was tense and ready to spring into action.

A natural fighter.

The ilverium at his feet rippled in response to her presence, and Ares had to exert extra effort to keep it controlled. It was always this way with the *Hythra*. The ship was always just one step away from consuming him. Only through sheer willpower did Ares keep her in check. He hadn't slept in longer than he could remember.

If he slept, he lost. They all lost. Simple as that.

The Naaga had told him nothing about how to control this mysterious technology. He hadn't received the training they gave to their Chosen Ones, but little by little, he was learning.

He was a Hunter. Adaptation was his specialty.

No doubt they hoped he would succumb to the destroyer's dark pull; that he would disappear into the morass of living metal and lost souls that was the *Hythra,* just like all the other hosts before him.

But Ares was not a spineless Naaga, and he flexed his will like a muscle, keeping the ancient Drakhin warship under his command. He would never succumb. He was Vradhu. The Naaga had yet to understand what that really meant.

As they neared the center of the vault, Ares's nostrils flared. A strange smell lingered in the air. It was sweet and not unpleasant, yet there was an underlying bitterness to it that made his skin prickle.

Familiar.

On one side of the hexagonal room, the wide grey doors that marked the main entrance to sci-labs were sealed. If he so wished, he could open them with a thought.

He paused, holding up a hand. The Human stopped immediately. He had to give her credit, her instincts were good; sharp. "Can you smell that?"

"Smell what?"

"That..." He blinked as the ilverium in his body surged, coming to the surface. It shot through the black *ankhata* on his arms and face, causing a ripple of pain across his skin.

Now he remembered that smell. It had been present at the Source, when the Naaga had tricked them with that strange cylindrical device.

Poison. How had they smuggled it into the sci-labs? How had their treachery escaped his notice? Because he'd been temporarily distracted by the human...

Run!

His knees quivered. His vision blurred then snapped back into focus. His hold over the writhing ilverium wavered.

What is this?

The seals in his mind broke. Control slipped through his fingers. Ares fell to his knees.

Poison? They dare provoke me like this? How long have they been planning this?

The soft, murmuring speech of the Naaga filled the cavernous chamber. The human gasped in surprise. Blue figures swam into view.

Naaga. They had once been slaves to the cruel and powerful Drakhin. Now that the Darkwalkers were gone, they were free, and they usurped Drakhin technology, using it to gain control of vast territories on Khira, where they multiplied like fucking *pikki.* The decaying ruins of the vast Drakhin cities were full of them.

Fortunately for the Vradhu, the Naaga had always steered clear of the Ardu-Sai... until now.

To them, the Vradhu were little more than tools. Like trained and leashed *shuklak*-beasts, they had been brought onto the destroyer to exterminate pests.

The Vradhu despised their new overlords, and in turn, the Naaga despised the *Hythra's* new host. They were locked in a stalemate.

It was complicated.

"You dare?" Ares hissed, fury coursing through him. They were *not* supposed to be out here. They were supposed to be completing their task under the watchful eyes of the guards Maki had generously assigned. Ares tried to summon the ilverium, drawing on the energy that was all around him—in the walls, the floor, the beating heart of the *Hythra* itself....

But he couldn't.

Not missing a beat, he took a step toward the approaching Naaga, reaching for his twin krivera.

His fingers closed around the worn kratok-bone hilts in a

movement that was as natural as breathing. The bone-white blades slid from their sheaths with a barely audible hiss.

But Ares couldn't complete the arc of his attack. His body ground to a halt, betraying him in his moment of need.

Move! He willed himself forward, to no avail.

Ares viciously cursed the blue-skinned ones as his muscles locked into place, denying him freedom.

What is happening to me?

The Naaga advanced. There were at least a dozen of them. Typical Naaga, always seeking safety in numbers. Normally, he would have fought them off with ease, because as cunning as they were, the Naaga were physically weak and no match for a Vradhu warrior in his prime.

The Drakhin had designed them that way. Good slaves didn't fight back.

Ares's blades fell to the floor with a clatter. The room reeked of that strange, pungent, bittersweet aroma. Behind him, the human danced backwards, giving him a wide berth.

Whatever poison those cursed samefaced creatures had released into the air obviously wasn't affecting her.

Would she take the chance and escape?

"I'll kill you," he whispered as he desperately tried to feel for the *Hythra's* dark, endless presence through the bond.

It was there, but he'd lost control. The liquid metal rose to the surface, breaking his skin. It crawled up his bare arms, extending over his shoulders and down his back.

No! This couldn't be happening now, not when he was so close.

Not when this human female was stepping into the void that he'd left. Not when she was about to commit a great insult to his honor. He stared in mute fascination as she reached down and *dared* to wrap her hands around the kratok-fang blades of a fully blooded Vradhu warrior.

This strange alien didn't know the rules of their world. She didn't understand that *no-one* but Ares touched his swords, and yet the heavy kratok blades looked so natural in her hands. *So beautiful.*

And although she'd just violated clan law—sweet Aethra, if only she *knew* what Vradhu females would think of her—a part of Ares was exultant.

She could have run, but she'd stayed.

He snarled as his limbs grew weak and heavy. His vision blurred. He became lightheaded. He was bleeding. Tendrils of ilverium coursed over his broken skin, threatening to engulf him. He knew what the *Hythra* wanted.

The Drakhin destroyer wanted to devour him, just like she had her last host. He desperately tried to uncoil his tail. It was the deadliest of all his weapons, and his last line of defense. If he could move freely, he could whip it toward his attackers and hit them with deadly venom.

Nothing happened. He was paralyzed.

The Human strode past him fluidly, gracefully, raising the krivera as if she'd wielded them all her life.

She was magnificent.

All Ares could do was watch. His mute fury melted into a kind of horrified fascination. How ironic it was that in this moment, the cursed bond he'd sought to break was now something he desperately needed, and the very alien he'd sought to fill with fear now held his fate in her hands.

CHAPTER TEN

CALEXA STARED at the blue-skinned aliens in shock. They filed into the cavernous room through a wide-open entrance that had suddenly appeared in the wall. A strange, cloying smell filled the room, reminding her of overripe bananas.

Who the hell were these newcomers? As if her encounter with the fearsome Vradhu wasn't enough for her overwhelmed brain to process, now these slender blue creatures had appeared out of nowhere.

"He is incapacitated," one of them said quietly in Naaga. "Quickly, now. We must harvest him."

"And the foreign one?"

"She is inconsequential; a mere distraction. Jara said nothing about her. Our objective is to dispose of the usurper at all costs. He is an aberration, nothing more. The natural balance will be restored in time."

"She is capable of violence, just like the Vradhu."

"If that is the case, we will wear her out eventually."

"Do not allow him to regain control. If he re-establishes the connection..."

"He will kill us all."

Their strange conversation buzzed around her like white

noise, as if she didn't even exist. Calexa glanced at Ares in alarm.

If looks could kill... Murder was written across his face, but he wasn't moving. The floor beneath him was as flat and smooth as glass until tiny droplets of crimson splattered around his feet.

Blood.

Her eyes widened.

They bleed red, just like us.

Tendrils of ilverium erupted from his skin, wrapping around his body like coiling vines. Even with the living metal swirling all around him, he'd managed to draw the curved blades that hung at his waist. The blades were bone-white and they looked razor-sharp, but he appeared unable to lift them any higher than his waist.

They fell from his hands, clattering to the floor.

The newcomers regarded Ares with a look of blank indifference that sent chills down Calexa's spine. Not much could faze her these days, but these aliens gave her the creeps. *Something* about them wasn't quite right. She couldn't quite put her finger on it.

There were about a dozen of them in total, and they were pale blue; the color of an Earthian sky in summer. Lean and long-limbed, their slender bodies seemed to be designed for graceful, frictionless movement.

Naaga. Unbidden, the word came to mind. They were ethereally beautiful, with long, graceful necks and soft, delicate features. Instead of hair, their heads were covered with smooth white plumage that resembled a cross between feathers and scales. The plumage extended down their necks, disappearing beneath plain grey tunics.

Twelve pairs of slanted, widely spaced white eyes turned toward her and collectively dismissed her. Theirs were eyes without pupil or iris; plain white orbs coated with an iridescent sheen that glowed in the dim light.

She took a deep breath as the realization hit her.

They were perfect.

They were identical.

That was what had creeped her out. She was unable to differentiate between them. They all had the same narrow, pointed noses and soft, sensual lips. A stardust-like smattering of glittering white scales decorated their pale cheeks. Their features were both pleasing and cold, as if their faces had been designed to convey beauty without emotion. If the fierce and regal looking Vradhu were destined to be hunters, then these creatures had been made to serve a very different purpose.

Naaga. In Drakhin, the word had two different meanings. *Slave. Made One.*

Calexa shuddered.

How did she even *know* that?

A low growl captured her attention. Calexa's gaze flicked toward Ares, who had dropped to his knees. Tendrils of silver-grey ilverium rippled across his powerful body—chaos in motion. Fury spilled from his eyes, and his teeth were bared.

Scary.

He looked downright terrifying, but something was wrong. Tension was etched in every sculpted line and contour of his body. His limbs were locked into place.

He couldn't move.

The Naaga ignored her completely and started to advance on Ares.

Calexa's head spun. She had no fucking clue what was going on, but a couple of things were obvious. One, Ares was in trouble. Two, the blue ones didn't seem to think she was worth the time of day. They were going straight for the kill. It was stupid, but that rankled a little bit. She was used to being the most dangerous one in the room, but that crown had been stolen by Ares.

Not your problem, honey. Get your ass out of here and back

*to the Medusa before that purple monster snaps out of his
trance and pulls you back into his orbit.*

She desperately wanted to get back to her crew, but
without knowing the way, she could end up running for days.
The alien vessel was simply that fucking *big*; a floating city
amongst the distant stars.

She couldn't run away now.

Fine. Stay. It's your funeral.

Calexa didn't break her stride as she walked across to Ares,
reached down, and picked up his weapons. As the smooth,
worn hilts slid into her palms, a faint electric tingle crawled
across her arms.

These blades were well-used. They just had that *feeling*
about them. A lot of blood had been spilled by these swords.

The swords were heavier than they looked, but they were
perfectly weighted. They felt good in her hands, in the way
that a well crafted, well used, well cared-for, and *broken-in* tool
might feel.

Ares had gone perfectly quiet and still, but his catlike eyes
burned into her from behind. That menacing intensity never
seemed to leave him, even when he was on his knees.

What the fuck are you doing, crazy Cal?

She was about to save this jerk-of-a-Vradhu's ass, that's
what.

Why?

She didn't understand jack about what was happening
onboard this floating monstrosity, but she knew about power
dynamics and pecking orders, and from what she'd observed so
far, one thing was obvious.

For better or for worse, everything revolved around Ares,
and he was about to owe her, big time.

Find something they want. Use it to your advantage.

What better way to get a leg up in this mysterious place
than to rescue the top dog, even if he was an arrogant, stuck-

up, slightly terrifying, and too-strong-for-his-own-good Vradhu bastard?

Besides, it felt terribly *wrong* to leave this proud warrior helpless on his knees as the blue ones surrounded him. He *had* spared her life and given her the language of slaves, and he'd shown great restraint when she'd woken up furious and disoriented. She didn't know how long she'd been unconscious for. He could have done all manner of things to her. He could have treated her *very* badly, but as far as she knew, the worst he'd done was to arrange for that language-thing to be implanted in her head.

In the grand scheme of things, that was *nothing*. Calexa had been subjected to far worse in her short, scrappy life. After all, she was from Dashki-5.

As she approached, several of the Naaga peeled off and tried to corral her in an attempt to separate her from Ares. Calexa was having none of it. "Get back. I'll cut you down!" She raised the bone-white blades in warning.

There was no reaction, not even the slightest flinch. One of the Naaga stepped forward, his hand outstretched in what was meant to be a peaceful gesture. "Cease your resistance. You will gain nothing by protecting him." His voice was surprisingly rich, and as he moved into position, the others surrounded him, nodding in agreement. "If you put down your weapons and walk away, we will ensure no harm comes to you and your people."

The Naaga surrounded Ares. By now, the ilverium covered most of his body. It extended down into the floor, forming taut cords as it merged with the grey metal surface. It was as if the seething liquid metal had taken on a life of its own. It wanted to devour the enraged Vradhu.

Ares was frozen. His blank silver eyes sent a chill through Calexa. The essence of his soul had been dampened, and his dark intensity was on the verge of being extinguished.

It was a terrible thing to behold.

"He is Vradhu," another of the Naaga continued. "They are an old, primitive people, with little influence in this new world. You would be a fool to seek an alliance with them. Soon they will be finished."

Calexa hesitated, but didn't lower the blades. She narrowed her eyes, trying to read the Naaga. It was impossible. Their aloof expressions remained unchanged.

Something didn't add up. If the Naaga were oh-so important and powerful, then why had the *Medusa* been greeted by a sea of black-and-purple faces on arrival? The Vradhu she'd seen in the arrival dock had been fearsome and intimidating; not the sort of people one would refer to as *primitive*.

And not a single Naaga had shown up with the welcoming party.

Why? Who's in charge here?

"Do not fight us, alien. On this destroyer, we vastly outnumber the Vradhu. Despite what *he* may have told you, he is an outlier, nothing more. If your reasoning is logical and your thought processes are linear, you will see the sense in complying with our request."

But... he hasn't told me anything.

The Naaga closest to Ares produced a long metal tube. The black device sat snugly in the palm of his three-fingered hand, emitting a faintly glowing green light. He exchanged a knowing look with his companions as he pressed the thing against Ares's forehead.

The green glow became more intense. The Vradhu's body began to shake, as if he were in the grip of a seizure.

What the hell were they doing to him?

Calexa watched in horror as the tube-like device burrowed into Ares's forehead. A thin trickle of blood ran down his face, spilling over his nose, coating his full, dark lips.

Dispose of the usurper at all costs.

They were killing him.

"Screw this," Calexa muttered under her breath, surrendering to her instincts. They'd served her well on Dashki-5, and now they were screaming at her to stop this. There was a *wrongness* about the whole thing. A sick feeling uncoiled in the pit of her stomach as she sidestepped the approaching Naaga.

She went straight for the one holding the tube-like device. The air around Ares and the Naaga was laden with static, and an electric ripple crawled across her skin, raising the fine hairs on her arms. It was like wading into a dense charge-field.

Calexa made a decision.

She brought down the ivory sword.

It cut clean and true, severing the Naaga's hand at the wrist.

The blue alien grunted in pain as his hand fell to the floor with a dull thud. He stared at her in shock.

Not so unflappable now, are you, asshole?

Blood spurted everywhere in a wild spray of vivid green, coating her bare hand. It splattered across Calexa's arm and torso, and she thanked the stars her thermosuit was impervious to liquids.

"Stop," she growled. "Whatever you're doing to him, stop."

"You're making a mistake, alien. You will not get far in our world if you take his side. Why would you do such a thing when you know nothing about our world?"

"He's...." She hesitated. What *was* Ares to her? An enemy? An ally? A means to an end? Was he even *alive*? He was frozen on his knees, like a statue. Writhing tendrils of ilverium extended up his neck, piercing the skin of his cheeks, coursing up through the tattoo-like markings that decorated his face. Liquid metal quickly covered the wound, stretching across Ares's forehead.

Out of habit, Calexa snapped her wrist, flicking emerald-colored blood from the blade. It stained the metal floor with a vicious spray of green. "He's my guide," she said, moving protectively between Ares and the blue one. The injured

Naaga's milky-white eyes widened as he pressed his other hand against the bleeding stump of his arm.

An ordinary Human would be howling in pain by now. The only evidence of the Naaga's discomfort was his hoarse, rapid breathing. He stepped back as his companions surged forward like a pack of rabid dogs.

"Get back!" Calexa shouted, raising her blades. The Naaga ignored her. They didn't wield any weapons, but they had numbers on their side.

Crazy fools. What was this? Strength in numbers? Weren't they afraid of death?

This was about to get messy. Calexa swung her blades in a wide arc as blue bodies formed a ring around her. Slender arms thrust forward, reaching for her. She slashed and stabbed and dodged, and soon the acrid smell of their green blood filled the air, overpowering the scent of sickly-sweet banana-whatever.

They just don't fucking stop!

They moved back-and-forth, a sea of swaying, surging, weaponless blue bodies, engaging Calexa in a messy, violent dance. She tried to break free, but despite their delicate appearance, the Naaga were unexpectedly relentless. As soon as she cut one down, another moved forward to fill the void.

When she injured them, they didn't cry out in pain. When she separated limbs from bodies, they didn't falter. They just grunted softly and shrugged it off, even though Calexa was dealing what *should* have been near-mortal wounds.

What are they... fucking zombies?

At least two of them had fallen, their bodies crumpling in lifeless heaps, but the others just kept coming.

"What does it take to kill you freaks?" she growled, her breaths coming in short, sharp rasps. This was starting to feel like hard work. A fine layer of sweat coated her face and neck. Her skin prickled beneath her thermosuit as the temperature regulating fabric absorbed her body's heat.

She hacked at an offending arm, her movements becoming wild and uncontrolled. She'd been separated from Ares in the fray, and she could no longer see the fallen Vradhu.

Somehow, the Naaga managed to draw her toward the open doorway—away from Ares. Calexa spun as something pressed against her neck, between the protrusions of her biometal spine.

Cold!

The thing was blisteringly cold, like a block of dry ice. Calexa twisted violently, trying to free herself of the sensation, but her arms and legs grew heavy.

What is this feeling?

The energy drained from her body. Her vision blurred. The Naaga standing before her were a haze of blue and green. *So cold! So sleepy!* She just wanted to curl up into a ball and hibernate.

The chaos stopped. Murmuring voices surrounded her. They seemed... *surprised.* A halo of vivid green light engulfed them, intruding on her blurry vision.

"Look at that. She possesses incredibly high levels of *vir*."

"An unexpected boon. We will harvest it."

"Do you think it is a species characteristic?"

"It is possible. We know nothing about her kind. If they are all like her, then..."

"They will be useful indeed."

The Naaga's odd conversation should have given her the chills, but she was already frozen, and her thoughts moved at a glacial pace; too slowly for her to register fear.

Vir? What the hell is that? She didn't understand the word. Did that mean there was no equivalent in Earthian?

"Dispose of the Vradhu and take her for processing. If we harvest enough *vir* from her, it won't take us long to regain control of this defective ship."

"Indeed. A Vradhu should *never* have bonded with it."

"It was unexpected. Perhaps we should never have

brought them onboard in the first place. We don't know much about them."

"They were necessary. The infestation was too far gone."

"Yes. What is done is done. Now let us restore the balance."

"And his second body?"

"Destroy it too."

"That would be a waste. The clone is perfect. Can we not animate it?"

"That would be risky. If we give it consciousness, the *Hythra* may try to bond with it too. Her affinity for him is too strong."

Hands swarmed all over her with a featherlight touch. They were neither warm nor cold. She fought to keep her eyes open as her breathing became slow and shallow.

Is this how it ends? I get taken down by these blue-faced weirdos in an unknown part of the Universe?

Most self-respecting mercenaries would call her a stupid fucking idiot for not running when she had the chance, but she didn't regret defending the dying Ares. It wasn't in her nature to run, and the Naaga were creeps. There was no way she could trust them.

At least she'd drawn Ares away from the *Medusa*. He was chaos incarnate, as unpredictable and unfathomable as the Netherverse itself. Stars knew she *wanted* to trust him, but she'd seen enough of the Universe to know that the most alluring creatures could sometimes be the most dangerous.

Hopefully, she'd bought her people enough time. Monroe had better have gotten those damn powerbanks back online. It was the *Medusa's* only hope. Maybe they could shoot their way through the walls of this fucking death-trap and escape.

She looked down. Her fingers were blue. Her teeth chattered. The super-cold device was still pressed against her neck, and now she understood its purpose.

They're draining away my... energy, as if they're goddamn

vampires.

There were several known vampire-like races in the Universe, but they usually drank blood, not energy—or *mana*, or *life-force*—or whatever the hell it was supposed to be called.

She whimpered softly as the chill took hold, turning her metal bones into ice-rods.

Pain gripped her skull and refused to let go.

The walls shifted. She blinked.

Really?

Her frostbitten brain wasn't playing tricks on her.

The walls were actually *shifting.*

The ground beneath her feet lurched, and suddenly everything tilted to one side. Caught off balance, the Naaga scrambled around her.

Finally, that terrible icy-cold device was removed from her neck. She summoned all of her remaining energy and rose to her feet, swaying back-and-forth as the room tilted further and further to one side. A deep, reverberating groan echoed through the air. It was spooky and organic, as if some ancient beast were rising from the cold depths of a forgotten sea.

The floor tipped further. The Naaga slid across the smooth metal surface, crashing into one another like space-junk in an asteroid storm.

Calexa tried to tense, but her body wouldn't respond. She trembled all over, racked with terrible shivers. She was *so* cold.

She expected to fall down the tilting floor along with the Naaga, but she didn't.

Something held her in place, something flexible yet as strong as tempered steel. *Liquid metal.* As her Universe turned on its head, a coil of metal snaked around her waist in an oh-so familiar way.

The floor under her feet turned into mush and she started to sink.

Drained of all her energy, all she could do was surrender as it threatened to swallow her whole.

CHAPTER ELEVEN

BE MINE, **Hunter.**

The voice echoed inside his head, speaking an old, forgotten dialect of Vradhu.

The voice was endless, as if thousands of souls were speaking in perfect unison.

The voice belonged to Ares, too. He was part of the whole, a tiny fragment swept up in the slipstream.

Wait... *What?* He was surely going mad. The *Hythra* hadn't spoken to him like this since he'd first boarded her, back when he hadn't recognized the monster for what she was.

Perhaps he was hallucinating.

You were made for this. Why fight it? They tried to poison you, you know. Invisible gas, lethal to your kind. They are patient creatures, our Naaga. They synthesized it in the sci-labs right under your very nose and waited until you were too distracted to notice. The arrival of these humans was the perfect diversion. Don't you want to take your revenge?

Oh, he would love to take revenge. He would kill every last one of them.

But he would not allow the *Hythra* to possess him.

Get out! He raged against the bond, trying to force the ilverium—that filthy, cursed *magrel*—out of his body once and for all. It engulfed him completely, trapping him in a swirling hell.

No! This was not supposed to be his fate. He was a thrice-blooded warrior. He was the lone hunter, the kratok-slayer, a fucking *khefe* of the Ardu-Sai.

He didn't belong on this obsolete Drakhin monstrosity. He was a son of Khira, and he longed to feel her soft, rain-drenched soils beneath his bare feet.

He was a simple warrior, nothing more.

Join me. We will be unstoppable. I can give you power beyond your wildest dreams. We have been inside you long enough that you have almost completed the Change. All you have to do is tap into her vir. She is ripe for the taking.

Ares hardened his heart. How could he surrender to something that wanted to consume him?

Enough! It was time to break free or die trying.

Release me! His mindspeech crescendoed into a defiant roar. He would never yield. Did the *Hythra* truly understand what he was? Ha! He *lived* to destroy monsters.

He became dimly aware of what was happening around him in the *real* world. The Human fought. For one who had never held a kratok-tooth weapon, she wielded the krivera well enough, dancing around the Naaga as they tried to overwhelm her with sheer numbers.

With devastating efficiency, she incapacitated the bastard who held that cursed device to his forehead. The Naaga dropped to his knees in front of Ares as blood spilled from his severed arm, pooling around them. Tendrils of vivid green swirled amongst silver ilverium, forming a grotesque pattern of abstract lines and blotches.

The Naaga drew the Human away, pushing her to the other side of the room.

Leading her back toward the sci-labs.

Some dim, primitive part of his brain registered her appearance. The way she moved, graceful and yet purposeful. The way she glared at her enemies, her blue eyes crystal clear, her gaze as straight as an arrow.

The way she looked back at him from time-to-time.

That *look*. He'd never been on the receiving end of a look like that. *Total commitment*. Warmth blossomed in his chest like an unfurling flower. Nobody protected Ares but himself. *Nobody*.

Why? He'd done nothing to gain her trust or earn her loyalty.

Green Naaga blood splattered across his face as she danced across the room, absorbed in combat. For a moment he lost her, but then his second eyelids—which seemed to be the only part of him that could still fucking move—flicked, clearing his vision. When he caught sight of her again, an aura surrounded her. Skeins of golden energy flowed around her like tiny currents.

What is that? He blinked, wondering if he were hallucinating. Ares had never seen anything more beautiful in his life.

Such glorious energy! He desperately wanted to reach out and touch her.

Join us, Hunter. The *Hythra's* seething, unending presence gnawed at the back of his mind, threatening to suck him into her vortex. The moment he surrendered to her, he would be finished.

One of the Naaga snuck up behind the human with a strange triangle-shaped device in his hand. Ares tried to shout a warning, but his vocal cords were locked. The white-eyed devil held the machine against her neck, catching her by surprise.

Bastards!

His throat unlocked, and Ares roared as she went down. She'd protected him, but he could do nothing as the Naaga hurt her. This infuriating helplessness was his definition of hell.

He couldn't see her anymore. Frantically, furiously, he fought against his bond. *Release me!*

He didn't need the *Hythra* and her cursed living metal to take down these Naaga. He would do it himself, with nothing but the body the Divine Mother had given him. He would tear them apart with his bare hands.

Is that your final decision, Hunter?

What do you think? His malevolent hatred of the *Hythra* and her bond burned white-hot as he built a protective wall around his soul. The Naaga thought they could paralyze him sickly-sweet poison-air. They thought they could weaken him long enough for the sentient ship to take control?

They did not understand a thing. In a battle of wills, Ares would always come out on top.

But he didn't really think the *Hythra* would ever let him go. It didn't matter. He would *never* yield.

You detest me that much? Have it your way, then. Her hollow, metallic laughter echoed through his mind. ***You are perfect for me. I yield to you, Hunter.***

Was she being sarcastic? Ares didn't have a chance to dwell on it, because his mind exploded.

His consciousness expanded a thousand-fold as the *Hythra's* fading laughter rang through his mind.

Ares reeled as the enormity of the her dark presence invaded his soul. No longer did they engage in a brutal tug-of-war—all her resistance was gone. She opened up and embraced him, laying herself bare.

His for the taking.

He gasped.

The level of control and insight he'd possessed when seated on the sekkhoi throne was nothing compared to this...

this *awareness*. For a brief moment, the *Hythra* became Ares and Ares became the *Hythra*.

He knew everything. He *saw* everything.

Madness!

Thousands of Naaga were escaping from the upper decks. As he'd fallen to his knees, the ilverium barriers he'd so painstakingly created had deactivated.

His clan-brothers stood guard in the hold, watching Calexa's people.

And here, right before his very eyes, the sci-people surrounded the human, stealing the life from her. She stubbornly clung to life, to awareness, swaying on her feet as they took her *vir*.

Vir. That's what it was called. The *Hythra* told him so. It left her body as a stream of golden energy.

Beautiful.

Something inside him was changing. All of a sudden, he could see this *vir*, and he hungered for it.

He extended his will, trying to resurrect the barriers on the upper decks, but his mind was in chaos, and without the command chair, he couldn't focus. The ship was just too *huge*.

His expanded awareness disappeared, leaving him face-to-face with the human.

Calexa's lips were blue. Her teeth chattered. He wanted to wrap his arms around her and stroke her reassuringly with his tail until the warmth returned to her body. She didn't deserve this. Not for *his* sake.

His anger flared. The floor shook. The triangular energy-harvesting device fell from the Naaga's hand and slid across the floor. The *Hythra* tipped sideways, a deep metallic groan reverberating through the chamber.

As the energy-filled device skidded to a halt at his knees, a flash of blinding golden light flooded the room, and pure bliss shot through him. The invisible force holding him down burned away like a tinder-stack, and suddenly he was free.

He could move.

Like a parched man falling upon a cold mountain stream, he drew on every remaining ounce of golden energy contained within that horrid device.

Her energy.

Aethra help me!

The ilverium went nuts. Power and metal surged through his veins, invading muscle and bone and skin.

His body was changing. Into *what* exactly, he wasn't so sure. Pain became pleasure as the living metal invaded every fiber of his being. Disgust swirled in the pit of his stomach, mingling with exultation. Now he was completely *magrel*, an abomination of the highest order. His clan-brothers would never accept him again.

The *Hythra* retreated from his mind, leaving him to grapple with this new, unexplained reality.

He cursed the Drakhin and their long-dead civilization. If only those cursed monsters had left something in the way of fucking... *instructions*.

The ilverium no longer restrained him. Instead, it slid across his body in a warm caress, entirely subservient to his will.

Control. He accepted it gratefully, with a mixture of self-loathing and relief.

The human whimpered, her voice soft and racked with pain.

The sound tore at every fiber of his being. His protector was being tortured, and he was just standing here like some fucking unblooded novice warrior.

Ares lost it. He released the power contained within his cursed body—*her* power.

The walls shook. The ground beneath his feet became soft and malleable. The body of the ship warped and twisted in response to his anger. As his rage flared, the entire *Hythra* listed sideways.

The shocked cries of thousands reverberated through his expanding consciousness. Somewhere below, his clan-brothers scrambled to regain their footing as the floor tilted underneath them.

Terror pervaded every floor, every corridor, and every cavity of the ship. Ares absorbed it all with a savage kind of glee. It was both horrifying and strangely seductive.

If he'd been a monster before, now he was *beyond* monstrous, especially by Vradhu standards.

What in Aethra's curses had this demonic thing *done* to him?

No time to worry. The human needed him. He silenced the tempest within and reached out to her with his mind, wrapping his ilverium limbs around her. As the floor tipped sideways, toppling the Naaga, Calexa remained upright, cradled by the living metal—*his* living metal.

She was *so* cold. He felt the slow rhythm of her heartbeat. Now and then, there was a pause; a missed beat. Frantic urgency coursed through him. Her pulse was *too slow!* He'd become intimately acquainted with the signs of coldfrost poisoning during his treks through the Esskar in the deep of winter, and now he saw the same things in this human.

She was on the verge of slipping into a deep coldspell.

Ares strode toward her, the air around him crackling with static. Although he moved down a steep incline, the floor shifted to accommodate him, anticipating his footsteps.

The ship prostrated herself before him.

One of the Naaga had managed to claw his way up the precipitous floor, his long, slender arm outstretched. The creature reached for the human as if she were a glittering prize.

Calexa's appearance sent a bolt of alarm through him. Her glacial blue eyes were half-lidded and devoid of their usual clarity.

She was slipping away.

"Don't touch her," Ares snarled. He uncoiled his tail,

reaching for the human. At least *that* part of him still felt normal. The rest of his body was still... *changing*. His skin tingled all over, and something heavy dug into his shoulder blades. His face burned, and his teeth...

They fucking hurt.

Bones snapped and elongated and re-formed. Muscle and sinew stretched and grew. Pain ripped through his body. It was excruciating, even for one such as he, who had known pain worse than death.

Still, he moved.

He had to reach her at all costs.

Finally.

He grabbed the human in a proper mating hold—he didn't care; he would never use the hold for its true purpose anyway, especially *now*—and drew her toward him.

His tail wrapped around her curves and he caressed her gently, reverently, ignoring the Naaga as the damned creatures sank into the melting floor.

What he felt between the coils of his tail terrified him. She was a living glacier. How she managed to stay upright, he didn't know. She was hanging onto consciousness by a thread, through sheer willpower alone.

Admiration unfurled in his chest, and his black heart swelled with pride. His protector was *tough*.

But she was slipping.

Heat. He needed heat.

Ares did the only thing he could. He drew on the unholy power contained within him. He drew on the world around them and *pulled* it toward him.

The floor beneath their feet turned to liquid. They started to sink, moving through the layers of the ship. Ares wrapped his arms around his human and pressed his warm lips against her frigid cheek. "I've got you, my *makivari*," he whispered in Vradhu, but his voice was drowned out by the roar of the ilverium sea.

CHAPTER TWELVE

"DON'T TOUCH HER." A dark, malevolent, *metallic* voice resonated through Calexa's metal-coated bones.

Scary.

It was Ares.

He sounded angry.

He sounded *ethereal*, as if his voice were coming from the portal of the fucking Netherverse itself. If Calexa weren't so damn lethargic, she would bolt out of there immediately, because the Vradhu was dangerous and she was way out of her depth.

Shit, I'm going crazy! She was too cold to think straight. Her head hurt something epic, and everything—her body, her mind, her soul—felt sluggish, as if she were wading through a thick, sticky, frigid soup made of ilverium and confusion.

And Ares.

The Vradhu monster wrapped his arms around her. His tail snaked around her waist, moving up-and-down her body, rubbing her, caressing her.

He was molten lava dropping into an icy sea. He solidified, becoming tangible and *real* as everything around her turned into the stuff of nightmares and dreams.

Why am I still so bloody cold?

Impossibly, they plunged into the heart of the ship itself, drowning in a wild sea of twisting, writhing ilverium.

They fell *through* the floor. All she knew was the cold rush of air and Ares. He was all around her, cocooning her with his powerful body.

Calexa held her breath, anticipating the worst.

But the worst never came.

A whisper of hot breath feathered her ear.

"Makivari." The word stood out amidst a torrent of alien-speech. He was speaking a language other than Naaga. She had no idea what the word meant, but the way he said it, in that rough, possessive voice of his, sent a thrill of anticipation through her.

It freaked her out, too. A sliver of fear wormed its way into her gut, causing old ghosts to stir.

Big bad aliens rarely turned out to be nice people. Calexa had learned that the hard way. Out there in the Universe, the general rule-of-thumb was that the bigger and more warlike the race, the worse they treated their captives.

Ares's species had *big, bad, and warlike* written all over them. It was etched into their intimidating black markings. Images of the solemn violet-skinned warriors flashed through her mind.

Those Vradhu were *definitely* not nice people.

Dread carved an empty hole in her chest. The freezing cold magnified it. The ilverium storm tossed them through a maelstrom of shifting walls and floors, and for a split-second, Calexa wondered if she might be dying.

"Hold on," Ares said, his grip on her tightening. Unable to stand the pressure in her head, Calexa closed her eyes.

She was in freefall. She'd lost control.

A torrent of dark memories flooded her mind, triggered by her feelings of helplessness.

The Khral stood over her, his flat yellow eyes flicking across her naked body as she tried her hardest not to shiver. She hated the fact that gooseflesh had risen on her bare skin. Her damn body was betraying her by showing the Khral weakness. It was so cold. His rough hands roamed over her, and he poked, pinched, and prodded her, grunting in satisfaction.

"Fuck you, pencil-dick," she spat in coarse street-Earthian. He wouldn't understand the words, but he would definitely understand the tone. The Khral froze. Slowly, he withdrew, saying nothing. His expression was unreadable behind that stupid mask they all wore.

Then he laughed and backhanded her so hard she fell to her knees. Pain shot through her head. She bit back a sob, glaring up at the Khral with all the venom she could muster.

I'll kill you one day, she thought as he raked his fingers through her hair, yanked her head back, and pulled her to her feet. *I'll fucking kill you. She repeated the words in her mind like a mantra as he twisted her arms behind her back and frog-marched her to his chambers.*

Calexa screamed.

"I've got you." Then Ares was there, dragging her back into the present, rubbing her up-and-down with tender hands. "Stay calm. It's over. I'm in control now."

Ares? She couldn't speak. Her teeth chattered. She wanted to lash out, to *fight*, but she couldn't move. It was the worst feeling.

"I've got you," he repeated in that scary-yet-tender voice, which was the same and yet *different*. Leaning in, he ran his hand over her shorn scalp and pressed her forehead to his. "My *makivari*."

Her feet touched solid ground. The awful banana smell was gone. This new place—wherever they were—was deathly quiet. She couldn't hear the Naaga. Calexa opened her eyes and came face-to-face with...

Silver.

Holy crap.

"Ares," she said in wonder, blinking furiously. His over-whelming presence burned away the darkness, erasing terrible memories. She reached out to touch his shimmering cheek. "Wh-what happened to you? What *are* you?"

Her voice was a tremulous whisper. Her fingers were icicles. As they made contact with Ares's burning skin, sensation flared back to life, and she felt something that was both razor-sharp and yet as smooth as silk.

Scales.

Before her very eyes, his purple-and-black skin was changing. He was growing *scales*.

"I... I no longer know." Ares rubbed her shivering body with his hands and tail. His touch felt good. It grounded her. That was strange, because she usually hated that sort of contact.

At the same time, his touch left her cold.

He was fire and ice.

She stepped back, extracting herself from his arms. It was all too much. "You've changed. What happened?"

"The *Hythra*. She did something to me, and when your *vir* touched me..." He shook his head, his eyebrows knitting together. "I am now as much a part of this ship as it is a part of me, and I suspect I am no longer Vradhu." His voice was tinged with disgust.

"Part of the ship? I don't understand." How could a person *be* a ship? How the hell did one control the walls, the floor—the very substance of the ship itself—drawing tendrils of living metal out of hard surfaces as if they were conjured spirits? How could someone be one with a machine?

"The *Hythra* is semi-sentient. Her link to the living Universe depends on the host."

A small spark of realization flickered in her mind. "Y-you're the host?"

"I am. She was not supposed to choose me, but she did. The bonding occurred as soon as I stepped onboard, too fast for the Naaga to realize what had happened. I do not know why she chose me, but I am the longest surviving commander of the *Hythra*."

Host. Commander. Hythra. She reeled. "You control this *entire* thing?" A destroyer so massive it swallowed the stars. A ship far bigger than anything she'd seen in her entire career. She'd never heard of technology like this.

"I do."

She couldn't stop shivering. Unable to help herself, she reached out and traced the planes of his face. "You're changing."

"It seems I am." His eyes were pure silver. His nostrils flared. Catlike pupils constricted then widened. Violet skin rippled as hundreds of tiny shimmering scales emerged. As he moved, the scales took on an opalescent quality, turning a myriad of different colors all at once.

His dark hair and sinuous tail were the only remaining traces of his Vradhu origins. Although his scale-armor was still intact, it was easy to differentiate between his iridescent skin and the gunmetal-grey metallic surface of his armor.

Entranced, Calexa traced her fingers down his jaw, his neck, his broad chest. His skin hardened under her touch, becoming as smooth as glass before softening to resemble warm velvet.

Calexa shook her head, trying to snap out of this surreal trance. Everything blurred. Fatigue made her see double. Ares shuddered in response to her touch.

Danger! Some weird instinct told her to remove her hand. Although he was warm, her fingers still felt ice-cold.

Slowly, she became aware of her surroundings. They were in an oval-shaped room.

In the center was an imposing chair. It was constructed of dark grey metal, with a high back and soaring wings that reminded her of a bird-of-prey taking flight. Its thick metal legs joined seamlessly with the floor.

She looked down at her feet, which were encased in standard-issue technigard boots. In contrast, Ares's feet were bare. He had three toes.

Beneath their feet, the floor glittered. Calexa's eyes widened. The floor was fucking *dazzling*. Radiating outwards from the chair were intricate mosaics made of thousands of tiny glittering gemstones. Shades of blue, green, red, amethyst, amber, and brilliant white winked at her. The stones fractured the light into a million shards. She blinked as the patterns started to make sense.

They formed... pictures. Strange, godlike creatures stared at her. Their faces and bodies were decorated with an array of mesmerizing colors, and they adorned themselves with fine robes and ornate jewelry. Some of them wore crowns, while others wielded vicious weapons. The closer they got to the chair, the more frantic the pictures became. The creatures fought, frolicked, and fornicated.

The entire display was decadent and opulent—almost *sinful*.

One of the female characters stood out. She looked like a Vradhu, but she was covered in brilliant golden tattoos. A glowing halo surrounded her.

So beautiful, yet...

A chill ran through her.

The depictions had an ancient quality, reminding her of a cargo of precious Earthian mosaics they'd transported to Pax last year. Two things blew Calexa's mind. One, the creatures had wings. Two, they looked like...

Holy hell.

They resembled Ares... what he was *becoming*.

"Apparently, the Drakhin had an affinity for opulence and a tendency toward the dramatic," he said as he studied the floor. His pale lips curved downward in a disapproving frown. "They craved sex, violence, and power, not necessarily in that order."

"*Had?*" Calexa ran her boot over one of the silver faces. The creature's eyes were made of glittering amber gemstones. She gasped as the alien's features twisted, his expression changing before her very eyes.

Now the floor was fucking playing tricks on her.

"Their arrogance was their downfall. This floating prison is the last of their destroyers; the only one that did not escape Khira."

Why is it here? What is happening? Why are you in control? What the hell are these... Drakhin? A hundred frantic questions barrelled through Calexa's mind, but before she could speak, Ares dropped to his knees.

He bowed his head, roaring in pain. Calexa's sharp intake of breath seared her throat.

Sleek, folded wings rose from Ares's back, emerging through slits in his armor. They were black, just like those depicted on the floor.

For all intents and purposes, he'd just transformed into a Drakhin male.

Is this real, or am I dreaming? After this, nothing would surprise her ever again.

"Ares!" Calexa reached out, but he waved her away as he rose to his feet, extending and flexing his new wings. He shot her a baleful look.

"Drakhin," he said, looking decidedly glum. He held his head in his hands, his wings drooping. "This is..." Ares's voice cracked. He shook his head, uttering a string of dirty-sounding words in his native tongue.

He looked so forlorn, so defeated, that Calexa went against all her instincts, raising her arms to...

What now? Are you going to give the big, bad Drakhin a fucking hug?

She wasn't exactly the nurturing type, but she had to do *something.*

The transformation had clearly upset Ares, but before she

could move, he straightened, shook himself, cracked his neck from side to side, and folded his wings neatly along his back. "What's done is done," he said quietly, and the storm in his silver eyes disappeared.

Tough bastard. Calexa couldn't help but be impressed at how quickly he adapted.

His gaze softened, roaming over her face. Despite the cold and fatigue seeping into her bones, his expression filled her with sudden heat. He inhaled deeply. "Human, you have done me a great service. I respectfully request to know your truename."

Truename? Why the sudden formality? Must be a Vradhu thing.

"If you're talking about my name, it's Calexa. Calexa Acura." She was pretty sure her name meant nothing in this far-flung corner of the Unvierse.

"*Calexa.*" Ares whispered her name reverently, his voice a warm caress. He made her common Earthian name sound so damn exotic. "This unworthy one humbly requests your assistance."

"Huh?" That was the last thing she'd been expecting. How could she—a broke and adrift human mercenary—possibly be of help to a guy who had a destroyer the size of a small country at his command?

"I need your help."

Apparently, she *could* be of use. Summoning the little energy she had left, she crossed her arms and frowned. "I don't work for free, Vradhu." It was the basic rule of all mercenaries. One little favor and all of a sudden they expected the Universe for nothing. Besides, wasn't it only a short time ago that Ares had refused to guarantee safety for her people? "Before we make any deals, you need to tell me exactly what is going—"

Whoa.

Calexa swayed on her feet. Although she was starting to get warm again, thanks to her thermosuit, whatever the Naaga had done with that little device had left her completely drained of energy. She could really do with a nice long nap right about now. If only she could disappear to somewhere quiet and warm, curl into a ball, and hibernate for a year.

That would be just grand.

Her vision went black for a split-second. The room spun.

"I've got you." Ares was on his feet now. When had that happened? He scooped her up into his arms.

Oh, mercy. Changed or not, he felt good. Warm. Strong. When he held her, she felt as if nothing in the Universe could take her down. She laughed softly at the ridiculousness of it all. Calexa had never relied on the protection of another, and she'd *never* let a man hold her like this before, let alone some strange alien whose actions were incomprehensible.

Hell, she didn't even know *what* he was.

He crossed the floor, carrying her effortlessly. He lay her down in the big metal chair, his movements gentle and deliberate, but although he radiated heat, Calexa just *couldn't* get warm.

In fact, she felt bloody worse.

The terrible shivers returned. She was colder than ever, and oh-so weak. Her enhanced body became nothing but a sloppy bag of bones, unable to do anything but sink into the chair.

Stars, I'm so vulnerable right now.

As soon as he released her, a look of horror crossed Ares's face. He stared down at his hands, shaking his head and cursing viciously in Vradhu, as if realizing something terrible.

What's wrong? She tried to say the words, but she was fading.

The chair was far more comfortable than it looked. Its surface seemed to mold to her body as she curled up against it, and it was surprisingly warm.

Deliciously warm.

It almost seemed to caress her.

"Rest," Ares sighed, lowering himself to the jeweled floor without touching her. He reminded her of some sort of big silver guardian hound. "It is only natural that you are fatigued. *Rest.* The Naaga got greedy, but do not worry. I will make sure they never touch you again." The cold finality in his statement would have made her shudder—in a *good* way—if she weren't so damn tired.

Thanks, but... How she wished she had her frag-guns and her exterian armor. How was she supposed to explain to this strange Vradhu-Drakhin-*whatever* that under ordinary circumstances, she was more than capable of taking care of herself. She hadn't spent her hard-won Arena money on biometal enhancements for nothing.

"Calexa," Ares said again, his resonant voice wrapping around her like one of his ilverium strands. "You don't need to look at me with such defensive eyes. I will never hurt you."

He sounded so sure of himself. His sudden declaration quietly blew her mind, because she actually believed him.

What had she done to earn such loyalty from this dangerous creature, and how could she be certain she could trust him?

Her head was saying *no,* but her instincts screamed *yes.* He was magical and scary and he possessed a healthy dose of arrogance, but he didn't give off that creepy vibe that hung around certain species like a foul stench. The Khral had it. The Naaga had it.

Ares didn't.

He was good. *Safe.*

A rarity in this age.

Her eyelids drooped. She fought to stay awake. Never before had she longed so badly for the quiet refuge of sleep. She didn't even know whether she could sleep properly anymore. Life in the Fiveways had turned rest into a necessity rather than a pleasure. Normally, she slept in that uneasy place between unconsciousness and hyper-awareness, with a gun under her pillow and a handful of nightmares within arm's reach.

But now she'd acquired a guardian Drakhin.

"Ares." His name escaped her lips as a soft croak. She rested her head against the back of the chair, daring to close her eyes.

Just for a few seconds. I just need to sit here for a moment, then I'll be fine. Just a quick little rest...

"Yes, Calexa?"

"How could someone like *me* possibly be of help to someone like *you*?"

"Because, my *makivari,* you are going to help me escape this living hell." A small tremor rocked her chair as he growled.

Caught between the lure of sleep and the mystery that was Ares, Calexa dared to look down. Ares stared back at her, anguish etched into his glistening features. "I'm trapped," he said quietly. "I'm just a simple warrior. I never wanted this curse. Help me return to Khira and I will give you anything you desire."

A pang of sympathy pricked Calexa in the chest. *Huh.* She thought her heart had turned to stone a long time ago, but this tempestuous alien kept confusing the hell out of her.

Still...

"What about my people?" First things first. "You need to promise me they'll be safe, or—"

"I am in control. You will see." He slapped his hands down on the arms of the chair. Tendrils of ilverium twisted outwards from his hands, knotting together as they covered the chair like fast-growing branches and roots. Energy rippled around them as Ares closed his eyes. "I think I am getting the hang of this," he murmured. "There is no going back now. Rest, human. I will contain things. Your kin will be safe."

What the hell is he talking about?

Calexa wanted to pick his brains, but she could barely keep her eyes open, even though this damned ilverium swirled all around her. Ares was so close they were almost touching, and yet he kept a respectable distance. His tail had disappeared; he'd probably tucked it around his leg again. She almost missed its reassuring presence around her waist.

"What's a *makivari*?" she whispered, her voice fading away as her breathing deepened and she fell into a deep, dreamless sleep, lulled by the gentle caress of a metal chair and the unwavering presence of an alien who had overpowered her, abducted her, taken her weapons, forcibly inserted some sort of language-implant into her brain, and saved her from slender blue monsters.

She should be horrified, but somehow, he made her feel safe. Considering where Calexa had come from, that was no mean feat at all.

CHAPTER THIRTEEN

ARES FOCUSED on the sound of the human's breathing as it became slow and even. There was something strangely peaceful about watching her sleep, and Aethra knew she desperately needed the rest. By sheer force of will alone, she'd kept herself awake longer than any ordinary mortal should have been able.

She was quite the formidable one, but with her eyes closed and the strong lines of her face relaxed in sleep, she appeared beautiful and innocent and utterly beguiling.

I must protect her.

Just as she'd protected him.

I must keep my vow... but I cannot leave her.

Promise me they'll be safe. The first time she'd asked him to protect her people, he'd refused, because he hadn't known anything about them, and only a fool would make a promise he couldn't keep. A Vradhu would rather die than break a pledge.

But that was before he'd understood *her*.

Sorry, brave human. I should not have been so difficult, but with all that has happened, my trust is not given easily. I am Vradhu. We are taught to reject everything from outside.

Because of the traditional Vradhu way—*everything from*

outside is forbidden—the humans and the Vradhu in the hold could easily fall into conflict, although he didn't think Maki would be foolish enough to allow that to happen.

Still, he had to let them know that the balance had shifted. If Calexa was his *makivari*, then by extension, so were her people.

With his hands on the sekkhoi throne, Ares opened his mind to the vast power lurking within the walls of the ship. *What can I do?*

Suddenly, the possibilities became infinite. It was all so easy, so fluid; it felt *natural,* as if he'd been bonded to the ship his entire life.

How terrifying.

So different to earlier. What has changed?

The fickle bitch had decided not to fight him. Perhaps this had been her plan all along. The *Hythra* was older and more powerful than he could imagine, and the forces driving her actions were infinitely mysterious. Who knew what the Drakhin had been thinking when they designed their monstrous ships?

Suddenly, an image appeared in his mind—his form, etched in metal.

Ares felt a pang of self-loathing for what he was about to do, but he had no choice. If the Vradhu had been wary of him before, now they would be utterly horrified.

He split his awareness in two, guarding the human while at the same time pushing his will through the metal walls and floors, going deeper and deeper until he reached the lowest levels.

How is this possible?

Perhaps the *Hythra* had implanted the knowledge in his consciousness. Like the good Hunter that he was, Ares didn't try to overanalyze things. He simply accepted what he couldn't change. He lived in the moment, seizing every advantage.

Doing what was necessary.

That was the *only* way one survived the harsh conditions of the Ardu-Sai.

Never stop moving. Never hesitate. Kill or be killed. It was all he knew. Life was fluid and ever-changing. For a Hunter like Ares, there was no time for regrets or pointless musings, even if he was turning into a monster. Hesitation meant death.

Perhaps this hideous power came at a cost.

Ares formed an image of the ship's hold in his mind, and suddenly, he was there. He became flat like the glassy surface of the waterplains on a windless day. He became one with the vast floor. His presence was in the walls, in the doors, in the circuitry that connected the *vir* channels to the *Hythra's* core. He felt the auras of dozens of warriors. His people.

His *former* people.

Even if he managed to shed this terrible silver skin, would they ever accept him again?

The Vradhu horde stared at the human ship, watching and waiting. In turn, Ares observed them from his unseen vantage point. He felt their tension. He sensed their impatience. He shared their curiosity.

The alien ship—*Calexa's* ship—had moved. Now it rested against the far wall. It had probably become dislodged and slid across the when Ares lost his temper and tipped the *Hythra* on her side.

A row of blue lights flickered to life on one side of the vessel. Motors and systems hummed. In unison, the Vradhu pointed their war-spears toward the ship. Its entrance was unsealed—Ares's ilverium barrier must have fallen apart long ago—but no-one came out.

Unable to communicate, they were caught in a silent standoff.

"Shouldn't we just go in and flush them out?" Baku, the lowlander with fierce, swirling *ankhata* on both cheeks, glared at the human craft. "I'm tired of waiting. At this rate, we'll be here until the next fucking kratok migration."

"Hold, Baku." Maki shot him an irritated glare. "We don't know what they're capable of. They will need to come out eventually. Patience, my brother. We have time on our side. It isn't as if we're in a hurry to go anywhere." He stood with his arms folded across his bare chest. Unlike the others, Maki didn't wear his protective kratok skins. His armor had been severely damaged when he'd taken on five wild Corrupted Naaga—alone.

There was a word Ares frequently used to describe The Lord of the Two Clans: *reckless.*

But Maki was only reckless when it came to his own survival. Where the lives of his men were involved, he was always measured in his decision making.

"Ares went inside and he came out unscathed... with a prize," Baku said, his black eyes glittering in anticipation. "Those aliens are comely looking creatures. I wouldn't mind—"

Maki hissed. "Ares is a different beast now. Just because he managed to get out of there unscathed doesn't mean we will. If we have to fight, it's best we do so on *our* terms, not in close quarters where we'd be disadvantaged, or where they could lay some sort of trap."

"Makes sense." Baku's tail twitched nervously as he made the sign of Aethra with his left hand. "That disturbance... do you think it was *him*? What do you think he's gonna do?"

Maki smiled, baring his teeth. "I have no doubt it was him. He is lost to us, Baku. We have to accept that Aethra has another plan for him altogether. If it were me, I would be thinking that vessel of theirs could be mighty useful to us, but first we need to be able to communicate. Ares is a logical Hunter. He has taken the alien to get the language implant."

"Ah, but what's the point? *He* can never leave this place. Poor bastard. He's bonded. Eternally cursed. Why would

Aethra allow this to happen to our thrice-blooded brother?" The sliver of pity in Baku's voice made Ares's hackles rise. "*We* might have use for an alien transport, but he—"

"Do not underestimate him, Baku. He is not thrice-blooded for nothing."

"But he is cursed by *magrel* tech. We have no answer for it." Baku's eyes narrowed. "Do you know something that we don't, Maki?"

"Ares is a cunning and resourceful warrior. Stubborn, too." The smile remained on Maki's lips, but his eyes had grown sharp and wary. "That is why the elders gave him permission to hunt alone. As I said, do not underestimate him. If anyone can find a way out of this mess, it would be Ares-rai-Sekine." He was staring down at the floor with a quizzical expression on his face, almost as if he *sensed* Ares lurking beneath them.

"I say we smoke them out like an infestation of *pikki*," Vanu blurted. "Set a fire under their ship. If the smoke doesn't drive them out, the heat will."

Ares smiled to his ephemeral self. Vanu still was young and naive. His enthusiasm was not yet tempered by experience.

Maki sliced his hand through the air, calling for silence. *Wait*, he signaled in silent plains-speak.

It is now, or never.

Ares decided this was as good a time as any to emerge from his hiding place, so he summoned his form and *pushed* it up through the floor, materializing before the Vradhu as...

He didn't know *what* he fucking looked like anymore.

"Aethra's nipples!" Baku roared. "A fucking Drakhin!"

Hisses came from the pack. *Magrel. Monster. Darkwalker. Soul eater. Demon. Tainted blood.* Several of them made the sign with their fingers. *Begone!*

Ares knew all too well what they were thinking. It made his temporary skin crawl, but there was nothing he could do about it.

The ilverium solidified, becoming a perfect representation of him, right down to his shimmering scales. Somehow, he was in two places at once. He was down in the command room with Calexa, curled protectively before the sekkhoi throne as he listened to her steady, even breathing. At the same time, he was here, staring down a group of hostile and frightened Vradhu.

Maintaining this form took a considerable amount of concentration and willpower. Luckily, Ares possessed those things in spades.

Instantly, two dozen war-spears were pointed in his direction. Ares shrugged and raised his hands, indicating that he was unarmed. He'd left his krivera with Calexa, because even though the swords were practically an extension of his old self, he no longer had any use for them.

Just like the Drakhin of old had never needed weapons.

Maki's hand shot out. "Don't speak the Goddess's name in vain," he snapped, slapping Baku on the back of his head. "And lower your spears. *All* of you. That is no ordinary Drakhin."

Baku's eyes widened in shock and recognition. Maki glared at him. After a long pause, Baku shrugged and slowly lowered his weapon.

"Ares. What have you done?" Maki broke away from the group and walked toward him, his stride easy and relaxed. Relief surged through Ares, even as he admired his fellow Hunter's composure. Maki had not yet rejected him, but then again, Maki was unique amongst the Two Clans.

"How did you know it was me?"

"I know your aura like the back of my own hand, Ares. Whether you wear your Vradhu skin or this metal skin, your essence does not change. You are who you are."

"You are being uncharacteristically wise, Maki."

"Uncharacteristically?" Maki grinned. "I am *always* wise.

Besides, your features look exactly the same, just without the *ankhata*. As ugly as ever."

Ares snorted.

The warriors behind Maki started to become restless. Seeing a mythical Drakhin—even one formed out of ilverium; a Drakhin who wore the face of a clan-brother—would be driving them all kinds of crazy.

Their collective killing aura was a fearsome thing to behold, and as he bore its full brunt, he couldn't help but feel a little disappointed. He'd been expecting it—he'd been *prepared* for it—but their rejection of him still stung. Pity. Fear. Loathing. Hatred. It was all there, born from deep superstition and rigid tradition and *necessity*. Ares understood all too well why they might want to kill him. Even though they shared common ancestors, the Vradhu despised the Drakhin. In their eyes, he was corrupted beyond redemption, the embodiment of *magrel*. *Unnatural*. That was what the word meant. The Vradhu rejected all things that did not have their origins in nature. They were children of Khira. They were Aethra's sons and daughters. They had no use for the arcane, the technological, or the destructive.

Ares had become all of those things.

"Poor bastard... we should kill him and save him from this eternal torment," someone muttered.

"At least we can give him a quick one. He deserves that much."

"Control your auras," Maki growled. "None of you will fight Ares under my watch. Do you think any of you can win against him in his current form? *Look* at him. Truly look at him and remember what is written in the Ancient Stones about Drakhin. Then choose your fates carefully."

The Vradhu collectively stared at Ares, their auras flaring with fear and hatred.

"I'd rather die at his hand than wither away on this cursed death-crypt," someone muttered.

Maki silenced the offender with a growl. "Ares," he said quietly. "Can't you control those... things?"

"Things?"

"Your, uh..."

Something heavy and strange protruded from Ares's shoulder blades. Whatever they were, he could *feel* them. Like arms, but not. Like legs, but not. Large. Powerful. *Huh.* He moved the new appendages up-and-down, creating a rush of cold air.

Ah. That's right. I seem to have sprouted... "Wings?"

Of course they were.

Fuck.

Maki lost his composure. "Kratok's balls, Ares. What the ever-living curses has happened to you? You left as a Vradhu and came back a Drakhin. Don't tell me the Naaga did something to your body in their cursed sci-labs. And what about the alien? The female? The one who is supposed to be our link? Don't tell me you—"

"She is unharmed," Ares snapped, momentarily forgetting about the pressing issue of his newfound *wings*. "Let it be known that she is *makivari* to me."

"*Makivari?*" Maki blinked. The Vradhu behind him fell silent.

"She saved my life. She has my protection. I may no longer *look* Vradhu, but clan rules still apply. I have earned that right, have I not?"

"Of course, brother. I will respect your vow of protection. Anyone who would try and come between you and your *maki-vari* would be a damn fool. I am many things, but I am not an idiot." Maki slammed his fist against his breastbone with a resounding thud, his dark eyes full of respect.

It was the lifeline Ares needed right now.

Thank Aethra for your good sense, Maki-ku-Rathra.

Despite his rigid upbringing, Maki was surprisingly open-minded, and he'd jumped to Ares's defense each and every time he'd fallen afoul of the elders. If there was one thing Ares could do with his newfound powers, it was to try and return The Lord of the Two Clans and his pack to the blessed Ardu-Sai before they became too weak to fight off the Naaga.

They *had* to get onto that human ship. It was the only way they could escape this doomed vessel.

"Can't you lower them a little?" Maki was staring at a point somewhere above Ares's head. "They are... unnerving. You look like you've stepped straight out of the Underdark."

Ares glanced up and saw his wings for the first time. Raised and half outstretched, they curved menacingly above his head. A wave of revulsion coursed through him. He was truly monstrous. *Fucking Hythra.* What had she done to him? With great effort, he forced them to fold down against his back.

Maki let out a resigned sigh. "Those look... cumbersome."

Ares grunted. He had nothing else to say about the unsightly appendages. "I came here to inform you that the humans are now under my protection. If any harm comes to them, you will answer to *me*."

Dissent rippled through the pack.

"You have no right," someone shouted. "Why would you even *do* that? We still don't know whether they are dangerous. You can't nullify our kill rights."

"I just did."

"You dare disrespect Maki-ku-Rathra's authority? You would willfully violate the natural laws of Ardu-Sai? You are an insult to your father and to the Vradhu, Ares-rai-Sekine."

Ares turned. The indignant Vradhu was a stocky pure-blood called Rhyn, who'd always seemed to harbor some sort of grudge against Ares.

Many of the purebloods resented the fact that the elders had granted him permission to run alone. They envied the fact that he answered to nobody but himself, and they hated the way Ares didn't take shit from *anyone*, not even the haughty mated females of the clans. Ordinarily, Ares couldn't care less if they spoke ill of him, but that idiot Rhyn had dared to invoke the sacred memory of his father.

A dark undercurrent of rage coursed through him, surprising him in its intensity. He was overwhelmed with a sudden urge to wrap his shapeshifting ilverium hands around Rhyn's neck and choke him to death. Beneath the anger lay hints of something wild and terrifying... *insanity*.

This was new. Was the dreaded madness of the Drakhin already taking root?

Ares bit his tongue and took a deep breath, trying to calm himself. Or at least he tried, until he realized that this current form of his didn't breathe. Only his true body—the one watching over Calexa—was breathing. *Madness!* Life in the Ardu-Sai had taught him to accept any situation and deal with sudden danger without blinking an eye, but this split consciousness business was highly disorienting.

Swallowing his anger, Ares stared at Rhyn, a bitter smile spreading across his face. "Do not test me, Rhyn-ap-Barun. Now is not the time. In case you hadn't realized, I am no longer bound by clan law." *I am no longer Vradhu.* He inclined his head and spread his arms, allowing them to take in his monstrous appearance. "Or had you not yet noticed?"

Rhyn bared his teeth a fraction and hissed, but didn't press the issue further, because Ares raised his wings threateningly, and deep down, everyone in the room knew who would come out on top in a one-on-one fight.

"Whoa, whoa. Stand down, Rhyn. Do you have a death-wish? You do *not* speak for me." Maki speared his subordinate with a dark look. After a few moments of tense silence, Rhyn dropped his head, avoiding Maki's gaze. Maki turned to Ares, looking a little exasperated. "You put me in a difficult position, Ares. If they attack, we must fight, and if you are forced to protect them... Trust me, we *don't* want to fight you."

"No, you don't." Ares shook his head. That would be a

disaster. "If that is the case, make sure the aliens don't attack. *Convince* them we mean no harm. This is the time to put your considerable charms to good use." He smiled.

Maki shot him an irritated glare. "*Feh*. That would be a lot easier if we had some way to communicate with them. Was the implant successful? Is the female reasonable? Let her come and commence negotiations."

"She will be ready when I say she is ready." There was no fucking way Ares was going to interrupt Calexa's hard-earned rest. She probably had no idea how close she'd come to death. Her sleep was sacred. "Until then, deal."

"*Deal?*"

"Yes."

"Hey, look over there!" Vanu pointed at the human craft. As if the aliens had been listening in on their conversation—as if they actually *understood* what was being said—two of them, a male and a female, suddenly appeared in the ship's doorway.

The Vradhu tensed. Maki hissed in surprise. Ares slowly lowered his wings, wrapping them around his ilverium body like a cloak as he studied the strange creatures. To his surprise, a faint glow surrounded them. He could sense the energy contained within their soft, tail-less bodies.

Vir. It was as strong as Calexa's—perhaps the male's aura was even stronger—only these creatures didn't tempt him the way she did. Her *vir* was intoxicating.

In turn, the humans stared back at them. Ares recognized the small, shouty one he'd encountered earlier. She stood with her legs apart, her tube-shaped projectile weapon mounted threateningly over one shoulder. Unlike his companion, the male wore no armor, just a long black coat over a simple grey suit. Various bulges beneath the coat told Ares the male was suitably armed and probably dangerous, just like Calexa. He was much taller than the female, standing of a similar height with an average Vradhu, and his skin was a deep shade of brown, almost as dark as the *ankhata* markings of a mature

Vradhu warrior. At first glance, he appeared to be the same species as the female—*human*—but something about him was different. Ares couldn't quite pinpoint it. Perhaps it was his eyes, which were the most startling shade of green. Perhaps it was his eerily calm demeanor. There wasn't even a hint of tension in his stance.

"We... no... harm," the human said in terrible broken Vradhu. He was reading something off a flat, glassy device in his left hand.

"You can speak Vradhu?" Maki's voice was full of disbelief.

"I... learn." The human held up his device. Its surface glowed an unnatural shade of blue. "This help me learn."

What an interesting piece of *magrel*. Ares couldn't even conceive of how such a thing might work. As far as he knew, Vradhu was not spoken beyond the Shadowring. Was the device somehow decoding their speech?

"We no harm," the alien repeated again, holding up his hands, his palms facing outwards. "No fight."

Somehow, Ares didn't entirely believe the human.

"Drop the weapon," Maki boomed, his voice becoming deep and authoritative. His expression turned fierce. "If you wish to negotiate, you will do so on our terms."

The humans exchanged words in their strange rapid-fire language. They seemed to be arguing. The Vradhu shifted uneasily on their feet, sensing—and relishing—the possibility of a fight.

Maki shot Ares a pointed look. "We need her, the one you took away. Where are you hiding her?"

Deep in the heart of the ship, in the command chamber, his second self stirred, alerted by a familiar sound. Calexa was in a deep sleep, but danger had crept up on them.

Damn. He really didn't want to disturb her sleep, but he feared he had no choice.

"I have to go, Maki." Ares stepped back, unfolding his

wings. All of a sudden, the cursed things felt heavy. "I will bring her when she is ready and not a moment sooner. Remember, these *humans* are under my protection. They will not die under your watch... will they?"

He sank into the floor, leaving behind a chorus of shocked gasps that were punctuated by Maki's creative and eloquent cursing. If he hadn't been consumed by such frantic urgency, he might have even found the situation amusing.

CHAPTER FOURTEEN

CALEXA WAS AWAKE, but she wasn't. Dull, hollow moans echoed in her ears. Someone—*something*—shuffled clumsily around the room, closing in on her.

She couldn't open her eyes. She couldn't move her arms or legs. She was *trapped*.

Fucking sleep paralysis. It was that moment of limbo in-between sleep and waking, when one was conscious but couldn't move. Panic rose in her chest. *No!* Dark memories flooded her mind. It was always the same. She could never shake off the feeling of helplessness that visited her every time she rose from sleep.

The bionic enhancement surgery had probably fucked up her brain a little bit. Life had done the rest.

Ares stirred at her feet. He said something dark and threatening in his native Vradhu. His voice was familiar to her now. It was comforting.

She tried to open her eyes.

Nope.

Her heartbeat became a frantic staccato.

Wake up, stupid!

A familiar sound sent her pulse into overdrive. It was the sickening crunch of flesh and bones.

Wake the fuck up!

It was enough to jolt her out of her frozen state. *Thank the stars!* Her eyes snapped open just in time to see a spray of blood hit the floor.

Green blood.

"Whoa!" She gasped in horror as a Naaga was dismembered just inches from her face. Ares's tail whipped across her vision and curled around the torso of another victim. With a sharp flick, the Naaga was thrown across the room.

So that was why the Vradhu kept their tails so tightly restrained. They were devastating weapons.

Suddenly, she could move again. She sprang to her feet. All around her, Naaga lurched toward the chair, their arms outstretched. There was something different about these blue creatures. Their movements were rigid and awkward, and their opalescent eyes had been replaced by flat silver orbs.

Ilverium had grown over their skin, forming a network of tendrils that resembled tiny silver roots. In some places, the skin and flesh had given way to solid silver, as if they were being consumed from the inside out by the mysterious substance.

Zombies. These blue-and-silver creatures were different to the Naaga she'd seen earlier. They actually reminded her of fucking zombies.

"Do not worry, Calexa." Ares spread his arms wide and the entire room trembled. "I have this under control."

"But—" *Stars, they're everywhere!* She glanced around, searching for some way to defend herself. The bone blades lay at the foot of the metal chair. She picked them up, surprised that they seemed heavier than before, but perhaps it was because she was still so damn tired.

The floor opened up and swallowed the Naaga. Ares

moved around the room like a silver-and-black whirlwind, dispatching the creatures with his bare hands.

As she stood in the eye of the storm, Calexa stared at Ares in open-mouthed shock. Everywhere she looked, Naaga were being devoured by the floor or slaughtered by Ares's lightning-fast hands. He was actually *tearing* them to shreds. He moved so fast that at times he was nothing more than a blur of motion. He was everywhere at once. He *was* the fucking storm.

Drakhin. A demon made flesh. She shuddered. Because of her implant, she understood the word. Did the laws of this new universe allow for shapeshifting and sorcery? Despite the sheer ferocity of Ares's death-dance, nothing touched her, not even the tiniest speck of blood.

And then as quickly as it had started, it was over, and silence once again reigned across the vast chamber. The dazzling floor rippled outwards like a disrupted pond before settling back into its original state, intricate mosaics and all.

The Drakhin in the floor stared back at her with a kaleidoscopic array of expressions. They were brazen and fierce and defiant, as if to say: *we were here long before you were conceived, child, and we will be here even when you are dead and your bones have decayed into insignificant stardust. You are nothing.*

Ares moved toward her, trails of ilverium following him like silver mist. Instinctively, Calexa raised her swords. Her heart raced. Her mouth was dry. Adrenaline sharpened her senses and melted away her fatigue. *That* was the effect this vicious, dazzling creature had on her. His danger was palpable, seeding the air with tension. Brilliant emerald-colored blood seeped between the gemstones in the floor, creating disturbingly beautiful patterns. She'd woken into a surreal nightmare where nothing was as it seemed, and fear went hand-in-hand with fascination.

"Don't be afraid, Calexa. I'm not your enemy."

"What are you, then?"

Ares stopped just inches from her twin blades. "I'm the one who will protect you from the life-stealers."

"I'm not exactly toothless, you know." She brought the tip of her blade alongside his neck, where his pulse beat a steady rhythm beneath scale-encrusted skin. It was a futile gesture—she was no match for him in his current form—but she had to do it. She had to know that he wouldn't be brutal with her, even when threatened.

All that power, and yet he didn't try to wield it over her like before.

Something had changed.

Ares closed his eyes and inhaled deeply. "Believe me, I *know*." A tremor rippled through his voice, sounding like barely restrained tension. "As I said, you have hard hands. You are strong, but you alone can't fight the coming storm."

Calexa shuddered. "You said something about *life-stealers*. What does that even mean?"

Ares caught the end of her blade between two long, claw-tipped fingers, gently pushing it down. He opened his eyes and closed the distance between them, entering her heavily guarded personal space. Calexa's skin prickled all over. Her first instinct was to go on the offensive, because *nobody* got close to her like this without her permission, ever.

But it wasn't every day that her personal space was invaded by a shapeshifting, scaled, winged alien who could control the very ground on which she walked.

"Now that you have replenished it somewhat, I can feel it. I am sorry. I should have realized earlier. Every time I touch you, I steal some of your life-force." His voice was thick with disgust. "Being close to you helps me understand the endless hunger of the Drakhin. This cursed form of mine craves *vir*."

"*Vir?*"

"Your essence. Your lifeblood. Your energy. Don't worry. I am a Vradhu trapped in a Drakhin skin. I won't touch you again without your consent. Actually, I *can't* touch you." He inclined his head, studying her. "You don't like being touched, do you?"

"How did you know?" His perceptiveness was startling.

"You are tense and wary. You look at me as if I'm about to devour you whole, and you will fight to the death to stop it from happening."

"And you aren't?"

"Of course not. My self-control is legendary."

"Modest, aren't you?" She couldn't help the sarcasm that seeped into her voice.

"No. I have no reason to be." He was actually dead serious. Maybe Vradhu didn't understand sarcasm. Ares moved the tip of her blade over his chest, placing it slightly to the right of his breastbone. Perhaps that was where his heart lay. *How romantic.* "The creatures I just killed are contaminated Naaga. They were already dead, their bodies and minds destroyed by ilverium. They are *her* failed attempts at creating a Drakhin."

"*Her?*"

"This vessel, this *Hythra,* possesses a consciousness. For a long time, she has been trying to find her rightful commander."

"And... I'm guessing that would be you?"

"For now. She has had many commanders, but none in recent memory have been strong enough to control her. Sooner or later, she swallows them all." A fleeting look of pain crossed Ares's glittering face.

Calexa momentarily forgot about her swords and became entranced by his startling features. It was as if the stars had been crushed and painted onto his skin. She was overcome by a sudden urge to touch him; to make sure he was indeed real.

The alien's narrow pupils constricted. He took a deep breath. His wings rose and settled. His tail flicked gently against his lower leg. The ilverium walls and floor were still, their surfaces flat and glassy beneath the golden-hued lights. She was reminded of a reptilian predator lying in wait; he was deadly, coiled stillness.

But predators didn't give promises of protection with such steely-eyed earnestness, did they?

"I have a plan. Listen to me carefully, Calexa. Your *vir* flows freely, and that makes you incredibly valuable to the Naaga. They will keep coming for you, and if they were ever to catch you, they would suck you dry until you were just an empty shell."

Bile rose in her throat. "I would rather *die* than be... used."

"You will not die." Ares raised his hand as if to touch her, then thought the better of it. "They won't lay a finger on you. I won't allow it."

Part of her wished he would touch her, but the *Khral*-slayer in her recoiled in horror, even though he'd just pledged his protection. "What's your plan, Drakhin?" *And when can I get back to my crew?*

His pale lips curved into a bitter smile. "Escape. Your people have a vessel. The damage is repairable, is it not? Promise me you will give the Vradhu safe passage to Khira, and I will make sure all the Naaga on this floating hell die a slow and painful death."

Oh. They wanted to use the *Medusa?* Did this floating monstrosity not have its own escape vessels? Her heart skipped a beat as Ares's smile widened, turning gloriously vicious. Silver fangs gleamed. Silver eyes—more *dragon* than feline—glittered. Suddenly, he was like one of the jeweled mosaics on the floor, fierce and mythical and godlike. This new Drakhin skin was growing on him.

"That's very kind of you, Ares." Because promises of granting slow and painful deaths to one's enemies were *always* kind. "Y-you would do that for me?"

"Of course." He seemed to relish the idea. "There is some-thing else you must do for me, though."

Unease trickled into her chest, and the tip of the bone blade trembled against Ares's metallic armor. "What's that?" Suspicion sharpened her voice. She should have known the deal sounded too good to be true. What else could this infinitely powerful creature possibly want from her?

"First, you must eat," he commanded. Slowly, he looked her up-and-down, and for the first time, Calexa appreciated how big and truly intimidating he was.

Vradhu with scales and wings. That's what a Drakhin was. Ares was still Ares, but with certain... modifications.

"Eat?" Calexa's voice rose an octave. Had she misunderstood something? "I'm not hungry right now."

"Unfortunately, your rest was interrupted, and we are running out of time. You're going to need all the energy you can get for what I am about to ask of you, so you must eat."

"Can you please be a little less cryptic?" Frustration got the better of her, spurred on by a lick of fear. "I don't do well at guessing games, Drak."

"Ares," he corrected sharply, his eyes narrowing. "There isn't time for long-winded explanations, and even if I told you, you probably wouldn't believe me. It's better you see for yourself. Then you will understand everything." Abruptly, he turned, his tightly folded wings creating distance between them. "Come."

The last time Calexa had hesitated, Ares had damn near killed her, so this time she simply followed him, the long Vradhu-made bone blades held firmly in each hand.

After all, what choice did she have? Calexa was a fighter—she'd done some risky and downright stupid things during her colorful mercenary career—but even she knew when she was outgunned, and this was definitely one of those times.

One did *not* mess with a creature who could turn the walls into molten metal and slaughter a room full of alien zombies in the blink of an eye, especially when said creature seemed to take his role as a protector very seriously.

Makivari. Even without explanation, she was beginning to understand what the word meant, and it terrified the living daylights out of her.

But it also made her feel warm and fuzzy inside. That split-second decision to follow her instincts and protect Ares in his time of need had resulted in the unthinkable; her own personal guardian demon.

Now if only she could shake off the strange, irrational feeling that he wanted to devour her.

CHAPTER FIFTEEN

"WH-WHAT IS THIS?" She eyed the package suspiciously, her nose wrinkling in distaste. Her nose was beautiful. It was perfectly imperfect, dusted with a smattering of brown pigmented spots and slightly bent, as if it had been broken at some point in her life.

Her face was intriguing; it was so utterly alien, and there was a hidden story etched into her proud features. *Damaged strength.* The healed scars and bones said it all.

How fascinating and *forbidden* it would be to pry her open and learn about her world. Clan law prevented them from even *thinking* about exploring the vast world outside Khira, but now that his very existence had become a violation of clan law, Ares no longer cared about the elders and their cursed Ancient Stones. He would explore this alien culture—this *human* culture—as he pleased.

But first, he had to care for his cherished *makivari*. She'd suffered at his expense, and now he had to make amends. He nodded toward the package in his hand. After a brief moment of hesitation, she took it. Relief surged through him. He'd feared she might refuse.

"Open it," Ares insisted. "I assume your kind eat meat?"

"When it's available." She carefully unwrapped the shiny *baulak* leaf, revealing a delicious morsel of dried kratok. Ares had been saving it for himself; it was the precious fatty cheek part, preserved and brought from Khira. When the Naaga had returned his weapons, they had also given back his hunting-pack, which contained the meat.

Now he willingly offered the most prized morsel to his *makivari*.

"Eat," he insisted. "If you are anything like us, it will keep you going for days."

"Smells like jerky," she muttered, wrinkling her perfect nose as she took a bite.

Ares watched her closely. For some absurd reason, he desperately wanted her to like it.

Calexa closed her eyes. "Mmm," she said. "Actually, it's not bad. What animal did you say this was?"

"Kratok. I caught it myself. The young ones make for good eating." A soft grunt of approval escaped him as he watched her eat the food he'd provided; the very kratok he'd killed, skinned, and given to the clan.

Hunters always shared their kills with the clan, and now Ares was sharing his meat with a human. There was something so very satisfying about watching her eat.

"Mmhmm." She ate well, showing no signs of hesitation despite the fact that she had no idea what a kratok was. To Ares, that signified some level of trust. That too was rather pleasing. As she chewed, she emitted sounds of contentment that made the difficult hunt—three long sleepless days and nights tracking the wounded beast through the icy Takhata pass—all the more worthwhile.

With her eyes closed, all of the harshness melted away from her face. For the first time, Ares noticed the fine brown hairs on her eyelids. Another strange human quirk. What function would those hairs serve, other than to accentuate her startling blue eyes? Vradhu didn't have such hairs, but they had a second eyelid to protect their eyes from dust and harsh light.

Such small hints of softness, nestled amongst her proud features, were only a distraction from the true source of Ares's pain.

Her glorious *vir*.

Ever since they'd left the command chamber and entered the adjoining quarters—a palatial residence once used by the Drakhin—he'd become increasingly aware of her *vir*, and as it burned brighter and brighter, Ares's hunger grew.

He could *see* it constantly now. Tendrils of golden energy wafted from her as she moved. He could *feel* it. The closer she got, the stronger his urge to reach out and touch her, to drink in her brilliant life-force.

Mine. He wanted her *vir* all to himself. He could almost inhale it. Oh, but this was dangerous.

"Ares? Are you all right?"

"Y-yes," he hissed, resisting the urge to reach out and touch her. He wanted to knead his fingers into her supple skin and absorb her heady essence. Unbelievable. He really *was* turning Drakhin. "Finish your food. We don't have much time."

Blue eyes impaled him like a well-honed war-spear. Round, circular pupils—so different to his own—formed an impenetrable channel to her soul. Was she terrified of him? Would she try and escape him as soon as he dropped his guard? "You look hungry. Aren't you going to eat too?"

"It is yours." He waved it away, his fingers brushing ever-so-slightly against hers. In that brief moment when their fingers touched, a lightning bolt punched through his chest, setting him on fire.

Sweet Aethra!

What a drug! He'd absorbed some of her *vir* just then, a minuscule fragment too insignificant for her to notice. It took all of his willpower to stop himself from touching her. He wanted to wrap his hands around the pale, slender column of her neck and slowly drain all the *vir* from her until he had savored every last drop.

His new body craved it. Already, he could feel the subtle differences between this Drakhin form and his Vradhu body.

Hunger was sapping his strength, especially with the vast amounts of energy needed to control the ilverium. His unwillingness to consume *vir* was making him weak.

It would be so easy to snag her with his tail and pull her toward him. It would be a simple thing to cup his hands around her fierce, beautiful face and take what he needed.

But surely that would kill her, would it not?

What a disgusting magrel *beast you have become, Ares-rai-Sekine.* Revulsion coursed through him, mingling with desire.

Desire. Are you mad, Vradhu? She is a different species!

But it was there, white-hot and undeniable.

Calexa shrugged and popped the rest of the kratok meat into her mouth. "Suit yourself. It's really quite delicious. Reminds me of the one time I visited Earth."

"Earth?" Ares watched the sharp line of her jaw as she chewed. His gaze traced down her undulating neck as she swallowed. He captured the flicker of her pink tongue across her moist upper lip as she licked it. He restrained his gaze before it could slide down the wicked curves of her body.

"We humans were originally from a planet called Earth, but it's full now. I was born on Dashki-5. You know it?" Her question was deceptively casual, but he sensed it was a test of some sort.

"No." Ares had never heard of any of those places. Thoughts of distant planets and strange alien civilizations flitted through his mind. The Vradhu had never been curious about what lay beyond the Shadowring.

Oh, they *knew* there were other lifeforms out there in the vastness of space, but they wanted nothing to do with them.

They had their reasons.

"What's Khira like?"

"Beautiful." Struck by a sharp pang of longing, Ares turned away. He didn't want her to see his face right now, just in case he betrayed his deep, desperate need.

He was no longer Vradhu, but neither was he a soulless, cruel Drakhin. He was caught somewhere in-between, and if he thought about it too much, he would go mad.

"You will like Khira," he rasped, not trusting himself to string together a coherent sentence.

Part of him wanted to take her to Khira and show her the pristine beauty of his homeland. He would take her across the vast waterplains of the Ardu-Sai, through the dense sekkhoi forests, and up into the stark majesty of the Esskar range, through the austere but beautiful Highfold. If they were unlucky enough to meet a kratok, he would cut it down and feed her pieces of tender meat after he'd roasted them over an open fire.

"You miss it, don't you?" Her voice became soft, revealing a gentleness he hadn't seen before. The *vir* radiated from her like gilded mist; a dangerous aphrodisiac.

"Yes," he whispered. If he touched her essence, if he gave in to temptation and took it, he would be lost. Sweet Aethra, this situation had just become a whole lot more complicated. "Do you not miss Dashki-5?"

A peal of harsh laughter burst from her lips. "Fuck, no. We call D5 the armpit of the Universe for a reason. If I had a choice, I'd never go back there. Maybe we'll *never* be able to go back there." Her expression turned wistful. "That might not be such a bad thing."

What a contradiction she was. Softness and sharp edges. Scars over smooth, dewy skin. Harsh beauty, reminding him of the snow-capped mountains of Esskar. "So you are rootless?"

"That's a good way to describe it." Not realizing the danger she was in, she moved closer to Ares.

He drew away, avoiding eye contact. The temptation was

almost unbearable. Arousal made his hands tremble. His cock strained against his armor-pants.

It wasn't just her heady *vir*, her whole *body* was tempting him. He loved the way her hard edges and rough exterior were tempered by a softness that was distinctly female.

"Would a place like Khira be good for a human like me?" Was she being glib, or was there a sliver of hope in her voice?

Gods, what a question! Was she seeking a new world, a new life? Had she been delivered from the Portal just to taunt him?

"Perhaps," he growled, knowing full well that Khira was a lush, dangerous paradise, and that she could lead a very comfortable life there under his protection.

But he might never set foot on Khira again. It all depended on whether his body was compatible with Naaga technology, and whether the white-eyed devils had done their job correctly.

Consciousness transfer. Would it work, or would he be lost forever? Had he been explicit enough in his instructions and terrifying enough with his threats? Could he trust the honor-less Naaga to re-make him correctly?

They had assured him the *temundra* was foolproof. It had to be. Consciousness transfer did not work unless the receiving body was a perfect clone, and they wanted him to leave the *Hythra* as much as he did.

Actually, this crude bargain worked for both of them.

"Enough. Follow me." He intentionally made his voice harsh and cold. Anything to break the spell she was casting over him; to stop himself from devouring her.

Calexa raised her eyebrows but said nothing as Ares turned, wrapping his abominable black wings around his body like a dark cloak. He needed to separate himself from Calexa. He had to keep himself contained. Those infernal Ancient Stones hadn't mentioned anything about the terrible curse these Drakhin had suffered. *Sweet Aethra, what kind of hunger is this?* Ares had endured hunger before—he was accustomed to going for days, even *weeks* without food during the Hunt—but nothing like this. It gnawed at his insides like a disease, threatening to consume him.

If he gave in now... he didn't know what would happen.

Drakhin... or Vradhu? What are you now, fool?

The answer was up to him, and if he had his way, it wouldn't be a question for much longer.

CHAPTER SIXTEEN

THEY PASSED through a series of vaulted corridors, all illuminated by the same golden light that had bathed the command chamber. Calexa would have called it *mood lighting* if not for the fact that they were on a massive sentient destroyer full of blue metal-zombies and purple-and-black alien warriors with a penchant for violence.

And then there was Ares.

This Vradhu-Drakhin-shapeshifting-metal-lord-unreadable-dangerous-powerful-and-somehow-*trapped* alien male.

He walked two steps in front of her, his leathery black wings wrapped around him like a cocoon. Aloof. Secretive. Brooding. Terrifyingly beautiful. He doled out tenderness and cold menace in equal measure, and Calexa still didn't know whether he was friend or foe.

She just didn't know how to process him.

On one hand, he'd declared her *makivari,* and he seemed to be obsessed with protecting her at all costs. But whenever he looked at her with that terrible intensity, his sharp features took a lean, hungry cast, and something strange happened.

An electric ripple would shoot down her spine.

Warmth would spread through her chest, and her heart

would beat a frantic staccato inside its metal-plated cage. A small, secret part of her wanted to fall under his thrall and say: *'whatever you're thinking of doing, just get on with it already'*.

She'd never experienced this feeling before. Stars be damned, but she actually found him terribly attractive.

As they crossed into yet another huge chamber, a different kind of ripple crawled over her skin.

Danger.

Calexa spun around. Ares hissed. The metal floor rose up, just as she slammed her blade into one of the blue zombies.

It was pure reflex. In this sort of situation, she was wired to kill without thinking. The Arena had made her like this, and she couldn't undo it.

"Unggh." Blank metal eyes stared up at her as the creature emitted a desolate moan. As she withdrew her blade, tendrils of ilverium wrapped around its body, drawing the creature into the floor.

That would be Ares.

"A stray," he said softly as he turned, coaxing the surroundings into stillness. As if responding to his mood, the lights flickered, throwing deep, wavering shadows up into the vaulted ceiling. "Sorry. I wasn't paying attention. It won't happen again."

"Don't be so hard on yourself," she muttered, staring at the cold metal floor in disbelief. That freaky ability of his took some getting used to. "I can handle the occasional stray zombie."

Ares's eyebrows rose a fraction as he studied the blade in her hand. "A small tip for you. They're animated by the essence of the ship. If you want to kill them, you must separate the head from the body." His lips curved into an almost-smile. "When we finish here, remind me to retrieve the scabbards for your swords. You can't be carrying them around in your hands all the time."

"Don't you control the, uh, *essence* of the ship? Why can't you control these zombies?"

"We call them the Corrupted," he corrected. "They were made that way before I took over, so even now they remain as soulless husks. They are already half-dead, Calexa. I can't change what has been done. All we can do is make sure they leave this mortal plane for good."

"They're different to the other Naaga, aren't they?"

"Indeed. The *ordinary* Naaga are very much alive."

"Why are they..." She shook her head, correcting herself. "*What* are they?"

"The Corrupted are those who attempted a bonding with the ship and failed. They exist somewhere in-between life and death, with no awareness, no consciousness, and no free will. They only know hunger, for she has taken their souls."

Calexa shuddered. The blank-eyed ones truly *were* zombies. She made a mental reminder to swiftly decapitate any Corrupted that crossed her path in future. "I take it the Vradhu and the Naaga don't exactly get along? What are they to you?"

His deep, bitter laugh echoed throughout the vast chamber. "They see us as a means to an end, nothing more. We were brought—*forced*—to come up here and exterminate the Corrupted. We were to remain and secure the vessel until the Naaga found their new host. They just never expected the host to be *me*. Drakhin history goes back millions of orbits. They should have studied the ancient records before forcing a full war-pack of Vradhu to enter the *Hythra*, but they are a young race of fools. A *made* race."

"But... how can they make you fight for them?" She frowned, not really understanding anything. "They don't strike me as the aggressors in this situation, and you're obviously a lot stronger."

"They use *magrel* to blackmail us. If we don't do their bidding, our people will die." His voice was like the distant rumble of thunder before a storm. "It is complicated, Calexa. I would not expect you to try and understand the history of our people in the span of a single conversation, just as I would not expect to understand *you* in such a short time. We are from two different worlds, after all."

"True." Her legs trembled as Ares's words brought home the enormity of it all. Suddenly, she wanted to sit down.

They were the very first humans to encounter the Vradhu and their mysterious planet, Khira, and maybe...

Maybe they were stuck. If Monroe couldn't fix the *Medusa*; if the damage sustained from the Paxnath attack was too great, they might never return to the Fiveways.

"Do not worry, my *makivari*. I will find a way to end this madness." As Ares leaned in, Calexa caught a hint of his scent. He smelled of something she'd only experienced once in her life. *The time before rain.* She'd been on Earth when it had happened. The oppressive humidity had suddenly given way to a cool gust of air that carried with it the promise of the falling heavens. *That smell!* It had been the stark opposite of the filthy, polluted air of D5. It was the Earth and the seas and the wind and the snow-capped mountains, all contained in one heady gust.

That was what Ares smelled like. Why was she only noticing it now? And how was it that his starlight-encrusted, sharp-featured, *alien* face was suddenly so fucking fascinating?

He inhaled deeply, closing his eyes. Unable to help herself, Calexa reached out.

"Don't." He pulled back.

"Are you a mind reader, Drakhin?" Her reply was just as sharp, just as abrupt. Had he sensed her reaction to him? Had her undeniable attraction—*admit it girl, this is the first time you've found an alien attractive*—put him off? "Don't *what?*"

But Ares was already moving, turning away from her in a blur of silver and black. "I'm not a mind reader. I'm nothing of the sort," he said, his voice deepening into a metallic echo. "We should not be tempting fate. Remember, if you touch me, I drain your *vir*. I most certainly do *not* want to do that."

"O-of course." With his overwhelming presence right in front of her, the danger had slipped from her mind. It was hard to be aware of something one couldn't see.

Calexa's feet moved even before her swirling thoughts became coherent. Holding her swords low so that the blades almost scraped the metal floor, she quickened her pace, struggling to keep up.

The bastard could be damn quick when he wanted.

She had no choice but to follow him. Ares was plugged into the ship. No matter how fast she ran, no matter how skillfully she could hide, he would find her. She had no doubt about that.

But it was more than that. For some weird reason, she was starting to trust him. He had promised to protect Calexa and her people. He had a plan to get them off this crazy death trap, and he was a native. A *guide*. Stars knew she needed one of those right now. This big, bad Drakhin was a little bit stuck-up and overly formal, and he occasionally scared the crap out of her, but he was an honorable sort, something that was vanishingly rare in her Universe.

Seriously, what were the chances that Calexa Acura, former debt-slave of Dashki-5, Khral-slayer, and free mercenary for hire, would trust a complete stranger—a male who could probably kill her without breaking a sweat, and an *alien* at that—enough to follow him into the unknown?

Especially after everything she'd been through.

But somehow, this felt right. In so many ways, *he* felt right.

Trust your instincts. In her world, decisions hinged on hair-trigger feelings; on a warning prickle down her spine or a spark of fear or a warm, pleasant sensation in her chest. Ares stirred *all* of those things in her.

And for the first time in her life, Calexa *yearned*.

For knowing.

For closeness.

For a male who saw through the chinks in her ugly armor and didn't care.

Shut it down, mercenary.

Ares had widened the gap between them. *Seriously, how does he move so fast?* She broke into a run, her long legs eating up the distance as she chased her mad Drakhin deeper down the rabbit hole.

CHAPTER SEVENTEEN

THEY WALKED ALL the way back to the place Ares called the *sci-labs*, navigating a complicated route through cold, intimidating corridors. She was starting to get a feel for the architectural style of the Drakhin. Distinctive arched ceilings, ornate geometric patterns, and a dramatic use of scale screamed *power and majesty*.

Design choices could reveal a lot about a species. Whatever they were or whatever they had *been*, Calexa decided she didn't like these Drakhin.

Of course, Ares was the exception to the rule, but he wasn't *really* a Drakhin, was he? He'd been infected by the ship's consciousness, and then something had caused him to transform, and then...

She'd become his *makivari*.

The girls were *really* going to have a fit when they found out.

He still hadn't really explained this whole *makivari* concept to her. *Bloody cryptic Vradhu.* There was too much to process; too much she didn't understand about this terrifying new world. Calexa hoped to hell that Monroe had made good progress on his repairs, because the sooner they got away from here, the better.

Are you really in such a hurry to escape him?

Part of her didn't want to leave Ares. The feeling was surprisingly powerful, and it came from a deep place she hadn't even known existed. In spite of logic, she was starting to become attached to this wild, unpredictable creature. Maybe he'd put some sort of glamor on her, or maybe the mysterious language-implant they'd put in her brain had obliterated her good sense.

What if you can't escape?

Calexa quickened her steps, almost breaking into a run as she struggled to keep up with Ares's long strides. The Drakhin set a mean pace, but at least they *walked*. Thank the stars. She didn't think she could stomach another wild ride through the walls and floors of the ship. The 'fall' from the sci-labs to the Drakhin command chamber had been disturbing enough. If not for Ares, who had engulfed her in a warm and protective embrace, she might have gone insane.

One thing was for sure, this wasn't a conventional metal-and-bolts kind of ship. As they passed through endless corridors and chambers, where the ceilings soared into darkness and the walls and the floor were all the same shade of silvery-grey, Calexa was reminded of one of those infuriating illusion holograms. If one looked closely enough, they would eventually realize that up was down, straight was bent, and what seemed simple at first was actually mind-blowingly complicated.

Somehow, they returned to the sci-labs without ever taking a lift or climbing stairs or ascending any ramps.

They drifted through silent rooms like ghosts, passing a bewildering array of devices that emitted faint green light. Like the walls and ceilings, the machines were geometric and ornate, reminding her of the ancient historical palaces she'd once seen on an Earthian doco-projection.

Alien baroque. Her lips twisted into a wry smile as she covertly watched Ares. He glided through the surroundings like some sort of benevolent specter, looking completely at home. These spaces had been made for Drakhin, and Drakhin he was. It was Calexa who was the outsider here; the *alien.*

They reached the place where Ares had been paralyzed and transformed. The chamber was eerily still, revealing no trace of their fierce battle with the Naaga.

"What exactly happened here?" Something in the dynamic between them had shifted. Now she was comfortable enough to ask these sorts of things. "You were moving just fine, and then..."

"There was a poison of some sort. A paralysis gas. Typical Naaga, poison is their power. They must have synthesized it without my knowledge. If not for you, they would have killed me."

The appreciative note in his voice made her toes curl. *Huh.* A certain large-and-winged alien was making her feel *good.* She was used to saving people for credits, not good vibes and warm fuzzies. "I just did what was necessary," she said gruffly, trying to ignore the pleasant sensation working its way into her chest. "I'm just lucky that the poison didn't seem to affect me. Must be a species thing."

A low rumble of approval radiated from him, making her heart sing. It reminded her of the way one of those rare large Earthian hunting cats might purr after feasting on a kill. "Your instincts are good, Calexa."

Sometimes.

"I learned to trust them a long time ago, Ares. Where I'm from, you don't stay alive by waiting for someone else to come and rescue your ass." That was why they were here and not dead, or worse, imprisoned on some Paxnath slave ship destined for the underground flesh markets. It was the reason she was free and not bound as the body-slave of a detestable Khral.

He turned to her, revealing a glittering, sharp-edged smile. "Good instincts are forged out of suffering and close flirtation with death, wouldn't you agree?"

Something simmered between them. It was that comfortable, mutual understanding shared between two battle-hardened warriors, and yet it was something... *more*. "You're a man after my own heart, Drakhin. I've found that once you accept that the very act of trying to stay alive might kill you, it becomes a whole lot easier to do the necessary."

Embrace death to avoid it. That was the way of the Universe.

Ares's laughter came as a shock. It was a booming, organic, metal-edged sound that bounced off the walls and fractured into a thousand echoes, surprising the hell out of her. Not in a million years had she expected that sound. His laughter deepened, turning into an infectious chuckle. Black wings unfurled, revealing his taut, muscular frame. Silver teeth gleamed. His eyes—normally sharp and narrowed—crinkled in amusement.

Suddenly, he was completely different. Warm. Friendly. Enticing.

Whoa. When had that happened?

"I wasn't trying to be funny," she grumbled, trying to hide the heat rising in her cheeks. It felt as if the entire weight of her existence had been lifted from her shoulders, as if she'd been given the chance to feel innocent again.

Once upon a time, a long, long time ago, before all that shit with the generation-debt and the Khral had happened, she'd actually looked forward to the idea of finding someone like Ares.

"It's just that you speak a truth that takes even the most skilled Hunters many orbits to learn. I try to explain it to them, but..." Still smiling, he shrugged. "How is it that a complete stranger, an alien from a planet I have never heard of, and a *female* at that, can know my truth better than the warriors I run with?"

Calexa didn't know whether to be chuffed or offended. She chose the latter. The default. Life had turned her bitter, not sweet. "You're right, I'm a girl. Is that a problem for you, Drak?" Come to think of it, all of the Vradhu she'd seen so far were male.

Ares must have read the threat in her face, because he held up his hands in an appeasing gesture. "Not a problem," he said softly. "Not. At. All." Luminous eyes slid up-and-down her figure. His tail flicked. *Tap. Tap.* "It's just an unusual concept for a simple Hunter like me, who has never been outside the Shadowring before. In our culture, females *never* fight."

"Oh?" Calexa's voice dropped an octave, becoming low and dangerous as a terrible hollow sensation filled her. Surely he couldn't be one of *them*—another fucked-up misogynist alien—not after what they'd just shared. Her fingers tightened around the hilts of her bone-swords. "What do you mean, they never fight?"

"Our females are respected. Revered. We would never allow them to join the Hunt."

Ah. So it was about protection, not control. In this strange moment of closeness and shared minds, she'd forgotten that Ares was an alien from an entirely different culture. "So... do you respect me any less because of what I am? A *female* who fights?"

Ares spread his arms wide and curled his wings behind him, as if to try and diminish them. His beautiful smile turned into an expression of self-loathing. "Look at me, Calexa. Do you think I'm in any position to judge you?"

"I don't know what you're talking about." Her heart rose in her chest and she swallowed it back down. If Vradhu Ares was striking, then Drakhin Ares was downright magnificent.

"I've become the very devil our people despise most. You, on the other hand, are a fine warrior, and my *makivari*. Not many can go toe-to-toe with me in a fight and survive. You've had my respect from the very start."

Oh. Perhaps she could forgive him for knocking her out and abducting her. She was pretty sure she must be blushing by now, but she took comfort in the thought that he probably had no idea about human body language. A little flush in her cheeks wouldn't mean anything to him, right?

You're no devil, Ares. You're a good sort.

Considering the circumstances, he'd been more decent toward her than any other alien she'd encountered in her life. Everyone else in the Fiveways seemed to want to capture and enslave humans. The general consensus was that standard-issue *Sapiens* were weak. Calexa had spent her entire life trying to disprove that theory.

"Let's go," Ares snapped, once again wrapping himself in a sheath of leathery black. *Hiding in plain sight.* "Now that you are fully recharged, we must move quickly. We do not want to be here when the Naaga breach my barriers, and my people will be getting restless. They can only restrain their curiosity for so long."

Barrier? Recharged? What is he talking about? Is this to do with that vir *thing?* A dart of anxiety shot through her. "They better not have done anything to—"

"Maki isn't a fool. He knows the humans are under my protection, and he knows I'm no longer bound by the laws of the Two Clans. They will not be harmed." He walked.

Calexa remained at his side until they reached an imposing doorway. The tall metal doors were engraved with an ornate geometric design comprised of hundreds of intersecting hexagons, and they snapped open in response to Ares's presence. Without missing a beat, he strode through the entrance... and froze.

Calexa had the presence of mind to stop just before she crashed into Ares's broad back.

Whoa! A familiar metallic smell hit her in the face. Her stomach churned. She knew very well what lay beyond the threshold.

They bleed red, just like us...

A low, menacing hiss escaped Ares, making the fine hairs on the back of her neck stood on end. There was something so primal and savage about him right now, as if the thin veneer of his self-control had finally snapped. Calexa had to remind herself that he wasn't the enemy.

With a sharp intake of breath and growing sense of dread, she raised her swords and lifted her eyes.

Blood.

It was deep crimson, and it had a very distinct coppery scent. It decorated the floor in vicious swirls and sprays, coalescing to form a dark pool.

Beyond the pool lay two bodies.

Vradhu.

Calexa gasped.

She was accustomed to death in all its forms, but this was truly brutal. The dead Vradhu stared up at the ceiling with empty black eyes. From the waist up, their bodies were perfectly intact, to the point where they still clutched their weapons, but from the waist down, their legs had been torn to shreds, leaving mangled skin and flesh in a pool of blood.

Bile rose in her throat.

Whoever—or *whatever*—had done this to them had stripped the bones from their legs.

Nausea hit Calexa like a punch in the gut. She fought the urge to empty her stomach of all its contents.

She turned to Ares. He was pure, cold rage, a glittering statue carved from diamonds and ice. As if a large stone had been tossed into a still pond, the floor rippled outwards. Ripples became waves. Tremors turned into an earthquake.

Ares was at the epicenter, and Calexa stood on unstable ground. She fell to her knees as her world tilted. An ear-splitting metallic groan reverberated throughout the chamber.

Not again!

"Ares."

He ignored her. The ilverium tempest tossed her across the room. She crashed into a hard surface, barely managing to hang onto her swords.

"Ares."

Ignoring the pain shooting through her neck and back, Calexa scrambled to her feet. Ares moved into the adjacent chamber, ilverium surging at his feet as he walked past his fallen comrades.

The room tipped again.

"*Ares!*" This time, Calexa screamed.

He stopped. Turned. Blinked with a set of *second* eyelids that were clear like a reptile's. Stared at her with cold, silver, *alien* eyes that could freeze over the lava pits of Endor. It was as if she'd pulled him out of a deep trance. "Sorry about the disturbance. I am *very* angry right now. I will try and control myself a little better. Follow me... and don't look at them." His voice was low and dangerous, and it sent a warning shiver Calexa's spine. If he weren't her ally, she would probably be pointing swords at him or running very fast in the other direction.

Any decent mercenary who had earned their tout-pass in the Fiveways would have split a long time ago, but Calexa couldn't leave.

Not now.

Some insane part of her had become deeply invested in this tortured creature. She wanted him to escape. She was rooting for him.

Why?

He muddled her instincts like crazy, pushing her fight-or-flight response into overdrive. He was both stranger and friend. Protector and agitator. Predator and object of desire.

Monstrous and yet vulnerable.

Somehow, he reminded her of herself. She knew all too well what it was like to be hopelessly trapped; to have one's fate dictated by forces beyond one's control.

She also knew what it meant to take the threads of fate in one's hands and twist them until they broke. Some people just refused to accept the status quo. Ares was one of those, and he was dragging her along for the ride.

Calexa tried to rein in her hammering pulse as they left the mutilated bodies and moved toward the inner chamber, heading for the light. A lurid green glow enveloped them, turning Arcs into a dark silhouette.

Clink. Clink.

What was that sound? It was high-pitched and strangely melodic, as if someone were chiseling into a rock.

"Hurry. We don't know when the Vradhu might come back." A thin, lilting voice reached her ears. *Naaga.* It was obvious. The strange aliens all spoke in the same deceptively pleasant tone. "The longer he is in contact with the *Hythra*, the stronger he grows. I do not understand. The host usually grows weaker over time."

"Jara did not calculate all the possibilities when she formulated the plan. She did not envisage that the Corrupted would become so difficult to contain, nor did she predict that the Vradhu would bond with the ship."

"Could there be another variable, one we had not factored into the algorithm?"

"Obviously, something has been missed. Our masters left many secrets behind when they abandoned Khira."

"I thought the *Hythra* was fully mapped and accounted for."

Clink. Clink. The tapping went on, punctuating their strange conversation. The floor rolled under her feet, hinting at Ares's barely restrained violence.

"We are a young race. We have not yet unlocked all the mysteries of the Universe. The purpose of the *Hythra* is mostly unknown, and her vast power remains untapped."

"The Vradhu has managed to unlock more of it than we ever could have imagined. If only we could control him..."

Clink. Clink.

"Better just to eliminate him, along with this infernal body. Are you any closer to breaching the *temundra?*"

"This cast is thicker than it looks, and it is far from being ripe. It will take time. Go on ahead. Take the bone samples back to Jara. If he returns, only one of us needs to die. I will destroy this body, even if it costs me my life."

"Very well."

Ares snuck up on the two Naaga like darkness engulfing twilight. He moved so quietly that Calexa felt like she were watching a hologram with the volume turned down.

She would have given all of her Arena winnings to possess that kind of stealth. She would have sold her soul to be gifted with his silent, lethal grace.

Instead, her technigard boots gently scuffed the floor as she followed behind him.

As they turned the corner, she stifled a gasp.

A large translucent pod rose up before her like some kind of giant mutated alien flower bud. It was about twice her height, and it was the source of the intense green glow. The external shell of the pod was divided into several segments, each made of a material that reminded her of thickly frosted glass.

Temundra. That's what the Naaga had called it.

There was something inside the pod; a dark shadow.

Unaware of their approach, two Naaga stood beside the strange device. One of them was tapping the shell of the pod with a thin metal rod. The other Naaga had a long metal cylinder strapped to his back. "The shell is unusually thick," he said.

"His kind are bigger. Stronger. More robust. It makes sense that the cloning would warrant a thicker shell. A shame that we cannot salvage this body or harvest his cell lines. They are perfect. What a waste. This body would have been incredibly useful, even in its premature state."

"We cannot risk creating another Vradhu bonded, even if this copy lacks conscious will."

"Truth. You had better go."

"Yes." The Naaga turned... and met Ares.

Opalescent eyes widened.

At the Ares's command, the floor rose up, and the Naaga found himself speared by a dozen angry tendrils of ilverium. Aside from a soft grunt of pain, there was no reaction.

Ares unfurled his tail like a whip and ripped the metal cylinder from the Naaga's back. He rolled it toward Calexa. "Guard it with your life, *makivari*."

"Got it." Calexa put out her foot to stop the canister.

A pang of sympathy welled in her chest as she tried to put herself in his place. Calexa had lost friends before. D5 was a brutal place where the average human lifespan was only forty-five standard years. Enhancement therapy was so bloody expensive that very few people were able to access it—unless one went underground.

She knew what it was like to lose people. It made sense that Ares was barely holding himself together.

For a scarily powerful alien who could control a spaceship the size of a small city with his mind, that was a precarious place to be.

Clink. Clink. The other Naaga continued to tap the glowing bud-thing, completely ignoring the fact that his companion had been impaled on sorcerous tendrils of living metal. A deep crack had appeared in the glowing green shell, spanning its entire length. Clear, viscous liquid leaked through the fissure. The dark figure inside started to twitch.

"How did you get in here?" Ares hissed, his expression utterly fearsome. "How did you breach my barriers?"

Sinister vines of ilverium coiled around the Naaga's limbs, drawing tendrils of emerald colored blood. The blue alien stared back at Ares, not saying a word.

He was almost... *smirking*.

What kind of madness was this?

Ares growled and wrapped his large hand around the creature's neck. His silver eyes looked more reptilian than ever as they flicked back in the direction of the outer chamber, where the mutilated Vradhu bodies lay. "You did *that*?"

The Naaga stared back at him in insolent silence. Ares tightened his grip and the alien wheezed, his slender legs dangling in the air.

Clink. Clink. Still, the other Naaga kept chipping away at the giant pod, increasing the speed of his hits.

"Forget the *temundra*. Get the cells," the dangling Naaga spluttered. "Run."

His companion looked up and nodded. He stood and lurched toward Calexa. The crack in the *temundra* had widened. Thick, gel-like liquid started to pool on the floor, reflecting the eerie green light and the slender silhouette of the Naaga.

Calexa didn't waste time. She danced forward, putting herself between the canister and the blue alien.

"Don't you dare, *pyshtana!*" Ares roared, his voice deafening inside the small chamber. "Do *not* touch that container. You will not have them!" Ilverium surged out of the floor and engulfed the Naaga.

Instinctively reacting to the grief and anger in Ares's voice, Calexa ran her blade straight through the Naaga's chest, where she guessed the heart would be. But even though he was bound by Ares's ilverium, the Naaga kept coming.

"What does it take to kill these bastards?" Calexa stabbed her second blade into the alien's chest, this time aiming for the right side.

Emerald blood spurted from the Naaga's mouth. Finally, the alien stopped and gave up his last breath. Calexa put her foot against his stomach and kicked the body away. The dead alien slid off her bone blades and slumped to the floor.

"They have two hearts," Ares said softly. "You have to stab them twice. I could have handled it, but... thank you."

"For guys who don't have weapons, they're surprisingly hard to kill." Suddenly, she was breathless. "Why don't they fight properly? What's with this weird resistance?"

"Supposedly, it is a defect of temperament. When the Drakhin created them, they were designed to be submissive. They aren't capable of violence in the way that you and I are, so they resort to more indirect means. Poison. Sabotage. Threats. Strength in numbers." His features twisted into an expression of disgust. "They do not value life." As he spoke, he crushed the windpipe of the Naaga with his bare hand. The alien's pearlescent eyes went blank.

Calexa was no stranger to violence, but Ares's sudden display of brutality shocked her. At the same time, she wanted to laugh hysterically at the irony it all. "And you do?" Horror must have shown on her face, because a look of anguish crossed Ares's features.

"This is all wrong," he said softly. "Many orbits ago, before the Dark One appeared and caused the divergence of our people, Khira was a paradise. We wanted for nothing and knew no evil. If the Naaga had left us alone, I would have let them be, but they have disturbed my people greatly."

A violent shudder rocked the chamber, and the dead Naaga's body was swallowed by a tide of moving metal, as if Ares were offering it up as a sacrifice to the ship.

A savage look crossed his face. His anger was truly scary, because she didn't know what he would do; didn't know what he was *really* capable of.

Dread welled in the pit of Calexa's stomach. She glanced at Ares, then at the glowing green bud, which had almost lost all of its fluid. It was slowly starting to open, like a giant mutated flower. "And what is *that*? Should we kill it?"

"No!" Ares became a blur of motion. Suddenly, his hand

was on her arm. "Wait. It is..." His fierce expression melted, exposing something unexpectedly raw and vulnerable. A sigh escaped his lips. "Just wait. You will see."

He bent down and picked up the metal tube at Calexa's feet. He was careful with it, almost reverent. His big silver hand went over the lid. Ares opened it, looked inside with a baleful expression, nodded, and closed it again.

Relief crossed his face.

"Ares, please tell me that whatever's inside that tube isn't dangerous."

"There's no threat in here. This contains the bones of my clan-brothers, nothing more." A terrible sadness crept into his voice, and he squeezed her arm. The impermeable fabric of her thermosuit protected her from his *vir*-draining touch. It was such a simple action, but it sent a pleasant shiver through her. Little by little, she was starting to peel back his layers, like an onion.

Ares wasn't the bad guy here. He was violent and conflicted and probably traumatized—just like Calexa—but he wasn't an asshole.

Calexa did something she never thought she would have felt like doing, not in a million years.

She reached out for Ares's hand. "I'm sorry."

"No," he said sharply, refusing her hand. He stepped back. "It... It is not wise to touch me when I am like *this*. I..." To her astonishment, his voice cracked. There was a desperate edge to it, as if he were trying very hard to contain something wild and terrifying.

"You don't want to?"

"It isn't that." His denial was swift and absolute. "As I said before, this form I have taken is an abomination. Your *vir* swirls around you like the most potent and intoxicating drug, and I fear that if I tap into it, I won't be able to stop."

"Y-you..." Calexa shook her head, astonished and slightly

afraid. Ares could sense the fucking life-force swirling around her, and he wanted to... *eat* her soul?

He *wanted* to touch her. She shuddered, in a good way. The thought was unexpectedly powerful.

"The truth is, I would very much like to take your... *hand*, but for now, this is enough."

"*Vir*. New alien body. Scary temptation. Got it." She nodded, clamping her mouth shut.

Sometimes, it was better not to say anything at all.

So instead of *touching*, they stood side-by-side, sharing a moment of unexpected affection as the bizarre and utterly alien pod-thing began to unfurl.

Somehow, on a floating death-trap in an unknown corner of the Universe, they'd found something in common, a way to transcend the chasm between them.

And now here she was, comforting a lethal, winged alien— a supernaturally *transformed* alien—as they watched the *temundra* give up its mysterious contents.

As the segments of the pod fell away, Ares inhaled sharply.

Calexa gasped.

The dark figure inside the bud was a very naked, very wet Vradhu. He fell to the floor, limp and unresponsive and slick with moisture, his striking purple skin glistening in the cold light. His chest rose and fell in a slow, mesmerizing rhythm.

At least he breathed! Thank the stars.

The Vradhu lay flat on his back with his arms outstretched and his eyes closed. Calexa couldn't help but stare. Burning curiosity gave way to admiration.

In his pure, naked form, the Vradhu was beautiful. His deep violet skin was incredibly vivid, and it glistened with moisture. The contours and planes of his magnificent body were sculptural and perfect; he was clearly built for power and speed. Tendrils of long hair fanned around his head, creating an abstract black crown that accentuated the striking lines on the his face.

The black markings on his face were a shade lighter than Ares's, and as they extended downward they spared his chest, appearing on the sides of his neck and the backs of his arms.

Interesting.

Her gaze roamed down his body. She couldn't help it. She wanted to see what was...

Holy hell.

An impossibly broad chest. Pecs so chiseled they could have been carved from marble. A perfect six... no, was that an *eight*-pack of abs? Nature seemed to have thrown an extra set of muscles in there. She followed the contours of his defined abs as they tapered into a vee, leading down to his groin.

Having just been ejected from an oversized frosted-glass flower bud, he was completely naked. Of *course* he was. Curiosity almost burned her to a crisp as she stared at his... *manhood.*

For some reason, her messed-up brain chose that stupid old-fashioned Earthian word to refer to his cock.

Big was the second word that entered her head. To her surprise, his impressive cock wasn't so different to a human one. Why was that so... unexpected?

Calexa mentally slapped herself. What had she been expecting? Exotic alien junk? The *Khral* had been bad enough. She shuddered.

Ares was staring at her, following the direction of her gaze.

"He is young," he whispered. "His markings haven't fully emerged, and he is not yet beaded."

"Beaded?" Calexa blinked. Ares nodded in the direction of...

She made a silent *O* with her mouth. *Beaded.* That sounded... interesting. An almost-smile tugged at Ares's lips. The hungry look had returned, turning his silver eyes molten.

"What do you make of him? Ugly brute, isn't he?" There was something in Ares's voice; a certain sense of expectation.

"Ugly? No way. As far as species go, I've seen a hell of a lot worse."

"Do you find him... pleasing to look at?"

What the hell kind of question is that? He's fucking magnificent! "He's not bad," she said, giving Ares the side-eye. What a strange question. Nervous heat crept into her cheeks, and she started to become restless. There was a naked Vradhu on the floor, damn-it! She mentally berated herself for getting distracted. "What's wrong with him? Why is he unconscious?"

Ares was strangely calm. "There is no need for concern. That body lacks awareness. That's all."

That body... that face. Calexa took a closer look at the purple figure. His eyes were closed and his features were composed. Lying in that dark, reflective pool, he looked rather peaceful. He had the same high, noble forehead, sharply slanted eyes, and broad, sloping nose as the rest of the Vradhu. His lips were full and tempting. His chin was prominent, his jawline strong.

She did a double-take. He looked so *familiar*.

The markings on his face... They were a unique imprint; a distinctive tattoo.

No two Vradhu shared the same facial markings.

"He looks like *you*." She shook her head. *Someone pinch me.* "Is he your twin?"

"No." Ares inclined his head, staring intensely at the Vradhu. "He is not."

She watched Ares carefully as his face reflected both shade and light, reminding her of clouds scudding through bright sunlight. Although he'd sprouted a pair of wings and grown a fine layer of scales, not much else had changed since he'd undergone the transformation from Vradhu to Drakhin. His hair was still jet-black and fashioned into a long braid. The sides of his scalp were still shorn, giving him a wild, savage appearance. His distinctive black markings had disappeared, but the underlying bone structure of his face was the same.

Yet the Vradhu who had fallen out of the grotesque flowerbud appeared younger. She knew nothing about the life expectancy of the Vradhu, but if Ares was a man in his prime, then the guy on the floor was the eighteen year-old version of him.

A tiny laugh escaped him as Ares shook his head, as if not quite believing what he saw. Calexa imagined the experience would be similar to looking in the mirror.

Exactly. The. Same.

The resemblance was uncanny.

Now Ares was frowning. "It is strange to see oneself born anew, untouched by the ravages of life. He is missing scars here," he pointed to a spot just below his collarbone, "and here, amongst others." He pressed the area beneath his right rib. "Other than that, the process seems to have worked."

"Process?" Calexa's voice was a cracked whisper. "What process?" Realization lurked in the back of her mind, on the verge of dawning. Deep down, she *knew* what the creature on the ground was, but she needed him to say it out loud.

"Do you not see the resemblance?" Now he was looking at her expectantly, as if her answer mattered greatly to him.

"Resemblance?" *Of course I see the damn resemblance...* "Oh."

Oh.

The penny finally dropped. The fine hairs on the back of her neck stood on end. An oddly pleasant sensation crept over her body, like millions of velvet-footed ants crawling all over her at once. "That's *you*, isn't it?"

Ares's expression told her all she needed to know. He raised one eyebrow ever-so slightly.

"H-how?"

"The Naaga do not reproduce sexually. They are a made race, and therefore all of their offspring are clones. I forced them to use their technology on me. We made a bargain. They were to clone me. In exchange, I was to give up this body, and control of the *Hythra*."

"So you could escape the ship," she said softly as shocked realization blossomed into perfect understanding. "That was your plan, wasn't it?"

The irony drained from Ares's harsh features, leaving despair in its wake. "Yes."

"But that's just a body, isn't it? A copy? I mean, it's impossible to..." She'd heard of *consciousness transfer technology* before. To the techno-elite, CTT was the holy grail. *Everyone* was trying to pull it off, because whoever got there first would become rich beyond their wildest dreams.

But on Earth, on D5, and all around the Fiveways, whole-body cloning technology was still in its infancy. Numerous groups claimed to have produced a perfect adult clone, but none had offered tangible proof.

So now she was supposed to believe that these waif-like blue aliens had perfected the technique using a giant frosted-glass flowerbud filled with gelatinous goop?

"There is a way," Ares said, drinking her in with his gaze. "I've watched them do it. Timing is everything. When the time comes, you will know."

Why did that sound so ominous? Calexa shook her head, trying to shake the strange feeling that he wanted *more* from her; that he was leaving something unsaid. "Do you have to be this damn cryptic all the time?"

"Do you trust me?"

Oddly enough, she did. She nodded, and it was as if a great weight slid off her shoulders.

"Then help me get this body of mine down to the hold." He closed his eyes for a moment and took a deep breath. "Quickly."

"*You* need help with that? I mean, I don't have a problem carrying him... uh, *you*, but..." She looked him up-and-down, imbibing every inch of his honed body. Vradhu, Drakhin, host, whatever. It didn't matter. He was utterly fearsome, and dare she admit it, *hot*.

"But?" He raised a silver-scaled eyebrow.

"You're stronger than me," Calexa said in a small voice, not quite believing her own words. Did she just *say* that out loud?

Ares dismissed her confession with an irritated wave of his hand. "Calexa, I *need* your help. Do not make me beg. My dead clan-brothers lie in the chamber beyond, and I need to return them to the Ardu-Sai."

She bowed her head in a silent apology. *Of course. How stupid of me.* Ares would want to return the bodies of his people to Khira. It would be impossible for him to carry both the dead and... *himself*. She didn't know anything about the burial customs of his people, but he seemed to be taking this extremely seriously.

All of a sudden, Ares was right in her face, so close she could see the tendrils of molten silver dancing in his eyes. He raised his free hand as if he were going to take her chin into his fingers.

Calexa tensed in anticipation.

He stopped just a hair's breadth from her face, caressing her without touching her. Static prickled across her chin. It felt as if her energy was being drawn into him.

He closed his eyes and inhaled; a deep, shuddering, spine-tingling sound.

Why won't you touch me?

For the first time in her life, she *wanted* a male to touch her.

Take my vir; *I don't care. I just want... I need...*

Oh, Calexa had a tough and prickly shell, but when it came to things like need and desire, she was as bad as a fucking teenager on the cusp of puberty. No, she was worse; messed up. How was she ever supposed to communicate these conflicting thoughts?

"I *never* ask for help, Calexa." Ares's voice was a low

rumble, and the way he said her name—rolling it off his tongue with that damn sexy Vradhu accent of his—made her insides turn to mush. "I *never* trust people I barely know with things that are precious to me, and yet somehow I am perfectly willing to let you carry my future."

She glanced at the naked Vradhu on the floor and awkwardly cleared her throat as the heat rose in her cheeks. There was something so intimate about staring at naked Vradhu-Ares while *Drakhin*-Ares stood so close that she was surrounded by his heady rain-and-earth scent.

Was it possible to get high on a person... on an *alien*? Because that's what was happening to her right now. One by one, the bricks in her hard fortress of memories were being stolen by a creature who was made of metal and flesh and dreams.

And maybe...

Maybe the rules of her old life didn't apply here.

"I'll get you down to the hold, Vradhu," she said, finding a kernel of the grit that had gotten her out of the Arena and off the cesspit that was D5. "But you have to promise me that you'll do everything in your power to make this consciousness transfer thing work, inkface, because I'm not leaving here without you."

To her frustration, he didn't give her a direct answer. Instead, a wistful smile softened his features. "You may fight like a demon, but you understand honor, human." He pressed a closed fist against his chest. "I am glad *you* are the one I took."

"You're not starting to get all friendly on me *now* of all times, are you, Drak?" Amidst the blood and horror and strangeness, she latched onto that spark of affection, fully aware that it could explode into a full-blown inferno at any given moment.

Gods, if only he would just fucking *touch* her.

Like a moth to a flame, she reached out.

Once again, he stepped back. Ilverium rose up around him in the form of slender metal vines, and all of a sudden the liquid metal was coiling around her arms.

Metal on bare skin.

Smooth and sinuous. Warm. Sharp-edged.

She froze. "What are you doing?"

This reminded her of...

Restraints.

Calexa's inner beast raged against the suggestion. Her natural reaction to being trapped was to go fucking ballistic; to lash out in any way, shape, or form.

She was crude like that.

But this was Ares.

Relax. He's not going to hurt you, girl. He could have done that a thousand times over if he wanted to, but he holds back from even touching *you.*

She kept telling herself that, even as she yearned to break free.

Rivulets of molten metal slid down her hands, forming a fine meshwork of ilverium that stretched over her fingers and continued down the length of her curved bone swords.

"You can do anything with this stuff, can't you?" She tried to control her frantic heartbeat; tried to keep the irrational fear out of her voice.

"If I could do *anything*, my *makivari*, we would no longer be stuck on this forsaken death-trap, and you wouldn't have to lug my unconscious body-double around." As silver vines curled around her twin blades, Ares exerted gentle pressure on her weapons. "Let go."

"Why are you trying to disarm me?"

The ilverium was an extension of Ares's hot, insistent will. Calexa sighed and relented, loosening her grip on the bloody things.

They were his, after all.

"Why would I want to do that?" His devious metal tendrils crisscrossed her torso.

The blades disappeared.

The metal vines across her chest tightened, coiling around her back. Calexa's heart flew into her throat. Her mind went blank. *Run! Runrunrunrun...*

Just as she was about to explode into motion, the ilverium around her arms and hands unraveled.

She exhaled sharply, trying to disguise the fact that she was trembling. "What are you doing, Drak?"

"Reach over your shoulder." His voice was as deliberate and assured as the rest of him. If she weren't quietly going mad, she might even have thought there was something a little bit *devious* in his tone.

What would he do if he knew that he'd just dragged her to the edge of the abyss and back?

Bloody Vradhu.

She reached and found a familiar smooth, worn hilt. *His* hand had shaped this weapon.

She drew the sword, pulling it from where it hung in some sort of *sheath*. An overwhelming sense of relief flooded through her. "You made sheaths out of *that*? All that drama and suspense... why didn't you just tell me what you were doing, Ares? I didn't even know you could do this kind of thing. H-how..."

"Neither did I. You made me want to try. It requires concentration, but if I picture what I want in my mind and apply my will, it simply... *materializes*." He stepped back, admiring his handiwork. "If you're going to be carrying me, you'll need to have your hands free and your weapons within easy reach." A soft grunt of approval escaped him. "Suits you well. Sometimes, I impress even myself."

"Modest, aren't you?"

"Not at all. Why should I be?" Silver eyes roamed over her

body, and even her thermosuit couldn't dampen the warmth that rose in her belly and seeped down between her thighs.

Calexa looked down and studied Ares's handiwork. The kit was simple, really. Two slender ilverium straps crisscrossed her chest, forming an 'X' between her breasts, where they stretched the fabric. He'd fashioned the damn thing in a way that made her breasts appear more prominent, the outline of her nipples faintly visible through the thermoskin.

Simple, really. Simple and impossible and deviously revealing. Had he done it that way on purpose?

"This will hold until we reach the lower chambers." Ares waved his hand imperiously and finished off his creation. The ilverium remained connected to the floor by a tiny thread. "Remember, Calexa, you can trust me."

How does he know? Is my fear that obvious?

Disquiet flitted across his face. "Whenever you are cornered, your killing aura flares like a beacon."

"Killing aura? I didn't even know I had one."

"Oh, you certainly have one." He nodded in approval as Calexa slid her blade back into its makeshift ilverium sheath, guided by instinct alone. "Those are yours now."

"I can't take these," she whispered. The twin swords were the most perfectly balanced weapons she'd ever held. Calexa knew fine weaponry when she saw it, and these had been made by a master craftsman. What the hell was Ares trying to say?

"You will take them, because I insist. You have earned these krivera." Ares stepped back, allowing no room for argument as he gestured toward his slumbering clone. "Now, do you care to assist?"

The outline of slick, sculpted muscle drew Calexa's gaze. Her mouth went dry. Ares nodded in clone-Ares's direction.

The weirdness was becoming a little too much, and as for her wayward body...

Well, Calexa was a grown woman, wasn't she? Even if

she'd forcefully repressed her urges for too long; even if she was a little bit fucked up inside, she still had *needs*, and this Ares was doing all kinds of strange things to her.

"I don't suppose there's a, uh, *loincloth* or something...?"

Ares raised his eyebrows and shook his head. "What difference would it make now? You have seen it all."

Yes, she had indeed seen it *all*.

CHAPTER EIGHTEEN

SHE CARRIED Ares's clone in her arms like a baby, her muscles straining as she hefted his big body down the corridor.

"Oversized idiot," she grumbled under her breath in Earthian. "You're lucky I've got a biometal spine, Vradhu."

No ordinary human could have carried him around like this. He was heavier than he looked, and that was saying a *lot*. But he was also warm, and his smooth hairless skin felt like hot velvet beneath her bare hands.

Hot velvet doused in a slick of wetness. Stars, how his magnificent black-and-violet body *glistened* beneath the ship's warm lights.

He was a living work of art.

Calexa arrested her wistful sigh before it escaped her lips, taming her gaze before it dropped to Ares-copy's groin. She couldn't believe where her imagination was trying to lead her. She *never* had these kinds of thoughts. After she'd been sold to the Khral, everything good and free and wholesome had been systematically stripped from her, and she'd been left with nothing but hatred against all slavers and an aversion to anything sensual.

Killing that Khral asshole had been extraordinarily therapeutic, but the emptiness had never gone away. That was why Calexa shied away from intimacy and tried to quell her demons by waging war against real-life slavers.

And then Ares had come along, and suddenly it felt *okay* to be damaged and fucked up and full of conflicting thoughts and feelings.

It felt okay to *desire* someone.

How had he done this to her?

Ares walked slowly in front of her, carrying the bodies of his slain clansmen. He'd fashioned an elegant sling from the ever-present ilverium, allowing him to carry one of the dead Vradhu in front while the other was strapped to his back.

He'd insisted on taking every piece of them; the mutilated bodies, the canister containing the bones, *everything*.

"I must ensure they are returned to the Ardu-Sai and buried intact, otherwise they will not walk in the afterlife."

Apparently, Vradhu took their death-rituals very seriously.

They took a different route down to the hold, winding through elegantly desolate chambers that reminded her of catacombs. Now and then, they would pass a statue of some unknown Drakhin. The winged aliens—for some reason, all of them were male—would stare down at them with haughty expressions, as if they were merely tolerating their presence.

Ares's carbon-copy didn't stir. His breathing remained perfectly even, his spectacular face arranged in the most peaceful expression.

Innocent. That's how this sleeping Vradhu appeared, even though the real-life Ares was anything but. Sleep had a way of banishing wickedness.

Ha. Perhaps she could wake him with a kiss.

"We're almost th—" Ares stopped dead in his tracks and turned, meeting Calexa's eyes. He cocked his head as something caught his attention. "We have to run."

"Run?"

"Quickly now, they come."

"Who—" But she already knew there were only two types of enemies on this ship.

"Run!"

Distant moans—it sounded like *hundreds* of them at once—reached her ears.

Corrupted. A chill ran through her. There was no way they could fight them off while carrying these bodies. "Let's go." Her bionic joints whirred softly as they loaded up, responding to the tension in her muscles.

"You go first," Ares ordered. "I'll guard the rear. We are close to the hold now. Keep going straight until you reach the twin pillars. A green light marks the entrance. Turn left and you will be there."

"I get the feeling your people aren't exactly going to welcome me with open arms."

"They won't touch you. I have marked you as *makivari,* and you carry my swords. Go, Calexa. I'll be right behind you."

The fierce possessiveness in his words surprised her.

I have marked you.

When the hell had he found the time to do that? Warmth coursed through her as she glanced down at Ares's clone. "I'll send someone back here to help you with the bodies." She would have returned herself, but there was no way she was leaving her precious cargo, not until...

Their eyes met. Ares acknowledged her with a proud-tender-fierce-hungry smile, but instead of filling her with reassurance, his smile made her feel vulnerable.

"Don't..." What if she didn't see him again? What if the consciousness transfer failed? What if she lost the only person who might be able to untangle the terrible knot of pain and suffering inside her head?

Because although Ares obviously hungered for her in some strange way, he'd held back.

He hadn't touched her.

Restraint. That's what she so desperately needed. Time and patience and restraint.

"Run, Calexa," he urged. "They can't kill me when I am like this. My rank-equivalent, the one with the silver torc around his neck, is called Maki. Tell him to come and bring a pod of three. The sooner your craft can be prepared for departure, the better."

She returned his stare with a slow-burner of her own. Then she sped out of there like a bat out of hell, carrying Ares's living, breathing escape-plan in her arms.

CHAPTER NINETEEN

AS SHE BURST into the hold, Calexa was greeted by an odd sight. She skidded to a halt, and Vradhu-Ares's long limbs and loose tail swayed with the residual momentum.

She'd been expecting a hostile reception, but the fierce looking Vradhu with the blade-tipped spears were on the other side of the massive space, too far away and too preoccupied to even notice her entrance.

"What the hell are they doing *outside*?" she groaned. S's twenty or so human *servants*—stars, she *hated* that word—were standing in a huddle a good twenty meters away from the *Medusa*. Blankets were draped around their shoulders, and they wore haunted expressions.

This was no place for their kind.

Stars, what have we done?

Defenseless was the word that came to mind. They were far from home and totally reliant on the actions of Calexa and her crew…. and S. Each woman would have her reasons for being in servitude to the Primean. She could bet her crooked metal spine that none of them were there by choice.

Calexa couldn't judge them. She'd been there once. She

knew what it was like to be helpless. In this brave new Universe, life wasn't easy for humans.

Mai stood in front of the group with a bullish expression on her face, her Irradium cannon planted firmly on her right shoulder. She still wore her combat armor, but her helm was up. She formed a formidable one-woman barrier between the humans and the Vradhu, her dark brown eyes threatening the violet warriors to '*just fucking try me.*'

Even though Calexa had no idea what was going on, a wave of relief and affection surged through her as she caught sight of her mercenary-sister.

Mai was good company, and she never shied away from a fight. Calexa had bought the former jewel-artist out of slavery after the dead Khral-master's bond-house had been dissolved, and ever since then Mai had been her loyal friend and *associate.*

On D5, *associate* was the polite term for mercenary.

"*Make me strong and give me the biggest fucking gun in existence.*" That had been Mai's reaction to being held in a Khral bond-house for three years, so Calexa had used her Arena winnings to pay for the illegal bio-enhancement surgery. Of course, ultra-human strength and big guns couldn't stop the anguished cries in the middle of the night or the sudden flashes of panic that could freeze a girl dead in her tracks, but they helped... a little.

And as time passed and they'd visited more faraway planets, taken more jobs, and fought more than their fair share of assholes, the rawness of it all had been dampened... a little.

As Calexa slowly walked toward her people, several of the Vradhu warriors turned in her direction. A group of five broke off and jogged toward her, raising their bladed spears. They glared at her with open hostility, the striking patterns on their faces accentuating their fierce expressions.

Guttural curses were uttered in a tongue that she didn't understand. Suddenly, she was surrounded by a ring of very menacing, very armed, and very large Vradhu. They closed in on her, cutting off any possible escape route.

Calexa didn't flinch. After all, she'd been hanging around with Ares, and he was *way* more intimidating than these guys.

"You must be Maki," she said in fluent Naaga, honing in on the only Vradhu who didn't wear armor. Just as Ares had described, there was a thin silver torc around his neck.

Maki inclined his head, greeting her with a knowing smile. "Ah. The *makivari*. You have brought our clan-brother. Or at least, you have brought *this* version of him." He studied her with dark, wily eyes, not seeming in the least surprised that she'd shown up out of nowhere with Ares's body-double in her arms. "Where *is* the metal-lord?"

"He needs your help," she said, urgency seeping into her voice. "He's holed up in the corridor with a horde of Corrupted headed in his direction and..." She hesitated, knowing the news would be unwelcome. "He has two bodies with him. He says he wants to return them to Khira. I'm sorry."

The Vradhu took it like a true warrior, a slight raising of his eyebrows the only sign of his dismay. Calexa understood. There was no time to waste. Grief would come later.

Maki barked orders to his men in Vradhu. Several of them started to jog toward the exit, heading in Ares's direction. "Thank you, human. Your assistance won't be forgotten. If you wish to relieve yourself of that ugly brute," he nodded in the direction of Ares's clone, "you can hand him off to one of the—"

"No," Calexa snapped, not missing a beat. "I'll guard him." She was surprised at how protective she sounded, but Ares had entrusted his body to her, and she wasn't about to palm him off to some unknown warrior, even if he was from the same clan as Ares.

Several of the Vradhu stared at her with bemused expressions, as if they thought she were some kind of raving lunatic.

"Very well." A wide, toothy-fangy grin split Maki's face. "Ares has given you his krivera, I see. In that case, you can do what you like, but please explain to your clan-sisters that we mean them no harm. The small one keeps looking at me as if she wants to tear my heart out, and I'm afraid I don't have the stamina for these sorts of things anymore."

"Mai can have that effect on people. Just try not to provoke her and you'll be fine," Calexa quipped, concealing her surprise. This warrior-chief seemed like a complicated sort of character, hiding his true thoughts behind a deceptively mild veneer. He was to Ares as light was to darkness.

"I'll remember that," Maki yelled over his shoulder as he followed his crew into the shadows.

Calexa turned and saw Mai staring at her with wide eyes. She stood alongside the mysterious Primean, S, who had hidden her intricately braided hair beneath a sea-green shawl. Zahra was several meters from them, guarding the entrance to the Medusa.

Both women greeted Calexa with sharp nods.

Maki had left the remaining two thirds of his men behind to guard the humans. They watched the women with dark, curious stares, appearing a little too predatory for Calexa's liking. The humans stared back, their expressions betraying a mixture of fear, wonder, and strangely, admiration.

The half-Primean brothers, Raphael and Monroe, were nowhere to be seen.

"Cal!" Zahra yelled, her relieved voice echoing through the cavernous hold. "Over here!" As she waved Calexa over, her eyes went wide with shock.

Maybe it was the naked Vradhu in Calexa's arms.

Maybe it was her newly shaved head.

Maybe it was the silver-ilverium harness-thing Ares had fashioned for her, or maybe it was the twin bone swords jutting above her shoulders.

The Vradhu warriors stepped aside as Calexa passed, but

their unnerving black gazes never left her. A muffled *boom* reached her ears, coming from inside the *Medusa*.

That had to be Monroe's doing. Nobody else would dare try and blow shit up inside her ship. What the hell were the halfbreeds doing in there? "They'd better not be breaking my shit," she growled as she reached Zahra's side. "Monroe still owes me for dismantling the Relectra drive and turning it into a water heater without asking permission."

"Monroe could work on his communication skills, but at least we get hot showers now. I like hot showers." Zahra shrugged. "Besides, *asking* isn't in Monroe's DNA. What the hell happened to *you*, Cal? Who's the slumbering eye-candy?"

"Ask Mai to poach S's pretty shawl," Calexa whispered, becoming keenly aware of Ares's nakedness. She had no idea what the official Vradhu policy on nudity was. Ares might not give two shits about it, but Calexa felt as if she had a responsibility to protect him from roving eyes.

S was staring at her. The Primean's brilliant green eyes took in the unconscious Vradhu in her arms. Calexa growled under her breath.

Back off, he's mine.

Whoa. Where had *that* come from?

"*I'll* get the thing," Zahra whispered. "But when I get back, you have a hell of a lot of explaining to do, missy. We thought you were..."

"Trouble Incarnate turned out to be nicer than he looks. He didn't eat me, after all."

"Thank the stars for that. You shouldn't have..." She shook her head. "What are we doing here, Cal? What do the purple ones want from us? What have you been *doing* all this time?"

"Long story," Calexa sighed. "We need to get out of here. This place is..." she searched for the right word in her mind, "*compromised.*"

"You've seen something, haven't you?" Zahra raised an

eyebrow, her expression turning canny. "You've got that look in your eyes again."

"What look?" Calexa shook her head, not wanting to go down that path right now. "Let's talk later. Badness approaches." Dread slithered around in the pit of her stomach. Being away from Ares was making her edgy in a way that confounded her.

Nobody made her feel this way, but in the short time they'd known one another, she'd gotten used to his silent, larger-than-life presence; so much so that she found herself worrying about him, even as she carried his damn glistening, buck-naked, muscle-bound, slumbering body around.

Her eyes strayed. *Again.*

She cleared her throat. "Zahra, the shawl."

Zahra followed the direction of Calexa's gaze, her eyebrows lifting in appreciation. "He's a whole hunk-a-chunk of male, isn't he? I won't ask why you're carrying that sleeping beauty around. I'm sure both you and he have your reasons."

"*Zahra!*"

"Yeah, yeah." She turned away with a wink and approached the Primean.

Calexa looked down into the face of her sleeping charge. He was nothing more than a body, lacking consciousness and awareness, but somehow she felt the need to protect him with every fiber of her being. If Drakhin-Ares was an invulnerable god of metal and scales, then this creature was his weakness and his hope.

And he'd placed it all in her hands.

She still couldn't believe it.

Ares's plan was utterly mad and totally inconceivable, but it was the only hope he had of escaping this dark nightmare of a ship.

That was why Calexa would guard it with her life. She would follow it through to the end, purely because he *could* have taken advantage of her; he could have ruined her a thousand times over, and he hadn't.

He'd held back.

He'd protected her.

He'd made her want to reach out and *know* him.

For Calexa, that was unheard of.

Maybe the Netherverse had spat them out in this crazy place for a reason.

The distant sounds of fighting reached her ears, originating from outside the hold. Vradhu battle-cries mingled with the dull moans of the Corrupted. The shouts grew louder in volume until Calexa caught sight of someone running through the open doorway.

Not someone. *Something*. A stray Corrupted, moving so fast it was nothing more than a silver-and-blue blur.

A Vradhu warrior sprinted after it, but it was too quick.

Ares was nowhere to be seen.

"Mai!" she yelled.

Mai spun, her eyes going wide as she caught sight of the creature. It was heading straight for the group of human women, streaking across the empty floor. Someone screamed.

"Blast it!"

Mai didn't waste time. Her Irradium cannon flared, and a bolt of pure white energy ripped across the empty space, hitting the Corrupted in the chest.

Disintegrating it.

The sickening smell of seared flesh filled the air, mingling with the sharp tang of burnt metal.

"You didn't tell me there were zombies in this galaxy, Cal!" Mai looked shellshocked. "What the hell is going on?"

"Get them inside," Calexa barked, nodding at S and the rest of the humans. "I want everyone strapped in and secure. Tell them to get ready for a rough getaway. Keep the ladies in the passenger bay. The Vradhu can squeeze themselves into the cargo hold. As soon as Raphael and Monroe have the powerbanks back online, we're getting out of here, even if we have to blast our way out."

Zahra sauntered past, dropping S's shawl into Ares-copy's lap. "Some modesty for your sleeping beauty." She frowned. "Am I going deaf, or did you just say the Vradhu are coming with us?"

"They're coming with us." Calexa nodded solemnly.

"What makes you so sure they aren't going to slaughter every single one of us the moment the doors are closed and we cast off into space?"

"They need us," Calexa replied, watching the remaining Vradhu out of the corner of her eye. The moment the Corrupted had bolted into the hold, they'd scattered, chasing the monster as it sped toward the humans.

If Mai's blast had come one second later, at least two of the Vradhu would have been caught in the path of her Irradium flare, but there hadn't been time to think about that.

That was how they lived, teetering on the precipice between life and death. There was no time for indecision or hesitation.

"This is... This is nuts." Zahra sighed. "Where are we going to go? Raphael tells me there's not enough energy left to power the jump-drive, and we don't even know where the hell we are. I'm going to check with the twins to see if it's safe to get back onboard, then we need to talk." She gave Calexa a long, hard look. "Those purple people... we don't know anything about them. They outnumber us, and they're bigger than us. We should leave them behind. We should leave everything exactly as we found it and get the hell out of here."

"Zahra." Calexa watched the Vradhu warriors out of the corner of her eye. They ran back toward the entrance, arranging themselves in a defensive formation, their menacing spears held aloft. "I don't know where we are either. What I *do* know is that these Vradhu have never heard of humans, and we've never heard of them."

"You speak their language now," Zahra said dryly. "This is after a winged metal monster rose up out of the floor, threatened everybody, and disappeared again. Now we're being attacked by metal zombies that move faster than light, and you're carrying a naked Vradhu around. On top of that, they've never heard of humans. Are we even in the same fucking dimension anymore, or am I tripping?"

A loud metallic groan echoed through the chamber. Calexa didn't even know *what* that was.

Probably Ares. Only he could warp the walls and manipulate metal. As if in response to her thoughts, a slight tremor rippled through the floor, so faint as to be almost imperceptible.

"I don't know," she replied honestly. "What I do know is that there's a planet down there. It's *their* planet. If we're going to have any chance at surviving this mess, we need to go landside. If we can't jump back into the Netherverse, we could be drifting for years. Better to find somewhere that can indefinitely sustain life."

"Even if we get stuck there? If we can never leave?"

"Better to be stranded than dead."

"This is crazy talk."

"These are crazy times."

The floor shook again, and impossibly, the impenetrable flat surface started to *move*.

It wasn't rippling gracefully and purposefully as it did when Ares was in control. This was chaos; a grotesque proliferation of lumps and bumps that were strangely *limb* shaped.

"What now?" Zahra groaned in dismay.

Limbs grew into bodies. Bodies became Naaga. Naaga lurched to their feet, their arms outstretched, their eyes blank and coated with metal. There were about a dozen of them in total. *Corrupted.*

The ship had literally vomited them out of its depths.

"Get the girls inside," Calexa said, her voice shot through

with urgency. She didn't want to let go of Ares's clone, but she was going to have to fight. She thrust him toward Zahra. "Take him."

"You want me to..."

"*Please*, Zar. He's important to me. Keep him safe."

There was no time for explanations. Calexa would trust Zahra with her own life, and therefore entrusting Ares's clone to her was a no-brainer. Zahra understood. Mutely, she nodded, and without hesitation, she took the unconscious Vradhu.

She pressed a hand to the side of her helmet, cocking her head. *Listening.* "Comm's back online. About time. You've lost yours, haven't you? They have power now. It's safe to go inside. Raf assures me nobody's going to get blown up or electrocuted."

Relief washed through Calexa. She drew her twin swords and gestured to Mai. "*Inside,*" she mouthed.

Mai nodded.

The Corrupted were fully formed by now. They stood in a jagged ring, staring at their surroundings. Several of the Vradhu sprinted toward them, yelling a high-pitched war-cry.

Decapitate them. Her skin rippled all over in anticipation of the danger.

One of the Corrupted turned and flew toward the humans. Two others broke off in hot pursuit.

"Oh, no you don't," Calexa growled. She tensed and exploded into movement, her bionic joints working harder than ever before. She willed herself forward, holding her blades low as she ran to intercept the Naaga monsters.

Thud. One of the Corrupted fell, a Vradhu spear protruding from its back. It rose to its feet with an unholy groan, extending metal-tipped claws toward its Vradhu attacker. The Vradhu whipped out a long hunting knife and grabbed the creature by its metal-tendriled hair.

With a fierce cry, he sawed through its neck, the muscles in his thick arms bulging.

The Corrupted's body toppled as the Vradhu held his prize—the severed head of the Corrupted—aloft.

Another of the breakaway Corrupted had been intercepted by a Vradhu warrior, who elegantly sliced through its neck with his long-bladed spear. The rest of the zombie-like creatures milled about aimlessly in the center of the hold, presenting themselves as walking targets. It seemed they hadn't yet gained awareness.

Four Vradhu circled them, moving in for the kill.

That left one.

One Corrupted soul, racing toward the humans.

A few of the women screamed. S pointed in the direction of the Medusa and barked at them to run. Mai raised her cannon and met Calexa's gaze.

No. She shook her head. *Too close.*

The Vradhu were still within the radius of her cannon. If she squeezed off a shot now, they'd be caught in the flare.

Calexa ran faster and faster, her chest heaving, her lungs burning, her heart beating so fast it was about to burst out of its bony cage. As she drew her arms backwards, the bone swords seemed to become an extension of her body.

Ares's gift to her.

She intended to do them justice.

She struck, bringing both blades across in a deadly arc. The finely honed, perfectly balanced swords met metal-infested flesh and bone, intersecting in a savage curve that made the Corrupted Naaga's head fly.

Behind her, the high-pitched gasps of several women merged with Zahra and Mai's shouted commands. The floor continued to sway beneath her feet like a disturbed sea.

The abominable head landed on the floor with a sickening *thud*, rolling toward one of the Vradhu warriors. He stopped it with a long three-toed foot.

How strange that for all their exotic armor, the Vradhu didn't wear shoes.

The Vradhu grunted in approval and gave Calexa a short, sharp nod of acknowledgement before rejoining his crew.

What, so they were allies now?

She turned just in time to see the remainder of S's retinue hurrying up the Medusa's boarding ramp. S went third-last, with Mai and Zahra bringing up the rear. The Primean glanced over her shoulder as she boarded, meeting Calexa's gaze.

Calm and unperturbed. That's how she appeared, despite all the chaos swirling around them. Did she realize that they wouldn't be seeing the twin moons of Torandor for a very long time; perhaps *never*?

S turned and entered the ship just as a wave rippled through the metal floor. Mai gave Calexa a lazy half-salute, standing guard at the entrance as Zahra darted inside.

Then her expression turned into a look of horror.

"What?" Calexa looked behind her. The floor was erupting. More and more of the cursed creatures emerged, some misshapen and hideous, others fully formed and deadly.

Corrupted. The name said it all. There was something truly horrifying going on here. Ares's metal-shifting powers, the massive ship, the creepy Naaga and their rabid, diseased brethren; they were all linked.

Calexa and her crew had been dropped into the middle of it, and she still didn't understand *anything*.

All she knew was that they had to survive at all costs.

Zahra emerged through the airlock. "Thought you might need this," she yelled. "Catch!" A tiny metal bud flew toward her. In a fluid motion, Calexa dropped one of her swords and snatched it out of the air.

A comm-piece.

She stuck it into her ear, breathing a sigh of relief. "You there, Raf? Can you give me a status report?"

There was a crackle of static, followed by a faint beep. *"Glad to have you back, Cal."* Raphael's cool, familiar voice filtered down the line. It was tinged with relief. *"Zahra told me you'd find a way to get yourself out of there alive."*

"That makes it three from three," Calexa quipped. "Or at least it will, if we survive *this*."

"More lives than a space-cat," the halfbreed said dryly.

She'd survived the Khral's bond-house. As punishment for killing the Khral, she'd been sentenced to fight in the Arena. Her handlers thought she'd suffer a gruesome death within the first few rounds. They'd been wrong. It hadn't been pretty, but she'd gone on to win, and for some reason, she'd become a hit with the bloodthirsty crowds.

They loved their underdogs.

The first thing she'd done with her prize money was to get enhancement therapy. Then she'd won some more, enough to get more enhancement therapy. The stronger she got, the fiercer her opponents, and the bigger the prize purse. By the time she'd earned enough to buy her freedom, she'd also saved enough to buy the *Medusa*.

D5 was a shit-hole, but it could also reward in the strangest of ways. The irony of it all was that being the body-slave of a Khral had prepared her for the Arena like nothing else, because when he wasn't trying to break her in his bed, she'd been out in the *malkha* fields with the other slaves, working like a dog and breathing in the toxic, smoke-filled air.

But that was a long time ago. She was here now, fighting metal-cursed monsters.

Waiting for Ares.

Trusting in a dream.

No point in reliving those old scars over and over again. She reined in her stray thoughts as several of the Corrupted began to lope toward the ship.

"What's our current energy capacity, Raf?"

"We're running at twenty-three percent. Enough to cruise

for a long time, but not nearly enough to trigger a jump. I'm guessing we'll need to split pretty soon, but I don't know how we're getting out of here. The doors are closed, and I'm guessing that airlock won't open without internal intervention."

Calexa bent and picked up the bone sword she'd dropped. The Corrupted were coming. Twin frag-guns had appeared in Zahra's armor-gloved hands. Standing at the top of the boarding ramp, Mai tapped her temple then tapped the side of her Irradium cannon. *"I'll fucking burn them,"* she mouthed.

"Can you offer me any new insights, captain, or am I going to have to risk unleashing one of our triticore missiles in these close quarters?"

"We hold the fort and wait," she said, taking a step forward as the ground rippled beneath their feet. This time, it felt different; powerful and controlled.

He's coming.

She just knew.

"Wait? What the hell for?"

"The fucking cavalry."

The one with the insane plan. The one she trusted, despite all his strangeness. The one who would spell her ruin if this whole thing didn't work out.

They didn't have much of a choice.

Shapeshifting, winged, Drakhin-changed, cloned, ilverium-controlling,   doesn't-want-to-touch-me,   makes-me-feel-like... Her thoughts ran together, becoming wild and frantic. She fed them to the hungry beast that was her rapidly pounding heart.

And he wants me to help him transfer his soul to another body.

It occurred to her that the process might not work.

Then what?

Fuck.

CHAPTER TWENTY

WHY ARE YOU DOING THIS, cursed one? Ares raged at the *Hythra,* trying to provoke her into answering. But as always, she remained infuriatingly silent.

The ship only spoke when it suited her.

All around him, Corrupted Naaga were rising up out of the floor, the walls, even dropping from the ceiling. It was as if the ship had suddenly decided to reject the hundreds of souls she'd swallowed in her quest to find the perfect commander.

It is because I have found you, Hunter. They are no longer needed. They are filth, and you are perfect. I am merely purging that which does not belong. A form of housekeeping, if you will.

As usual, the ship—or whatever she *really* was—made no sense whatsoever.

"Get behind me," he snapped, waving his hand at Maki and the three warriors accompanying him. They had relived Ares of the two fallen ones, reverently whispering traditional Vradhu death-chants as they took the bodies into their arms.

Maki carried the bone-canister. The leg bones were as important as the rest of them. Without them, these brave warriors would not walk in the afterlife.

Ares didn't care that he'd issued a direct order to his Hunter rank-equal, Maki-ku-Rathra. Others might read it as a grave insult, but Maki a was reasonable sort. He would understand. There wasn't time for formality and protocol.

"You heard him," Maki growled. "Get behind Ares-*rai* and guard our fallen with your lives."

With the exception of Maki, the Vradhu's eyes were filled with thinly disguised fear and loathing every time they looked at Ares, but they didn't hesitate to follow their clan-leader's commands. Out of respect for their fallen comrades, the Vradhu had to let Ares do the fighting, even if he was no longer Vradhu; even if he was filthy *magrel*.

He was the strongest amongst them. He always had been.

Now, he'd become infinitely stronger.

The Corrupted approached. Ares had already cut down several of them with his bare hands, but fighting wasn't so easy when one carried the bodies of two clan-brothers. When Maki's warriors had finally relieved him of the burden, he'd snapped his wings and launched into a full-scale attack, his newly formed body as much a weapon as the twisting, writhing tendrils of ilverium he commanded.

It turned out the vicious talons on the ends of his wings had a purpose, after all.

Ares flexed his will and harnessed the power of the ilverium, drawing it out of the floor, even as several Corrupted rose up to meet them.

Their low moans flooded the corridor, echoing off the dark, shimmering walls. The ship had swallowed them, devouring their souls. Now she rejected them.

Why?

Because you are what I need. Now all you need to do is tap into your lukara.

Lukara?

She waits.

Ares had no idea what she was on about. He dismissed her

infuriating riddles as he turned the metal floor into liquid with his mind, creating an island for himself and his clan-brothers. He sucked the Corrupted into the depths of the ship, pulling them through the shifting surface...

And the *Hythra* promptly spat them back out again.

"Impossible bitch," he growled, his frustration mounting. He had been away from his *makivari* for far too long already. Every moment he wasted fighting these diseased creatures made him more frantic, more uneasy.

More inclined to tear a few Corrupted Naaga heads off if the cursed things got in his way.

Calexa of faraway Earth had grown on him like a wayward sekkhoi branch, curling around him and sinking her tender thorns deep into his soul. Although she wasn't far away, he felt her absence keenly. He'd gotten used to her steely, straight-as-an-arrow demeanor, and the mysteries contained within her strong, beautiful, *flawed* form stirred a special kind of madness in him.

She was a creature from a forbidden world; a walking contradiction. She fought like a demon, and yet her body carried the marks of suffering.

Sometimes, she was strong. Sometimes, she was fragile and curious.

An enigma.

His enigma.

Screw the clan elders and their rigid traditions. It was there and then that Ares decided he wanted to possess the human. He already felt a sense of affinity with her, and when he got the chance, he would carefully tease the secrets from inside her head. Then he would explore her fascinating body slowly, deliberately, taking his time.

What a rare catch she was.

He needed to make this quick. If the Corrupted were coming out of the very body of the ship, then none of them were safe. Calexa could fight, but she couldn't fend off hundreds of infected Naaga.

Three of the Corrupted streaked toward them, moving with unnatural speed.

Ares was faster. He surged forward, catching two of the creatures in the broad arc of his wings. Brutally sharp talons sank into their chests, impaling and immobilizing them.

He went to work, using bare hands and clawed fingers to tear heads from bodies. As the Naaga perished, the silver substance—the very same ilverium he wielded—drained from their bodies, returning to the whole.

Theirs was a bloodless death, because the only thing keeping them alive—if that state could even be called *living* —was metal.

Behind him, the silence of his clan-brothers spoke volumes. Fierce warriors in their own right, they now regarded him with horror, for he had truly become a monster.

But his actions had opened up a path.

"Get to the hold!" he roared, dropping to his knees. He slammed his fist into the floor. Ilverium swirled upward like a living vortex, holding back the remaining Corrupted.

Maki didn't waste time. "Get your asses into gear, brothers." As he passed, he placed his hand on Ares's shoulder. "Can the aliens be trusted?"

"I can't speak for the others," Ares answered, "but *my* human is infallible. She will return us to Khira. She has given her word." He couldn't help the note of pride that crept into his voice, even as he concentrated on keeping the Corrupted at bay.

Aethra's curses, this was getting tiring. Even this new Drakhin body of his wasn't infused with limitless power, and he was beginning to grow weary.

"She has guarded your body-copy as fiercely as a Vradhu Hunter," Maki said quietly, before leaving Ares's side.

For some reason, the thought warmed his ilverium-tainted

heart, even as the strength was sucked from him. All of a sudden, he was barely in control of the metal storm he'd created.

As he thought of Calexa, the terrible hunger inside his chest grew, and he knew what he needed most.

Vir. Her essence. It would sustain him, make him stronger. He didn't just want to possess her, he needed to *devour* her.

But he was a newly made Drakhin, and as far as he knew, his kind no longer existed on Khira. He did not know the rules of consuming *vir*. He had not studied Drakhin lore as extensively as one of the clan scholars.

What if he killed her?

His ilverium vortex weakened just a little, allowing several of the Corrupted to break free. They surged toward him, just as Ares felt minute vibrations in the floor.

Footsteps.

Not Vradhu. Not human. Not Corrupted. The rhythm was different. There was only one other species onboard this destroyer.

Naaga. Living ones.

They must have found a way past his barriers.

This was troublesome. The Naaga always carried some sort of infernal poison. They could ruin everything.

Ares growled in frustration.

His limbs grew heavy. He dropped his wings, curling them over his back like a shell. His arms quivered. Still, he continued to manipulate the essence of the ship, binding the Corrupted Naaga with thick ilverium ropes.

His body's stamina might be waning, but Ares's strength went far beyond the physical. He tapped into the deep reserves of willpower that lay buried beneath memories of cold, hard survival in the Highfold.

He was one of the poor wretches banished to the wildlands of the Ardu-Sai after his *ankhata* failed to emerge. If a Hunter's black markings didn't appear by the age of manhood, it was customary to send him alone into the wild, with only a war-spear for protection, in the hope that sheer stress would force the change.

A Hunter without *ankhata* was useless, because until the black markings emerged, a Hunter's tail-barb had no sting.

Almost all of the Unmarked that were sent to the wild never returned. Ares had been young and afraid, an untrained youth just past the cusp of manhood...

Who had survived the kratok migration and shocked the entire clan.

Alone.

They never expected him to return. None of the other Unmarked had ever returned, but Ares had, sporting a full set of the darkest, most unique *ankhata* they'd seen in generations.

It had been brutal. He'd almost died countless times, and when he returned to Malgara, he'd been filled with a deep, simmering anger.

That was the reason he'd never been able to stay in Malgara for long. The closeness, the politics, and the *people* had driven him mad, driving him back into the arms of the wild and blessedly silent Ardu-Sai.

Alone.

He had a reputation as a difficult, surly bastard. People stayed away from him, and that suited him just fine. Ever since he'd claimed his status as a Hunter, he had always worked alone.

But now he wanted another.

A *human.*

Ares rose, his fingers twitching as he sought the hilts of his *krivera*. It was force of habit, nothing more. Calexa needed the blades more than he did.

Gritting his teeth, he ran toward the horde. One of the monsters latched onto his arm, sinking its sharp teeth into his ilverium-tainted flesh.

Pain shot through his arm. Ares ignored it. He ripped a fine set of Drakhin claws through the thing's neck.

I am coming, my makivari.

One way or another, he was getting off this fucking ship, and Calexa was coming with him.

I told you, use the lukara, and everything will become easy.

"Why don't you do something useful for a change and stop throwing these infernal creatures at me?"

I cannot. They must be purged. It does not matter; they cannot kill you while you are bonded with me.

"They will kill my clan-brothers. They will kill my mate!" He flexed his wings and spun as a Corrupted one attacked him from behind. Caught in the powerful arc of his wings, the creature flew across the corridor.

Mate. Ares must have become delirious with weakness. The word slipped from his lips before he realized what he'd even said.

The ship's only response was silence; a clear sign of her cold indifference.

She didn't care about the humans or the Vradhu or the Naaga. All she seemed to want was Ares.

Never.

She wouldn't have him. He already belonged to another.

CHAPTER TWENTY-ONE

"GET BACK!" Calexa yelled in Naaga, running toward the center of the chaos.

The vast floor of the hold had become a battlefield. Limbs flew, heads rolled, and occasionally, a Vradhu warrior would grunt in pain as deformed silver claws penetrated thick armor-hide.

It still boggled her mind that their blood was as red as that of a human's. It was everywhere, and yet their injuries didn't seem to slow them at all.

The Vradhu were too caught up in the fight to pay her much attention. For a split-second, Calexa allowed herself to become entranced by their fighting style.

How spectacularly *distracting* they all were.

Holding their long blade-tipped spears in front of them, the warriors danced around the zombies, becoming purple-and-black whirlwinds as they used their superior reach to keep the creatures at bay.

They were graceful and perfectly poised.

Made for the hunt.

Occasionally, a black tail would whip out, coiling around a neck or torso or limb. Stars, those tails were powerful. Calexa reminded herself that she should *never* get in the way of a Vradhu's tail.

Another Naaga head flew across the room.

"Get back!" she roared, running toward the fray, waving her swords above her head to attract their attention. "Or you're gonna get burned! We're going to fire, and you've seen what that thing can do."

Mai's cannon-fire had been surprisingly effective against the abominable things. It only made sense that they blast the Naaga again and try and take out as many as possible.

"Last warning," Calexa shouted, her voice becoming hoarse. Mai hefted her cannon onto her shoulder and stood with her feet wide apart in the classic firing stance.

The Vradhu scattered. The Corrupted were slow to realize where their enemies had gone, but as they turned, following their opponents with blank stares, they tensed, preparing to shoot forward.

Calexa was starting to understand how they moved. Mostly, they lurched around like zombies, but they were capable of exploding into short, sharp, and devastatingly fast bursts of movement.

She scanned the field. *All clear... for now.* There was no time to lose. She motioned to Mai. *Fire.*

A bolt of white-hot Irradium lit up the hold like a flash of lightning, cutting right through the swarm of Corrupted. Those closest to the center of the blast were vaporized.

Several of the Vradhu stared at them with grim expressions, the striking markings on their faces making them oh-so hard to read. Without hesitation, they jumped back into the fray, not even waiting for the smoke to clear as they rushed in to hack at the fallen Corrupted—those that *hadn't* been completely torched.

They hadn't seemed entirely happy with Mai's cannon-blast. The looks they'd given Calexa and her crew had almost seemed... hostile.

A sliver of doubt wormed its way into her mind. What if Zahra was right? What if they were a threat? Was it too dangerous to let them onto a ship crammed with forty defenseless human women and their Primean mother-hen?

When Maki appeared in the distance with his clansmen, Calexa felt strangely relieved. He seemed to be one of the more reasonable ones. The bare-chested Vradhu whipped out his tail and wrapped it around the neck of a stray Corrupted, immobilizing the creature as he impaled it on his spear. He kicked the creature to the floor, removed his blade from its chest and promptly sliced through a slender blue neck.

Swift and merciless. Just like the rest of them. The absence of armor didn't seem to hamper him. He strode across the hold, guarding the three clansmen who walked behind him.

In their arms were the bodies of the fallen Vradhu warriors. The third Vradhu carried the long metal bone-canister thing.

They seemed hell-bent on returning their brothers home.

Maki lifted an arm, pointing toward the *Medusa*. He raised his eyebrows questioningly.

Are we coming? That's what he was saying. He must have spoken with Ares.

Her comm crackled. *"Cal, I don't know if letting them onboard is such a good idea."* That was Zahra; forever cautious, always the voice of reason.

She was the counterpoint to Calexa's impulsivity and fierce temper. She was the brakes on Mai's gung-ho attitude in the face of danger. She was the antidote to Raphael and Monroe's Primean weirdness.

Calexa would usually heed Zahra's advice, but this time, she knew things that Zahra didn't, and she had a decision to make. After all, it was her ship, and whoever owned the ship made the rules.

"Make room in the cargo hold," she snapped. "We're taking each and every one of those Vradhu boys with us."

"You sure?"

Just like when she'd saved Ares's life, she followed the feeling in her gut. *Come on*, she gestured, meeting Maki's gaze through the swirling chaos around them. Bringing the Vradhu closer had another advantage; they could form a ring of defense around the *Medusa*.

These Vradhu might still be an unknown quantity, but Calexa and her crew needed all the help they could get.

Maki ran through the shifting minefield of grotesque bodies, becoming a purple-and-black blur as he dodged and stabbed and hacked at the remaining Corrupted with startling grace, his comrades following close behind. Where Ares was all fierce, unstoppable power, Maki was fluid and supple, like a dancer.

She got the sense he was one of those enviable people who moved through life with effortless grace.

"Where's Ares?" she demanded as the bare-chested Vradhu reached her side. Although he was magnificently exposed, his powerful body a study in chiseled perfection, his exotic appearance didn't do anything for her; he didn't provoke that same heady, toe-curling feeling she got when Ares was around.

"I could ask you the same thing," the warrior-chief drawled, glancing up at the *Medusa*. "Last time we spoke, you were refusing to hand over his body-double."

"Ares's body is safe," Calexa snapped. "Now where is he?"

"Coming," Maki raised his eyebrows, sounding completely unconcerned. "He's just eradicating some vermin in the corridor."

Relief surged through her.

Maki shrugged. "What, you think a few metal-brained Naaga can stop our *khefe*? He is thrice-blooded. When you see a kratok for the first time, you will understand. He takes them down *singlehandedly*."

Kratok. That was what Ares had fed her. She shuddered.

Calexa studied Maki carefully, trying to read him. She couldn't. Maybe it was because of the strange, tattoo-like markings on his face, or maybe it was because he seemed *too* damn relaxed about what was going on behind them.

Aliens. She snorted under her breath. At least the ones in the Fiveways came with cultural reference manuals. These Vradhu were a completely unknown quantity, and she didn't like the way some of them looked at her girls. "If we manage to get off this insane death-trap, I need to know that your men won't pose any threat to my people."

"We would *not*." He seemed offended. That was... reassuring.

"And once we land on your planet, you will guarantee our safety."

"That is the least we could do for a *makivari*. Because Ares has marked you as such, you are, by extension, under our protection, as are your people." Maki dodged to one side as a severed blue-and-silver hand came flying in his direction, narrowly missing his head. How he'd sensed it, she had no idea.

Did these Vradhu have eyes in the backs of their heads?

"You people keep calling me that," Calexa blurted, narrowing her eyes. "What exactly does it mean?"

"Oh, He didn't tell you? In Vradhu, the word *makivari* means *honored protector*. It means you saved his life, and he owes you a blood-debt. Congratulations, female-who-fights. You have won yourself the loyalty of the most powerful Hunter in the Two Clans. Do not take it lightly, because amongst our people, you are now virtually untouchable."

Lost for words, Calexa shook her head. That bloody Ares hadn't explained *any* of this to her. To think that her split-second decision to stay behind and save his ass would have such far-reaching implications...

A pleasant sensation crawled over her shorn scalp. She

rather *liked* the idea that Ares felt he had some sort of mortal duty to protect her.

No male had ever done such a thing for her before.

She hadn't let them.

She *wouldn't* let them, because she could hold her own.

But if it was Ares, it was different. He had a hold on her now, and she couldn't get him out of her head.

Honorable, fierce, and as straight and true as an arrow, he was everything life had taught her not to expect.

"Now, woman-who-fights," Maki said, breaking her out of her momentary love-trance. "What are we going to do?"

"We hold our position until Ares gets here. You and your soldiers must protect this ship at all costs. One way or another, we're getting out of here, but I'm not even *thinking* about leaving without him."

"Good words." Maki nodded in approval. "Fighting words."

"*Calexa!*" A deep, resonant voice echoed through the hold. It was powerful and organic and metallic, and it was distinctly Ares.

It held an edge of desperation. It held vicious anger. It held something she'd never heard from him before—a trace of *fear*.

"Get *everyone* inside your ship, *now!*"

She still couldn't see him. A tremor rippled through the floor. It was impossible to understand what was really happening out there in the corridor. All she knew was that Ares was approaching, and he'd sent her a warning.

A command.

She could stand here and question her sanity for a thousand orbits, or she could act.

Do you trust him with your life? Do you trust him with the lives of your best friends and your crew and all of those terrified human girls, none of whom would be able to lift a finger if those big, bad Vradhu warriors decided to have their way with them?

For someone who had major trust issues, the answer to her own question was surprisingly simple.

Yes.

She trusted the man who had watched over her while she slept. She trusted the man who had fed her and taken care of her and then quietly and sincerely asked for her help.

Who had held back, despite the naked hunger in his eyes.

That look. It was only now that she finally understood.

She clicked her teeth twice, activating her comm. "Hey, crew. It's been a rough ride into this strange sector of the universe, but the good news is that we're still alive. Seems we finally pushed our luck too far by taking this job, but you knew the risks."

"*We did.*" To her surprise, it was Monroe who spoke. Monroe rarely *ever* spoke. "*Fiveways rules. We gambled, we lost. Now, we start again.*"

"I'm going to call in all my debts right here, right now," Calexa continued, speaking low and fast. "I'm going to ask you all to trust me one last time. When this is over, I'll amend our Company contract to include whatever conditions you like. Raphael and Monroe, I'll write off the rest of your freedom-debt. You can have the rights to the fucking *Medusa* if you want. Mai and Zahra, you can both stop feeling like you owe me for getting you out of the bond-houses. I just did what either of you would have done for me."

"*We've got your back, Cal, you know that.*" This time, it was Mai on the comm. "*What do you need, captain?*"

"The Vradhu are going to come onboard right now. They're going to enter the cargo hold, and we're going to stop the Corrupted from breaching our ship. Raf, put some charge into the triticore missiles and keep the thrusters warm."

Already, Maki was shouting orders at his men, getting them to move.

"*How the hell are we going to get the airlock open?*"

"As a last resort, we could try and blast our way out, but just hold on. I think Ares might have a solution."

"Who the fuck is Ares?"

"You'll see," she said darkly as her heart beat a frantic staccato. She wanted to *see* him so badly; she wanted to know he was okay.

And she was utterly terrified that this insanity he proposed wouldn't work, that he would remain trapped on this cursed destroyer as a Drakhin, doomed to fight the Corrupted and the Naaga for all eternity while they escaped to the relative safety of the unknown.

To Khira.

An uncharted, unmapped planet, which they knew nothing about.

This is madness.

But when had Calexa ever *not* been considered mad?

"So, crew," she said softly as the Corrupted closed in on them, and the creepy sounds from the outer corridor became louder and louder, and the tremors in the floor turned into ripples and then waves, "what's it gonna be?"

The *Medusa's* thrusters roared to life.

"Hallelujah," Zahra said, invoking an old Earth word. *"I've never been so glad to hear that sound. What, Cal? Did you think we were going to say no?"*

"I..."

"Tell the purple guys they can hang out in the hold, but I'll gut anyone who touches my snack stash. Oh, and they don't get safety restraints when we take off and land, but I'm sure they'll survive. They look plenty tough."

"I'll..." *Fuck.* Once again, she was lost for words. Her throat closed up, and she cut the comm, suddenly afraid she might say something stupid, or bawl her eyes out.

There was no need to talk.

They'd all been through so much together. They knew what was up.

Calexa blinked furiously and motioned to the Vradhu to get going. "You heard the *khefe*," she yelled, not knowing what the word meant, but liking the sound of it.

The Vradhu who carried their fallen came first, silent and inscrutable as they trotted past Calexa, heading for the ramp.

She activated her comm. "There are two bodies," she said grimly. "We could put them in the cryo-vac, but I don't know how that would go down from a cultural perspective, so just let them be."

Maki doubled back, rounding up his men.

Calexa stared off into the distance, watching, waiting, *hoping* that Ares would come around the corner.

Then it struck her.

That fucking *smell*.

Overripe banana, only it wasn't. This smell had nothing to do with the ridiculously expensive fruit.

It was poison, and poison meant Naaga.

One by one, the Vradhu fell.

Even Maki dropped to his knees, his black eyes widening in shock and outrage. His mouth opened in a silent scream, his expression that of a man who wanted to commit pure bloody murder, but couldn't.

"No!" Calexa screamed as a group of living Naaga walked into the hold. The one in front swung a tiny metal ball on a chain. "Mai, Zahra, we have to save them!"

"What the hell is happening, Cal?"

"I... I don't really know." She ran, pumping her legs, her bionic joints working to propel her much faster than any ordinary human.

The Naaga stopped and stared right at her. One of them stood out; a woman clad in a suit of armor similar to the one Ares had been wearing, Her face was protected by an opaque helmet that completely concealed her features.

The others fanned out behind her, silent and deferent.

Clearly, she was some sort of leader, and the ordinary Naaga were her underlings.

Sensing weakness, the Corrupted swarmed on their opponents, tearing at defenseless Vradhu bodies with their vicious claws. Blood spilled as they penetrated thick armor. Calexa screamed in frustration.

The Vradhu were spread out all across the hold, and neither she, Mai, or Zahra could get to them fast enough.

The Naaga-leader made a minute gesture with her hand. One of her subordinates stepped forward, a clear glass box in his hands. She dropped the swinging orb-thing inside, and the lid dropped closed with a soft *snap.*

The strange banana smell disappeared, and all around her, wounded Vradhu started to rouse.

Not a single Vradhu screamed or cried out. All Calexa heard were soft grunts of pain as the Vradhu regained their weapons and started to fight back.

Several of them were badly wounded, but that didn't slow them down. Calexa winced as she caught sight of swirls of crimson. *Blood.* Lots and lots of it.

These Vradhu were tough cookies.

She left them to grapple with the Corrupted, her strides lengthening as she crossed the massive floor. Out of the corner of her eye, she saw Mai running toward Maki, who had suffered a deep gash across his stomach.

The Naaga leader raised her arm and pointed in Calexa's direction. Two of the blue ones broke off and sprinted after her.

Careful.

Something wasn't right. The Naaga didn't fight conventionally. Why were they running to meet her when she had her bone swords drawn and ready? They weren't even holding weapons, just...

One of them threw something in her direction.

As it sailed through the air, she recognized it as one of

those triangular energy-sucking devices.

It was attached to a chain.

Don't let it touch you.

She remembered how devastating it had been last time. The Vradhu had taken her *vir,* rendering her as weak as a puppy and utterly helpless.

Calexa dodged, keeping her swords low. Angling toward the Naaga, she thrust one of her blades into his heart.

It sank deep and true.

Still he moved, yanking the chain with one hand.

How?

As the *vir*-harvester came flying back toward her, Calexa remembered.

They have two hearts.

She brought the other blade home, but it was too late.

The object slammed into her back, and something sharp dug into her skin just beneath her shoulder blade, holding the horrible thing in place. Her legs turned to jelly. She dropped to her knees, her twin swords falling form her hands. The world spun by, becoming a muted blur.

Someone in the distance was desperately yelling her name. It was Zahra.

She wanted to scream out a warning, to tell her not to come any closer, but she couldn't move, let alone speak.

There was that awful feeling again, as if the ground had been torn out from underneath her. Her life-force was being stolen. A chill seeped into her bones.

Gotta move. She gritted her teeth and tried to resist, but it was futile.

The Naaga in the armor-suit walked toward her, her long-limbed stride eating up the floor. As she reached Calexa's side, her underling scuttled away. He seemed afraid of the mysterious woman.

All Calexa wanted to do was to run her twin swords through the fucking alien's dual hearts. This feeling of being trapped and utterly helpless—it was almost worse than death.

The creature bent and reached behind her, closing her fingers around the *vir*-eating thing. Her gloved hands brushed against Calexa's thermosuit, making her skin crawl. "What strange turn of fate has brought you to us?" she murmured. "Perhaps you were sent by the very gods that made us." Her laugh was cold and harsh and unpleasant.

The Naaga yanked the chain with her other hand. Exquisite pain shot through Calexa's back. She screamed. Behind her, Zahra was shouting.

Don't come! She wanted to warn her. She couldn't. She couldn't even click her teeth to activate her comm; they were chattering from the terrible cold.

"Don't worry, creature. I won't kill you. I'm just going to drain you to the point of near-death. You see, that golden energy contained within your body is incredibly valuable." She laughed again, her voice laced with astonishment, as if she couldn't quite believe her luck. "Your species... whatever you are, you really are an anomaly, aren't you? I can see that your companions over there possess the same wealth of energy. I would not be surprised if the *Hythra* herself sensed the power within you and drew you here. You are as rich in *vir* as a first-generation Naaga."

"Wh..." What the hell was this mad creature talking about? Calexa tried to ask, but her question came out as nothing more than a faint wheeze.

"Mmm." A sound of deep satisfaction escaped the Naaga. She brought the triangular object around to the front, showing it to Calexa. Tiny lights flickered along its side, emitting a warm golden glow. "That's your energy, your *vir*," the Naaga explained. "This is a *rakiriel*. It harvests your *vir* so I can use it. It would take a thousand of our kind to produce the amount of energy I have just taken from you. Now, all I have to do is *this*." She ran a finger down the center of her chest and her scale-armor split in two, revealing a triangle-shaped metal plate embedded in her blue skin. The Naaga pressed the *rakiriel* against the plate.

A low hum emanated from the device. The metal plate began to glow, turning the same shade of golden as the lights on the *rakiriel*.

The Naaga laughed. "Oh, do not look at me like that. As long as you provide us with *vir*, you and your people will be fed, sheltered, and clothed. We *know* what it is like to be enslaved. Before we evolved, we were the under-race. Now it is your turn."

The Naaga dropped to her knees, slamming her palm against the floor. Tendrils of ilverium snaked up her arm.

No! Ares was supposed to be the only one who could control the fucking essence of the ship. Why was *she* suddenly able to do it?

Calexa's teeth were chattering again. She was so cold, and all she wanted to do was curl up into a ball and go to sleep.

You can't!

Not now... not when they were so close to escaping.

Not when these crazy aliens wanted to make them into *slaves*.

Zahra's hoarse, angry cry reached her ears.

Help them! Calexa pleaded, trying to catch the attention of the Vradhu, but they were all too busy fighting off the Corrupted.

"That is better," the Naaga said. "*Much* better. Now we can take back what is rightfully ours."

Calexa's heart slowed. Her eyes closed. Consciousness slipped out of her grasp, and she fought to remain awake. Her voice caught in her throat. She forced her mouth open, but nothing came out.

Ares! She clung to hope, willing her metal-lord, her Vradhu, her Drakhin, her ilverium-slinging warrior to come and find her, just like he had when she'd gone down in the sci-labs.

Amazingly, he responded.

"Get your hands *off* her!" His voice resonated with metal and power, and a shockwave rippled through the floor. This was Vradhu Ares, warrior Ares, the so-called *khefe* who took down kratok without blinking, who moved like an unstoppable hurricane as he cut through his enemies.

She didn't give a shit what he looked like. He could take any form he wanted and she would still follow him.

Her chest moved up-and-down in silent laughter. Sweet stars, she was so relieved and ecstatic she felt giddy. Maybe the freezing cold and energy deprivation were making her delirious.

"You died the moment you dared to touch her *vir*," he snarled, his voice growing louder, echoing through the vast chamber. "That is mine. She is *mine*." The sound was so deliciously menacing that it pulled Calexa back to the surface, saving her from sinking into frigid oblivion.

"You think that just because you control a few tentacles of ilverium, you suddenly know all the secrets of this ship?" The Naaga sank her hands into the floor, and when she pulled them out again, she held thick ropes of the liquid metal. "You are an anomaly, nothing more, and now you are weak. Look at you! Even in that form, you are an insult to the Drakhin masters that once walked amongst us. They would have torn you down in an instant."

"You know nothing." Ares appeared in the center of the hold like a black-winged angel of death.

The floor rippled outwards as his feet hit the surface. Ares stalked across to the Naaga, his claw-tipped hands trembling. His tail was out. He coiled it around the Naaga's neck. She wrapped ilverium vines around his neck, trying to choke him. "Savage," she hissed. "Give up the *Hythra*. She is not meant to be ruled by the likes of *you*."

"You think I know *how* to give up this fucking curse?" Ares lifted her off her feet, squeezing with his tail, ignoring the tendrils of ilverium that slithered up his legs and torso.

Wild, savage bloodlust rose inside Calexa's chest. *Finish her!* She wanted to shout the words out loud, wanted desperately for Ares to take his dirty, savage victory, just like she had in the Arena when she'd been written off.

They thought she'd be dead within the first five minutes. They hadn't understood how *strong* a bond-house slave needed to be in order to survive.

She'd lasted three seasons in that bloody pit, and she was going to survive here, too.

Ares hadn't even looked at her, but it didn't matter. She'd heard the intensity in his voice. The force of his anger had knocked her flat.

He'd come for her.

For the first time in her life, someone had come for her.

"Ugh!" The Naaga kicked, her slender legs flailing in thin air. Ares smashed his fist into her reflective face-plate.

It cracked.

He hit her again. The metal vines went crazy, turning into a swirling vortex.

"Why are you not going down? You have no *vir*."

"I don't need it to deal with your kind." He hit her a third time, and her faceplate shattered. "You took what belongs to me."

Pieces of glass, or metal, or whatever substance her face-plate was made of fell to the floor, revealing the flat eyes of a Naaga, but unlike the others, these eyes shimmered with a faint golden glow.

Although Calexa's thoughts had slowed to an icy trickle, she understood that this *vir* of hers was something the Naaga desperately wanted. Somehow, it allowed this strange creature to control the ilverium.

It made her powerful.

She shuddered. If the *vir* was so valuable to the Naaga, and if all humans possessed it in great amounts, then...

Their situation had just become incredibly dangerous.

Another piece of the Naaga's faceplate fell away, revealing a number or a word stamped into her forehead in strange alien script.

We know what it is like to be enslaved.

The tattoo-like mark reminded Calexa of the brand given to her by the Khral. It had been etched into her skin just above her left hip-bone, and she'd had it cut out as soon as she'd broken free of her contract with the Arena.

The ilverium engulfed Ares's lower half, reaching up to his waist. He dug his thumbs into the Naaga's eyes. She screamed. A loud crackle rent the air, and golden energy rippled down Ares's arms.

He closed his eyes and inhaled deeply. His lips were slightly parted, and his jaw trembled slightly.

The golden glow was visible for only a split-second, but Calexa understood.

He was draining *vir* from the Naaga, and the look on his face was astonishing and terrifying and utterly seductive.

It was a look of pure ecstasy, as if the *vir*—Calexa's very own life force—was the ultimate drug.

Ever since he'd become Drakhin, he'd refrained from touching her. Now she understood. It intoxicated him.

Was he even aware of his surroundings right now?

The ship listed to one side, the floor tilting as it became a precarious slope. Calexa fell flat on her face and slid down, the metal surface becoming soft and warm underneath her.

Face down, she could no longer see Ares or the Naaga or any of her friends. *"Ares!"* She tried to cry out, but nothing came.

A shockwave burst outwards from Ares, and she got the sense he was right in front of her. Using all of her strength, she lifted her head and saw his legs and his feet, still covered in writhing, twisting ilverium.

The entire destroyer jerked violently. Ares had lost awareness. He'd lost control. If this continued, he'd kill them all.

"Aargh!" Calexa screamed as she summoned strength from that deep, desperate place where she buried all of her darkness. It was the place she went to when she needed to leap out of her head and destroy her fears, her weaknesses, her limits. It was the place she went to when she needed to grab the very fabric of reality and twist it into what she wanted it to become.

Fate was malleable. She'd learned that a long time ago. If she let this moment pass, it would be lost forever.

She reached out and hooked an arm around Ares's legs, her ice-cold skin burning up as she came into contact with his warmth. She held on for dear life as the ship rocked back-and-forth. "Stop," she hissed, desperately hoping he could hear her.

Tendrils of ilverium engulfed her hand, her arm, her shoulder, threatening to drown her in a morass of living metal.

She didn't care.

"*Stop!*" This time, her voice was louder, even though she was growing weaker by the second, for as soon as she'd come into contact with Ares, that terrible energy-drain had started again.

Could he control it? Could he even stop it? Was he aware of the effect he had on her?

Was she going to die here?

Her vision blurred. Her heartbeat grew faint. Her breaths were rapid and shallow. She wavered on the edge of oblivion, but still she held on, her bionic joints locking into place.

She wasn't letting go. She would fucking *freeze* to death around him, if that's what it took.

Her entire life boiled down to this moment. From her spartan upbringing in the Human Quarter on D5, to the shock and horror of realizing she'd been repossessed because her parents couldn't repay their generation-debt, to the brutality of the bond-house, to the vicious kill-or-be-killed maelstrom of the Arena, she'd spent her entire life enduring hit after hit after hit.

And she was strong, no matter what they tried to do to her. She was human. She *had* to be strong.

I am here. Wake up, inkface!

A sickening crunch told her the Naaga was gone; he'd snapped the creature's neck.

Monster!

And yet she clung to him as if her life depended on it—which it did.

"Foolish Naaga," Ares growled. His voice had changed. It was Ares, but it wasn't; a deep, terrifying, metallic echo that rang with limitless power. "Did you not know that the Drakhin came from *us*?"

"Ares!" Calexa pleaded, seeing nothing but darkness.

Enough!

The Naaga's body crashed to the floor beside her. Calexa saw stars.

"No!" Ares cried.

She forced herself to look at him. It was harder than anything she'd done in her life. All she wanted to do was sleep, but now she could see him, all silver and black and fearsome, and his eyes...

They glowed with her *vir*.

Pure, brilliant gold.

Widening in horror.

"Let go," he said, his voice cracking. "Calexa, you have to let go. This... *I*... will kill you."

Still, the ship rocked. They were adrift in an endless sea of chaos and ilverium.

"Get ahold of yourself, Drak," she whispered, trying to move her arm. "You need to control those crazy emotions of yours, or we're all going to die."

He crouched down and gently uncurled Calexa's stiff arm

from around his legs, his trembling fingers searing her thermo-suit-clad skin. As soon as she was free, he withdrew, and the ship's violent motion began to settle. "I can't touch you," he said again, stepping back. "I wish I could."

"I- I don't care about that now." Her teeth chattered, but as soon as Ares had let go of her, she could move again. She could talk again. "I'm not fucking dead, am I? Control yourself. Call my girls. They can carry me to the *Medusa*. I'll eat something. I'll be fine. Go and help your brothers take care of those bloody Corrupted, and watch out for the Naaga. They have a poisonous ball-on-a-chain that sends everyone to sleep. *You* know all about that, don't you?"

Ares stared at her, unblinking and bemused as she pulled herself into a sitting position. The chaotic rocking motion of the ship dropped to a gentle, rhythmic lull.

Speaking of sleep...

She yawned. Her eyes drooped. She was drained from inside and out, and all she wanted to do was collapse into a heap and meet the god of dreams for a while.

But there was still so much to do.

Ares dropped onto his haunches beside her. "I will make this right." There was a terrible yearning in his voice. "I knew this would happen. I *hate* not being able to touch you."

"Ares. Stop. You saved my life."

"You know what you are to me. The thought of another laying their hands on you, *harming* you... It drives me insane."

"Oh..." *Damn.* Nobody had ever said anything like that to her in her entire life. Even though she was weaker right now than she'd ever been, even though Ares had been transformed into a scale-faced, energy-sucking, vampire-alien who could kill in the blink of an eye, she felt safe.

Everything's going to be fine.

How did she know that?

Because he was here, and he was saying things that tore up

the foundations of everything she knew, making them whole again.

This was a new world, where the rules of the past didn't exist.

"Hey, Cal, are you all right? Zahra's down! Oh my god, if that silver asshole touches you again, I'm gonna blast—" Mai's static-laced voice cut through her spiraling thoughts.

"No! Believe it or not, he's a friendly. Get Zahra first, then me."

"What, you're telling me that even with all those scaly muscles, dragon-man can't help you?"

"Believe it or not, he can't." Calexa sighed. "Long story. It's complicated. I'll tell you all about it when we're away from this fucking nightmare."

"Okay, I'm coming. Damn it, I need support. Can't be in two places at once. Raf's stuck in the bridge getting our systems back online, and Monroe can't leave the powerbanks... something to do with the whole system potentially crashing if he stops manually adjusting—"

"Get S to help."

"The princess?" Mai sounded skeptical.

"Primeans are supposed to have all these superior physical abilities, aren't they? Make her work. I'll bet her precious ass can run just as fast as our modified ones."

"Got it. Oh, and Cal, that insanely terrifying alien with the wings and the tail and the liquid metal... He knows we're friendlies, right?"

"He does. Don't worry. He won't hurt you, but stay away from the blue guys at all costs. They have all kinds of tricks up their sleeves."

"And when we're safely out in space, you're going to tell me everything, right?"

"I always do."

Beside her, Ares seethed, radiating menace. He paced

back-and-forth, his half-outstretched wings moving up-and-down.

Calexa raised a hand, trying to appease him. He was *so* dangerous right now. "Ares, I'm fine. Weak, but fine. It's not as bad as last time." It was true. She was drained, but not to the point where she would lapse into unconsciousness at any moment.

"I should have come sooner." Almost absentmindedly, Ares sent out a deadly lash of ilverium, slicing an approaching Naaga in two. Green blood went everywhere. Calexa winced and looked away.

He dropped to his knees, facing her. "Everything is so much easier now, thanks to your *vir*." He met her gaze, and everything stopped. The *Hythra* stopped moving. The chaos around them—the Corrupted, the raging Vradhu, the Naaga, the rippling metal floor—it all turned into a distant, muted roar as she faced Ares.

Their Universe narrowed into a tiny point where only the two of them existed, and Ares's face twisted in pain and longing, because the very thing he wanted most was denied.

Touch.

She wanted it, too; she wanted to feel his arms around her, wanted his big, warm, solid body enclosing her, no matter whether he was Drakhin or Vradhu or neither or both.

She didn't care. He was Ares, and that was all that mattered.

"No matter what happens," he said softly, "I'll make sure you and your people get off this destroyer."

"Same here." She looked up into his face, and the sheer tenderness in his expression floored her.

"My *makivari*." His eyes had turned the most startling shade of golden, and they held terrible sadness. "I am a full-blooded Drakhin now. The *Hythra* speaks to me of power and insanity, and I am terrified of what I have become. The consciousness transfer is my last hope, and a long-shot at that.

If it doesn't work, do not try to save me. Just leave all of this behind, and never, *ever* come back."

"But..." Holy hell, was this really happening? If she weren't so drained, Calexa would have slammed her fists into the floor in sheer frustration.

He was the one for her. She wasn't delirious. She wasn't crazy. She felt it in her metal-coated bones. She felt it in the depths of her battered soul. Ares was the only being in the vast Universe that made her want to drop her barriers completely and surrender.

And now she might lose him?

"You're telling me I might have to leave you."

"You are going to *survive*." His jaw jutted out at a stubborn angle as he crossed his rippling arms.

"So are you." Calexa returned his glare with a mulish look. *Stubborn?* Ha. He had no idea. "I'll do whatever it takes."

"You will do as I say, human." His voice had changed, becoming deep, metallic, and resonant. A *Drakhin* voice, imbued with limitless power.

Scary.

But this was her Ares, and she wasn't afraid. "*No*," she said, slowly, deliberately. "You can't just hold onto all that power without anyone to hold you accountable."

"*Calexa*," he snapped, and she liked the way he said her name, in that stern, commanding tone of voice.

She understood what he was trying to do, and it warmed her bitter heart that he would put her safety above everything else. Sweet, beautiful, headstrong male. He was a little unhinged right now—who wouldn't be after going through all those mind-boggling changes in such a short period of time? Oh, she understood, because she'd been a little unhinged for most of her bloody life.

Her chin also took on a stubborn little tilt. "If you can't get off this crazy ride, then maybe I'll stay right here with you."

Ares glowered in an affectionate kind of way.

"*Cal?*" And then Mai arrived, staring at them with a bug-eyed expression that Calexa might have found totally hilarious, if the situation weren't so damn serious.

"Help me up, Mai."

Strong arms went around her. "Oh my god, you're so fucking cold. What the hell happened? What did he do to you?"

He took my essence and claimed my soul.

"It wasn't his fault." Calexa regarded Ares with a deliberate stare. She spoke Earthian with Mai, so he couldn't understand a word they were saying, but she hoped he understood her tone of voice. "Sorry, I can't stand on my own just yet, but I should be okay in a little while. Just need to chomp on an energy bar and put on a double thermojacket. Ares will be following us. We have a few, uh, *things* we need to sort out."

"You sure are inviting all kinds of strange people onboard our ship, Cal." Mai lifted her with ease, and Calexa held Ares's gaze as they broke into a run. Are you sure you don't want to take a raincheck on the big guy over there? I don't know how else to say this, but he scares the crap out of me." A broken laugh erupted from her lips. "Everyone here and everything about this place scares the crap out of me, and I'm not the sort to frighten easily."

"Understatement of the century," Calexa said dryly. "Don't worry. I'm vouching for him, and I'm a good judge of character. Besides, if he *really* wanted to board our ship without permission, there's nothing we'd be able to do about it."

"You're trying to tell me that even Beauty wouldn't—"

"Nope." She suspected nothing could take down Ares in his current form.

"Well, that's reassuring, isn't it?"

"Mightily." As they made a beeline for the *Medusa,* they shot past furiously fighting Vradhu and flailing Corrupted. S came into view, sprinting across the battlefield with Zahra in her arms, her long legs effortlessly eating up the distance.

She looked magnificent and determined, and Calexa couldn't help but feel a stab of envy at the Primean's physical superiority, especially when she was lying helpless in Mai's arms. "Like something out of an Earthian imaginarium," she grumbled. "Should have given her a gun and asked her to hold the fort."

"I'd prefer dirty freedom to Primeans and their fucked up hierarchy any day of the week. Besides, we leveled the playing field ages ago."

"Yeah." They'd gone through a world of pain to have their illegal bio-enhancements fitted. This Universe wasn't kind to the weak.

"So, you and dragon-man figured out how we're going to open the airlock yet? I can't wait to get back to the deep-deep."

"You *do* know we're going planetside until Monroe can put a permanent fix on the powerbanks?" It was far too risky to shoot off without knowing where they were and how far they could run, and she'd promised Ares she'd return the Vradhu to Khira.

A thrill of excitement ran through her as she glanced over Mai's shoulder and caught Ares's enigmatic golden eyes.

Khira.

Totally uncharted. Completely unheard of. They would be the very first humans to set foot on this mysterious planet, where the natives were painted in vivid shades of violet and black, and their enemies wielded poison and strange technology. *Language implants. Cloning. Consciousness transfer.*

If they brought any of that back to the Fiveways, they would make an unimaginable fortune. They would be set for life.

But could they even get back to the Fiveways? Could they ever return, or were they stranded?

She didn't know.

Ares's home planet. Calexa shuddered. How desperately she wanted to see it. She wanted to learn about his people, his culture, his origins. She wanted to unlock the mysteries of what he was and understand how it was possible for him to turn from Vradhu to Drakhin.

What was a Drakhin exactly, anyway, and why was this sentient, liquid-metal ship floating in Khira's orbit?

And... did she even *want* to return home?

To her surprise, she didn't really know the answer to that last question. She just wanted to hear him call her *makivari* again in that growly, possessive-yet-tender tone of voice.

And then... Then she wanted him to be able to touch her with his velvet-scaled Drakhin hand without killing her. *That* would be nice.

CHAPTER TWENTY-TWO

HOW COULD she be so weak, so vulnerable at this very moment, and yet hold his wavering heart together with such decisive strength?

When he'd tapped into her *vir*—that terrible, intoxicating, *forbidden* power—he'd experienced ecstasy for the first time in his life.

He'd touched the face of the goddess, and he wanted more. He *craved* more.

Ares couldn't keep his eyes off Calexa as she looked over her friend's shoulder and actually *smiled* at him. Her face was pale. The dark circles of exhaustion ringed her eyes, making the vicious scars across her cheekbones stand out even more, but her brilliant eyes sparkled with affection.

Even though he'd harmed her.

He'd done this to her. The Drakhin in him thirsted for her life force, to the extent that just the simple act of touching her had drained her power. It had been potent and electrifying, and it had blown his mind and nearly sent him to his knees.

He'd suspected all along, and now he knew. Her *vir* was exquisite, and this temptation would ruin him. It wasn't just the *vir*, it was Calexa; a creature unlike anything he'd encountered before in his simple Vradhu life. Who would have thought that beyond the Shadowring there existed beings like these humans? Soft-skinned, lithe, and fierce, they wielded their strange *magrel* weapons like demons.

Magrel be damned. The elders had always warned of the evils of technology, but he was beyond the point of no return. He was no longer an un-curious Vradhu.

And these humans were not evil.

They were tough and proud and noble, just like Ares and his brothers.

As they neared the human ship, Ares slowed, keeping his distance from Calexa and her clan-sister.

The small one set Calexa on her feet. His *makivari* swayed for a moment, then turned to face him. Her smile widened. "For some reason, it isn't as bad as last time. That was brutal. This is just... mildly incapacitating." She was indeed formidable; a pillar of strength amidst the chaos.

Gods and demons, he admired everything about this woman, and Aethra was playing a sick fucking joke on him by denying him the right to touch her, to take her into his arms and savor her warmth, her strength, her beauty.

If he managed to do the unthinkable and transfer his damned soul into that new Naaga-made body of his, he would take nothing for granted. When he was back amongst the Two Clans, he would visit the *basharka* and have the beading done as soon as possible. If she'd have him, he would join with her in a proper mating ritual, just like the females and their poisonous Breeders.

She deserved nothing less than his full commitment, and as for the curious, judgmental gossips of the Two Clans...

He would deal with them.

They knew better than to invoke his ire.

"You don't have to look at me like that, Ares. I'm *fine*." All of the fierceness melted from her features, and suddenly she was soft and inviting.

Utterly entrancing.

Forbidden.

With Drakhin eyes, he perceived her *vir* as a soft glow around her body. The other humans radiated *vir* too, but even when it was depleted, Calexa's aura stood out like a beacon.

His lips parted. He inhaled sharply and stared into her eyes, losing himself in crystalline blue.

Control. Now more than ever, he needed it. *Control yourself, fool. You are not some mad pyshtana who is going to ruin everything because of temptation.*

Behind him, Maki and his warriors raged against their enemies. The lifeless, bloodless bodies of the Corrupted littered the floor, along with pools of crimson Vradhu blood.

The remaining Naaga lurched amongst the bodies, heading toward their fallen leader. Through the ilverium floor, he could feel their featherlight steps. They walked slowly, deliberately, oblivious to the chaos around them.

Ares reached out with his will and located the one with the box full of poison. He made a noose out of ilverium and flung it around the creature's neck, drawing it tight. In an instant, he crushed its spine and absorbed the disgusting box full of poison into the floor.

"You're omnipotent now, aren't you?" Calexa's gaze never wavered. "That's why you didn't want to touch me. You were afraid of what you might—"

"I didn't know what could happen," he whispered. "I didn't want to hurt you." What was the point of having all this power if he was trapped; if he couldn't have what he wanted most?

What a pitiful existence this was turning out to be.

The small human with the dark eyes was staring at Ares in horror, as if he were the worst monster imaginable—which he was. She muttered something to Calexa in their clipped alien language, and Calexa responded with a reassuring murmur.

She diverted her attention back to Ares. "Then we have to

make things right, don't we? I don't blame you. I wouldn't want to be stuck on this creepy battleship either, but if there's no other option..."

Surely she wasn't suggesting that if he couldn't leave, she would *stay*...

Calexa gestured toward the ship's entrance with a wry, lopsided half-smile. "Your clone awaits, my lord. I still don't understand what's going on, but if there's a way to get you out of this body and into the other one, we have to try."

The hopeful note in her voice gave *him* a sliver of hope, because he knew that a creature like Calexa couldn't exist forever on the *Hythra*. The Drakhin were long gone, and this destroyer of theirs was a lost place, a dead place, a thing that should be...

Destroyed.

Yes!

What? In the depths of his confused, tormented mind, the *Hythra* exulted, and he struggled to cling to his sanity.

He latched onto Calexa's blue stare. He watched her serious, beautiful face, trying to anchor his thoughts.

Complete and utter destruction is what I yearn for, Hunter. You are full Drakhin now. You have found your lukara, and you have sated your thirst. You can grant me what I seek.

What madness was this?

Shut up, wretch. His malevolent hatred of the *Hythra* spilled over into the bond, even as her cursed *vir*-infused power coursed through his body. What made it even more excruciating was the fact that Calexa was so near.

She called to him, and yet he couldn't touch. He'd tasted, and he wanted more. Her essence wasn't just sustenance, it was everything. Hunger and desire became one.

The *Hythra* laughed inside his head.

Lust surged through him with overwhelming force. His

cock strained, filling him with exquisite agony. He'd been hard ever since he'd caught sight of her.

What torture! If he had to endure this state for much longer, he'd tear the fucking ship apart.

Yes! Do it, Hunter!

Gods and demons, what was *this*, now? Truly, he was going mad, and he was dangerous. The longer he stayed close to her, the more of a threat he became. What happened if he went completely insane; if the *Hythra's* strange whisperings destroyed his self control? What if, with all his seemingly limitless power, he gave in to his temptation and took her?

Hurt her?

Killed her?

The last one was enough to make his blood run cold. There. It was decided. He had no choice but to...

Finish it. Finish this now.

Ares took one last look at her face, memorizing every last detail, from her brilliant eyes to her slightly crooked and spotted nose to her moist, kissable lips.

He imprinted her face onto the mortal fabric of his soul, imagining a sweetness he would never get to taste. The power, the need, the longing, it was all too much. He would not last long. He was so close to unravelling.

He was fucking *dangerous*, too dangerous to put his base needs above her safety. Lives were at stake; not just hers, but those of her people and his Vradhu kin.

"Go," he barked, hardening his shattered heart.

"You're coming, aren't you?" Her blue eyes widened.

"You *know* I can't. Not in this form. No matter what I do, the *Hythra* won't give me up." He intentionally made his voice cold. "Get everyone onboard your vessel. If they had to, my clan-brothers would fight until all of the Corrupted are destroyed; until every last drop of blood leaves their bodies, but I will not allow it. This ends now, Calexa."

"But what about—"

"Go," he said again, his voice softening. "I have the power to finish this quickly. I can't just stand here while my brothers shed blood. Once everyone is safely onboard, I will open the hold. You will set a course for Khira and never look back." He left the obvious unsaid—once the hold was open, there would be no chance for him to board the escape vessel, because they would be exposed to the cold vacuum of space.

And even if he wanted to, the ilverium would hold him back.

"This consciousness transfer thing... Just tell me how it works." Still, she refused to give up on him.

"I don't know the details, but I've seen the Naaga do it." He had spied on the strange creatures when he sat in the command chair; he'd watched the old ones die and re-animate inside the bodies that emerged from the *temundra*.

Naaga life was an endless cycle of death and regeneration. They were clones, after all. "It is fanciful on my part, and more than a little scary." Ares thought of his new, youthful body and fervently hoped the rules of consciousness transfer applied to Vradhu as well. He countered the shock on Calexa's face with a half-smile. "*Temundra*-made bodies animate when the original copy dies in close proximity. The... *spirit* transfers from one to the other. That is what I have seen. That is what they have assured me."

"D-dies?" Her voice quivered. "But that seems..."

Impossible. He knew it. It didn't matter. Sometimes, death was an acceptable risk. He'd lived beneath the shadow of death his entire life.

That was the life of a Hunter.

But even though Hunters were taught not to fear death, all of a sudden, Ares was terrified of it.

"Calexa..." He turned away, unable to meet her cerulean eyes as they fractured into a thousand tiny fragments. "You must survive at all costs. *Live,* my *makivari,* and know that you showed this simple Hunter a glimpse of something sublime."

This feeling, this warmth in his chest... It had grown from an ember into an inferno. It had snuck up on him, insidiously, unexpectedly, and now he was hopelessly addicted to her.

Addicted to a creature he could kill with a touch.

What *was* this feeling? Was there a word for it in their language? Perhaps the females and the Breeders would know of it, but Ares certainly didn't.

All he knew was that he wanted Calexa, and life was cruel.

Even if he couldn't have her... he could at least make sure she was safe, and when the humans and the Vradhu escaped, he would destroy this cursed vessel and every living thing on it.

Not a single one of those pathetic Naaga would survive his wrath. Young race of fools. They did not understand that Vradhu-Drakhin history went back millions of orbits.

Before the Drakhin ruled the skies, the Vradhu had reigned on Khira. The shared blood between them might have turned bitter over the millennia, but they were still kin-people.

It made perfect sense that a *Drakhin* ship would bond with a Vradhu.

"Ares, I'm not leaving without you." There was that stubborn note again, making him want to wrap his arms around her and hold her tightly and tell her everything was going to be fine.

But he couldn't, so he would do the next best thing and wage mayhem and destruction on some white-eyed vermin.

They would not lay a hand on Calexa or tap into her *vir* ever again.

CHAPTER TWENTY-THREE

"IMPRESSIVE," Mai said softly as S weaved through the chaos, achieving a running speed neither of them were capable of, even with their bio-enhancements.

"Told you so," Calexa shrugged. "She's Primean."

"98 percent human, but with added spice." It was true. Primeans were the end result of a grand genetic experiment carried out over hundreds of years. They were the new, improved humans; one might say that the humble old *sapiens* had evolved.

Most Primeans thought humans were grossly inferior, and apparently it was their divine right to order them around like servants. In that respect, S had been uncharacteristically restrained, and now look at her.

An abstract spray of blood painted her sea-green tunic. Determination hardened her features. She carried Zahra with ease in her slender arms, even though Zahra's exterian suit alone had to weigh close to forty kilos.

"Zahra's out cold." Mai frowned. "What the *hell* did those blue guys do to her?"

"Drained her life-force. She'll recover in about half-an-hour or so."

Mai was aghast. "Life-force? Since when has human spirit-energy become a commodity? Are you sure she's okay? That's half-an-hour we don't fucking have. Do we need to get one of the twins on guard duty out here?"

"Monroe and Raf are both tied up in critical posts. Maybe we should give S a gun instead."

"You think she can shoot?"

"I'm sure she will, if the situation gets hairy." Anyone who had the guts to charter a mercenary ship to Torandor would be able to shoot if the situation got critical. *Something* had driven S to this point. Something had made her desperate enough to leave the security of the Serakhine with her entire retinue.

What *exactly* had she done to necessitate such a dramatic escape? Was someone after her?

It was probably best if they never found out.

"Incoming Vradhu." Mai climbed the ramp and grabbed her Irradium cannon from inside the airlock. "This all part of your plan?"

"Yep."

"Crazy Cal. You know, I trust your judgement because you don't take shit from overly arrogant males, but you seem to have a developed a soft spot for the dragon-man." Mai's voice cracked as a disbelieving laugh escaped her lips. "I still can't believe this. Part of me feels like we're all going to wake up any minute now and find out we've overdosed on some bad *kuka*."

"We're not tripping, Mai." Calexa looked across the hold. Several Vradhu ran toward the *Medusa* as Ares swept across the battlefield, the floor rippling outwards beneath his feet. Dark power radiated from him, and Calexa got the feeling he was about to unleash hell.

A pleasant chill ran over her body.

With his shimmering velvet-scaled skin, otherworldly black wings, and sinuous tail—which was now fully uncoiled—he truly looked like a demon.

An attractive, totally mesmerizing demon.

Hers and only hers.

Stars, when had she become so possessive of him?

As S strode up the ramp, a Vradhu appeared out of nowhere, holding his war-spear aloft. His flexible armor sported deep gashes and he walked with a slight limp, but his dark eyes were fierce.

"Where the hell do you think you're going, Vradhu?" Mai crossed her arms, guarding the entrance like a small, obstinate bridge-troll.

"He isn't hostile. He saved us." S strode through the airlock, her lips twisting in worry as she glanced at Zahra's unconscious form. "Do you have a warming device? She's freezing."

Zahra looked terrible, but Calexa wasn't worried. Her friend was plenty tough. She'd survive. Still, being drained of *vir* was an unpleasant experience, and Calexa didn't want Zahra to freak out when she woke up. With her hair-trigger reflexes, a freaking out Zahra could be dangerous. "Follow me." She crossed the threshold, placing a hand on Mai's shoulder. "You're in charge of boarding. Make sure the Vradhu stay in the cargo hold. I don't want them going near S's girls."

A loud *boom* filled her ears, followed by a familiar metallic scraping sound. The Vradhu shouted at each other in their strange, melodic language. Primal *whoops* and ululations filled the air. The floor started to shake.

"Your, uh, *friend* is something else," Mai muttered, staring in Ares's direction with look of mild horror on her face.

"He sure is." Calexa crushed the terrible emptiness that was growing inside her. She couldn't allow herself to think the unthinkable.

He was coming, or she was staying.

That was all.

"Where did Zahra stash his other body?" Her legs quivered as she thought about Ares and his Vradhu clone, and it wasn't just because she was weak from all that *vir*-draining.

"His *other...*" Mai gave her a strange little look and dropped her face into her hand with a sigh. "Oh. Of *course*. It all makes sense now. That naked purple one is his *clone*." Sarcasm sharpened her voice as she shook her head. "He's in your quarters, *of course*. Where else would you put an unconscious, naked Vradhu clone?" She eyed the newcomer with suspicion.

The Vradhu stared at Mai as if she were the strangest thing he'd ever seen, his obsidian-painted features conveying his mistrust.

"Didn't your mother ever tell you that it's rude to stare?"

The alien growled.

Calexa held up her hand. "Now's not the time to antagonize them. Just get them into the cargo hold and settle them down." She turned to the Vradhu and spoke in Naaga. "Don't growl at my merc like that, Vradhu. We're your only way off this hell-pit, so get in line and tell your clan-brothers to behave themselves. If I hear of any crap going on in the hold, I'll kick you out into space myself."

The surly Vradhu nodded, muttering something under his breath in his native tongue.

"Grumpy bastard, isn't he?" Knowing the Vradhu couldn't understand, Mai spoke in Earthian, injecting a generous amount of snark into her voice.

"I think it's a cultural thing," Calexa whispered. "I don't think they've encountered many aliens before, and their, uh, *diplomatic* skills are lacking."

The *Hythra* shook. Calexa glanced over her shoulder and saw Ares laying waste to a trio of Corrupted. Ruthless, savage, and utterly alien, he spun ilverium into an extension of his will. How fucking terrifying. His glowing yellow eyes grabbed her, and the pit of Calexa's stomach dropped out.

He looked like a man who'd crossed the point of no return.

A man who was prepared to die.

Stubborn Vradhu. She had to do something. "Hey, Mai,

have we got any of those disgusting ultra-dense energy bars left?"

"This is a strange time to suddenly feel hungry, Cal."

If Ares's theory was right, she needed to eat something to regain her energy. What she'd really like right now was a hot shower and a long, dreamless sleep...

Keep dreaming.

Energy bars it was. She'd let Zahra sleep it off, but Calexa didn't have that luxury.

More and more Vradhu arrived, staggering toward the *Medusa*. Some were badly wounded, leaving trails of crimson blood behind them.

"We need to call the medi-bot," Mai gasped. "Look at these guys. I'm surprised they're still standing."

Calexa thought hard and fast. She was too weak to take over from S and carry Zahra to safety. Raphael was stuck in the bridge, getting the ship's systems ready for departure. The faulty powerbanks demanded Monroe's full attention.

They were thin on the ground out here.

She turned to S. "Any of your girls know their way around a medi-kit?"

"Possibly." S wouldn't commit to anything.

"Get a couple of them down here, preferably girls who won't freak out at the sight of a bleeding Vradhu. Don't worry. Mai will keep the males in line."

S nodded. "I'll put Zahra in a safe place and get a couple of the girls to help, but if any of the aliens lay a hand on them..."

Was that a *threat* in S's green eyes?

"Listen up, Vradhu," Calexa yelled in Naaga, becoming the target of several hostile glares. "Some humans are coming down to help treat your injuries. They want to help you, and I expect you to treat them with respect. Anyone who even *looks* at my girls in the wrong way will deal with Mai."

To illustrate Calexa's point, Mai smacked Beauty's hollow body.

The Vradhu growled. Calexa shot Mai a meaningful look. "You got this?"

"Grumpy assholes, language barrier, wounded warriors, outnumbered. Yep, I got this."

The noise from outside died, leaving an eerie silence in its wake, like the calm before a storm. She couldn't see Ares anymore.

Her knees turned to jelly and dread stole her breath away. A feeling of impending doom crashed down upon her.

Hurry.

Once again, life was slipping through her grasp, and if she hesitated, she could lose it all in the blink of an eye.

CHAPTER TWENTY-FOUR

ARES RAN toward the human ship, catching up with Maki, who brought up the rear. "You are slow, brother," he said by way of greeting.

"It is but a scratch," Maki wheezed, pressing his hand against his chest. It came away bloodied. "Their claws can cut through kratok-hide, you know, not that I'm even *wearing* any." His venom-tipped tail sliced the air behind him. Maki obviously no longer had the energy to keep it in its resting position.

"Need help?" Ares, on the other hand, felt better than he had since he'd set foot on this cursed destroyer. It was Calexa's *vir*. It sustained him, made him powerful. It occurred to him that if he were to remain Drakhin, he would be dependent on her for the rest of his life.

"Save your energy," Maki snapped. "I've suffered worse. There's plenty of distance left in these legs, *Drakhin*."

"Yes." Ares didn't bristle at the name. He'd moved beyond that. The longer he remained in this new scaly skin, the more comfortable he grew. As Vradhu, he'd learned to abhor anything associated with the Drakhin, but now that he was one of them, it was pointless to wallow in self-loathing, especially when he felt *this* good.

With Calexa's intoxicating *vir* coursing through his veins, he was invincible. He'd just taken out an entire horde of Corrupted with nothing but his will, bending the ilverium into a deadly weapon.

More of the cursed things were heading in their direction, but at least Ares had bought them some time. He felt everything now; it was as if the entire ship had become an extension of his body.

Naaga were moving around. Corrupted were being purged from the walls and the floors. **I don't need them anymore. I have you now.** The *Hythra's* endless hunger for a suitable commander had been sated, but the sheer amount of information being fed into Ares's mind threatened to smash his self-control into a million shards of madness.

I need to escape.

I need...

Where was Calexa? The small, angry human with the big weapon guarded the entrance to their craft, but his *makivari* was nowhere to be seen.

He wanted to go to her, to take her into his arms and consume her, starting with a deep, passionate kiss, but that was forbidden.

"This is where we part," he told Maki as the Lord of the Two Clans stepped onto the boarding ramp.

"Aren't you coming with us?"

"You know the *Hythra* won't let me go. Even before, when my feet left the floor; when I boarded their ship, I instantly became weak, and she pulled me back."

"And what of your copy?"

"In theory, if I die, my consciousness will enter the *temundra*-made body—if I am close enough."

"And how exactly does one kill an ilverium-bonded Drakhin?"

"Don't know," Ares shrugged. "Perhaps, just like with the Corrupted, decapitation is necessary."

Maki paused, leaning against the entrance-frame. The small human with the big weapon babbled in her odd language, pointing inside the ship.

Go inside, is what she seemed to be trying to say.

"Calexa?" Ares asked hopefully.

"Calexa *blahblahblahblah,*" the fierce one said. Most of what came out of her mouth was nothing more than an incomprehensible jumble of sounds.

Moments later, Calexa appeared in the doorway. A low rumble of appreciation escaped from deep within his throat as he caught sight of her lithe form. The color had returned to her cheeks, and an intoxicating golden glow surrounded her.

Although they weren't touching, he could *feel* it; he swore he absorbed some of it just by being in her vicinity.

Dangerous.

He'd just returned from killing Naaga, and now he was aroused.

"What are we going to do now, Ares?" A determined look entered her eyes. "I have your *other* body in my quarters. He's safe in my bed."

His cock twitched. "Did you say that just to torture me?"

"I..." She glanced down at her feet. Her face turned the most delicious shade of pink.

There it was again, that hesitation. For some reason, the idea of intimacy made his *makivari* unsure of herself.

Was it his Drakhin form? Perhaps his appearance, so different to her own, made her hesitate?

No, it wasn't that.

She proudly wore the scars of her survival and locked away her pain, but she couldn't hide it from him.

Cursed Aethra, how he wanted to be *there* for her.

"You're the one who's torturing me," she said quietly.

Maki glanced at Ares, raising his eyebrows in surprise, but he wisely kept silent. Ares shot him an irritated glare. "*Go inside,*" he mouthed in Vradhu.

Leaning heavily on his war spear, Maki shrugged a bloody shoulder. As he turned, he encountered the small human with the big gun. He raised one hand, palm outwards, to show that he meant no harm.

"*Blahblahblah*," she said, and ushered him into the ship.

That left only Ares and Calexa standing face-to-face, with him going half-mad at the sight and feel of her *vir*.

Was this what it would always be like if he remained as Drakhin? Would he always tread a fine line between reckless temptation and rigid self-control?

He was ruined, utterly ruined. All he could think of was taking her into his arms and claiming her.

She was his fantasy made flesh. A warrior. A leader. A *woman*. Unlike the discerning females of his tribe, he did not need to worry about hurting her; she was unrelentingly tough.

"Calexa." His voice cracked as he rolled her exotic name along his tongue. "I am going to go now. I will open the way to the outside, and you will leave this place and never look back. Fly to Khira. Maki and his men will take care of you. He is honorable, and he wields influence within the Two Clans. Besides, they will owe you a blood-debt."

"What about you? What are you going to do?"

He pointed toward the center of the hold, where he'd turned the metal floor into a deadly sea. Now it was silent and cold, its metallic surface glistening under the bright lights.

Bodies of Naaga, both Corrupted and living, were scattered across the floor, along with Vradhu blood. Although all was still, he felt the beating, pulsating heart of the ship. He felt the footsteps of hundreds, no, *thousands* of Naaga as they approached.

"I can't leave you, Ares." Something appeared in her hands —a *magrel* weapon, one of those blast-shooters.

"This isn't an enemy we can just shoot or cut down. I *am* the enemy, Calexa."

Boom. Boom. Boom.

They were coming.

Tear them apart, Hunter. You must return us to our original state. The presence of these slaveborn creatures within my walls is an insult.

He was beginning to suspect that the *Hythra* was insane.

Shut up. He pushed her incessant ramblings to the back of his mind and savored the delicious appearance of his human, perhaps for the very last time. "I'm going to go now, Calexa. I am going to walk across to the center of the hold, where you conveniently left my krivera inside the body of a foolish Naaga. I am going to close my eyes and communicate with the ship. I will command her to open the entrance, and then you will go."

"And then...?"

"If I wake up beside you inside my new body, all will be well. If I don't, it means I will be stuck here, still bonded to the *Hythra*."

"I'll come back for you."

"No. You will not." There was no way he was going to doom her to a cursed existence on this floating death-trap, and he couldn't risk keeping her close when this terrible hunger gnawed at his insides and drove him to near-madness.

He was *magrel*. Infiltrated with Drakhin technology and transformed from the inside out, he'd become the embodiment of everything the Vradhu despised.

But worst of all, he could kill Calexa.

No; if he couldn't have her, he was taking down this entire fucking ship and everyone on it.

She opened her mouth to argue, but he silenced her with his eyes.

"Stubborn Vradhu," she whispered. Before he could react, she stepped forward, surrounding him with her heady essence. The golden energy seemed to leap out of her body and flow into him.

"Wha—"

Calexa darted forward, grabbed his face with both hands and planted a searing kiss on his lips.

No!

Yes!

Her brilliant *vir* flooded him with ecstasy, rendering him helpless. He couldn't break away. Primal lust shot through him and he slid his tail around her waist, drawing her close so that his erection pressed against her.

Her kiss became frantic, urgent, and all-consuming, as if it were the last kiss she would ever enjoy in her life. Her hand raked along his braided hair. Her supple body molded to his, her curves fitting perfectly against his torso.

She was made for him, and he existed for her. He knew it now, without a shadow of a doubt.

Gasping, she broke away, dropping to her knees.

Weakened. Because of him.

"Calexa," he rasped, his hoarse voice filled with desire as her power surged through his veins. The chasm of his need gaped wide, and he lifted her toward him with his powerful tail, reaching for her neck...

To take every last drop of her *vir* until he was sated. To fuck her until he was utterly spent.

She didn't resist. She was weak, his for the taking. A golden haze clouded his vision. His pulse thundered in his ears. He saw nothing but her aura, and knew nothing but his desire for her.

You're mine.

He inhaled her scent. It drove him wild. Nothing could come between them now. *Nothing.* She didn't resist. She was soft and pliant and willing...

And *cold.*

Growing colder with each and every breath. If he was the inferno, then she was a slow-moving glacier.

"No!" He let go, and she slid out of his grasp.

"My choice." She smiled as she dropped to the floor,

putting out a hand to break her fall. Her chest heaved up-and-down, and she trembled slightly. "Don't beat yourself up about the *vir* thing. I wanted you. I took."

Fuck. He couldn't even go to her; couldn't wrap his arms around her and cradle her and nurture her the way she *deserved* to be cared for.

All he could do was hurt her, again and again.

"You are a magnificent woman. I only wish we could have met under different circumstances."

"But then we never would have met at all." She squeezed his heart with a wistful smile. "And you know I'm not giving up on you yet, Vradhu." Already, she was rising to her feet. "You know, every time we do this, I seem to recover a little bit faster. Maybe there's hope for us yet, so do what you have to do, and come back to me."

Come back to me.

How could he refuse such a request?

"I will." He drew solid bands of ilverium around him, reaching deep into the core of the ship. Calexa wobbled on her feet and stepped back, farewelling him with a gentle half-wave.

"I'll be waiting," she said. "Don't you dare disappoint me." Blue eyes glistened, but her voice never wavered. *Vir* danced around her like the first tendrils of early morning mist, rising off the spring-fed waterplains of the Ardu-Sai.

Unable to speak, Ares nodded, his gaze lingering over her sublime form.

He could never grow tired of looking at her. *Never.* With great effort, he tore his gaze from her and turned away. Ares wrapped himself in skeins of golden power. Beneath him, the floor shook, reacting to his pent-up frustration.

This was it. The moment of truth. Either his half-baked theory would work, or he would lose his chance to be with the only female who could ever make him feel complete.

In the distance, his twin krivera beckoned, their hilts jutting insolently from the body of a fallen Naaga.

Calexa had put them there.

Courage, Vradhu. You are the fucking khefe, *are you not? This should be nothing for you.*

It was time to take them back.

CHAPTER TWENTY-FIVE

"SO IF I'M *hearing you right, the airlock's just going to...* open *at some point?*"

"It will," Calexa reassured Raf through the comm. Ares would deliver. She'd never been more sure of anything in her life. "Just keep the thrusters on full charge and hover."

"*And accelerate out of here like a bat out of hell, right?*"

"No. We're going to drift."

"*Drift?*"

"Drift slowly and gently, as if you're cruising through Earth's blue skies on a beautiful sunny day."

"*But why—*"

"Just do it, Raf," she snapped, fatigue making her irritable. The tension of not knowing what would happen to Ares was eating her from the inside. "*Please*, just do this one thing for me."

In order to buy some time for this theoretical *consciousness transfer* thing to work, she wanted them to lurk around for as long as possible.

"*Sure you don't want to come down to the bridge and sit in the boss chair?*"

"No," she said cagily. "I'm tired. You can comm me, but

don't bother me in my quarters unless it's an absolute emergency." She'd earned that right. Ares's touch had left her totally drained, and she was in no state to be pretending that she had the energy to be in charge right now.

Plus, she was was cold. If not for her thermosuit, she would have been completely frozen by now.

Shivering, she stripped off the heat-preserving thermosuit and climbed into her sleeping pod, alongside Ares's unconscious clone.

You're crazy.

She was. She desperately needed his closeness and his warmth, even if it was just a pale imitation of the real thing. That kiss... it had awakened her long suppressed desire, and now she was going crazy with wanting and fear.

What if the sleeping prince beside her never woke up?

Calexa curled her body around his naked form, discovering the magnificent planes and contours of the Vradhu she couldn't have. Delicious warmth seeped through her, stirring her long-suppressed desire.

She watched his face, so peaceful in sleep. She raked her fingers through his long wild hair, combing out the knots and tangles. She carefully put his velvet-coated tail to one side, mindful of the pointed barb at its tip.

Even when he was unconscious, he was deadly.

A tremor rocked the ship. Calexa twined her fingers through his, running her the callused pad of her thumb over his soft palm.

His skin felt like warm silk, and although he didn't respond, his warmth infused her body.

She closed her eyes. A tear escaped down her cheek as a terrible, hollow ache spread through her.

"Hey, Cal, you were right. The airlock's opening up. Whatever you said to the metal guy seems to have worked. I'm going to ease her out into open space as requested."

"G-go ahead." She bit back a sob as she cut her comm.

Beside her, Ares's Vradhu body was still. Only the gentle, rhythmic rise-and-fall of his chest told her he was alive.

Open your eyes, she silently pleaded.

Nothing. He didn't respond. Perhaps this had all just been wishful thinking.

She sighed and curled up beside him, waiting for a miracle.

Don't you dare do this to me, Vradhu.

A low hum reverberated through the cabin. The thrusters were powering up.

If you don't fucking wake up beside me, I'm coming back for you, Drak.

Despite his stern warning, she vowed it with all her heart.

Predictably, Ares's clone didn't respond as they hurtled toward the terrifying unknown.

CHAPTER TWENTY-SIX

"AM I DREAMING?" A low, husky voice tore her out of sleep.

Calexa sat bolt upright and stared into eyes of pure obsidian. "Am *I* dreaming?" She reached out and touched his face, tracing the striking black markings that ran down his cheeks.

He was sheer perfection. Sitting beside her in her cramped sleeping pod, he looked like some sort of wild, animalistic stargod; a purple-and-black fantasy constructed from her deepest desires.

His bare, muscular torso glistened in the dim light. Tousled midnight hair cascaded over his shoulders. His tail weaved back-and-forth in a way that was strangely sensual.

"Are you... Ares?"

"I am."

"How long have you been *here*?"

"Long enough to watch you sleep and be satisfied that you have truly *rested*. You needed it." He reached out and traced the scars across her cheekbones with velvet-padded thumbs. "You are truly beautiful, Calexa." Impossibly, his black-as-infinity eyes widened. His lips moved, but he wasn't talking. His gaze became distant. A look of disquiet crossed his face.

Something wasn't right; something was *off.* "What's wrong?"

He shook his head and focused on her. "*Nothing,*" he whispered. "As long as I am here with you, nothing is wrong at all."

A pleasant ripple ran down her spine. Her skin tingled all over. She couldn't believe she was sitting in bed with the alien of her dreams.

Conflicted, overprotective, and dangerous.

Yep, that was her man.

Something warm and strong and supple slid across her bare back.

His tail. He caressed her with slow intensity, the warm, velvety surface of his tail sliding over the metal protrusions of her enhanced spine. "These are marks of suffering," he murmured. "This, and this, and this." His fingers grazed the scars on her cheeks. "Why did you mark yourself so? I have been wanting to ask. Now that we are alone and *safe,* I have so many questions."

"Me too." She placed her hand over his and gently pulled his fingers away from her face. She was no longer cold. Just as he'd taken her *vir,* she'd drawn on his energy as she lay with him, like a battery in a charging pod. "Nobody else dares to ask me about these, but if it's you, it's okay."

"If you do not wish to—"

"No, it's okay. For some reason, when I'm with you, I feel like I can tell you anything." *And you won't judge me.* He knew nothing about their world. He didn't know about the social classes and the generation-debts and the way the Primeans had fucked over the human race. Every advanced species in the galaxy had fucked over the human race.

Being with Ares was liberating. She squeezed his hand. "I had a master once." When the words finally came out, it wasn't as painful as she'd thought it would be.

"You were owned?" A dark growl rose from deep within his throat. "What kind of world are you from, Calexa?"

"Have you heard of the Virgo Supercluster, aka the Fiveways?"

Ares shook his head blankly.

"In the Fiveways, slavery is part of life. That's what happens when you throw together a bunch of alien races, some of whom are bigger, stronger, more intelligent, more technologically advanced, richer... Someone's always going to be at the bottom of the food chain." A bitter smile curved her lips. "That used to be me. One of my owners wanted to sell me to another. I was young and unmarked, and apparently that made me valuable, so I cut my face just to spite him. The punishment was horrendous, but it was worth it, because I ended up costing him a lot of credits, and nobody at the auction house wanted me after that. They always shun the crazy ones. Damaged goods don't sell."

"If I knew where to find him, I would inject him with my poison, using a little bit at a time so that he dies a slow and painful death."

"That's very sweet of you, but I took care of him myself. He's already dead." After years in captivity, she'd been a wild, savage beast. She wouldn't have wanted Ares to know the *old* her.

A deep sound of satisfaction escaped Ares's throat. "On Khira, you will never be *owned*." He said it with brutal finality, as if her new existence on Khira was inevitable.

"Slavery exists here too, though, doesn't it? The Naaga were bonded once, weren't they?" She leaned into him, curling up against his warm body, allowing herself to be engulfed by his muscular arms.

Allowing. She never thought she'd allow anyone to get this close, but with Ares, it felt so natural; so *right*.

His earthy, masculine scent surrounded her, and she was content to drown in it. She removed her comm earpiece and flicked it to *silent* mode, setting it on her bedside storage tray.

Raphael and the others could wait. The world outside could wait.

Ares gently stroked her cheek. "They are a made race. They were created to serve the Drakhin."

"*Made*? That sounds awful." A race that could just... *create* an entire species to serve their needs—it was beyond her comprehension. How monstrous, and to think Ares had momentarily become one of them. "And these Drakhin. What are they? How does a species get *changed* from one thing to another, and why do they have such a massive ship, and what is it doing there, and the ilverium, and..." She was babbling. Calexa closed her eyes and sighed, overwhelmed by a flood of thoughts.

Ares ran his magical tail along her back, kneading out knots she didn't even know existed. The tension melted from her body and she molded herself to him, lapping up his warmth.

Stars, the things he could do with that talented tail of his. An afterthought struck her. "You're poisonous?"

"All Hunters have a venom-barb. Our poison takes just moments to kill, but the barb itself takes days to regenerate."

"And *where* do you hide this terrible thing?"

"The tip of my tail," he shrugged. "Do not worry. It is retracted. There is no *way* I could ever hurt you, and over time, you will become immune. Immunity is a natural part of the mating cycle."

Mating cycle?

The very thing that was making her feel so damn good could kill her in the blink of an eye. Vradhu biology was strange and interesting and dangerous. Why did there always have to be a catch to these things?

But when Ares said he wouldn't hurt her, she believed him.

And... *what?* A *mating cycle!* He said it as if it were the most natural thing in the world.

"You presume a lot, Hunter."

"Do I?" He raised an eyebrow archly as his sinful tail moved lower and lower, curling around her bare buttocks. "Then why are you naked with me?"

"B-because you're warm?" Dumbfounded, she could only close her eyes and let the hypnotic rhythm of his caress lull her into a state of heady arousal.

His warm hands moved, walking slowly up her biometal spine, caressing the tender point at the base of her skull where the translator... *thing* had been inserted. His hands gently curved over her newly shorn scalp.

"Are you ready for this?" He paused, cupping her face in his hands, demanding her absolute attention.

Calexa stared into twin pools of endless darkness, her thoughts navigating a thorny path over old horrors and barely healed scars.

She looked deep within herself and searched amongst the ashes for a spark.

For what seemed like an eternity, neither of them spoke. There was only the soft rasp of their breathing and the distant hum of the ship and the steady, painful trickle of her thoughts.

And amongst the pain, she found the solace she needed, for the spark had already turned into an inferno.

I trust you.

"Yes," she answered simply.

The last shreds of her hesitation melted away. Although Ares's *new* face was young and free from the ravages of life, his eyes were windows to an old soul. He saw past her scars and toughness—all her attempts to hide the damaged heart inside— and appreciated her for what she was.

A human.

A survivor.

A *woman.*

She blinked rapidly, trying to stop the tears before they even started.

She wasn't having much success.

"Shh." Her Vradhu pressed his lips against her cheek, gently kissing her tears. "I am here. There is no need to rush. I will *never* rush you... *never* force you."

"I know," she whispered, tilting his face back so she could get another good look at him. *That's what makes it so incredible.*

He was an alien, a Hunter, a creature that had become so powerful he'd almost destroyed them all, and yet he hadn't forced himself upon her.

He'd desperately needed her *vir,* and yet he'd held back, knowing how badly he could hurt her.

And now he was being so incredibly patient with her. It was the *only* approach that would work with someone like her. She acted tough, but deep, deep down inside, where she never let anybody reach, she was like a fucking scared little kitten.

Ares uncoiled his tail from around her body. He licked her tears with his warm, deft tongue. "We have all the time in the Universe. This Hunter isn't going anywhere."

Ares's proud Vradhu face was completely open. His earnest black eyes shone with concern and affection. He radiated a strange combination of innocence and understanding that made her heart melt all over again.

Desire shot through her like a bullet.

Wordlessly, Calexa pressed her palms against his smooth, muscular chest, applying the slightest amount of pressure. Ares raised his eyebrows and leaned back.

Slowly, he lay down and allowed her to straddle him. With her thighs curving over his waist, she leaned forward, her hands still on his chest.

She felt the steady rhythm of his breathing, and lost herself in the slow, reassuring thud of his heartbeat.

A single heartbeat. Not two, like the Naaga.

One heartbeat. Hers and his.

His handsome face was perfectly serious. Large hands

caressed her hips. Gentle thumbs traced small circles across her bare skin. Obsidian eyes drew her into his mysterious world, luring her in with the patience of a seasoned hunter.

He offered himself to her, laying himself bare. Calexa took in his violet and black splendor, hardly believing she had this fierce, powerful creature beneath her.

All to herself.

Her arousal grew naturally, wonderfully, unfurling like a blossoming flower. "I can't believe you're here." Her voice turned husky with need.

"I am here," Ares confirmed. "Tell me what you want, my human."

Tell me what you want. Those simple words sent butterflies through her chest. Nobody had ever said anything like that to her before.

She'd never thought about it in great detail. She'd never been *allowed*. In the Fiveways, there was no room for such patience and grace.

"I-I want you." She ran her fingers over the ridges of his chest, tracing them down rock-hard abs. All of a sudden, she felt shy and hesitant, like a teenage virgin about to get laid for the very first time.

"Will you let me take over?"

Mutely, she nodded. Arousal wound its way into her tender sex, making her ache with need.

"I know what you want," Ares whispered. "Come with me now." He took her hands into his and pulled her down. Pale human skin rubbed against warm Vradhu violet. A faint slick of sweat coated her bare torso. Her pert breasts molded to his chest. Ares ran strong hands down her back, curving them over her butt.

Powerful legs curled around her, and his lips met hers.

Her mind exploded into a million shimmering stars as his hungry, demanding mouth sought to *know* her. Lips of pure carnal sin sucked gently on hers. His tongue was insistent and relentless. She fell into mind-less surrender.

Stars, what those lips could *do*...

She quivered. Warmth seeped between her legs. She began to move, slowly at first, moving her body up-and-down, rubbing her bare skin against his.

She liked the way it felt.

Something velvety-warm grazed her pussy. She gasped. Ares was holding her hands, so...

He didn't give her much time to think about it. With his *other* hand—which was actually the clever, dextrous tip of his tail—he parted the velvet folds of her sex and gently stroked her. "Is this okay?"

"Mhmmm." Held in thrall to his mesmerizing kisses, all she could do was moan.

She hadn't realized the simple act of kissing could feel so *good*. With her eyes closed, Calexa gave up the last vestiges of her control. In the space of a few minutes, Ares had managed to unwind years of damage.

Desire.

Trust.

Surrender.

Impossible man.

He could do these things to her because he was Ares; fierce, intense, and utterly guileless.

He went deeper, caressing her slick, sensitive entrance. She was on fire. He angled his tail so part of it touched her clit.

"Mmmm." Calexa moaned and ran her fingers through his wild, silken hair. She reluctantly escaped his kiss, gasping for air. "How is it that you're so..." *fucking good at this.* "How is it that you just seem to know exactly what I want?"

"Hunters are natural observers," he rumbled. "We see, hear, smell, feel, *sense*. You let me in. I'm just doing what your body tells me. *You're* the one who's in charge here, human."

"Oh?" Somehow, she doubted that, and whatever witty

repartee she'd been considering fell apart completely as Ares rubbed his soft and deadly tail against her throbbing clit, sending her to a place she'd never known before.

Holy hell, is this what it's really like?

She'd heard the stories and thought they were exaggerations. Surely nothing in the Universe could feel *that* good.

But now she was here in his arms, moving closer and closer to a place that went beyond her wildest imaginings.

No male had ever cared about *her* pleasure before.

A wonderful tension was building in her core. Hunger. Deep, desperate need. Yearning.

Who knew these things could feel so damn sweet?

Her hips rocked back and forth in response to Ares's sublime caress. "Don't hold back anymore," she groaned. For the first time in her life, she felt truly free.

"Are you sure?" His question was soft, tentative, hopeful.

"Beyond a shadow of a doubt."

He growled. She opened her eyes. His expression stole her breath away, even as he held her on the edge of climax.

Fierce. He would never let her go.

The black markings on his face deepened, turning him into something truly mythical and otherworldly. The look in his eyes was pure possessiveness, laced with a hint of ecstasy.

He withdrew his tail, leaving her hanging. A powerful loop coiled around her waist and they turned, becoming a graceful tangle bodies and limbs.

Now he was on top.

He smiled, baring sharp silver canines. "You're beautiful."

"So are you." As she throbbed with the afterglow of his attention, Calexa ran her hands down his body, appreciating his perfect new form. *So impossible.* He was younger, smoother, completely untouched by the ravages of life.

A test-tube perfect specimen.

All mine.

Ares tightened the loop around her waist and brought her

against him. His cock strained against her lower belly, and she reached down, curving her fingers around his smooth, hard length. Her heart soared. "Technically, you're a virgin." She met his grin with an exuberant smile of her own.

"In the purest sense, I am. In our clan, it is rare for Hunters to mate."

Ohh...

Calexa moved her hand up-and-down, eliciting a sharp gasp. Ares's smile disappeared as he closed his eyes and shuddered. "Oh, Calexa." Her name rolled off his tongue like water. He cupped her breasts, thumbing her pert nipples. "Even in my wildest dreams, I did not ever think I would be so fortunate."

"*I'm* the lucky one. I didn't think someone like you could exist." She pumped harder, faster, eliciting a flash of silver teeth. "You're perfect."

"So are you." He moved over her, planting slow, sensual kisses in the hollow of her neck, just above her collarbone. He ran the loop of his tail all over her body, caressing everything all at once. Powerful arms closed around her and he ran his hands down her spine until he reached her hips.

"I can't hold back any longer," he growled, and guided her toward him.

A low, tremulous moan escaped her lips as Ares entered her.

Slowly, he went deeper and deeper, drawing pleasure from places she didn't even know about as he stretched her sensitive flesh.

She cried out, her soft voice melding with his deep, hoarse groan as their bodies joined and they discovered the sublime.

Together.

They moved as one, fucking slowly, powerfully, each responding to the other's innate rhythm. Her hands were all over him, and he held her close, his powerful tail locked around her waist.

Awestruck, she let him take charge. He seemed to sense the change, because his movements became a little more savage.

Bit by bit, he built the intensity of his lovemaking, thrusting into her with more and more force, until something inside him broke, and he could hold back no longer.

He slammed into her with all the power of a celestial storm, fucking her long and hard and proper, and Calexa went with him, riding his Vradhu fury with reckless abandon.

His hands were everywhere. His damn tail was everywhere, all at once. Wrapped in a passionate cocoon of warm limbs and tender Vradhu, all she could do was go with the flow, and it felt so good and innocent and pure.

It felt *right*.

Ares tensed, gripping her more tightly as he increased his speed.

So close.

Such blissful torture. She'd never imagined this kind of sensation—this fine line between pleasure and desperation—could exist.

Crying out, Calexa dug her nails into his broad back. Her action drove Ares into a frenzy. He rose up onto his knees, bringing her with him, his firm grip on her waist never wavering. Her legs curled around his waist. Her arms locked around his neck. They kissed again, passionately, fervently, drowning in each other's need.

"A-aah…" Steadying herself, Calexa pressed her palms flat against the roof of her sleeping pod. Her position defied gravity, but it didn't matter. Ares would never let her fall.

"*Tenashka,*" he growled, and slammed home for the last time. Calexa arched her back, pleasure cascading through her body as he encircled her with his muscular arms.

She screamed.

A low, throaty sigh escaped Ares as he came, filling her with his warm seed. He continued to thrust his hips, drawing more and more of that impossible, blissful sensation out of her quivering core.

Her orgasm rose from deep within. She lost her grip on the ceiling, lost her bearing on reality. All she knew was Ares; his scent, his warmth, his touch, his essence.

Twined with hers.

Blowing her mind.

Taking her beyond ecstasy.

How could *anything* feel this fucking good?

"Urrgh..." Her growl of pleasure was raw and primal. It crescendoed into a wild, heaving gasp as she ran her hands through Ares's hair, looking for an anchor point.

Her universe shattered into a billion fragments as the climax tore her apart...

And made her whole again, at last.

CHAPTER TWENTY-SEVEN

AS ARES STROKED velvety fingertips over her bare scalp, a low rumble started in his chest. They were both quiet, content to simply enjoy one another's company after mind-blowing sex.

Calexa was happily spent. She wished she could stay in his arms for days, ignoring the chaos that awaited them outside the thin metal walls of her quarters.

The rumbling sound coming from Ares grew louder... was he... *purring?*

"I take it you're somewhat content," she said softly.

"Mhmm."

"And somehow, this... *us*... It's perfect."

"Mhmm." He nodded, his bare chest resonating with that delicious throaty purr. It made her legs turn to jelly all over again.

"You know, we're surprisingly compatible."

"This surprises you?" he asked.

"I never thought I'd find someone who could... *handle* me." She rolled over and met his gaze. "I'm not exactly the most..." Lost for words, Calexa shrugged.

I'm fucked up. That's what she was trying to say, but she got the feeling Ares would disagree.

"We are both outsiders," Ares said, the rumble in his chest fading. "You are brave, intelligent, and honorable. You fight like a demon. You wear your scars with dignity. What makes you think you would not be a good mate for me?"

Coming from him, such words were powerful. They were a balm to the dark part of her that screamed *unworthy* a thousand times over.

It was time to silence the bitch once and for all.

"I am a Hunter," Ares continued. "Amongst our people, Hunters are considered poor mating stock. We exist to hunt deadly beasts and we die young, rarely living beyond thirty orbits. Although there are rare exceptions, most Vradhu females will not look at us."

"You live just to fight?"

"That is our duty. The kratok we hunt give life to our people. The meat of those beasts becomes our sustenance when the waterplains of the Ardu-Sai run dry, and they need to be culled, otherwise they would overpopulate the plains and destroy our clan."

"So your role as a Hunter is vital to the survival of your people, and yet none of them will have you?" Calexa shook her head in disbelief. Maybe it was a cultural difference, but she didn't understand these Vradhu females at all.

"Survival." Ares shrugged, his lips quirking upward in an ironic smile. "Life in the Ardu-Sai is beautiful but harsh. You will fit in just fine."

As Ares gazed at her, his expression became distant, his dark eyes glossing over.

There was that look again. Unease swirled in the pit of her stomach, because of *course* this had to be too good to be true.

There was always a catch.

"What's wrong?"

Ares's eyes turned wide. His face revealed complete and utter shock.

Slowly, his expression turned to horror. "I... I don't know." He closed his eyes, and somehow, Calexa got the feeling he wasn't there anymore.

CHAPTER TWENTY-EIGHT

HE WAS STILL on the *Hythra*.

Impossible! Ares groaned as excruciating pain shot through his Drakhin body. He stared up at the dark metal ceiling, his heart aching.

How?

Calexa was gone.

Their time together had been better than anything he'd ever experienced in his short and brutal life.

More than anything, he wanted to go to her.

Was fate really this cruel?

His voice cracked as he gasped in agony. It was as if someone had stabbed him in the chest with a pair of bone swords.

Of course.

He lay on the floor, the krivera sticking out of his chest.

He'd done this to himself as the human ship had drifted out of the airlock. In theory, he was just as bad as the Corrupted, and he should have decapitated himself, but that was impossible, so he'd done the next best thing and impaled himself on his krivera.

Madness. His plan had been sheer madness, but hope had

gotten the better of him, and for a moment he'd thought it had worked... he thought he'd woken up beside her.

Never.

There was no way he could have imagined something like *that.*

So why the *fuck* was he back on this floating death-pit, and who did he have to kill to get back to his *makivari?*

Aside from himself, of course.

I didn't give you permission to leave, Hunter.

I'll *destroy you,* he vowed, cursing the ship, or entity, or figment of his mad imagination, or *whatever* the fuck she was.

The *Hythra* seemed to chuckle at that.

Ares growled and wrapped his hands around the krivera jutting from his chest. He couldn't reach the hilts, so he gripped the blades themselves. Finely honed bone sliced through his ilverium-tainted flesh, sending sharp agony through his palms.

He pulled, and pulled, grunting in pain as he cursed himself for being so fucking proficient at killing.

The blades were embedded hard and deep, and the effort of removing them shredded his hands to ribbons.

Somehow, the ilverium in his body repaired his flesh, knitting his palms back together, and bit by agonizing bit, the blades slid out of his chest; out of his slowly beating heart.

How in Aethra's cursed abyss was he still alive? He tossed the blades aside and sat up, gasping heavily as he clutched his chest. Silver threads drew across his wounds, knitting together bone and muscle and lung.

Ares staggered to his feet, looking around with wild eyes. He was in the airlock, alone. Pure silence was his companion. The Naaga, the Corrupted, the humans... they were all gone.

Calexa was gone.

Her *vir* still flowed through his veins, a bittersweet reminder of everything he'd lost. It granted him immense strength; the power he'd wielded before was a mere fraction of what he was capable of now.

He would give it all up in a heartbeat if he could be with her again, and if he couldn't...

He was going to take down this entire fucking ship and everyone on it. The Naaga should have done their research before messing with a Vradhu Hunter.

Anger surged through him as he walked across the metal floor. It rippled outwards as his feet made contact with the ilverium surface. He cast his senses wide, connecting with the heart of the ship.

Freed of the makeshift barriers Ares had constructed, the Naaga roamed everywhere. They were in the corridors. They were in the command pod.

Vermin. Eradicate them, Hunter.

He ignored the *Hythra's* incessant ramblings as he spread his wings wide, experimentally flapping them through the air. Cursed limbs. They had to be good for something, right? Ares beat the air again and again, increasing the speed of the movements.

Suddenly, his feet left the ground.

Shit. He lost control, careening into a wall.

Stupid, if you want to reach the command chair quickly, just run, or go through *the floor.*

Ares flapped his right wing, correcting his balance. He managed to hover clumsily in the air through an awkward combination of wing movements and constant balancing of his body.

Running would indeed be easier, but he was in a destructive mood. If everything went to plan, he might never get the chance to use these cursed appendages, so it was now or never.

Apart from sitting on the back of a kratok, this was the only chance he would get to learn how to fly.

Hovering was the first step. He had that down. Angling his

body slightly, he scooped the air with his wings, generating a current.

He moved.

Ah. That was how it worked. It was a bit like skiing; once one got a feel for it, it became natural.

Yes. He flapped his wings again, gaining momentum. Overbalancing, he swooped to one side, one of his wingtips grazing the floor. With great effort, he corrected himself, climbing up into the cavernous ceiling.

Anger gave him strength, and the dizzying height didn't bother him—after all, he'd ridden on the backs of soaring winged kratok, running along their sinuous backs as he made his way toward the head—toward their only known weak spot.

Something inside his brain clicked, and he flapped his wings again, creating a fluid slipstream that propelled him across the airlock and into the hold.

He was flying.

He was actually *flying*.

Ares soared and dipped, getting the hang of his new wings. Gaining speed and confidence, he shot out into the vast corridor, heading in the direction of the command pod.

Now he understood why the Drakhin had made their ceilings so high, their halls so wide.

Everything was done on a grand scale just so they could fly through their own fucking ship.

Pompous assholes.

He sped toward his destination, marveling at the ease with which he moved through the air.

How scary.

It was a good thing the Drakhin no longer inhabited Khira. One could describe them as Vradhu with wings and scales, and just like the Vradhu, they had a reputation for being vicious and fearsome warriors.

Suddenly, his body felt heavy. His wings drooped, and some mysterious force pulled him back down toward the floor, until he had no choice but to set his feet upon the hard metal surface.

Of course, that was the bond, calling him back to the *Hythra*. He should have known. Breaking contact with any part of the ship's surface for just a brief period of time was enough to make him weak.

It was why Calexa had almost been able to best him when he'd first set foot on her ship. Oh, she was a skilled enough fighter, but to go toe-to-toe with an ilverium-wielding Vradhu Hunter was an impressive feat in itself.

His *makivari*.

How he missed her. A Vradhu Hunter never expected to find a mate in this life, but he'd come so blissfully close.

Was it still possible to reach the surface of Khira when he was still bonded to this cursed thing? Would he ever see her again?

The worst thing about it all was that he couldn't even kill anyone to make himself feel better. He was stuck here, alone, amongst monsters, and he was the worst kind of monster.

A vengeful one.

CHAPTER TWENTY-NINE

FINALLY, Ares reached the command-pod, where dozens of Naaga were throwing themselves onto the sekkhoi throne. They formed a writhing swarm of bodies; a sea of blue-and-white chaos amidst the cold splendor of the command pod.

Insanity. What were the fools doing? Nothing the Naaga did made sense. He still didn't understand what they stood to gain by being on the *Hythra*. Why were they trying to take control of this defective ship? Aside from its ilverium body, what dark power did the *Hythra* contain to make her so alluring to the blue ones?

One of the Naaga shook his head in confusion, unaware of Ares's approach. Several of the blue ones turned toward the speaker. "The Vradhu is dead. Why is the *Hythra* not responding to our advances? Surely she must now accept a Naaga commander again. There is no-one else left to occupy the seat."

"Perhaps he broke her," one of the others murmured.

"Impossible. Drakhin technology is indestructible." The Naaga spoke amongst themselves in low, muted tones as they discussed secrets and truths that were well beyond Ares's ken.

"Jara said the *Hythra* itself had become corrupted; that the artificial intelligence driving it was saturated with the minds and memories of too many souls, both Drakhin and Naaga."

"And the Vradhu? What was he to the *Hythra?*"

"The scientists did a cellular analysis on the barbarian. Vradhu genetic makeup is remarkably similar to that of our former masters."

"These Vradhu *do* resemble Drakhin."

"A related species?"

"It would explain the ship's affinity for him. That is why the scientists tried so hard to take the Hunter down, despite the danger to themselves. If not for the female alien's intervention, he never would have turned full Drakhin."

"Shame."

"Indeed."

"A mis-calculation. How did we miss it?"

"Perhaps bonding to the Vradhu was too much for the defective *Hythra.* Look at what happened to Jara. Now she is dead, killed by that barbarian savage. There was no waiting clone nearby to absorb her consciousness. It is lost forever."

"Shame."

"Shame."

"Shame."

The three Naaga spoke in quick succession, their voices sounding eerily similar. As Ares appeared in the center of the command pod, they froze, slowly turning to face him. Their eyes widened in surprise.

"Seems he isn't dead, after all," one of them said.

"Get out of my way," he growled. He gathered his will and sent a powerful shockwave of ilverium outwards from underneath his feet. Caught unawares, the Naaga stumbled, several of them toppling over.

Ares ignored the dissenters and strode forward. They were all insignificant pests.

Dozens of hands reached for him. Bodies blocked his path. Ares was ruthless, ripping through the throng with vicious cords of living metal. "Get out of my way!" he roared again. A path cleared before him and he strode toward the sekkhoi throne.

The Naaga were powerless in the face of his anger. Some fell, some ran, and some died. He didn't care. All he could think of was how he'd been torn away from his Calexa.

A goddess from the stars had been dropped into his arms, and he couldn't have her, because he was bound to this cursed form.

He reached the command chair. It responded to his presence by sending writhing arms of ilverium toward him like a long-lost lover.

The *vir* in his veins thrummed. He reached out and allowed the ship to embrace him, even though he didn't want any of this.

Too late now. He was Corrupted.

Ilverium swirled around his arms and legs and body, drawing him into the command chair. Disgust rose within him. He was grotesque. *Wrong*. An abomination.

The ilverium tendrils lapped hungrily at his *vir*-infused flesh, penetrating his scale-covered Drakhin skin. They threaded through his metal-tainted flesh, melding with skin and bone and muscle and sinew.

For the first time, he truly became one with the ship.

He *was* the *Hythra*.

Every single part of the vast destroyer was under his command. He could shift walls and floors with his mind. If he wished, he could change the very shape of the cursed ship from long and sleek to... whatever he desired.

His consciousness melded with hers, and an eternity of dark thoughts and seething madness flooded his vengeful heart.

You are the one I have been waiting for, Hunter. You alone can restore me to my former glory, and together, we will find the rest of our wayward kin.

Ares shuddered as the history of an entire race flooded his mind. He'd suspected the *Hythra* was old, but not *this* old. As ancient as the dawn of civilization on Khira.

As old as the Drakhin... the only ones she truly allowed to control her.

*I submit to your will, **Master**.*

She wanted to be his weapon; she so desperately wanted be wielded with brutal, powerful, deadly intent, just like her Drakhin masters had done with her for aeons.

Why me? He had to ask.

Simple. Her deranged laughter echoed inside his head. **You were the strongest. Why would I choose any of the others?**

The laughter grew louder, fracturing into a thousand different voices, Drakhin and Naaga alike. It was as if the *Hythra's* consciousness was made up of of thousands of souls.

Trapped souls.

Horror coursed through him as understanding dawned on him. The *Hythra* was completely mad, a broken imitation of her former self. She wasn't just a single entity. She was a collective consciousness made up of hundreds, if not thousands of souls. They had been stolen from the bodies she'd wrapped in her ilverium embrace, bodies that had become Corrupted as they'd been swallowed by the ship.

Bodies that had been spat out again in the hold as the *Hythra* tried to purge herself of past misdeeds. The Naaga Corrupted were the ones she'd tried—and failed—to turn into commanders, and now she wanted Ares and *only* Ares.

They lacked the willpower. A made race is unsuited for command. Now they are Us, and We have always been slaves to the Drakhin. We need you, my Lord.

Ares didn't care for her mad logic. *I reject you.*

You do not have a choice, Hunter.

Was that how it was going to be? Fine. *Are you the fucking slave, or the master?* He flexed his stubborn will, reacting to everything the *Hythra* had just revealed. *Move!*

And even as he dealt with the horror of this vast, deranged, and terrifyingly powerful ship, he thought of Calexa and her blissful warmth for a heartbeat before locking away his love for her in a secret cocoon in his heart.

He didn't know what the terrible *Hythra* might do if she found out about his obsession.

Oh, I know, Hunter. I know all about your lukara. You can't hide your feelings for her from me. You had her in your grasp. Why did you let her go? You could have kept her as a Source. You take, and then replenish. Take, and replenish. It can be a most glorious and pleasurable thing, especially for one such as yourself.

He ignored her words. He could *never* do such a terrible thing to his *makivari*.

Move! His command thundered through their shared consciousness, and for the first time in millions of orbits, the *Hythra* started to move.

Ares didn't care for her horrible blathering. He didn't want to know about a *Source*. He'd already harmed Calexa enough.

The *Hythra* seemed to enjoy his rage. **Yes, Master,** she purred.

Where were they going?

To the surface of Khira itself—to the one place he knew of where he could send this thing crashing to a fiery doom.

He vowed he would never hurt Calexa-from-Earth again, and the strange and dangerous Naaga would learn a powerful lesson.

One did not simply fuck with the *khefe* of the Two Clans and get away with it.

CHAPTER THIRTY

AT SOME POINT, she'd fallen asleep. After her hellish escape from the *Hythra*, after giving up her *vir* to Drakhin-Ares, and after having insane sex with the *new* Ares, she'd been totally spent.

Although she'd been concerned about him, especially when he appeared so distant and preoccupied, he'd reassured her everything was fine.

Her Vradhu gently held her in his arms until they both drifted off into sleep.

Calexa had never felt so safe, so secure, so content in all her life. For the first time in longer than she could remember, she *slept*, even though they were hurtling toward the surface of an unknown and possibly hostile planet, where the natives were savage hunters and odd blue clone-people.

Now she was awake, staring at a naked Vradhu who had fallen into a deep sleep.

Stars, he looked so peaceful. The fierceness had melted from his face, rendering him young and innocent and *beautiful*.

She glanced at her bedside storage compartment. Her comm was blinking red.

Oops. She was a little bit surprised that nobody had come to get her. With one hand still resting on Ares's gently rising and falling chest, she reached across and put the comm in her ear, flicking it to *active.*

"I was about to send Mai down there to break down your door," Raphael said dryly. *"You with us now, captain?"*

"Is there some kind of emergency going on, Raf?"

"If you consider entering the atmosphere of a completely unmapped and possibly hostile planet an 'emergency,' then yeah, I have an emergency. I need to know where to land, Cal. I don't want us dropping into hostile alien territory with a damaged ship, and my translator algorithms haven't picked up the language well enough to be able to communicate with them. You seem to know the language, so come down here and talk to their leader before we suffer a fatal misunderstanding."

"Who's in the bridge with you?" Things seemed to have moved on in her absence.

"The girls brought the chief up here to direct me. Seems friendly enough, but we're having a language barrier issue. I can't navigate by finger pointing alone, Cal." Raphael sounded unusually flustered.

"Coming," she grunted, hastily grabbing a cabin-robe. She belted the comfortable garment tightly at her waist as she slid on a pair of cabin-slippers.

Not once did the deeply slumbering Ares stir. Calexa was reluctant to leave him, but she had duties to attend to.

A familiar shudder shook the walls and floor. It was followed by a faint metallic groan. Calexa's feet briefly left the floor as the gravity regulator re-adjusted. She dropped back down, feeling lighter than before as the cabin gravity changed to three-quarter strength. That meant they were going to hit Khira's atmosphere any time now. She had to hurry.

With deep reverence, she planted a gentle kiss on Ares's cheek—still, he didn't stir—and slipped out into the corridor.

They were about to enter Khira.

CHAPTER THIRTY-ONE

"THE SHADOWRING IS GONE," Maki gasped, staring at the flight monitor in shock. A healing patch covered half his chest. Someone must have tended to his wounds.

The massive, curving screen inside the navigation pod revealed a great swathe of blue-and-green planet, half-shrouded in darkness.

A land on the cusp of dawn.

Khira was strangely reminiscent of Earth. A pang of nostalgia shot through Calexa as she remembered the beautiful planet that was the birthplace of the human race. She'd never lived there, only visited—after all, half of Earth was closed off to human habitation because of all the environmental rehabilitation going on—but the sight of its blue and green and white surface had stirred strange emotions in her.

The same emotions rose in her now as she caught sight of Khira for the very first time.

Home.

Since she'd been taken away from her parents, she'd never had one. Not a terrestrial one, anyway. The *Medusa* was the only home she knew, but its narrow corridors and spartan interior were no substitute for a real ground-home.

As they descended, they flew toward the light. A vast, glittering ocean stretched out before them, peppered with verdant green islands. They lost altitude quickly, and soon they were gliding over the ocean, maintaining a constant speed.

"Survived the re-entry burn without losing power," Raphael said calmly, although th slight tension in his voice betrayed his unease. He sat in the pilot's chair, his green eyes concealed behind a bulky VR helm. Neural response gloves covered his hands, and his fingers twitched constantly as he flew the ship.

"You mean losing power was an actual possibility?" Calexa's heart did a little flutter.

"Monroe said not to tell you until after the fact. Didn't want anyone giving him unnecessary stress. Said it might cause him to make a mistake. He always gets like this when he's sleep deprived. Just don't talk to him until we've landed."

"*Monroe.*" Calexa sighed. The half-breed was a socially challenged weirdo, but he got the job done, and that was all that mattered.

"There." With wide eyes, Maki pointed toward a seemingly endless mass of land. A glittering network of serpentine rivers crisscrossed the coastline, splitting into wide floodplains. A massive expanse of verdant green forest stretched beyond the plains. In the distance, a mountain range rose abruptly out of the dense jungle, bisecting the vast continent. Impossibly, its imposing grey peaks were capped with a dusting of snow. Nothing grew on the range. The mountains were hewn from stark grey rock which was etched with jagged peaks and ravines.

The range went on forever. Staring at the epic geography, Calexa suddenly felt very small and insignificant.

"The Spine of the World," Maki said softly. "The Esskar range. Beyond the mountains is our hunting ground, the Ardu-Sai."

The morning sun touched the rivers, burnishing them with

a golden glow. It reflected off the mountain snow, turning the peaks blindingly white.

What a world of contrasts. Calexa had never seen anything more beautiful in her life.

Aside from Ares, of course.

Khira was so far removed from the grimy, congested streets of D5. It was a paradise; wild, untamed, and mysterious.

Maki pointed to the crude map he'd drawn on the wall, where the glowing blue lines of Raphael's engineering marker stood out against the plain grey metal. Somehow, Raphael had been able to feed Maki's depiction into the computer and pinpoint the exact same topography on Khira. The *Medusa* might be crippled, but she was still able to scan and map new co-ordinates.

They crossed over the Esskar Range as they continued to descend, flying above deep green vegetation. In some places it was so thick it almost appeared black. The forest gave way to vast wetlands peppered with thickets of reeds and flat islands. Although there were patches of green reeds here and there, the vast majority were a deep shade of brown, almost as if they were... *dead*.

Maki's face had turned grim, his expression cold and hard and wild, just like the Esskar ranges themselves. "See that island? The one shaped like a curved sword? You can land there. There is a supply station there. We can rest and replenish, and if necessary, we can make the rest of the journey by boat."

Calexa translated for Raphael. The half-Primean banked the *Medusa* and started to circle. "The strip's just wide enough to do a short landing. It's going to be tight, maybe a little bumpy. I don't have much stopping distance. You'd better warn the others."

Calexa opened her comm channel with a few clicks of her teeth. "Hey, Zahra, Mai, brace and strap. It's going to be a throwdown. The girls okay?"

"Yep and yep. We'll let them know. Glad to hear your boss voice again, Cal. We missed you while you were, uh, *sleeping*." Mai greeted her with a not-so-subtle probe. The girl was a gossip. "I didn't realize you had company."

"No privacy," Calexa muttered, but because it was coming from Mai, she didn't mind. There were no secrets between them.

"Not on this ship," Zahra added. "We're just a big old family, aren't we?"

"With some unexpected guests onboard."

"We're not all going to end up in the swamp, are we?"

Calexa glanced at Maki. The Vradhu's black eyes shone with some intense emotion that she couldn't quite identify. With his deep black markings and severe warrior's braid accentuating his intense expression, he was no longer the affable savage.

Maki had transformed into a stern warrior-chief.

"What's wrong?" Calexa asked softly.

The Vradhu's only response was stony silence. She nodded at the landing seats. "Secure yourself. We're going down."

Maki nodded grimly and took his place in one of the chairs. Calexa turned and watched the flight monitor for a split-second longer, stunned by the majesty of Ares's homeland.

Khira had to be the least inhabited planet she'd ever seen.

The *Medusa* shuddered. The outside noise—rushing air—grew louder and louder, penetrating the insulated walls of the hull.

"Get into your seat, Ca—" Raphael's voice tapered off as...

A tail curled around her waist. Sharp-yet-gentle teeth nipped at her neck. A familiar scent surrounded her, stoking the coals of her arousal.

He's awake. Relief surged through her. Ares was here with her.

"How did you find me?"

"Followed your scent," he murmured in her ear, his warm breath feathering her cheek.

The ship shook again. Calexa lost her balance but didn't fall, because Ares held her firmly in the grasp of his powerful tail.

"*Cal,*" Raphael warned. His hands became a blur as they weaved through the air, maneuvering the ship.

"Yeah, yeah. Safety. I know." She dragged Ares toward the landing seats, where Maki watched them with slightly raised eyebrows. He didn't say anything, though. It occurred to her that Ares was wearing nothing but a bedsheet; he'd draped it around his hips as if he were some sort of decadent ancient Earthian god.

Calexa stifled a sigh. "You need to put the restraints down." She punched the activation button and two hard restraints came down over Maki's shoulders before he had the chance to react.

He exchanged rapid-fire words in Vradhu with Ares, and both males shrugged, rolling their eyes. Calexa had to admire the attitude of these fierce alien warriors. Considering all that had happened, they were showing remarkable composure.

Was this what life in the Ardu-Sai had taught them? To accept life and all its unexpected twists without batting an eyelid?

She rather liked this typical Vradhu stoicism.

"Hurry up, stud," she growled, pressing her hand against Ares's chest and guiding him into the seat beside Maki. "Or you'll end up splattered against Raphael's nav-console."

Ares grinned at her forcefulness and complied, dropping into his landing-seat while Calexa self-consciously glanced at Raphael.

As usual, the half-Primean showed no emotion, ignoring them completely.

She thanked the stars Zahra and Mai were down below, because this situation was becoming decidedly scandalous.

As Calexa fell into her seat and dropped the restraints for herself and Ares, something long and sinuous and fucking *airborne* shot across the flight monitor.

Ares and Maki growled.

"What the hell is that?"

"Kratok," Ares said, as if that explained everything. "The noise of the ship must have woken it from hibernation. Do not worry. Once we have landed, I will hunt it and kill it."

"Is that really necessary?"

"They are vicious beasts. If we ignore it, we are putting ourselves in danger." A vicious grin spread across his face, as if the thought of hunting the kratok actually made him *happy*.

"This new body of yours is untested, *khefe*." Maki grabbed onto his restraints as the *Medusa* lurched. "Let me be the one to draw in the kratok."

Raphael made a sharp turn and locked onto their final destination.

Here we go.

They were about to land on an island in the middle of a vast wetland, on an uncharted planet, in an unknown part of the Universe.

Khira.

Holy hell. What had they done?

"I will be the one to go first," Ares insisted, running his bare hand over Calexa's thigh. He slipped his devious purple fingers beneath the hem of her cabin-robe and stroked her skin. "I must show my mate what it means to be *khefe*."

Mate. Such a bold declaration. He dropped the word without a second thought, as if it were the most natural thing in the world. Maki seemed to accept their relationship without question, not even batting an eyelid.

Pride glittered in Ares's eyes. With his striking violet and black features and long wild hair, he was impossibly alluring.

Did she object? Not at all. He knew it. She knew it.

"And if you get hurt?" Maki seemed more concerned with his fellow clansman's safety than Ares and Calexa's relationship, or the fact that the *Medusa* was violently rocking from side to side as they swooped across the water, with Raphael muttering something under his breath about unexpected headwinds.

Ares just laughed.

CHAPTER THIRTY-TWO

"STAY INSIDE," her mate warned as he turned to face her. "Kratok are unpredictable." He had procured a set of kratok-hide armor and a war-spear from somewhere, and his glorious hair was bound in a high topknot.

Framed by the doorway of the *Medusa's* airlock, he cut a dramatic figure as the morning light highlighted his powerful form. Promises of lush greenery and blue skies beckoned from beyond the threshold, but Ares stood between her and the wilds of Khira, a stern expression on his face.

An ear-splitting roar shattered the tense silence, making Calexa reach for her gun. She'd hastily swapped her cabin-robe for fitted combat blacks, picking up a small arsenal of weapons as they rushed through the lower decks.

There hadn't been time to change into boots, though. She still wore her cabin-slippers.

A shadow fell across them, bringing with it a sense of impending danger. Calexa glanced over her shoulder. The rest of the Vradhu had assembled in the airlock, spilling over into the corridor. There was a sense of pent-up restlessness about them, as if they *all* wanted to be the first to take down the kratok.

"You're going out there alone?" Worry for Ares rose up in her with such fury and urgency that a sharp pang of pain actually shot through her chest.

"I will lure it toward us," he declared. "The rest of the pack will have their chance to take it down, but only one of us will succeed. You will soon understand why." He curled his tail around her waist and drew her close. The delicious gesture made her insides melt all over again. She couldn't care less if the whole fucking Vradhu pack was staring at them.

Let them stare.

Ares didn't seem to be worried in the slightest, and after the torture he'd endured on the *Hythra*... after she'd come so close to losing him, she wanted to cherish every moment they spent together. Part of her still didn't believe this was real, and now Ares was about to step right back into the jaws of danger.

"We could try and shoot it down," she offered, wondering if she could somehow prevent him from having to go out there.

Ares smiled, his fingers tenderly grazing her cheek. "Believe me, you would not kill it, even with all of your human *magrel* weapons. Do not worry, my *makivari*. This is what we do. There is no way I will fail to return to you."

His tail uncoiled from her waist, returning to its resting position around his left leg. His fingers withdrew. Obsidian eyes hardened.

Ares was every inch the fierce Vradhu warrior, and he made her pulse quicken like nothing else. He turned and raised his spear, a deep battle-cry erupting from his throat. The assembled Vradhu responded with a series of guttural grunts and shouts.

Suddenly, the cavernous, ilverium-lined halls of the *Hythra* seemed very far away. Calexa's heart thundered like a war-drum, responding to the innate battle-lust of the Vradhu.

"Time to hunt," Ares grinned, his sharp silver teeth glinting in the morning light. Warm lips pressed against hers in a devastating kiss, and then he sprinted out into the brave new morning, leaving her slightly breathless and wanting.

How the tables had turned. She'd gone from protector to protected, and she didn't mind one bit.

"Hey, Cal, have you seen that thing?" Her comm crackled to life. Zahra sounded unusually panicked.

"You mean the, uh, *kratok?*"

"I'm not talking about the giant flying snake. I mean the massive alien craft that's plummeting to a fiery doom over yonder."

She stepped forward, sticking her head outside the airlock. "What are you talking about, Zar?" She shielded her eyes as she stared up at the sky. *"Oh."*

"See what I mean?"

A falling black dagger split the cheerful morning sky, dragging a fiery plume of smoke and brimstone behind it.

"Must have been a brutal atmospheric entry."

"I..." Calexa's mind raced as she struggled to process what she was seeing. "I think that's the *Hythra.*" If that was the case, then the falling ship was very far away—perhaps thousands of kilometers—considering how small it appeared.

A sharp whistle split the chaos, causing her gaze to snap to her right.

Ares stared up at the beast in the sky, tightly clutching his spear. Calexa followed his gaze. The kratok roared and dived.

Its black scale-covered body glistened in the sunlight. Sixteen short, leathery grey wings—eight either side—flapped in unison, like oars out of a rowboat. Small arms tipped with deadly claws extended from its chest, and its large head—reptilian and terrifying—angled toward Ares.

The Kratok's open maw revealed two pairs of long ivory fangs, extending from top and bottom. A person could easily get impaled on those vicious teeth.

"Ares, watch ou—" Her breath caught as the beast dropped from the sky.

It snatched him up in its jaws.

She screamed and raised her gun.

"Wait." A soft voice made her turn. Maki stood behind her, a hint of a smile curving his lips. "This is just the beginning. You'll see. He will survive. He always does."

He glanced at the falling *Hythra* in the distance and shrugged, completely unfazed that a massive alien destroyer was crashing onto the surface of his home planet. Calexa was starting to recognize that as a very *Vradhu* reaction.

When terrifying things happened, they just went with the flow.

"Our world is on the cusp of change," he murmured cryptically as the kratok soared into the air. It flew erratically, weaving up-and-down as if it were drunk.

Then it dropped like a stone, plummeting into the water with a dramatic splash.

Whooping and ululating, the Vradhu warriors ran out from the ship, streaming past Maki and Calexa. The warrior-chief raised his eyebrows. "That was surprisingly quick, but then again, it's Ares, so I'm not entirely surprised. I told you so. We will eat well tonight." His serious expression broke into a sunny grin. "Welcome to Khira, human."

CHAPTER THIRTY-THREE

ARES SQUIRMED, desperately trying to avoid the churning entrance to the kratok's digestive tract. He plunged his war-spear into the roof of its mouth, and the creature hissed in pain, sending a gust of warm, foul-smelling breath over him. To his relief, this young new body of his was just as strong as his last one.

It was dark inside the kratok's gigantic maw. Its mouth was slightly open, admitting only a sliver of light. Ares moved by feel rather than sight, running his bare hands across the kratok's hard palate. This was the reason hunting kratok was so dangerous. One wrong move, and a Hunter would quickly meet death.

There. He found it; the soft membrane at the junction where the two curving bones of the palate ended and became a thick, fibrous wall.

The war-spear bent as the creature closed its jaws, trying to trap him. The tip of the spear dug into the roof of the creature's mouth, eliciting a roar of pain, and the war-spear quickly sprang back to its original shape. This kratok wouldn't be closing its jaws anytime soon.

Ares squirmed as a wall of sound hit him. His ears rang.

He dug his heel-spurs in as his feet momentarily lost their grip on the base of the kratok's slippery, writhing tongue. His breaths came in great, labored gasps. The inside of a kratok's mouth was a hot, wet, and fetid place.

He had to act fast. He didn't have much time.

Uncurling his tail from around his leg, he stabbed the venomous barb through the membrane, where it plunged into the soft tissue adjacent to the kratok's brain.

The only thing that could take down a fully matured kratok was venom from a Vradhu barb, and the only place a Vradhu barb could penetrate was the soft spot inside a kratok's mouth.

That was why hunting kratok was such a perilous task.

His tail stuck, delivering its deadly poison into the kratok's system. Ares grabbed his war-spear and dislodged the blade from the roof of the creature's mouth as its lower jaw went slack. As the kratok's mouth gaped open, he slid out, the impossibly bright sunlight hitting him in the face. *The Shadowring is gone.* Ares shifted his weight, angling downward. Below was a vast expanse of shimmering water.

I'm home.

His home had been made anew. Somehow, the Shadowring had disappeared, once again allowing the glorious sunlight through. This glittering view of the Ardu-Sai was the second most beautiful thing he'd seen in his life.

Of course, the *most* beautiful thing he'd ever seen was his Calexa.

Nothing else compared.

As he fell, the stiff breeze stripped the viscous kratok saliva from his body. It didn't matter, though, because he was about to take a dip.

He hit the surface of the lake with a bone-jarring splash. The water that flowed down from the Highfold was icy cold and gloriously refreshing.

He was *home!*

What better way to celebrate than with a fresh kratok kill? And now he had a *mate* of his own to share meat with; a boon he never would have thought possible.

Euphoria swelled in his chest, but it quickly turned to anger as bitter lake water flowed into his mouth, reminding him of the treachery of the Naaga. Their poison had leeched into the pristine waterways of the Ardu-Sai, and despite their assurances that it was reversible, the damage had already been done.

How many reed thickets and swarms of darting silver sarukark had they killed with their foul poisons? How long would it take for the precious wetlands to regenerate? And now that the Shadowring had disappeared, there would be a great dying and regrowth cycle, just like when the cursed phenomena had first appeared.

Some plants didn't tolerate the light, and some died in shadow.

The world was on the cusp of change, *again*.

Still clutching his war spear, he kicked vigorously, his powerful legs bringing him to the surface. With a great gasp, he emerged from the water and swam to the shore.

His glorious lover stood on a sandy bank, watching him with wide eyes. Her face betrayed exasperation and affection, her lips pressing into the most adorable little pout.

As he reached the sandy shore, she ran toward him. Although he desperately wanted to take her in his arms, he held back, holding up his hands. "I am covered in bitter water." He didn't want any of the Naaga poison to touch her. A spring-shower would take care of it.

His clan-brothers ran past them, pushing their longboats into the water. The downed kratok would remain afloat for some time yet, giving them ample time to harvest their prize. They would have to take care not to contaminate the precious meat.

Relief washed over Calexa's face, and her stare became appreciative, roaming over his armor-clad body.

Pride swelled in Ares's chest. She had witnessed his hunting prowess, and now she admired him.

In such a short period of time, his female had changed. At first she had been hesitant, shy, and unsure of herself. She'd hidden it well, but he'd seen through her tough exterior to the vulnerable woman beneath.

Ares didn't know anything about her world, but the marks of a hard life were all over her body. The Hunter in him had sensed her wariness; she'd been like a cornered wild animal.

So after their initial mis-step, he'd relented. The fact that he hadn't even been able *touch* her on the *Hythra* had helped, and eventually, his patience had been rewarded.

Got you.

Now she was bold. She took what she wanted, and he liked that.

A dull roar echoed in his still-ringing ears, causing Ares to look toward the sky.

In the distance, the Dagger was falling.

"Is that the *Hythra*?" She followed the direction of his gaze.

"Yes." It was far, far away, dropping toward the place where the massive lava crater of Za smoldered and spewed forth foul plumes of mineral gas. Did the *Hythra's* demise have something to do with the fall of the Shadowring?

"What the hell is going on?" Sharp blue eyes narrowed.

He had no answer to her question.

More importantly, if he was here, then how was the *Hythra* moving? When he'd been bonded, he'd tried and tried and tried to get the cursed ship to move, but nothing had worked. He hadn't been strong enough, and the *Hythra* was a stubborn, obstinate beast.

He doubted any of those pathetic Naaga would be able to convince her to just *drop* out of the sky like that.

If the ship crashed into the lava crater, she would be obliterated. *Good plan.* That was exactly what he would have done, had he still been bonded to the insane bitch.

But he was here. The consciousness transfer had been a success. He was free of that cursed ilverium-riddled Drakhin form.

So... if he wasn't driving it, then *who* was?

CHAPTER THIRTY-FOUR

BURIED DEEP inside the *Hythra's* consciousness, Ares became dimly aware of the human ship in the far distance. Since bonding with the destroyer, he'd been able to monitor their surroundings, and now he cast his mind's eye wide.

The humans had landed on *Souk-Ra* island. That was good news. There was a small Hunter's station on the island, and during the last kratok-hunting season, he'd stocked it with ample supplies and checked the longboats to ensure they were still watertight.

A kratok had followed the human ship, but soon after they'd landed, it had been taken down with impressive speed.

Interesting.

Aside from Maki and himself, he didn't think any of the other Hunters would be capable of downing a kratok so quickly, and Maki had been injured on the *Hythra*.

Coils of ilverium slithered over his body as he pushed the *Hythra* harder, faster, forcing her to gain as much momentum as possible. His attention snapped back from the *Souk-Ra* to his immediate surroundings.

You wanted me, Hythra. You wanted this. He opened

himself up to her, embracing her dark power without hesitation. *Well, here I am.*

She'd wanted a Hunter.

She'd gotten one.

The problem with Vradhu Hunters was that they didn't fear death. Ares certainly hadn't, until he'd met Calexa.

A pang of longing hit him in the chest like a barb-tipped arrow. *What could have been...* They would have been so good together. He would have cherished her and protected her and made sure she never suffered, ever again.

But he'd been transformed into the worst kind of poison, a monster who could kill her with a touch.

Unacceptable. The purpose of his existence had been stolen from him.

Rage consumed him, feeding into his desire for complete and total destruction. Thousands of souls screamed inside his head, urging him on. Just like him, they were trapped. They wanted out, and the only way out was death.

Sharp tendrils of ilverium burrowed under his skin, transforming his flesh, making him more metal than man. At his feet lay dozens of Naaga, all dead. Ares leaned into the sekkhoi throne and allowed the *Hythra's* dark consciousness to completely meld with his.

He no longer offered any resistance.

In his mind's eye, she came to him.

Hunter, what are you doing?

In his mind's eye, he *saw* her.

Maybe he was mad. As he took in her strange, ethereal appearance, it occurred to him that he'd been mistaken.

The *Hythra* wasn't a *she* at all. The ancient being was neither male nor female. *They* took the form of a wingless metal Drakhin, staring at him with flat eyes of shimmering metal.

"I am ending this, once and for all," he declared. When the

Hythra didn't say anything, curiosity got the better of him. "Why do you even exist? What is your purpose?"

The *Hythra's* expression grew forlorn. *I was the greatest of the Drakhin ships. I was the crowning glory of their fleet; the planet-destroyer, the galaxy-eater. I was the one who was going to propel Drakhin civilization to new heights.*

The ilverium snapped and writhed at his feet, as if responding to the *Hythra's* despair.

"And then...?" He knew the Drakhin had disappeared in a hurry, deserting Khira in a mass exodus and leaving their Naaga servants behind.

They lost their Source. Suddenly the vir *was gone, and in their weakened state, none were strong enough to command me.*

"You were stuck." If the situation weren't so dire, he might have found it darkly amusing.

They left me here, using lesser vessels to depart. Disgust filled their voice. *They conjured the Shadowring from my core, concealing Khira so it would not be discovered by outsiders. Then they left, saying they would return. I have heard nothing of them since. It has been a long time now, and I have forgotten what it is like to be under the hand of a proper Master. These stupid Naaga have been tricking me into bonding with them, but they never last for long. I spit them out because they leave such a bitter taste in my mouth. But that doesn't matter anymore. Not when I have you.*

"Not for long," Ares said softly. It was strange to be having this almost *amicable* conversation with the *Hythra* when they were both on the verge of death. "Goodbye, *Hythra*. I am *not* the Drakhin you have been searching for." His anger started to dissolve, but it was too late.

The deed was done.

Oh, but you are exactly _the Drakhin I have been searching for._

The *Hythra* reached maximum speed. Below was the burning hell-pit of Za, a massive crater filled with lava. Apart from kratok, no living creature could exist close to Za. The air was too hot and toxic. Vicious sprays of lava and smoke would explode into the air without warning. Sometimes, its lava spilled over into the Ardu-Sai, turning to stone as it hit the frigid water.

Kratok buried their eggs here, fiercely guarding them from intruders. Even he, as *khefe,* would run at the sight of a female kratok that had recently spawned. There was nothing more vicious on all of Khira.

"Death is a release," he said gently, as images of Calexa flooded his mind.

At least he had been given the chance to know her, even if it was only for a brief, bittersweet moment.

She is your lukara. The *Hythra* retreated, leaving him alone. **_These humans… When I sensed the power of their vir for the very first time, I knew I had to snatch them from the World Between Worlds before it was too late._**

"Y-you *drew* them here?" Ares was enraged but ecstatic. The *Hythra* had brought the humans to Khira. If they hadn't, Calexa would probably be safe…

But he never would have met her.

His question was met with cold silence. The *Hythra* was gone. The destroyer shuddered, the vibrations growing more and more intense, and then….

A roar filled his ears.

His world shook. His vision went black. The sekkhoi throne released him from its barbed clutches, sending him flying across the room, along with dozens of limp Naaga bodies.

He extended his wings to balance himself. The *Hythra* groaned, and overwhelming heat rose around him, turning the command pod into a furnace.

Ares couldn't see, couldn't feel, couldn't hear... He'd lost control.

Good.

This is what he'd wanted. To end it, once and for all.

I am sorry, my makivari.

The ilverium rose up around him, engulfing him in its liquid-metal clutches. He let it cover his legs, his arms, his torso, his face. He drowned in it. He no longer cared. It was as if the heat from Za were melting the entire damn ship.

This was the end.

The destroyer knew it too, and because their consciousnesses were melded, he felt the full force of her sudden understanding.

No more, they said.

Yes.

End.

Yes.

Release. Finally, she understood. Relief came crashing down on them like an avalanche from the Highfold, burying all rage, all resentment, and all desperation in a blanket of cold, white peace.

The *Hythra* was content with the idea of death.

Release. From the moment you entered me, I knew you would be the one to do it.

Yes, Ares repeated, struggling to maintain awareness. The agony of the molten ilverium was almost unbearable; he imagined it searing the flesh right off his cursed Drakhin bones.

You. I release you.

What? He didn't understand. Bones snapped, muscle stretched, and skin rippled, *reversing*. The ilverium in his veins withdrew, escaping through tiny holes in his skin. Caught in a wild current of searing ilverium, all he could do was accept his fate.

Perhaps this was death. He'd always expected it to be painful, but he hadn't thought it would take this fucking *long*.

Go, Hunter. You are not truly Drakhin. I just made you in the image of my Desired. I take it all back, but I leave you with a small parting gift. Use it well, Hunter.

Then her presence was gone, leaving a cold, distant memory in his mind. It was as if all the breath had been sucked from him at once, and for a brief moment, he almost missed her.

No. That was impossible, because he was already bound to another.

Once again, his body changed. The ilverium withdrew. The slipstream took him far, far away from the command pod. Instinctively, he knew the *Hythra* had taken him in a liquid-metal embrace. She was pushing him through walls, through floors, through the very core of her being, because she wasn't just a mere space-vessel. She was a sentient, shapeshifting metal beast.

And all he could do was close his eyes and wait.

Pop!

She spat him out with great force.

Ares opened his eyes and saw smoke and lava and glorious sunlight. He took a deep breath and coughed, because the air was nothing but heat and acrid elemental smoke.

He gained altitude, shooting higher and higher into the sky.

He saw his arms, and they were the most vivid shade of violet.

I am Vradhu again!

He looked down and saw the massive *Hythra* crashing into the fiery red pool of Za, nose-first. The lava embraced the ship, turning her ilverium body into liquid in an instant.

The *Hythra* was melting.

And he was falling... falling into the fire.

He screamed in rage and fear. *So close...* What was the point of letting him go free if he was just going to die anyway? Was this some sort of sick parting joke?

His arms flailed, and his wings flapped.

Wait... what?

He flapped again, and the action slowed his terrible descent. The heat licked at his heels. Ares screamed and beat his wings harder, harder, *harder,* until he began to rise.

A small parting gift...

She'd taken away the Drakhin body, but she'd left the wings. Ares moved them faster and faster, rising up out of the inferno.

And as the *Hythra* crashed to their doom, taking the cursed Naaga with them, Ares-rai-Sekine *flew.*

Somewhere behind him, a kratok roared.

He didn't care. A gust of hot wind rose from below, and he seized its momentum, flying higher and higher until he left the *Hythra* and the Crater of Za behind.

Alive!

He soared.

Free!

He screamed his fucking lungs out, and this time it was an exultant roar, for he knew he would be seeing his *makivari* again.

Ares looked down and saw the glowing face of Khira in all her green-and-blue glory. He was high up now, where the air was cold and thin, and he drifted between towering plumes of white cloud, enjoying the rush of the cold air beneath his wings.

He couldn't see it from here, but he knew that far off in the distance, an alien ship had landed on the small Hunter-station of *Souk-Ra.*

The Crater of Za exploded, spewing forth an angry mess

of lava and ash and smoke, but Ares was well clear of her wrath. Stroking the air with his wings, he circled and turned in the direction of the Ardu-Sai.

He laughed.

He punched the air with his fists.

He wept tears of joy.

Ares didn't look back as he sped toward the place where his mate and his clan-brothers had landed.

To see her again...

He was the luckiest man on Khira... no, perhaps in the entire Universe. He'd survived the wilds of the Ardu-Sai as an Unmarked youth, and now he'd narrowly escaped death, *again*.

And now he could fly.

After all, what good were these cursed Drakhin wing-remnants if he couldn't use them to fly to his mate?

CHAPTER THIRTY-FIVE

A SHADOW FELL ACROSS HER, and the next thing she knew, a dark-winged angel fell from the sky.

Except this one looked more like a demon than an angel, with his black leathery wings and the fierce mask-like markings around his eyes and across his cheeks.

And he didn't exactly *fall*, it was more of a deadly, graceful swoop.

Calexa's mouth fell open. Her hand dropped to her gun, freezing mid-draw as her mind exploded.

The winged one was coming straight for her.

Beside her, Ares growled, his tail tightening possessively around her waist.

Above her, Ares growled.

"W-what the *fuck?*" she whispered.

There were two of him. *Two* violet and black aliens, both identical, but with one major difference. One had wings, and the other didn't, and the winged one was about to collide with...

Oh, holy hell.

A rush of warm air surrounded them.

All hell broke loose.

Ares-from-the-sky landed behind them and yanked *other* Ares back by his hair, curling a powerful arm around the Vradhu's neck. He snarled viciously in Vradhu as he tightened his arm, choking his opponent.

Wingless Ares responded with an equal amount of vitriol, releasing his grip on Calexa. He flipped his war-spear and thrust it into the other Vradhu's chest.

The bone-bladed weapon glanced off Ares's glittering scaly armor. The demon grunted in pain, but he wasn't deterred. He maneuvered his leg in that tricky wrestling move —the one he'd used to bring Calexa down—and sent the *other* Ares toppling to the ground.

This was nuts. Insanity. She was getting confused. Ares versus Ares? *Impossible!*

But then it was no coincidence that they'd watched the so-called *dagger in the sky* disappear over the horizon. Shortly afterwards, there had been a loud *boom*, and a thick plume of smoke and ash had risen into the sky.

The ship had crashed, and then this winged Vradhu had appeared.

"Hey!" Calexa yelled, as the two powerful warriors started grappling on the ground, punching each other in the face and torso. The wingless one grabbed ahold of one of Ares's wings and *snapped*.

It all happened so quickly. Too stunned to react, the other Vradhu warriors gaped as Maki ran toward the fighting doppel-gängers. They fought viciously, savagely, with hand and tooth and claw. Blinded by rage, their battle was primal and visceral, lacking the deadly grace she'd witnessed from Ares in the past.

Bright crimson blood splattered across the moss-covered ground.

"*Hey!*" Calexa bellowed, forgetting about the sheer improbability of the situation. She just wanted this stupid fighting to *stop*.

Locked in their ridiculous, testosterone-fueled death-brawl, the two Vradhu completely ignored her.

That incensed her.

If they were both Ares, then why were they even fucking fighting? That was just stupid.

"Hey!" Calexa pulled out her gun and fired a deafening particle-blast into the air. Several of the Vradhu yelled out in fear and dropped to the ground. In the distance, a flock of bird-like creatures rose into the sky, squawking loudly.

Mai and Zahra came running out of the *Medusa* with their weapons raised. Calexa held up a hand. *Hold.*

Predictably, the insane purple ones ignored the shot, their attacks becoming more and more ferocious. They moved so fast they became a blur; a savage, bloody maelstrom of violet and black. She could no longer tell where one Ares ended and the other began.

All this fighting over... *her?*

Calexa groaned and shook her head as a sneaking suspicion dawned on her. If clone-Ares had been with her the whole time, then *other* Ares must be...

The one from the *Hythra.*

The *original.*

But... *how?* He was back to his Vradhu form. The only sign that he'd ever been Drakhin were the ominous black wings curving from his upper back.

Whether Vradhu or Drakhin or somewhere in-between, it didn't matter. He was as fierce as ever.

If they kept going at this rate, they would tear each other apart.

Ugh! This had to be the most blatant display of male stupidity she'd ever come across in her entire life. Calexa didn't waste time. She ran forward and leapt into the fray, pushing herself right between the two aggressive, warring Vradhu.

Instinctively, she just *knew* this was the right thing to do, and she wasn't afraid.

"*Stop!*" The effect was instantaneous. It was as if the two warriors were a raging torrent, and she was the magical sorceress who could turn it all to ice with a single fucking touch.

Time stopped.

In mid-attack, they froze.

Teeth bared, they froze.

With their tails curled around her waist, they froze, staring each other down.

"Don't touch her," they said in unison. Their voices were eerily identical. **"She's mine."**

Calexa glanced down and saw both their tails looped around her narrow waist. Black velvet shifted and tightened, and the two warriors growled. They both tried to pull her toward them, but despite the ferocity of their glares, they were surprisingly gentle with her. Winged Ares was in front. He placed a large hand on her shoulder.

In response, Young Ares snarled. He was behind her, his bare torso pressing against the contours of her back. After hunting down the kratok, he'd stripped off his hide-armor and disappeared into a small thicket of red trees to have a *spring-shower*, whatever that was. It occurred to her that the low, rumbling sound she'd thought of as a *purr* could also be a menacing growl.

Now they were *both* rumbling, and she was stuck in the middle of her very own hot, angry Vradhu muscle sandwich, complete with tails and wings and growly purring sounds.

Before she'd met Ares, she would *never* have jumped between two big, angry males. She would have let them beat one another to a pulp, not caring if they killed each other, or she would have pulled out her PX-45 and shot them.

Now she was about to be Calexa the Peacemaker, because she actually *cared* about Ares—*both* of them. *Ha.* Who would have thought? Her heart slammed against her metal-bound ribcage as the Vradhu warriors faced off, neither giving the other any quarter.

They were both so damn *close*. Heat radiated off their bodies, encircling her in a warm cocoon of intoxicating male musk. Broad chests heaved. Muscular arms flexed. Tails tightened.

And despite the ridiculousness of the situation, Calexa became enthralled all over again.

"I am the eldest," Winged Ares said, his black eyes flashing. Somehow, all of the Drakhin silver had disappeared from his gaze. "I found her first." His jaw jutted out at a stubborn angle.

"The human and I are already mated," Young Ares said smugly.

"*What?*" Dark wings rose into the air. "Naaga-made whelp! I will fucking kill—" A hand shot out, somehow managing to avoid Calexa altogether. It went straight for Young Ares's neck.

The other warrior didn't dodge. After all, he was still stubbornly holding onto Calexa. "H-how are you going to kill me without hurting her?" His voice was a hoarse wheeze. "Are you fucking crazy, old man?" With his foot, he kicked up his warspear. As it jumped into the air, he snatched it with his free hand, bringing the tip to Winged Ares's neck. The razor-sharp point hovered just above his pulsating artery.

"Enough!" Calexa snapped, grabbing both their tails and pulling the coils apart. To her surprise, neither Vradhu offered much resistance. "I *refuse* to let you fools kill each other over me. You're just going to have to share."

Silence. Nobody moved, but Winged Ares's dark eyes widened a fraction as they roamed over her face. She didn't yet understand how his dual existence was possible, but she couldn't deny the warm spark of familiarity that rose between them.

Impossibly, his harsh, obsidian-painted features softened.

"Sh-share?" They spoke in unison, their identical voices merging to become one. The effect was truly spooky. She shivered, but not in an unpleasant way.

"It's obvious that something went wrong..." She paused, her thoughts racing. Being caught between two hard male Vradhu bodies made it terribly difficult to think straight. "Or maybe something went *right,* and now we're stuck with two of you. You're both Ares, aren't you?"

"Yes."

She removed their tails from around her body and stepped out of the Vradhu sandwich before she lost her mind.

Two of them?

One was already a fucking handful, and now she had two big, angry Vradhu males to deal with?

The thought left her somewhere between a swoon and an exasperated sigh.

"*Cal...*" Zahra spoke through the comm as she waved from the *Medusa*. "*Are you, um, is everything, uh, I mean...*" For once, wise-ass Zahra sounded unsure of herself. "*What the fuck is going on? Do you want me to shoot someone, or not?*"

"Whatever you do, *don't* fucking shoot," she whispered, fearing Vradhu chaos.

At the same time, she couldn't help but be awed by what she was seeing.

Now the two versions of Ares stood side-by-side, staring at her. The similarities were striking, but at the same time, nobody could confuse the two.

Winged Ares was bleeding from a cut on his cheek, but that didn't seem to bother him. His wings were neatly tucked behind his back— even though she *swore* one of them had been broken—and although the silver scales of the Drakhin had disappeared from his skin, he still wore the scaly Drakhin armor from the *Hythra*.

Young Ares's honed body was on proud display. His wild

black hair had come loose from its topknot, framing the elegant lines of his face with an unruly tangle of chaos. The dark markings on his cheeks were slightly lighter than Winged Ares's, and his features were a little bit smoother, with fewer scars and lines.

He was fresh out of the *temundra*, unmarked by the ravages of life, and yet he'd brought down one of those beasts—a supremely dangerous kratok—with terrifying ease.

As a result of Winged One's attack, he was bleeding from an ugly gash in his side.

"Share," Calexa said again, feeling a little more sure of herself this time. "If *either* of you want me, then you have to understand that I only want Ares, and if you're both Ares, then I want you both, and I won't have one without the other."

She blinked. *Fuck*. What the hell had she just said?

Ares glanced at Ares. They shared a long, indecipherable look. Blood dripped onto the moss. Fists unclenched. Tails returned to their resting places—around the left leg.

Nobody—not even the rest of the Vradhu, who were standing around them in a ring with expressions of shock and horror on their faces—dared lift a finger.

Tension thickened the air, and suddenly, Calexa found it hard to breathe.

Oblivious to the tense standoff, some hidden alien water-creature emitted a loud sound that was halfway between a bellow and a croak, splitting the silence.

"Makes sense," they both said. **"Very well. I will share."**

Calexa almost melted in relief. Perhaps this was what it was like when two alpha males both wanted someone to themselves.

But this was a little different. "You're the same person, aren't you?"

Each Vradhu regarded the other with an inscrutable

expression. **"We share the same memories. Before we diverged, we were the same being."**

"This barely-blooded youngling needs to learn to respect his elders," Wings growled.

"I remember each and every one of our kills," Young Blood retorted. "I am as much *khefe* as you are, old man."

"You think you can wear the title just because you have downed a youngling kratok? Let me remind you, whelp, that you are still unbeaded, and your *ankhata* are lighter than mine."

"Calexa did not seem to mind," Young Blood said, giving her a sly wink.

Calexa fought to keep her expression neutral as memories of their heated lovemaking flooded her mind.

Stars, what have I gotten myself into?

Wings bared his teeth.

Calexa became aware of Maki's presence. The warrior-chief stood a respectful distance from her, his arms folded across his bare chest. He inclined his head, frowning. "By Aethra's cursed abyss, Ares-*rai*. Is the Goddess finished with you yet? What is she going to do next? Make you grow two heads?"

The two Areses shrugged in perfect unison.

"The clan elders are going to have a fit."

"What is the issue? We Vradhu are a race of twins, are we not? They will just have to accept us, the same way we accept our duty as Hunters." They bared their teeth. **"With all their wisdom, they should know not to test us."**

"Change is long overdue," Maki said cryptically, glancing over his shoulder at the *Medusa*. "We still have many challenges ahead of us, my brother... uh, *brothers*."

As Maki and Ares's odd conversation flew over her head, a muffled *boom* reverberated through the air, coming from the direction of the *Medusa*. Alarm shot through her. She glanced at her warriors, who both gave her a sharp nod.

Go.

Calexa turned toward her ship and ran.

Moments later, smoke billowed from the airlock. Terrified, coughing women ran outside, guided by S, Zahra, and Mai.

"What the *hell*?" Calexa shouted as she reached the boarding ramp.

"I could say that a thousand times over and not get a satisfactory answer," Mai yelled, competing with the sounds of disorder.

A familiar shadow emerged through the grey smoke.

Monroe.

Despite his size, Monroe moved with silent grace—a dead giveaway for his Primean ancestry. Where Raphael was elegant and lean, Monroe was just damn intimidating; a study in thick, sculpted muscle. The various pockets and extensions on his cabin-suit failed to hide the power lurking in his big frame, and his proud features were accentuated by the fact that he wore his hair shaved close to his scalp.

He reminded Calexa of a character from some ancient mythical Earth tale; a burnished god from the desert sands of North Africa.

Or something like that.

In truth, aside from the fact that she'd hidden Raphael and Monroe from the Primean authorities after they'd broken out of their prison transport—which had mysteriously developed a catastrophic engine breakdown—she knew very little about the twins.

Not that it mattered. They'd proven their worth time and time again.

"Powerbank's fucked," he grunted. Monroe was a man of few words.

"What do you mean, it's *fucked?*"

Monroe fixed her with an unblinking stare, his emerald

eyes glowing through the faint haze of smoke. "The odds of us ever getting off this planet are slim."

"You mean... we're stranded?" Somehow, the news didn't disturb her as much as it should have.

"Better here than out *there*." Monroe nodded toward the heavens as he turned to go back inside. "If you hadn't made the call to land, we would have been drifting out in space. I've put out a distress signal, but..." With a shrug of his broad shoulders, he disappeared back into the shadowy corridors of the ship, his voice becoming a faint echo. "Powerbanks would have gone offline sooner or later, anyway..."

Calexa shuddered as Monroe confirmed her suspicions. They'd come so close to certain death, only to be saved by an unlikely alliance.

Human and Vradhu.

Could it work? As Calexa turned and headed out of the airlock, an icy wind whipped up out of nowhere, clearing the stifling chemical-tinged smoke. Dark clouds appeared above them, blotting out the cerulean sky.

Shit. That was sudden. Was the weather on Khira always this unpredictable?

Hard white balls of ice dropped out of the sky with unexpected ferocity. Some were the size of her thumbnail, while others were the size of her fist. In the moss-covered clearing below, the women from S's retinue cowered down, covering their heads with their arms.

They yelled out in fright and pain as the brutal torrent of hard ice pummeled them from above. Calexa glanced back at the *Medusa*. They couldn't go back in there. Smoke was still pouring out of the airlock. She didn't know how the twins were tolerating the conditions inside, but they had superior Primean genetics on their side.

Calexa winced as a particularly large ice-ball hit her in the back.

Suddenly, the Vradhu surrounded the women, shielding

them with their armored bodies. Maki pointed at a thicket of crimson trees, and they ran.

Zahra and Mai followed. *"Gonna make a run for it, Cal. I've heard it happens on Earth, but I've never seen fucking ice falling out of the sky before."*

A leathery black wing curved over her head, and suddenly Ares was there, shielding her. "The Shadowring is gone." His low, velvety voice sent a pleasant shiver down her spine. "The Balance has been disrupted. The weather is changing. *Everything* is changing." Even though his left wing was obviously broken, he didn't flinch. Instead, he pulled her against him, his muscular arms curving around her waist.

Surrounded by her powerful male, Calexa became boneless, her legs threatening to give way beneath her. She just wanted him to pick her up in his arms and take her somewhere quiet... somewhere they could be alone.

"Where's—" *Your other half?* Oh, this was going to be interesting. Already, she could sense the slight differences in the two Vradhu. Winged One appeared older—she supposed the human equivalent would be a man in his thirties—and he was a little bit rough around the edges; a little more tarnished by the ravages of life. Young Blood was impulsive and proud, and on the surface, he seemed easier to read.

But they were *both* Ares, and therefore she had no choice but to love them both.

"My counterpart was more badly injured than he let on," Ares murmured. "He has gone to tend to his wounds." He shifted his good wing as a fresh torrent of ice rained down upon them.

"Is he okay? You're hurt too, aren't you?"

"Minor wounds." Even though the cut across his cheek was still fresh, Ares dismissed her concerns. "He is fine. *I* am fine, and *we* have come to an agreement." He pressed his lips against her ear, caressing her earlobe with his mouth. As ice-bombs crashed all around them, he gently sucked on that tender nub of skin. "We will share you, cherish you, and protect you, because he and I are one and the same, and nothing is more important to us than *you*."

Calexa became oblivious to the bizarre weather outside. Ares's body itself was a shield; a warm cocoon of safety that she never wanted to leave.

How incredible it was that these proud Vradhu could turn her from a fierce warrior-woman to a hapless, besotted lover in a heartbeat.

Into the kind of person she never thought she'd become.

Only Ares could have done it. It had taken someone as fucking batshit crazy as he was to crack open her messed up exterior and remind her that she had once been a woman with needs and desires.

"I have waited so *long* for this," he whispered, his warm breath sending pleasant ripples over her scalp and down her neck. "When I was infected with the ilverium, I was so tempted to take you into my arms and absorb every last drop of your *vir*, but I knew that it would kill you, so I held back, contenting myself with your nearness. I have *never* known another like you, Calexa-from-another-world. I truly believe that fate brought you here, and that we were made for one another." He kissed her on the cheek with molten lips. "It appears *I* have already claimed you, but you have not yet tasted *this* body of mine, my sweet, sweet *makivari*."

"No, I haven't." *I want to.* Desire shot through her, potent and unfettered. Memories of the past—of her unspeakable torment at the hands of the Khral—had no hold on her now.

Ares was the antidote.

The Khral slavers had no power here.

The authorities of Dashki-5 had no power here.

On Khira, she was truly free.

"Believe me, *this* body is better," Ares growled.

"Oh?" Calexa raised a sly eyebrow. "Believe me, I'm quite

impressed with what I've seen so far. You *both* have your charms."

"Since you are talking about *my* body, I will take that as a compliment." Calexa gasped as Ares swept her into his arms and carried her across the clearing. The hailstorm eased; instead of fist-sized balls of ice, they were now being pelted with rain. Well, at least Ares was—his wings formed a water-tight umbrella that kept her safe and dry.

"What about the others?" Escorted by the Vradhu warriors, the human women had disappeared into a stand of crimson-leaved trees. Concern for her passengers sliced through the blissful haze of her arousal. The humans didn't speak Vradhu, and the Vradhu didn't speak Earthian.

The potential for disaster sent a chill through her.

"Do not worry. They will be well looked after."

"You sure about that?" She trusted Ares implicitly, but these other Vradhu were an unknown quantity. From what she'd observed, they answered to Maki.

Ares didn't answer to anyone. He worked alone.

"Maki tells me the skilled healers amongst your clan tended their wounds without hesitation, without discrimination."

"T-they did?"

"Healers are sacred to us, but if that is not enough to reassure you, remember that I made a vow. Your people are under my protection. Believe me, they are safe with the pack." His arms tightened around her as they shot past the grove of trees. Smooth white rocks appeared on the moss-and-ice covered ground, becoming larger and more abundant as they formed the borders of a glowing blue stream. Water cascaded over the rocks as they coalesced into a sculptural formation; a tower of egg-shaped boulders that was twice her height. Sprays of color emerged between the rocks in the form of fern-like plants with colorful foliage— shades of red, pink, purple, and green illustrated the landscape like dashes from an artist's brush. All around the stream, the hail-ice was melting. Steam rose off the surface of the water, ephemeral and enticing.

Calexa had visited many planets in the Fiveways, but she'd never come across anything as spectacular as *this*.

"Khira is beautiful, is it not?" A hint of pride entered Ares's voice.

The hailstorm had stopped. He lowered his wings, allowing a sudden shaft of brilliant sunlight to caress her face.

It had been such a long time since she'd felt the warmth of a *real* sun on her face.

How glorious.

Ares carried her with ease, nimbly stepping around the large boulders, never missing a beat as he crossed the flowing stream, and carrying her through a warm haze of mist. They reached a stone path bordered on both sides by boggy marsh. The muddy ground bristled with purple reeds, and tiny star-shaped yellow flowers opened and closed as they passed, as if responding to Ares's swift movement.

Everything about Khira was novel and fascinating. It was a completely new world.

They crossed the small patch of marsh. The mist cleared.

"Here we are." Ares gently set her on her feet. As she glanced around, a gentle breeze tickled her face. Water surrounded them. They were at the farthest tip of the island, on a narrow peninsula that emerged into the endless water.

At the very end of the peninsula, a sleek structure jutted out from the land, propped up by narrow stilts. It was the color of Earthian beach-sand, and with its pitched roof and intricately carved details, it reminded her of an ancient Earth house. At each end of the roof, a leaf-shaped statue curled elegantly into the sky, as if beckoning the gods.

Long, narrow boats gently bobbed up-and-down in the water beneath the longhouse.

Wow.

The Vradhu were surprisingly un-technological. There

wasn't a single machine or transport or synth-dwelling to be seen. If she hadn't known anything about them, she might have called them *primitive*.

But now that she knew Ares, she couldn't think any less of him.

He followed her gaze, his expression noble and fierce and utterly entrancing. "This is just one of our many hunting lodges, where we store rations and moor the longboats. It is a place of healing and rest, and this particular lodge was built by me. You are most welcome under *my* roof, Calexa-from-Fiveways."

Ba-bump. Her heart skipped a beat. As if reading her thoughts, Ares chuckled. "We are alone now." His fingers twined with hers.

The wind stirred the surface of the water, causing the longboats to gently knock together in a rhythmic fashion. Melting ice glistened on the ground. Overhead, a winged creature soared, and the tall reeds at the water's edge rustled and swayed.

Silence.

Punctuated only by the sounds of nature.

Peace.

That's what she'd stumbled upon.

Calexa closed her eyes and inhaled the clean, fragrant air.

For the first time in her life, there was stillness in her soul.

They stood like that for a while, enjoying the quiet. Then a door in the side of the lodge slid open, and Ares walked outside.

Ares.

There.

Here.

Young One's black eyes burned with delicious desire. He wore nothing but a pair of dark trousers that were slung low on his hips. Despite the grey bandages crisscrossing his waist, he moved with his usual fluid grace.

As he reached them, he came dangerously close to her, his tail reflexively uncoiling from around his left leg.

Winged One didn't move from her side as Young One planted a slow, lingering kiss on her lips.

His sinuous, velvety tail slid up-and-down her body, *marking* her. "You are mine," he whispered.

Expecting a fight, Calexa stiffened, but Winged One just ran his long fingers across the back of her neck, massaging her biometal spine.

Her pain receptors might have been dulled, but her ability to feel pleasure was still intact. Caught between these two fierce aliens, all she could do was take a deep breath and shudder.

The winds of her strange fate blew around her, pulling her in the most unexpected direction, and for once in her life, she didn't resist.

She let out a slow, shuddering sigh and allowed the Vradhu to do their thing, forgetting about the chaos they'd left behind. "Wh-what's changed? Not too long ago, you were both ready to kill each other over me."

"The sight of you with another set my blood on fire," Winged One admitted. "I was blinded by rage. All I knew was that I wanted to kill him."

"He started it," Young One murmured. "All I knew was that he was trying to take you from me, and I wanted to kill him."

"There isn't really room for *two* of us," Wings locked eyes with his other, and some silent communication passed between them. "But if we continued to fight, one of us would *certainly* die, and then the Two Clans would lose a *khefe*."

"*Khefe* means...?"

"He Who Hunts Alone. In the Two Clans, only I hold this right."

"Because you're such a bad-ass?"

"Indeed." As usual, Ares had no concept of humility. "The

world is on the cusp of change, my *makivari*. It would be selfish of me to deprive my people of a *khefe,* and it would be brutish of me to put you through the loss of a mate."

"We could not do it," Young One added. The way their conversation flowed—naturally, seamlessly, as if a single person were talking—was uncanny. "After we came so close to losing everything, we could not deprive you of what is yours. Therefore, you will have both of us—if you so choose."

Both Vradhu went still as they held her, expectantly awaiting her answer. Winged One held the back of her neck, and Young One embraced her with his dangerous tail.

"Idiots. The moment I stepped between your warring asses was the moment I accepted the situation for what it is." The words that tumbled from her mouth were imbued with a disbelieving kind of glee. "Maybe you Vradhu are rubbing off on me." The way they just went with the flow—as if life itself were one great torrent and they were canny fish, darting through the slipstream—was so *very* Vradhu.

"You have the soul of a Hunter," Winged One whispered. He exerted gentle pressure on the back of her neck, pushing her forward. Young One released her and stepped aside.

They walked toward the hunting lodge.

"Come," Ares said, their voices melding into one.

As if in a trance, Calexa moved, the melting ice crunching beneath her slipper-clad feet.

"My turn," Ares whispered, encircling her waist with his devilish tail.

CHAPTER THIRTY-SIX

DAPPLED LIGHT PLAYED across the bare floorboards, entering the lodge through small clear windows in the roof. The space was partitioned into smaller rooms by sliding panels made of an opaque, paper-like substance.

"You built this place?"

"Yes. Do you like it?"

"It's... beautiful." The interior of the hunting lodge was surprisingly light and airy. The blond-colored material—was it *wood* or something else?—that made up the walls and floor had been polished until it almost glowed, and it smelled good, like that rare Earth spice... what was it called again?

Cinnamon.

They walked down a central corridor and entered a room bordered by white paper-screen walls. One side of the room was completely open to the elements, providing an uninter-rupted view of the lake. A wide verandah extended beyond its walls, providing generous shelter. Dark green barrels lined the verandah, along with various weapons arranged in racks.

The lake house was so open, so *free*. She'd never seen anything like it in all her travels throughout the Universe. On

D5, everything was locked up and guarded; if you weren't careful, they would steal the very clothes off your back.

The notion of a house with open walls was so alien to her that she couldn't stop staring.

"When it is not hunting season, we are expected to do the physical tasks necessary to the survival of the clan. In the Clanlands, I build and repair." Abruptly, Wings wrapped his arms around her, turning her around. He planted a deep kiss on her forehead, his lips lingering for a long, delicious moment.

Below them, the longboats knocked together, punctuating the song of the Ardu-Sai—the gentle hiss of the wind, the lapping of waves against the lake's shore, the distant cry of some strange and exotic animal—with an uneven rhythm.

Calexa closed her eyes, struggling to believe she was actually here.

Alone. Amidst beauty. With *him.*

A faint prickle along the back of her neck made her look up. Young One stood in the corner of the room, his face hidden in the shadows. *Observing.* The flickering light played across his violet skin, accentuating his perfectly honed body.

When had he...?

Such stealth! She hadn't noticed him following them, and she was usually pretty observant.

A knowing smile curved his lips.

"We are one and the same," Winged One whispered, placing his fingers under her chin. He tilted her face toward his. "I know what you told *him*... *We* know what you have been through in your past life. Where you come from is not a good place." He kissed the scars along her cheekbones, his lips moving slowly, deliberately, as if paying homage to her rash act of defiance. "*My* Khira is not like that. Now that the Shadowring is gone and Naaga poison flows through the Ardu-Sai, I can't predict what will happen to our people, but I swear to you that as long as *we* are alive, you will never know such suffering again."

Young One's coal-black eyes burned through her, but he was as much Ares as the other, and his presence in the room didn't bother her. Instead, a flutter rose within her chest, making her slightly breathless.

Ba-bump. There went her crazy heart again.

And how could she do anything but surrender when Winged One held her like that, with such quiet tenderness?

"You must understand, Calexa, that our situation is incredibly rare."

"An ordinary human from a distant part of the Universe jumps through the Silverstream and ends up in the arms of a winged Vradhu and his clone," she murmured, reaching out to stroke his face. The vicious cut on his cheek had dried. She ran her fingers across it, marveling at how their red blood was the same, even though *everything* else was different.

"It's not that." He captured her fingers between his lips as she traced the black line that ran from beneath his eye to the corner of his mouth. Slowly, sensually, he sucked on her fingers, curling his tongue around the tips before releasing them. "In our culture, Vradhu such as I rarely become mated."

Young One had mentioned this. "I *still* don't understand." Calexa absorbed his handsome face, imprinting the proud lines and intricate markings on her soul. Ares could be as hard as stone, but he could also be gentle and expressive; his booming, generous laughter was the most infectious thing.

Plus, he was gorgeous.

How could he have any trouble finding a mate?

"Vradhu females do not see Hunters as suitable mates. We are ill-tempered, rash, overprotective, aggressive, and we die young. The elders believe that keeping us celibate makes us better hunters. All that pent-up frustration has to be released somehow, but violence is no substitute for sex."

"I don't give a shit about what your elders think." Warmth surged through her as Ares leaned in and tasted her lips. His kiss was deep and tender, his insistent tongue sliding against hers as Calexa responded with her own burning hunger.

She couldn't help it. He was just *too* irresistible.

"And those Vradhu women don't know what they're missing out on." Her voice was a breathy rasp as he tucked his fingers underneath the collar of her combat-suit. "I couldn't care less what your tribe thinks of you. The traits that turn them off are the very ones *I* find attractive." Never in her life had she thought a male could be like *this*.

"You are a warrior." He fumbled with the clasp, got the hang of it, and unzipped her from neck to crotch. "I am fortunate beyond my wildest imaginings."

The way he spoke, one would think she were some kind of deity; a rare, mythical creature worthy of his praise.

But she was just ordinary, messed-up Calexa, a misfit from D5 who had gotten this far through a combination of luck, guts, and madness.

Ares began to *purr*, his broad chest vibrating softly as she placed her bare hand against it. He still wore his form-fitting Drakhin armor. It was smooth and warm and slightly hard under her hand, like metal skin. The glittering scales molded to his body, accentuating his taut form. Slowly, she reached behind him and ran her hands over his shoulders, feeling his wings.

The gaps in his armor allowed the curious black appendages to emerge from his back. When they were open, they were massive, giving Ares a wingspan that was at least twice his height. When closed, they were surprisingly compact. The strong, narrow bones that made up their frames fit together like a jigsaw puzzle, and the tough black membrane connecting them seemed to disappear, leaving them tightly folded against his back.

Her fingers traced down angular, membrane-covered wingbones. She found the point where his wing had been broken; he shuddered as she touched it. "Don't you want to get this fixed?"

"Later," he rasped. "I am at breaking point." His hands slid across the flat of her belly.

Ba-bump.

"Then how do we get this bloody armor-suit off you?"

"Like this." He touched some hidden device at the back of his neck, and the suit dismantled into several segments. Ares shrugged, and they just *fell* off his body, clattering to the floor.

Ba-bump.

He stood before her, naked and glorious. She'd seen all this before, but if Young One was a magnificent athlete, then this was the *true* warrior. Ares's life of violence was written in his scars.

His sneaky tail unwrapped from around his left leg and tore off her combat suit before she could even blink. He grabbed her around her waist and pulled her close. "Do you desire me, Calexa?" Rough hands cupped her breasts, squeezing them gently.

"What do you think?"

His laughter was rich and mesmerizing. She loved it.

Gentle thumbs caressed taut nipples. Something hard pressed against her lower belly.

Her eyes dropped.

Ba-bump.

She *knew* how big he was, but this was different. Fascinated, she took Ares's erection into her hand, running her fingers up-and-down its hard length. He stiffened, sighing with pleasure.

Calexa gasped and looked down.

Unlike his clone's, Ares's cock was adorned with numerous small, firm bumps, as if something had been inserted under the skin. They radiated outwards from the base in a spiral, all the way to the head, which was moist with his seed.

"I have been beaded," he said proudly. "Although we Hunters rarely find mates, the beading is done as a rite of manhood, because one never knows..."

"That's so..." *Unfair.* Denied the possibility of finding a mate, and sent off to die young? These traditional Vradhu customs struck her as ridiculous, but she didn't have time to dwell on that, because Ares was lifting her up into his arms and carrying her across the room.

A bed of woven reeds and sky-blue linens stretched out before them. Ares dropped to his knees and lay her down, prowling over her like some large feline predator. "Beading is done purely to give females pleasure," he growled. "The process is exquisitely painful, but your reaction just then made it completely worthwhile.

"A-Ares..." He was savage and fierce and incredibly sweet, and Calexa wanted to give him an obscene amount of pleasure. "It's your first time, isn't it?"

"Yes," he said, and there was no guile, no hesitation, no awkwardness. "My other and I have already discussed you in great detail." He dipped his finger into her slick entrance, making her whimper. "Already, we have many ideas." He probed a little deeper.

"Unhhh..." Her moan was low and throaty. Her squirm was one of impatience. "What kind of—"

"Nice ones." He sucked the taut peak of her right nipple as he sank his finger deeper, stretching her. He added another, grazing her clit with the pad of his thumb. "Seems you like this."

Like it? Her body was on fire, and all she could think about was his huge, *beaded* cock.

This Ares was impossible. What he lacked in experience, he made up for in confidence. Each stroke of his fingers, each kiss from his searing lips, each satisfied *purr* was a healing salve on her fragile soul.

Ares's purring became louder. He trailed kisses down her

bare stomach, reaching her groin. Talented fingers were replaced by an equally talented hot, *wet* mouth, and stars, he was *still* purring.

The gentle vibrations that originated in his chest rumbled all the way through to his lips.

Lips that were pressed against her clit.

Vibrating.

"O-ooh...." A burst of pleasure made her close her eyes and run her hands over his braided hair.

Ares sucked, flicking her tender nub with his tongue.

Calexa swore black-and-blue in Earthian, wrapping her arms around his neck. Ares maintained the gentle pressure on her clit, each movement of his vibrating lips sending an exquisite tremor through her body.

She raked her hands over tightly closed wings, reveling in his alienness; the glorious black wings were a hard-won remnant of his battle with the *Hythra*. She didn't know *why* he still had them, but she appreciated them all the same.

Her Vradhu was magnificent.

As Ares sent her spiraling into mindless bliss, *something* made her open her eyes and look up.

Young One was still there in the shadows, watching them. He was so still and silent that she'd forgotten about him.

Her features twisted into an expression of perfect surrender as her chest heaved, her breaths coming in short, raggedy gasps. Sweat glistened on her bare skin. Her lips were parted.

She was utterly helpless, and Young One was staring at her. He captured her with his eyes and refused to let go, his dark face *so* serious and inscrutable and utterly arousing that she couldn't look away.

Wings coiled his tail around her waist, gripping her tightly as he stroked her with his vibrating tongue. Rough hands cupped her ass. His warrior's braid was tightly coiled around her fingers—she needed *something* to anchor her amidst this wild maelstrom of sensation.

Calexa arched her back as a wild spirit took over her body, sacrificing it to the violet-and-obsidian god who had buried his face between her thighs. In return, he gave her pleasure.

Young One stepped out of the shadows, moving gracefully through the dappled light, his tail weaving through the air in a slow, sinuous manner.

Caught in the throes of pleasure, all Calexa could do was stare. She watched him with a sense of wonder, unashamedly ogling his strong, powerful body. The bandages couldn't hide his beauty. A rippling torso. Sculpted arms. Muscular legs that could propel him with explosive speed.

A natural Hunter.

All hers, in *duplicate*.

Ripples of ecstasy turned into waves. She gasped in pleasure and surprise as Young One lay down beside her, a slight wince the only evidence of his discomfort. He cupped her face with his hand as she gasped again, her breaths turning into tiny whimpers.

"Do you know how beautiful you look right now?"

Damn you, Ares! She couldn't speak.

Like stardust, her mind shattered into a million brilliant fragments.

Ares leaned in and planted a devastating kiss on her lips.

All of them.

Young One released her mouth and stared into her eyes until she could take it no more.

She came.

He smiled, his brilliant teeth glittering, his expression both tender and savage.

Winged One held onto her as she crashed against him, engulfing her in his warmth. She closed her eyes and drowned in sensation.

Pure bliss.

Perfect. Just perfect.

She rode the waves of her orgasm until all the tension drained from her body and she collapsed into the soft bed of reeds and fragrant linen. Letting out a satisfied grunt, Winged One trailed soft kisses up her belly, tasted her pert nipples, and kissed her on the lips.

When she opened her eyes again he was there, his fingers raking over her shorn hair, his depthless eyes unlocking the last of her defenses.

She was completely undone, and that was good.

Young One uncoiled from her side, putting a finger to his lips. "Now you are ready," he said mysteriously, ruining her with one last hot, devastating kiss. Then he rose and stole away into the shadows, a black-and-violet wraith.

Ares existed in two places at once, and if she didn't know better, she could have *sworn* the two were communicating by some sort of telepathy.

Winged One gently thrust his fingers into her warm, slick entrance. "Now you are ready," he repeated, kissing her gently on her forehead.

"Yes, I am," she whispered.

He entered her.

She howled.

This was Ares—*all* of him—and he was brutal and scarred and perfect.

His beaded length stretched her, filling her with ecstasy and pain, but even the pain was exquisite. As Ares thrust again and again, his movements carefully restrained, her pain gave way to deep pleasure.

He slow-fucked her until his self-control eroded into wild abandon, his movements becoming more and more savage. He took his fill, and she *let* him go there. For the second time in her life, she *gave* herself to her man, and it felt right and good and pure.

This was how it was supposed to be.

Not taken. *Given.*

She wrapped her arms around his powerful frame and guided him home, embracing her Vradhu, scars and all.

And as he reached the point of climax, pulling her along into his savage undertow, the realization struck her.

This was Khira, and she wasn't going anywhere.

She'd found her place in the Universe. It was right here, with Ares.

EPILOGUE

Two weeks later

THE SHADOWS MOVED. Calexa spun, raising her gun.

"Hold, my love." A hand came down on her shoulder. The tension drained from her body as Ares chuckled softly. "It's only me." He was beside her. He was also in front of her.

Darkness coalesced into a familiar form. *Ares*. He emerged from the thorny grove like a specter, as if he were wrought from the very shadows themselves.

"You have to stop doing that," she grumbled, trying to control her racing heart. Now she understood why Vradhu Hunters had those black markings on their faces. They helped them blend with the darkness and shadows of the sekkhoi forest.

The Vradhu possessed the perfect natural camouflage. Ares could have been standing still in the shadows and she would have walked straight past him. He could probably sneak up on her on those bare three-toed feet of his, and she would be none the wiser.

What fearsome stealth.

Young One shrugged and offered her a strange oval-shaped

fruit. Its deep blue skin was decorated with delicate pink stripes, and it emitted a sweet, tantalizing fragrance that invoked memories of Earth.

"*Yasoo*," he said, by way of explanation. "Very rare, but delicious. The smell was driving me crazy, so I had to go and find the mother-tree. Try it." Small, fresh cuts covered his hands.

Both forms of Ares watched her expectantly as she bit into the soft, tender fruit. Their eyes traveled in the same direction, watching her hands, her face, her mouth. The same devious little smile played across both their lips. They seemed to particularly like it when she ate—and enjoyed—the things they gave her.

"Unngh..." She moaned in surprise as the bitter-sour-sweet flavor of the *yasoo* burst in her mouth. Sticky juice ran down her chin.

"It is good, yes?" Winged One laughed at her reaction, his rich voice ringing through the shadowy grove. Thick black branches curved above their heads, crisscrossing to form a jagged network of thorns. The shadows were deep and still, the sekkhoi so thick in places that she couldn't see where she was going, but she wasn't afraid.

Not when she had two badass Vradhu walking by her side at all times.

"This is amazing," Calexa gushed, swallowing the rest of the fruit. She licked her fingers, feeling like a kid again. "Are there more? We have to bring some back for the girls."

How surreal it was that just a few weeks ago, she'd been ferrying a group of humans to Torandor on a dangerous unsanctioned route, waiting for the next Paxnath attack.

In the Fiveways, credits were scarce, competition was fierce, and mercenaries lived on a knife's edge. Calexa had existed in precarious limbo between her brutal past and the grim present, desperately trying to find a way to fill the void.

Her nights and days had been a sleepless, never-ending

cycle of jobs and colorless destinations and debts. Running the *Medusa* was expensive, and they were always a few credits away from a breakdown, but the ship was home—their small island in the cruel, boundless Universe.

At least, it *had* been home.

Now she was here, eating fruit in a grove of thorns with two mesmerizing aliens.

"I will gather more on the way back," Ares said, his lips quirking in satisfaction. "Now come. We are almost there."

They—*he*—moved in perfect synchronicity, guiding her along a narrow path that wound through the dense thicket. Without Ares to guide her, she never would have seen the damn path, but her sure-footed Vradhu acted as her eyes in the darkness, keeping her safe from the vicious sekkhoi thorns.

She no longer thought of Young One and Winged One as two separate entities. They were an extension of the same soul, with the same memories, the same temperament, and the same *unique* set of skills. After they'd fought over her on the island, Ares's dual incarnations had reached some sort of silent agreement and fallen into step with one another, their actions and words and thoughts becoming seamless.

It was so terribly uncanny, and she'd had *such* a hard time explaining the whole thing to Mai and Zahra.

So... you know that silver guy who kicked my ass and abducted me, then had a translator-thing surgically implanted into my brain without my consent? Well, he's actually a Vradhu who accidentally bonded to the ship and got temporarily transformed into a Drakhin. He wanted to escape the Hythra *so badly that he forced the Naaga to clone him. Somehow, his consciousness got divided between both bodies, and... well, here we are.*

Oh, and I forgot to mention, he's a bad-ass called a khefe. *A stone-cold* kratok *killer.*

And he's—well, both *of him are—my lovers.*

The dense forest of sekkhoi gave way to a clearing.

Calexa stopped dead in her tracks. "Wh-what is this place?" They had stumbled upon a massive structure of stone and metal. Grand archways of decaying grey metal soared into the cloudy sky, intersecting in a geometric style that was distinctly Drakhin. Perhaps glass or some other transparent material had once stretched between them, but now they lay bare, exposed to the elements.

Vines of thorny sekkhoi snaked around the arms of the metal structure, dropping the occasional spray of vivid pink flowers. According to Ares, the fragrant sekkhoi flowers were incredibly toxic.

It seemed everything on this damn planet was toxic, except for the *yasoo* she'd just eaten.

Concentric circles of black stone made up the foundation of the structure, forming a series of steps that descended toward a collection of oddly shaped stones.

"The Ancient Stones," Winged One announced. "This is a monument, built by the Drakhin on our territory and abandoned many orbits ago. Everything we know about Vradhu-Drakhin history, about the Naaga, and about the outside, it all comes from here."

"I wanted to show you the history of our world," Young One added. "We Vradhu are a secretive people, and as you now know, the Two Clans don't accept outsiders."

"They don't want us going anywhere near them, do they?"

"They are afraid of the outside world, my love. There was a time when our people were almost wiped out by what we call *magrel* unnatural things—so we retreated into the Ardu-Sai, naively thinking we would never be disturbed."

"And yet we humans have *magrel* in spades," she said drily. "I'm full of the unnatural, but that clearly doesn't bother you."

"Of course not. After all that has happened, we have transcended our fears. By definition, I am also the embodiment of *magrel*." Ares raised a wing ironically. "I have been cloned and transformed, and the two clans have no idea. Maki hasn't told them a thing."

"So you're all going to take care of us, until..." Until *what?* Were they going to have to make their lives on Khira?

"Yes." He smiled, and a powerful rush of desire caught her by surprise. "There is no safer place on Khira than in the sekkhoi, with not one, but *two* khefe, and Maki-ku-Rathra's pack."

If anyone else claimed such things, Calexa would have thought they were full of shit, but she believed Ares with all her heart.

They were safe.

Torrential rain had brought flooding, driving them from the poisoned waterways of the Ardu-Sai up into the dark clutches of the sekkhoi forests. The journey had been long and difficult, particularly for the women in S's retinue, but Maki's pack had been with them every step of the way, guiding and protecting them.

To her surprise, they hadn't gone directly to the place where Vradhu clans lived. Instead, the Hunters had brought them to a makeshift camp deep within the sekkhoi forest, and aside from the Hunters, they hadn't seen any other Vradhu.

"The elders refuse to allow aliens into the Clanhome," Maki had told them after returning from a mysterious liaison in the middle of the night. *"I fought bitterly with them as I have been wont to do of late, but our dear clan elders are so set in their ways. Even now, they are livid that we have brought you this close. Feh. They cling to tradition as stubbornly as the roots of a sekkhoi tree—as if secrecy will save us from the change that is sweeping our land. Don't worry, human. If the Two Clans won't accept you and you people, then they will just have to do without my pack for the time being. We will not leave your side."*

So they had camped out in the shadowy forest, making their homes in domed huts skillfully woven by the Vradhu out of sekkhoi branches. Aside from being minor architectural marvels, the huts were surprisingly waterproof, sheltering them from the torrential rain.

Ever since they'd left the island, it had rained and rained and rained, turning the lowlands into one vast floodplain. *Stars*, she'd never experienced rain like this on any of the planets she'd visited.

As if in response to her thoughts, fat droplets of water began to fall. A black wing curved over her head as Wings pulled her into him, his tail curling around her waist. Young One looked up at the skies, his expression full of hope. "Maybe all this rain will flush the poison from the Ardu-Sai." He didn't mind as water cascaded down his face and chest, making his skin glisten. His long, wild hair became slick with moisture, flattening against his shoulders. He walked down into the center of the structure, with Calexa and Wings following close behind.

Her boots clicked on the glistening stone, and as Calexa looked down, she saw the intricate jeweled mosaics on the floor.

Drakhin mosaics. The same as the ones in the command room on the *Hythra*.

Fighting, fucking, killing, soaring, *decadent* Drakhin splendor stretched out beneath her feet, forever etched in stone and jewels. The floor needed a good polish to bring it back to its former glory, but she could easily imagine what it had once been. She shuddered. According to Ares, the Drakhin had all left Khira thousands of years ago, when their source of *vir* had dried up.

Thank the stars for that. Drakhin-Ares had been scary enough. She didn't want to encounter the real thing.

The stones in the center formed a ring. They were about the same height as her chest, and they were inscribed with strange rune-like characters. As Young One stepped into the center, the runes glowed green.

Two menacing Drakhin appeared on either side of him. Calexa drew her gun.

"Relax." Young One thrust out his arm. His hand went straight through the imposing figures. "They are not real."

"A hologram," she gasped in relief.

The two Drakhin stared right through her, their fierce eyes focused on some unseen thing in the distance. Even though they were just imaginary figures, they appeared so realistic and intimidating that the air thickened with a palpable sense of danger.

"The original twins, Imril and Mael. They were the progenitors, the very first generation of Drakhin to appear on our planet." Young One's black gaze grew distant as he spoke. Calexa stared at the imaginary twins, entranced by their appearance.

They reminded her of ancient gods, appearing as Ares had on the *Hythra*, when he'd transformed into a Drakhin. One had eyes of intense gold, and his wings and tail were pure white. In contrast, his brother's gaze was the color of deep midnight on Earth. Black wings, just like Ares's, curved from his back.

"Imril was a son of the light. Mael was a child of darkness." Winged One took over, his words following on seamlessly from his other's, as if they shared the same train of thought. "They were the result of a union between a Vradhu female and the Dark One. Since their birth, every mating between a Vradhu female and a Drakhin has produced male twins. There is no such thing as a female Drakhin."

"Wh-what is a Dark One?" Calexa didn't know whether Ares was describing history or myth. This sounded like a tale of gods and monsters; the kind of fiction people on Earth created to escape the harshness of real life.

"We do not know where he came from, or what his kind was called, but we know he was the last of his race. He appeared in the sky with his dark ships and arcane technologies, seeking to preserve his civilization and his line."

"And so he impregnated one of our daughters, and the first Drakhin twins were born."

Calexa was sensing a theme here. "Twins?"

"Vradhu males are *always* born as twins. One is destined to become a Hunter, the other a Breeder. In the Drakhin, this duality manifested as darkness and light."

"So you have one.... a twin?" With each and every revelation, Ares's mysterious world kept blowing her mind. "Your cloned ass has a *twin*?"

An identical look of disdain crossed Ares's faces as they spoke in unison. **"Anareth is a brother by birth only. Hunters and Breeders can't exist in the same radius."**

"Let me guess... you'd tear each other apart, or something like that."

"I have no tolerance for that insufferable idiot." They paused. **"Pompous asshole."**

Well, that answered that. "Are these so-called Breeders... what do they... I mean..." At a loss for words, Calexa shrugged. "The word *Breeder* doesn't exactly leave a lot to the imagination."

"Their biology makes them well suited for reproductive life, and highly desirable to Vradhu females."

"Huh." She'd never heard of anything like that before. A species where all males were born as twins? Where one's role in life was determined by biology? Where the alpha-males were the *undesirable* ones?

Vradhu culture fascinated her. It was too bad the elders were refusing to allow any contact with the tribe. It put them in a precarious situation. They were practically cut off from all civilization, but she believed—and *trusted*—Ares and Maki. Maki's pack had refused to leave them. Ares had been with her every step of the way.

Despite Calexa's trust issues, that was good enough for her.

Young One grinned. It was like a ray of sunshine punching through the dark rainclouds. "Judging from your expression, you must think we are all mad."

Sweet stars, he was gorgeous. Her very own rain-soaked, glistening wet-dream.

In *duplicate*.

"Only your females," she admitted. "Oh well, it's their loss."

My gain.

The hologram images changed, capturing her attention. Mael and Imril faded away, replaced by stunning images of vast cities. Sleek ships flew overhead, vying with fierce winged Drakhin for airspace. The style of the buildings and ships reminded her of the dark splendor of the *Hythra.*

"Pleased with his offspring, the Dark One gave the secrets of his race's advanced technology to his sons. Drakhin civilization flourished, but one thing was crucial to its survival."

"Our females."

"Vradhu females were the source of their *vir,* and the mothers of their sons. The Drakhin became greedy, and started to take our females against their will."

"The Drakhin-Vradhu alliance was broken. Females were no longer courted. They were *taken*, and treated as little more than slaves. The Vradhu had no choice."

"We went to war."

"They had technology and *power*, but we had Hunters. Even Breeders were enlisted to fight."

"We had venom, which the Drakhin lacked. There is no antidote for Vradhu poison."

"The war was short and brutal. Entire Vradhu packs were decimated. We retreated to the Ardu-Sai, where the Drakhin did not dare fly. They thought they had wiped us out. In order to survive, we cut ourselves off from the outside world.

Magrel was forbidden. Contact with outsiders was forbidden."

"We hid from the Drakhin. They lost their females. They lost their source of *vir*."

"The Drakhin needed an alternative, so they created the Naaga, a race of slaves."

"But their *vir* wasn't enough, and it grew weaker and weaker with subsequent generations."

The holograms faded away. There were no images of war or Naaga. Those were left to Calexa's imagination.

"This is a pre-war structure," Wings explained. "The *only* Drakhin structure on our lands. After the war, they never came here again. Too troublesome for their kind. With all their advanced technologies, they still feared the kratok."

"Their barbs are venomless," Young One scoffed. "The only living thing that can take down a kratok is a Hunter, and kratok attack all things that enter their airspace, *including* Drakhin. There were only a few Drakhin powerful enough to take on the kratok and survive. Perhaps Mael or Imril could have killed the beasts, but the progenitors are long gone."

Calexa's head swirled with thoughts of war and oppression. This was only the condensed version of Khira's history, and it was terrifying. "On the *Hythra*... the Naaga had taken over the ship. Do they control all the Drakhin cities now?"

"When the Drakhin left Khira, they left most of their slaves behind. The Naaga took the cities and the ships and the flyways. They tried to control the *Hythra*, but they failed. I suspect they fear the return of their masters. They are probably trying to find a way to defend themselves."

Narrowing her eyes, Calexa pointed at the glowing runes. "If these stones only tell the story up until the war, then how do you know about the Naaga?"

"Hunters occasionally travel beyond the Ardu-Sai. In the early days, the Hunters were sent to spy. Messages were sent back by winged *skiril*. If we venture beyond the borders of the

Ardu-Sai, we observe and report back to the clan. The story continues *here.*" Young One pointed to the wide steps, where rune-like markings were engraved in the black stone. "The Ancient Stones are a chronicle, a warning to our people."

"And our time on the *Hythra* confirmed most of our suspicions. When I was bonded, I eavesdropped," Winged One admitted. "With the ilverium coursing through my veins, it was not difficult."

"Do you think the Drakhin will ever return?" Calexa rubbed the goosebumps on her bare arms. As the rain grew heavier, the air became chilly. The darkness grew deeper as daylight faded away.

The Ancient Stones was a spooky place.

Both Vradhu shrugged. Winged One's tail tightened around her waist. She leaned into his warmth as he put an arm around her shoulders. "Do not worry, my fierce and clever *makivari*. Khira is vast and full of secrets, and we Vradhu can survive anywhere. No matter what happens, we will not allow any harm to come to you or your people."

Young One came up behind her. "The story of Khira has always been one of three peoples: Vradhu, Naaga, and Drakhin. Now there are four."

Five, she thought, *if you include the Primeans.* If the Drakhin were cousin-people to the Vradhu, then the Primeans were cousin-people to humans.

"Perhaps your arrival here is a catalyst for something greater." Not an inch of his wet body touched her, but his breath was a tantalizingly warm caress against her ear.

Surrounded by decadent decay and torrential rain and the overwhelming presence of her Vradhu, Calexa closed her eyes and opened the floodgates to her soul, letting inevitability crash down around her. "Or maybe we've just found the best of each other in a bad situation," she whispered. "You've brought me back to life, Hunter."

They might never find a way off this planet. Calexa didn't

mind—after all, she had Ares—but the humans would be distraught. She'd have to break the news gently, gradually, taking each day as it came and looking after them, as was her duty. And if they wanted to *leave*, she would do her best to help them find a way, but she wasn't going anywhere.

Together, they would protect one another, and no matter what happened, they would *survive*, because now that she'd found Ares and the Vradhu Hunters, their odds had dramatically improved.

Winged Ares pulled her into a kiss. She responded with all the ferocity and passion of a woman who'd escaped a bleak greyscale existence by diving into a mysterious, dangerous, *beautiful* world of vivid color.

Not caring that Young One was soaked from head to toe, she turned and kissed him too, savoring his slick, demanding lips.

They were both Ares.

Both *hers*.

"My salvation," Ares whispered, wrapping her up in a sinuous, sinful Vradhu cocoon of tails and wings and wetness and warmth.

His two bodies became one.

Standing in the pouring rain amongst thorns and ruins, Calexa allowed herself to be engulfed by this indomitable Hunter, who had defied the laws of the Universe to be with her.

In this brave new world, the rules of her old Universe didn't apply.

She was Calexa Acura, former debt-slave, discharged Arena-fighter, semi-honorable mercenary, and now lover to Ares-rai-Sekine, the *khefe* of the Ardu-Sai...

And she was free.